FELINE FURY!

The alien whirled on him and caught the carafe on the downswing, gripping Riker's wrist in fingers that felt they would crush his bones. By degrees, Riker's hand let go of the carafe of its own accord, and Marik stood, still holding the wrist, glaring at him from inches away out of those terrible, pained, glittering eyes. . . .

The Trumpets of Tagan

THE TRUMPETS OF TAGAN

SIMON LANG

ACE BOOKS, NEW YORK

This book is an Ace original edition,
and has never been previously published.

THE TRUMPETS OF TAGAN

An Ace Book / published by arrangement with
the author

PRINTING HISTORY
Ace edition / July 1992

ISBN: 0-441-82576-1

Ace Books are published by The Berkley Publishing Group,
200 Madison Avenue, New York, New York 10016.
The name ''ACE'' and the ''A'' logo
are trademarks belonging to Charter Communications, Inc.

PRINTED IN THE UNITED STATES OF AMERICA

10 9 8 7 6 5 4 3 2 1

To the steady, the brilliant, the firstborn:
Mark, with gratitude and love . . .
and to the Lady Kimberly.

April 25, 1991

To the reader:

I began writing this novel in the last months of 1975, hard on the heels of *The Elluvon Gift*, for the enormous circuitous work I loosely term 'Einai' comprises some twelve to fifteen novel-length interrelated stories. By the end of 1978, I had virtually completed the book: the maps were drawn, the 3-D mock-up of the island of Tagan and the smaller I'a were complete down to the moss, and all the happenings choreographed and set down in their permanent form.

In the years since 1978, we've added seven children, lost several immediate family members, sold two companies and our ranch, and made a cross-country move.

In answer to my mail, I wish to state that yes, I *am* still alive and yes, I *do* intend to keep writing, including more books about the Einai and the personnel of *Skipjack* and *Hope*. I've just been awfully busy. Thank you all for asking.

In my former books, *All the Gods of Eisernon* and *The Elluvon Gift*, I respected the wishes of the people who assisted me, and omitted any thanks to them. However, I intend to thank some of them here.

First, to Al, for reasons best known to himself. Then to the Big Six, for the interest, the pride they take in my work, and the prayers. To wit: To Marco for the invaluable advice; to Kip, for his delicious wit; to Terri for her down-to-earth moral support; to Hans, for his broad-and-always-available shoulder; for Beth's laughter and holy joy; and especially to Gret, for her intelligent and sensitive editing and continuity checks, without which I might have been finished sooner, but not nearly as well. Especially without chapter 7.

To Sam and Maria, who typed, and discovered in me a world they had never suspected.

And to Mudge and Dad.

I'd also like to thank several persons to whom I'm not related, especially to:

The men at Pacific Telephone, Los Angeles, California, who proved beyond a shadow of a doubt that Ilai could not do now what he did then; my faithful friend Alice Laukert, who believes; Pat Cavallero, R.N., Yale/New Haven Hospital Triage Center; Nash Roberts, who is well known to people serious about meteorology and polled-Hereford cattle breeding; Eleanor Faller, of the Minerology Division of the Peabody Museum, but who swears fealty to Yale University as well; Ronald Ojinski, USN, Long Beach, California; Steve Waldman, of the New York State Athletic Commission; the men and women of the Jet Propulsion Laboratory, Pasadena, California, and the Manned Spacecraft Center, Houston, Texas; and everyone who has contributed his or her time, interest, and expertise to make this book a reality.

THE TRUMPETS OF TAGAN

PROLOG

THE HALABY CENTER for Spatial Segregation was situated squarely in the middle of the Great Glass Lake and was accessible only by helo or skimmer. Ground cruisers were unable to negotiate the mirrored obsidian surface, and sailing craft were forbidden to approach any nearer than ten kilometers to the Center's outer perimeter.

Breach of this widely publicized law was dealt with by the Marine Authority, who patrolled constantly in trim, Teflon-keeled cruisers. Punishment was swift and invariable: passengers and crew were turned over for questioning by PBI investigators, and the offending craft was phased out of existence. A maintenance crew was dispatched to repair any damage done to the lake's flawless green-black surface.

The Center's Controllers themselves, arriving by special skimmerbus, deplaned into a corridor containing a gauntlet of scanning devices which identified them by retinal patterns, voiceprint match, EEG alpha-wave base, and blood chemistry coding to the seventh factor. Incoming personnel not meeting the necessary identification were detained in situ by an array of lasers capable of slicing a would-be saboteur into several interesting but non-functional segments.

Nor was this stringent security a manifestation of paranoia on the part of the agencies involved in the Center. Quite the contrary. It was a measure of their sanity.

No one wanted another Sennimetl catastrophe.

During the most recent episode of the Federation/Empire War, which flared to violence and ground down to negotiations with interminable regularity, a Krail operative had made his way into the center of a key Federation military base, on a

1

densely populated planet known as Sennimetl. Within moments, the Center's control holograph had gone down and thirty-two unControlled vessels, a dozen of them multiwrap battle cruisers, had struck Sennimetl en masse just as they dropped out of warp at .2 lights. Sennimetl was pulverized and its moon was sent caroming into its nearest planetary neighbor—also heavily populated. Wholesale loss of life became meaningless by reason of numerical overload and cumulative horror.

The powers-that-be decided that the catastrophe was, viewed practically, essentially a propaganda problem.

There would be panic if the news were allowed to break all at once, they decided. There would be chaos. And with the Krail Empire forever at its throat, the Federation could ill afford the risk. Therefore the Council maintained a cool official silence, as though nothing had happened.

There were rumors, of course. Shipping had to be rerouted around the disaster area and the crewmen talked, but merchant seamen have always brought home tall tales. These new stories inflamed a lukewarm patriotism—but they spread no panic. Scientists were quietly informed, cautioned, and, upon occasion, threatened. It worked.

Nobody made waves.

Later, when the political climate had improved and the Federation was making strides (albeit short ones) at the negotiating table, useful bits of fact-cum-propaganda were leaked to the media. Tear-jerking tri-D articles pretended to cope emotionally with the grief of surviving relatives, and action films involving not much more than sound and fury in living color (augmented by audio recordings of cattle stampeding, and frequently interrupted by commercial messages) were cranked out by the score and pap-fed to an avid public.

There was a boost in the sale of telescopes, for gazing at the spot where Sennimetl ought to have been.

A toy company put out a "Sennimetl Game" for ages ten to adult.

There were plastex toys.

There were comic books.

Biff.

Pow.

And ho hum.

After a while it came to be said that the Sennimetl catastrophe just might have been a blessing in disguise, because of its impetus to the war effort. After all, the Federation had won the peace afterward. What more could you ask?

The Federation Space Agency, the public found, could ask a great deal more. Centers were relocated in less accessible areas, scanners were fine-tuned. The old six-hour shifts were tossed out. Controllers, all GS20s or better, worked two-hour weekly shifts at impressive salaries, linked to their ships by a featureless metal helmet (familiarly known as a "bucket"), the leads of which tied directly into the cerebral cortex by a process known as ion tophoresis. The Agency had made the Centers as safe and efficient as was humanly possible, with the exception of a just and lasting peace. However, as any politician might have explained, such a notion was so naive as to be absurd.

The famous FSA efficiency was evident this morning, as Martin Donovan switched his Control/Identity of USS *Plover* to his relief and heard her muttering, as she slipped into her bucket, the time-honored psalm of starship Controllers:

". . . if I take the wings of the morning and dwell in the uttermost parts of the Deep,
Even there also shall Thy Hand lead me, and Thy right Hand shall hold me.

"If I say, 'Let only darkness cover me, and the light about me be night,'
Even Thy darkness is not dark to Thee, the night is as bright as day; for darkness is as light with Thee . . ."

His week's duty done, and *Plover* safely orbiting, Donovan stretched hugely, making the transition from clean, cold space, with the luminous planet slowly revolving below and the unwinking stars standing sentinel all around, to the familiar Center, with its holograph of Eisernon glowing brightly in the middle of the room, and the helmeted Controllers busy at their boards. Each of them was the Control/Identity of one of the ships whose holographic image stepped away from gravity on the long, hard pull, or flashed away for rendezvous with its Jumpslot.

They were the natural evolution, he thought, of the old Mississippi River pilots who guided the tall ships (and later the churning paddle wheelers, and later yet, the nuclear clippers) past treacherous snags and sawyers, safely to port. Donovan was a history buff and it pleased him to think in those anachronistic and romantic terms. But then Donovan was an anachronistic and romantic man. He was also his own sort of a genius.

It was because of this genius, and possibly because of his other qualities as well, that the chief, Whitman, stopped him on his way out of the Center. He jerked a thumb over his shoulder in the general direction of his office.

"See you a minute, Donovan?"

"Sure. What's up?" He followed Whitman into the comfortable clutter of his cubby, tossed his jacket down on the spare chair, and leaned against the wall. "Problem?"

The chief lowered his bulk into the desk chair, pursed his lips, and shook his head. "Not exactly. What do you know about USS *Skipjack*?"

"Military. She's a sub. She was on that super-alien rescue last month. Supposed to be in dry dock for repairs. Crack crew."

"What's the scoop on the rescue?"

"You didn't hear." It was an astounded statement of fact, rather than a question.

Whitman shook his head. "I've been working on the Seddaj mess, out at Kilindoni."

Donovan spread his hands. "Well, the way I got it, Chief, and this is only hearsay, you understand, *Skipjack* was in deep space when she came upon a damaged alien lifeboat; not one of your Federation craft, but an extragalactic emissary no less." Whitman lifted his brows.

"Well, *Skipjack*'s second, the Einai gook, what's-his-name, Marik, he brings the beast aboard—it calls itself an Elluvon— and it turns out to be female and full-term prego at that. So they have to rendezvous with *Hope*."

"The hospital ship?" the chief wanted to know.

"The same. But that's not the heart of it, you see! For

because it's an extragalactic alien, the Feds want it, the Krail want it, and an old buddy of Marik's, who's now a pirate, he wants it, too. So they all come after it, and there's a huge donnybrook aboardship; some people get bad hurt, and the Elluvon gets soundly stuck somewhere in the tubes system.''

The chief whistled soundlessly. He knew about the tubes. Every large ship had a network of transit tubes under its skin, not only for swift transport of goods and personnel, but also to reinforce the structure of the ship itself. They worked on a system of air pressure, and any being caught in a shutdown stood a good chance of dying where it stood.

"And who should go after it but the Marik himself. Got her out, too." Donovan shrugged. "That's about it."

Whitman didn't lift his head. "Finish it." Donovan started to smile. He shook his head.

"I, ah, I don't know what you—"

"Finish it, Donovan." The big man hadn't moved, but the little pig eyes tracked him like a pair of gun muzzles.

"Oh. Well, *that.*" He grinned again, uncomfortably. "Lot of scuttlebutt about her next mission, but, ah . . ." He shrugged and looked away. "Why don't you fill me in?"

The chief shuffled a few papers, making a great show of getting the edges precisely aligned. "Classified, right? It doesn't leave the Center."

"All right, then."

"Scuttlebutt's right. Her next mission is a time warp, code name Timeslide, back to three distinct points in the Past. I got this part direct from Central. You see, the Elluvon was so grateful that she gave Marik her Egg."

"Ah—would you mind repeating that last?"

"Her Egg. She laid an Egg and she gave it to Marik. He's a telepath, she's a telepath, he saves her life, so she up and gives him this Egg. Seems like with the Egg aboard—and Marik to link with it—the ship can travel through Time anyWhen they want to. But when the Egg starts to hatch, she tells him, you'd better hightail it for home, because once the kid is out, you're stuck WhenEver you are. So there *is* a substantial risk attached."

"But it's actually *Time travel!*"

Whitman nodded slowly. "Not only that, she's going to Jump from here and we're going to be Controlling her."

Donovan flushed with excitement. "You're joking!"

Whitman ignored that. "Problem is, the Controller." He began turning a dirty glass ashtray round in short, precise quarter turns, keeping his head down. *Spin, stop. Spin, stop.* "It's a risky business. We're going to need a Controller who knows what he's doing."

Donovan's heart began to pound, slowly and painfully, in his chest. "Well, now, you've a whole crew of men like that, now, haven't you?"

"Yes and no. This is going to take somebody special." *Spin, stop.* "This is new stuff. Virgin territory. Never can tell what'll happen." *Spin, stop. Spin, stop.* "Of course," he growled, "a man could write his own ticket. That's something."

"And the adventure. You'd have to call it a hell of an adventure." The anvil in his chest threatened to shake him apart. "For the man you chose for it."

"Man's already chosen. You understand, a man could lose his mind, for all we know. Man could get his psyche dragged hell-bent-for-leather across space and time, too. He can always say no."

Donovan's jaw sagged and he sat down slowly on top of his jacket. "Wait a minute, Chief. Lay it out, now. Are you asking me—"

"Nobody's asking you anything! We're just talking about it!"

"Ooooh, yes you are," Donovan breathed, his eyes blazing. "I think that you—" he said carefully, spacing his words and savoring the fine, rich flavor of them "—Daniel J. Whitman—are asking me—Martin Michael Donovan—if I would like to Control *Skipjack*'s Timeslide. In fact, boyo, I'm convinced of it!" He spoke almost in a whisper. "*You're asking me if I want to* be USS *Skipjack*!"

Whitman glanced up at him through his brows and made a curt little nod. "Central wants your answer within twenty-four hours," he muttered.

"Then you give it to them, Chief, right away, right now. You tell them that Donovan himself says, hell yes, he'll Control the Timeslide, and thank you kindly into the bargain." He sprang to his feet, snatched up his jacket, flung it over his shoulder, and started off toward the Center. At the doorway he paused and turned. "Oh, yes, and you can tell them for me that himself'll get 'em there and back as safe as babes in their mothers' arms."

"Hey!" Whitman called after him. "Hey! Donovan! You're going the wrong way! You're headed back for the Center!"

Donovan kept going, walking backward down the corridor to talk to him. "I've got to set it all up!" he yelled back. "Call my home, will you? Tell Josie I said not to wait up, I've work to do." He grinned, pointing an impressive finger at Whitman. "Carving my niche in history—with a Controller's bucket!"

CHAPTER

I

THE SOUND OF distant trumpets carried cleanly across the water from no particular direction. Repeated twice, and then twice again, the two notes, low and rising, like the horn of some medieval huntsman, brought Paul Riker sharply out of sleep and to his feet on *Oriana*'s polished bluewood deck. Steadying himself against her mast, he rubbed a hand across his eyes and gazed about uncertainly for the source of the pervasive sound. He frowned at the open after hatch, the furled sails, the serene blue sky lavishly brushed with mares' tails. Where could it have come from?

The boat?

Dao Marik's sleek forty-foot sloop was a genuine lady of her class, teak and bluewood and gleaming white hull, with the inevitable wide-set eyes painted boldly on her prow just above the waterline. Clean, trim, and empty, she boasted no crew but himself—and Marik, cloistered in the comfortable cabin below, placing call after telecom call to his various search teams all afternoon, while Riker sunned himself on deck.

No music there.

The sea, then?

He squinted at the sunshots glancing off the chop.

Nothing.

Nothing but the dark smudge of an island on the horizon, a picturesque fishing *byela* churning out to sea, her nets extended on lateral booms like great coarse butterfly wings, and—he looked round—the Reef, of course, the long, curved arm of coral that stretched almost twenty kilometers into the Single Sea: the Reef at Bru-Riga.

It was an easy landmark, a popular sight. Anyone who had

9

ever seen a postcard of the planet Eisernon was familiar with
half a dozen views of the famous Reef. It was a mecca for
well-heeled tourists, and its few shoreline resort hotels were
always booked several years in advance. If it were not for the
fact of his being Marik's houseguest, Riker knew, he could
never have gotten within camera range of the Imperial Coast.
The prices were astronomical, and reserved only for the
socially select.

The lagoon proper—fifty fathoms of crystal-clear water that
effervesced mildly on the Earthuman skin—was noted for its
superb sport fishing, the scuba appeal of its thousand grottoes
and sea-floor spires, and its spectacular scenic beauty.

What it was not noted for, Riker recalled with a touch of
chagrin, was auditory hallucination among sober young starship captains on shore leave.

He shook his head to clear it and rubbed his eyes again,
feeling the motion of the boat through his feet and uncon-
sciously responding to it. Let us assess the situation logically,
he thought. Let us be reasonable.

The seas were running two to three feet here outside the
Reef, with a nice chop and a persistent cross swell shouldering
smoothly under *Oriana*'s port quarter. Combined with a cool,
shifting breeze and the hot golden sun, the sloop's easy rocking
motion had made Riker feel lazy and content. He smothered
another yawn. Had he imagined the haunting music? Could he
have dreamed it up from the fugitive recollections of a hundred
alien planets?

It seemed likely enough. The sound of those ghostly trumpets was more the stuff of dreams than of cold reality, even
here on Eisernon, where the mysterious and wonderful were so
commonplace as not to be discussed. A swim, he decided, was
definitely in order. Clear the cobwebs out, he thought.

He had totally forgotten Marik's warning.

He slipped over the side into the warm sea, enjoying the faint
momentary sizzling of his metabolism reacting with the water,
and dove deeply, hoping that the unbelievable beauty of the
lagoon side of the Reef also pertained to its seaward face.

He was not disappointed.

The wilder side of the Reef was a rugged underwater tumble
of coral outcroppings and unlikely convolutions that hinted at

ancient and overgrown wrecks, and Riker found himself wishing he had brought a camera. Among the phantom masts and crusted timbers were vast colonies of ruby sponges, and he could see hordes of tiny translucent blue cleaner shrimp moving cautiously among their scarlet frills, peering at him myopically and waving their antennae. A number of caverns, black and enigmatic, gave on to the sea from the slanted coral face, some of them merging with the limitless ultramarine shadows far, far below.

Nearer at hand, basking in the warm, smoky sun shafts that filtered down through the clear water above, a school of brilliantly colored fish moved through a series of intricate patterns. Riker put out a hand to touch them and they flashed off, halted less than a meter away, and regarded him with the astonished expressions of fishes everywhere. Beyond them, as far as the eye could see, other fishes in countless varieties fed among the coral, peacefully migrating from place to place like grazing sheep.

Far below, in one of the murky undersea caverns, something stirred. A sinuous, heavily scaled body lifted and slid, sending up soundless puffs of sand and debris. Fins flared silently open. Nostrils quivered, delicately sensing prey.

Riker hung immobile, fascinated. Although his instincts were beginning to remind him that Earthlings were, after all, an air-breathing species, he was attracted by the plantimals anchored in every sheltered crevice of the Reef, captivated by their myriad varieties. As he swam closer to admire a particularly large specimen, a school of little fish with bright red bellies and impossibly long ventral fins followed him, nibbling at his skin and settling in his hair. When he shook them off good-naturedly, they made a tight circle of their flight with equal good nature and came back again.

Riker put out one finger to stroke the plantimal's leaf—or what appeared to be a leaf—and was delighted to feel the responsive curl of the creature's tentacle pressing back against it. It was decidedly a pleasurable sensation and it expanded hypnotically, seductively, up his hand and partway into his arm, until suddenly he felt a painful acid tingle, a distinctly predatory wrench. He jerked his finger free from the grip of the lovely carnivore, but not before the acid bite of its digestive juices peeled off a strip of flesh, leaving a raw, red slash that made a rosy cloud in the water before it dispersed. It was then that he realized just how long he had been submerged.

It is probable that Riker, had he been conscious of the effect of that cloud on the huge creature slithering out of the shadowy cavern far below, would have made for the boat with considerable alacrity. As it happened, however, he felt only his need for air as a matter of urgency, and kicked steadily for the surface still unaware of the upward drift of leviathan.

He broke free into the sunlight some twenty meters from *Oriana*'s shining hull, taking welcome breaths of air, and rolled over lazily on his back, watching the thready tendril of scarlet describe a diffuse umbilical between himself and the primordial sea.

Odd, he thought, we think of it as an alien planet, and yet the sea is just as full of wonder as the seas of Earth, and the sky is bannered with the same misty cirrus, and the people—

"Paul?"

Dao Marik appeared on deck, immaculate in white trousers and deck shoes. Lean, dark, and muscled like a gymnast, he might have appeared Earthling if not for the inhuman balance and reflexes that brought him in an effortless vault to the coach top while he scanned the sea, and down again in one extended moment of power-checked control that on Earth belonged only to a few accomplished athletes, or to big cats at the peak of their prime. "Paul?"

It was only when he stepped down that the limp was perceptible, Riker noted idly, and the dueling scars that marred the otherwise flawless green-gold hide of his second officer. He smiled to himself, recalling the dueling incident, as Marik called again, "Paul? *Zarik tu kelec imm?*" Where are you?

"Here, Dao. *An-an son*," he called back, and suddenly there was a scintillating explosion of life around him, of fishes fleeing the Reef. They were hitting his entire body and he caught at them with both hands, laughing and surprised, as they fled in fishy panic. Incredibly, then, the air was full of them; the same little red-bellied fish that had adopted him among the coral were now springing into the air in terror, all fleeing in the same direction, stinging his face and neck and chest with flat, cold slaps. He caught a couple of them in his hands and held them, wriggling and flipping, toward Marik.

"Look what I've got!" he called, laughing, as another school blundered into his treading legs. "Hey! I can't believe the excitement around here all of a sudden!"

"Paul!" Marik's quick gray gaze scanned the agitated water. "You'd better come out of there, right away!"

Riker tossed first one fish and then the other as high as he could, making an iridescent rainbow against the sky as they spread their fins and sailed. "Oh, I don't know, Dao," he began, rather reluctantly, for the water was very pleasant indeed. "I think I'll stay in for a while longer."

"Get back here!" Marik's tone was icy and imperative. "Now!" There was no amusement in the alien's face as he stood tensely at the rail, white knots of muscle showing at the angles of his jaw; and after a disbelieving pause, wherein Marik stood watching him intently, Riker stroked strongly toward the boat, puzzled and annoyed. Granted, he had ignored Marik's express warning about swimming outside the lagoon—had forgotten about it, in fact, until he saw Marik on deck!—but there was no need to get testy about it. It was a big ocean, but he wasn't a child. Paul Riker—Captain Paul Whitfield Riker, commanding USS *Skipjack*—could take care of himself. Marik's obvious apprehension was almost an insult. The boat loomed above him, casting its white shadow on the water.

Suddenly he was struck by a submerged, fast-moving something that threw him against the hull, knocking the wind out of him. Black lights danced before his eyes and he sank weakly below the surface just long enough to inhale a faceful of water that sizzled in his throat. Whooping and gagging, he clawed blindly for the ladder, and Marik grasped his arm and unceremoniously hauled him aboard just as a violent surge heeled *Oriana* over to port and back again.

There was the sound as of a huge ivory scissors clashing shut behind them, and an ominous sustained gurgling rising from the sea. Riker, who had fetched up hard against the superstructure when the sloop rolled, scrambled to his feet bruised and dripping, and demanded hoarsely, "What was *that* all about? What the hell's going on?"

Marik tipped his head mutely toward a spot hard off the

starboard beam, where a heavy, serpentine coil flowed out of the sea and back into it again in a kind of a mobile, living arch. Rising a good four meters above deck level, Riker estimated numbly, the coil was part of a body so thick and muscular as not to bend at any appreciable angle; it simply emerged as a flowing loop, its considerable speed indicated solely by the emergence and subsequent submersion of multiple pairs of small and gossamer fins. It was close enough for them to have reached out and touched it, had they been so inclined.

"Ramper," Marik said shortly as Riker stared aghast. "You can't be too careful." He turned away and busied himself freeing up the sail, and Riker shook his head in perplexity.

"But"—he pointed to the sea—"but I was just swimming there! Right there!" he blurted, and Marik flashed his brief white grin over his shoulder.

"So was the ramper," he confided drily, working at a stubborn reef point. "Here, bear a hand with this, will you? We'll want to make for shore as quickly as we can." Riker glanced at the place where the shimmering flukes had at last disappeared.

"You think it'll come back?"

"The ramper? No, they rarely attack boats. I'm surprised that this one came so close to *Oriana*. Actually, they're usually rather shy."

Riker nodded heavily and started on the next knotted line. "Right." He winked exaggeratedly. "You just keep right on believing it. It may look like 'shy' from the deck, buddy, but when you're the guy in the water . . ." Their shared laughter drowned out whatever else Riker might have wanted to say, and Marik allowed that "shy" might have been a slight oversimplification of the fact.

"Granting all that," Riker wondered, "why are we headed back?"

"Message from ComFleet. It came through on a scrambler key, which is why they couldn't patch it through to us out here. We'll have to take it at the house."

The house, Riker thought, was an extremely casual way to refer to the magnificent pavilion—Marik's family estate, or one of them—that had once been the Summer Palace of his grandfather, the last Han emperor: the Han who had ruled the world.

The Han were nearly extinct now, Riker recalled soberly, freeing the last reef point and slapping the furled canvas. Marik was one of the last of a dying breed. Had his beautiful young wife lived, they two might have produced a dynasty of Han children. As it was, there was only one, whom Marik had never seen. Only one.

The last.

The lost.

"Any word on your baby?"

Marik made no immediate answer, but watched as the sail came up like applause in the freshening breeze, and *Oriana* tugged at her anchor, plunging a bit and eager to be off. Then he smiled introspectively. "Not quite yet. But presently, I think."

Riker, having hauled in the anchor, slowly coiled the rope between his hands, not looking at his friend. "I hope so," he said fervently. "I just hope you can find her, Dao, wherever she is." He made no mention of his real concern; but it had been a long and savage war, and small children tended to get hurt in a war. Hurt—or dead.

Marik, busy at the wheel as the sleek craft began to knife her way through the choppy green swells, slid that cool gaze his way, and an expression at once humorous and grim crossed his face. His slit pupils dilated with emotion, and he looked as deceptively relaxed as a leopard lounging on a tree limb. "Oh, I'll find her. Believe me! If she is alive, I'll find her!" He paused, his eyes narrowed, and said softly, with unaccustomed intensity, "I've *got* to find her, Paul! She's all I have left!"

After that there was just the sound of the sea, hissing past the hull, and the mournful creaking of the *standi* perched on the mossy wet rocks along the shore.

Marik tossed his gear onto the sumptuous divan in his study, crossed to the telecom set in one oak-panelled wall, and switched it on, indicating a comfortable chair, which Riker declined with a shake of his head. He crossed instead to the tall, many-paned windows and stood gazing out over the broad, well-kept lawns and stately trees that had been growing here

since before the Return of the Earthlings, while Marik settled
himself in a carved bluestone chair and punched the series for
ComFleet.

Riker, curious as to what message could require scrambling,
heard the familiar "will call" signal from the telecom, and saw
it go to black. Evidently Fleet was busy with weightier
concerns than Marik and Riker; they would have to wait. Fleet
would ring back when they got around to it.

"Hurry up and wait," Riker grumbled. "Four-word history
of the military." He strolled restlessly around the room, from
the hand-carved doors past the cold hearth, where a fire was
laid ready for cool seaside nights, and back again to lean on the
edge of Marik's desk. He regarded Marik with an attitude of
quiet amazement.

"Do you realize," he demanded impressively, "that we are
actually sitting in the Summer Palace of the Han emperors? I
mean, think of it! The sense of history here! The things these
walls have seen, the families, the music, the slaves—"

"Our word for 'slave' has a somewhat different connotation
than yours," Marik reminded him quietly, from where he sat.

"But think of it, Dao," Riker continued, warming to his
subject. "The centuries of civilization this place represents!
You read in the history books about the Summer Palace, you
see copies of its art in professional journals! Why,
it's . . . it's invaluable, it's beyond price! Do you realize,"
he continued, crossing to the south window and looking out
over the rose garden, "that under slightly different circumstances, this pavilion would be the center of the world? World,
hell," he amended, "the whole system, wasn't it?"

"The entire system," Marik agreed quietly. "Eleven planets. Not counting our colonies."

Riker smiled to himself, caught up in the enormity of the
thought. "The center of Eisernon, right here," he repeated,
fascinated, and another thought struck him. "And you, Dao,
would be—"

He broke off, flushing, and whirled on Marik, an apology
ready on his lips, but there was such an expression on the
alien's face that no further words were possible. Marik smiled.

"—the emperor," he finished for him softly. "Yes. The

thought has occurred to me from time to time. Especially here, in this room.''

Riker's face was flushed and earnest. "Dao, you must believe I didn't intend—"

Marik closed his eyes and nodded his understanding. "No problem, Paul."

The silence grew long and companionable. A bird warbled outside. Dust motes danced in aimless circles, like vagrant thoughts, in the last thick gold shafts of sunlight slanting in through the tall windows. Finally, in another mood altogether, Riker broke the silence. "What did they call him? the Emperor.''

"My grandfather? What do you mean? Your Highness, or Your Majesty, something like that?" Riker nodded. "No. No, we don't say that. They called him—" He broke off suddenly, and smiled. "On second thought, I don't think I want to tell you. I don't think I want to tell you that at all." Riker stiffened with mock indignation.

"Come on! What about that famous Einai hospitality we hear so much about?''

"It doesn't extend to suicide. Forget it."

"I'll find out eventually, you know," Riker told him complacently. "Law of averages."

The telecom chimed. "I think not," Marik replied as it chimed again, and he pressed the stud. The face of an ensign—young, blond, everything by the book—appeared. "ComFleet Headquarters. Ensign Gould, sir." The disinterested blue eyes looked right through him.

"Second Officer Marik, USS *Skipjack*. I'm returning Administrator Barren's call.''

"Stand by one, sir." He made an off-screen adjustment and there was scarcely a flicker before the bland, fleshy face of Administrator Edwin Barren filled the screen and froze electronically while someone—probably Gould—cleared up a recalcitrant squiggle, affording them the opportunity to study him closely at some length.

Marik required no such opportunity. He remembered Barren well. It was Barren who had destroyed Marik's Einai service record and medical certification, including his registry as a Priyam, "for the good of the service," while Marik, seriously injured, had looked on helplessly from his hospital bed. The only other copies of the lost documents reposed in the scuttled hulk of the hospital ship USS *Pacific*, which was in such precarious condition that entry would have been suicidal. There was talk of nudging it into a local sun, and Marik hoped to chance the recovery of his papers before that happened. In the meantime, he—a Priyam—had been serving as a mere second officer aboard USS *Skipjack*, the sublight vessel under the command of Paul Riker.

The loss to the medical profession of his inherited and specifically trained talents was staggering, he reflected without conceit. For no matter how brilliant and dedicated he might be, if a man were not empathic and telepathic, no amount of study would make him so. And without those prerequisites, he could never become a Priyam. Many with the necessary qualifications had failed. To date, there were exactly nine Priyamli left in the galaxy. And one of them, Marik by name, had been prevented from practicing by Edwin Barren.

In all fairness, he supposed, his situation might have been worse. Under Riker, he had been permitted a limited practice aboard *Skipjack*; and his position as second, or science, officer was no lowly rank. If not for Paul Riker, he mused, and the intercession of Priyam Mykar Sharobi, who ran USS *Hope*, he might very well have been relegated to some lonely Rim outpost where they counted meteors for a living.

In the same fairness, too, his situation could have been infinitely better. If not for Administrator Barren, he would have been a full Priyam again. If not for Barren, he thought darkly, seated in his grandfather's palace, and all the men like Barren, he would have been much, much more than a mere Priyam.

The figure on the screen flickered to life and Administrator Barren smiled. "Why, Mister Marik, it's good to see you again. And I'll bet you're glad to see me, eh? Got you the job on the *Skipjack*, fixed you up, eh? How's that working out?"

"Splendidly, sir. Thank you."

Barren leaned closer, evidently peering into his own screen. "Who's that over there? Captain Riker? Is that you, Riker?" And as Riker came reluctantly into camera range, he continued jovially, "How's our boy working out? Need any special help? No little racial problems cropping up, eh?"

"No, sir," Riker replied stiffly. "No problems. Mister Marik is the finest second in the Fleet, and I consider it a privilege to work with him."

"Well, of course it is, Captain," Barren purred indulgently, with a confidential wink, "of *course* it is. Just like an Earthling, eh? Like I always say, give one of them a chance, and you can hardly tell the difference." He leaned forward conspiratorially and winked again.

"Now, say, I'm not one to trade on gratitude or anything like that, I think my reputation will bear me out, but I have a little favor to ask of you, and I don't think it's too much to expect."

"How may we serve you, sir?" asked the man in the bluestone chair, his gray eyes steady on the screen.

"Well, I've got a bunch of people here who are involved in the Reconstruction—you know, politicians, military, people like that, and some of them have never been to Eisernon before. . . ."

"And you'd like to show them something of the flavor here," Marik interpolated smoothly. "A few good bars, the quaint little shops, the remarkable bargains." He paused. "The Summer Palace."

"There you've got it!" Barren beamed, slapping his thigh. "You caught the whole idea first crack out of the barrel! You certainly are quick for an Einai, Mister Marik!"

"You're too generous, Administrator." Marik might have been carved of the same stone as the chair. "Very well. How many guests shall I expect, and when will they arrive?"

"Well, I thought tonight was a little soon, short notice, you know, so I told them tomorrow night. How's that? About six o'clock. For, say, a dozen people?" Marik's quick, almost imperceptible gesture silenced Riker's hot protest before it exploded. "I thought maybe one of those eye-eye banquets, you know what I'm talking about? And maybe you could round up a few natives, a village headman or something. Nothing too primitive, you understand, these people are top drawer, but give it some local color."

"We'll color it for you, sir. If green is an acceptable color." Most Einai were green-skinned, and had Barren been a little less obtuse, he might have had the grace to be embarrassed. Instead, he laughed as if Marik had said something amusing.

"That's pretty good," he chortled. "Pretty good. So we'll expect the red carpet for these people tomorrow night. Or the green carpet." He cleared his throat pompously. "If I can make it, I might drop down, too, but don't expect me until you see me. I've been to this kind of thing before, and after a couple of times, it gets kind of stale, you know?" He winked again. "Don't worry about me. You just enjoy yourselves tomorrow night. Marik. Captain." He made a curtailed wave of the hand, as a politician might make to his constituents, and the screen went to black.

"Yes, sir," Marik said to the dead screen. "Thank you, sir."

"Son of a bitch!" Riker expostulated. "You aren't going to do it! You heard him—he invited those people here—to *your home*—before he bothered to even consult you about it! Of course, you're not going to sit still for that! Let him take his dozen politicians to the Shali-Rho.* That'll take the edge off their appetite for 'local color'! The colossal nerve of the man!"

Marik rested his head against the back of the chair. It was a long moment before he spoke. "We are an occupied people," he said at length, from a great distance, "and the Federation is making a sincere effort to offer restitution for the damage that has been done our planet. Shall I refuse the courtesy of my house to those who are working to help us? You underestimate me, Paul."

Riker pointed an accusing finger at the telecom's blank screen. "Edwin Barren," he replied, "is an ill-mannered, congenital, son of a—"

"And if he is," Marik challenged, cutting him off, "what possible bearing could that have upon *my* behavior? Would you have me function on Barren's level? I am Priyam Hanshilobahr *Dom* Dao Marik! Not some Erthlik"—he teetered on the edge of an epithet, then the superb control, like the pleasant green-gold mask, slipped neatly into place—"named Edwin Barren," he finished smoothly. Riker make a mocking half bow.

*The Hotel Shali-Rho, located in and named for Eisernon's planetary capital, was, at the time of this narration, the finest accommodation the planet had to offer. It has since been eclipsed by several more-modern resorts, e.g., *The Bru-Riga* (Marriott), *The Elv, The Hilton Imperial,* et al.

"Very nice," he commented wryly. "I almost didn't hear that."

Marik smiled pensively at this steepled fingers and resumed thoughtfully, "This man Barren—in his own way, much as I dislike him—and I have several very good reasons for disliking him—Edwin Barren is working for us, too. Perhaps these guests of his have a right to see something of Eisernon as it was." He interlocked his fingers slowly, lost in a brown study, and rested his forehead against them. "As it could be again," he mused quietly. "This house has much to say, if a man has ears to hear." He lifted his head and tapped the thumbs of his still-clenched fists against his lips for a long, thoughtful space, his eyes half-closed, drew a deep, steadying breath, and got up, pulling his resolve and his hospitality together with one word: "Tarangi?"

Riker, half-seated on the edge of Marik's charis-wood desk, shook his head without looking up from his examination of a Xhole artifact that Marik used as a paperweight, thought better of it, put down the artifact with great care, and followed Marik tardily across the richly veined flooring in time to hear him murmur to himself, "Properly managed, this visit could be a godsend to us."

He opened an elegantly carved cabinet and took out two stoneglass bowls, divided half the contents of a crystal decanter between them, and expertly rotated the bowls in his palms, warming their clear green contents. He read Riker's expression correctly and repeated, as though it were important that Riker understand—and believe it. "No matter how much it inconveniences me personally, Paul, I will not oppose anything that could help my planet or its people."

"All right!" Riker, still smarting, tapped the cabinet with the side of his hand, wetting his lip abstractedly. "Tell me just one thing! Now, I have stood by and watched you let people step on you right and left! You let them call you coward and blame you for Mishli's death, when we both knew it was my fault! You let that pirate Mennon beat bloody hell out of you on *Hope* because you had some screwy sense of loyalty!"

"Granted," Marik agreed calmly, still warming the bowls; but his eyes glittered blackly, so wide were his pupils, the dead giveaway that he was feeling much more than he was letting

on. Riker began to pace, continuing hotly, "Now this jackass
Barren comes along, this—this *bigot!*—and he takes you over
for his own PR! And you let him do it without so much as an
argument! Sure, walk on my face, sir! By all means, take over
my house while you're at it! Kindly give one of us a chance,
and we're almost as good as an Earthling! Not quite, of course,
but almost!" He wheeled on Marik. "Where's your pride, for
God's sake? What the hell's the matter with you, Mister? Are
they right? Are you basically a coward, after all?"

Marik's head jerked as if he had been stung. He set down
one of the bowls on the cabinet ledge for Riker and resumed his
place in the ornate chair. For a while, he gazed into the middle
distance, not moving when Riker muttered, "I'm sorry, Dao. I
didn't mean that; you're one of the bravest men I've ever met."
He shook his head in anger and chagrin. "It's just that you
have no more sense of self-preservation than a—a lemming!"

"My first responsibility is to Tadae," Marik retorted crisply,
"and my second is to my people. *I've got to do what I can for
them!*" Bitterly, "T'ath knows that's little enough." He set
down his tarangi and clenched his interlocked fists against his
mouth once more.

"And what about yourself?" Riker asked. "Free of your
people, Dao, what about yourself?"

"Self!" The word blazed out as Marik's hands hit the chair
arms hard, and it startled even Riker, who had a reputation for
steadiness under fire. Marik was on his feet in the swift, fluid,
feline reflex that betrayed his anger more forcefully than the
utter revulsion in his voice. "Self!" he repeated disgustedly.
"Do you people never get sick of hearing yourselves say
'self'? Do you never think of anyone else but your great god
'Self'? It's no wonder you Erthlikli have such a lust for
colonization, Captain! Each of you occupies a one-man world!
No wonder you need the universe to your 'selves'!" He turned
away and braced both hands on the windowsill, slowly bending
his head.

Riker stood astounded. Marik's reaction had shocked and
disturbed him. Selfish? he protested mentally. I? Half-
defensively, he reflected quickly upon the history of Earth, of
the Riker family, and of Paul Riker specifically, and a warm
flush crept under his jawline. Well, *yes*, but . . . he rational-

ized mentally, so maybe we're a little self-centered sometimes; but we've done a bit of good here and there, too, his mind protested defensively. We're not all bad.

It was then, at that thought, that he knew Marik was right. When a man felt he had to defend his goodness, even to himself, he couldn't be very sure of it. A truly good man, a superior man, wouldn't have to resort to defense. The superior man had no need of witnesses to his virtue, least of all himself. It was simply evident, needing no defense and recognizing no accuser.

And his accuser? He swung on Marik—and stopped.

The sun had set, and the run of silver dusk light on hair and shoulder and high cheekbone made him appear unreal, Riker thought, an image out of some dreamer's imaginings: alien royalty in white ducks and deck shoes, suffering our unbearable selfishness. And he's right about us, Riker pursued, there's the pity of it. He's right. How many inconvenient unborn did we massacre, how many unwanted and elderly did we pull the plug on (before they became suddenly valuable as immigrants and baby-sitters for immigrants, for—great God!—more colonization!), sacrificing how many millions of our Past and our Future to the god who predates our sporadic interest in Yahweh? The great god Self. Ask Cain, Riker thought ruefully. Better than that, ask Abel. Ask the ones who bleed. They'll tell you, down to the last drop, what it cost them for some of us to want a master race, a segregated society, an endless cornucopia to sate our insatiable greed.

Oddly enough it was his disdain for just such attitudes that had led Paul Riker to abandon the polo and lansquenet of his affluent cronies in favor of the clean, spare, egalitarian toughness of the Space Academy.

Riker clasped his hands behind him. "I'm sorry, Dao," he offered sincerely. "I deserved that. I am, after all, an Earthling, and I'm probably more selfish than I realized, both for myself and for my friends."

Marik lifted his head, pulled a deep, shuddering sigh, and turned back from the window where the first stars—wet, shiny, white discs—were beckoning. "No," he replied, once again the genial, effortless host, "what you deserve is an apology—and an answer. You are a guest in my house, and a worthy one

at that.'' He made a very humble and touching bow, a courtly
gesture that might have fit well in some medieval setting.
''*Buchat-ge, chom-shanami*,'' Marik murmured contritely.
''*Sint em ze domt en chomde'ze rak-tun al chomtun she'hai.*''
Forgive me, most honored friend. I will offer the merit of the
penance I perform for your own soul.

''There's nothing to forgive, for pity's sake. I deserved it!''
Riker made a disclaiming gesture, feeling embarrassed and
uncomfortable. ''Besides,'' he added awkwardly, ''you were
right.''

Marik straightened and flashed that brief white smile.
''That,'' he confided, ''has absolutely nothing to do with it.''
He picked up his tarangi from the desk, drank, and sauntered
back to the window, studying the sky. ''We're in for some
weather. I hope it holds off until the miligachin is harvested.
Bad time of year for a storm; this late, we get those small, fast
ones that do a lot of local damage.''

Riker made no comment to that, and Marik recognized his
captain's expression, the unwavering determination to keep the
conversation on course. With a quick gesture, Marik flung
away all the conversational trivia that might have insulated him
from Riker's trenchant question and the necessity of a reply.
What about yourself, Dao?

''You want your answer. And the answer is, I can never be
free of my people, Paul. I am all they have of an emperor, and
am therefore their servant. That, by and large, is the function of
emperors.''

Riker crossed toward him, weighing the concept in his hand.
''But—if you were! Please, a fantasy, now, a supposition. If
you were—!'' He invaded the alien's eyes with his earnest
brown stare, and after an introspective moment, Marik crossed
slowly to the bluestone chair, obviously deep in thought, and
sat down.

''Free of the responsibility of my people, Captain,'' he said
at last, ''and faced with the sort of a situation Barren has
presented in my life, I would find several options open to me:

''First, and most obviously, I could slay Barren out of hand;
but besides the fact that such a course would put me out of sync
with Tadae, it's an impractical idea.''

''I'm not so sure of that,'' Riker muttered darkly.

"What would I gain, Paul?" Marik countered. "My records returned to me? My position as a Priyam?" His voice dropped. "Mishli?"

And it occurred to Riker that had it not been for Edwin Barren's meddling in Marik's life, the lovely Hennem-mishli might still be alive and here, bringing constant spring to the Summer Palace.

"Of course not," Marik continued briskly. "And I would have to endure the guilt of sending someone to Tadae in Barren's condition. Tsk, tsk. Can't have that, you know." He sipped from his bowl.

"So, then, the second option: ah, there's the temptation, my friend. Not to *break* him, you understand, but a little judicious *bending* of the man . . . But there it is again, you see. Out of the question. Although, as I said," he reminisced regretfully, "one *is* tempted to *think* about it, from time to time."

"And you've come up with a good reason why that's impractical, too, right?"

Marik held him with his eyes. "Eight months on a hospital ship taught me that pain is never an answer—it's a question. And I couldn't impose that question on anyone else, Paul." Just the ghost of a smile. "I still have trouble enough answering it myself." Marik sipped again from the bowl in his palm, thoughtful, relaxed, seemingly done with talk.

Riker, on the other hand, felt annoyed with what he regarded as Marik's passivity, and fervently wished that he had been in a position of reply to Barren's summary appropriation of the Summer Palace. There had been a time, at home on Zerev, when, given an equivalent provocation, Paul Riker would have made a suggestion as to time and place (say, the Dueling Oaks, at dawn?) and sent over his second with a gauntlet.

Proper reprimands aside, he could still conjure up an option or two that Marik had overlooked, not that Marik had any options. Two choices, both of them impossible, was the same as no choice at all, he felt, and said as much. It was Marik's turn to be surprised. "I agree with you, Paul," he assured him sincerely. "Those choices are no choice at all. That's why I chose the third option."

"Which is . . . ?" Riker demanded.

"I forgave him," Marik said simply, and Riker let out a short explosion of laughter, half an astonished expletive.

"I believe it! Do you know—I believe it? Anyone else, no, but *you*!" He shook his head in exasperation, paced around the room, and then hesitated before Marik, who sat watching him with a tranquil feline air.

"You do not exist!" he accused, pointing a finger at him. "You aren't real! And this pavilion isn't real! Dammit, Dao, people just don't act like that! People just aren't that patient, that—hell, it sounds stupid, but people aren't that *good*! By all rights, you should have killed somebody by now, after what's been done to you! I know *I* would have under the same circumstances!"

"Tadae wouldn't like it," Marik smiled. "And besides, if I did what I felt, instead of what I ought to do, what would happen to—"

"What would happen to my people?" Riker mimicked in chorus with him. "Yes, I know. But somewhere there's got to be an end to it!"

"Oh, there will be," Marik assured him, suddenly grim. "Even a Han Einai has an end to his patience. If someone went too far, I would be obliged to correct his discretion."

Riker finished his drink and put down the bowl. "And Tadae wouldn't mind that."

"He'd love it," Marik said, grinning. " 'Admonish the sinner' and so forth. It just hasn't gotten bad enough yet."

Riker was stopped short of asking just exactly how bad it had to get, before it was 'bad enough,' by the chime of the telecom, and the cheery face of a middle-aged Einai woman appeared on the screen. Her merry yellow eyes described hemispheres, as if she saw only the top, or better, half of the world and those in it, and her cheeks were as round and shiny as green apples. The lower half of her face was painted a clear, even pale blue, the distinctive Shimshen caste mark, and Marik's hearts squeezed a little at this. Mishli, too, had been a Shimshen, dedicated to Life. In the background, they could hear the voices of very small children at play. Marik reached forward with a hand as steady as marble and opened the switch.

Marik could not have guessed that miles away, in the dingy back room of a nondescript bar, a small group of determined men was watching him on an ordinary telecom. For a space, the pickup caught a tight head shot of him as he bent toward the set in his study, then the image leaned back in the carved bluestone chair.

"Dao Marik," he identified himself quietly. The remarkable gray Han gaze seemed to regard them with a calm self-possession, making some of the men uneasy until they reminded themselves that it was his caller Marik saw, and not their intrusion. As Marik opened the switch, the other half of the split screen bloomed into light and the woman—from Marik's point of view—became visible.

"A Shimshen," one of the men, an albino swamplander, murmured. "This could be what we're waiting for." He brushed his snowsilk hair out of his eyes and squinted against the glare of the set. Someone muttered assent, but there was no comment from their leader, a tall, bearded Einai who absently fingered the thin white scar at the base of his throat. He stared back at Marik with unvarnished hatred in his tiger yellow eyes, lost in thought; then he pulled a deep breath and lifted his chin at a lean, fair, young Krail, standing against the far wall.

At the Einai's signal, he went through a door leading into a cellar, and from there into a subterranean conduit that had been broached by skillfully placed thermite. Catching the eye of a small, shaven-headed man dressed in the uniform of the Public Service Utility who was working atop a ladder at the telecom cable, he scarcely nodded before turning back the way he came.

The bald man climbed down and made his way along the conduit to a jury-rigged junction, lit by electronic torches, where a burly giant of a man—Jek by name—was holding two Public Service workers against the wall with a minimum of effort. The bald man paid them no attention, but hurried to a makeshift console set against the curving wall and switched off several toggles, reset a rheostat to its normal setting, and pulled his patchwork out of the main trunk line. He left everything as he had found it, with the exception of the illegal extension of Marik's telecom line no engineer would have believed he could rig. He removed his coverall, gave Jek a sign (whereupon the giant removed his restraining arm from the two workers, warning them with one pointing finger to remain hugging the wall), and the two left, locking the cellar door behind them. By the time the workers broke it down, the bushmen would be long gone and the bald man's patchwork would have self-destructed automatically.

The woman on the other half of the split screen moved. Her dimples deepened and disappeared, and her eyes lighted, but there was a steely glint behind them. When she spoke, it was in High Eisernai, and very respectfully.

"*Chom-ala,* Hanshilobahr *Dom* Dao Marik," she greeted him, making the *chom-ala* gesture as of old, the silent clap-and-spread of both hands, which Marik echoed gravely. "My name is Sofyan of Elv, and I have only just heard of your search for the little one." She nodded wisely. "You have searched far, my lord. Your people are very thorough."

Thorough? He considered the word. Ten provinces had been searched in four days; in a month, the entire protectorate. The continent, if need be. Anywhere there could be a street called Raintree. The search, which would have been tedious under any circumstances, was made infinitely more difficult because of the chaos left by the most recent installment of the war. Records had been lost, files destroyed. Those city maps remaining often showed housing where now there were vast fields of rubble. Wild fern and coreliae vines were beginning to cover raw, blasted earth where villages once had stood. And worse, virtually every settlement larger than three or four huts had a Raintree Street.

The raintree was native to Eisernon, growing wild on the mountains and gracing public parks, and the name was as common to the planet as Ruro-Yal was to Minsoner, or Main Street to Earth. Marik pulled a deep sigh. Raintree Street. So far Raintree Street—all the Raintree Streets, in all the cities and towns and villages—had been a series of dead ends.

She was waiting for his answer. They all wanted him to talk: the media people, the sincerely interested, the bored, the cranks. They all wanted him to give them something, lend them something, share his personal life and his agonizing quest for his child. Several women had proposed marriage; many had offered alternatives less exalted and a good deal more enthusiastic.

What no one seemed to understand was that all Dao Marik wanted was his child, alive and well, and a little peace and quiet. So far, the only respite he had had from this inundation had come aboard *Oriana*, with the sea anchor out and the telecom shut off, praying for word of his baby.

Thorough, the Shimshen had called the searchers? They had better be, at the very least, thorough, Shimshen.

"That's to be expected, don't you think?" he asked in the split second after her comment. "After all, she is my daughter."

Although, he reflected, there was no assurance that his child was a girl. It might be a son, for all he knew. Kles Mennon, the pirate who had been first to let him know she existed, had referred to her merely as "the baby," but there had been a feel about it, a mental flavor, an—oh, call it an *essence*—that marked the thought unmistakably as being that of a little girl. He thumbed the hidden "record" stud and the screen immediately locked onto the call and printed out the location and telecom code of the caller.

As the information printed out on the monitor set, miles away, the five men in the room reacted. No one spoke or moved, but their expressions sharpened. They came alert. The giant bushman, Jek, blinked slowly at the Krail standing by the alley door, and the youngster allowed himself a death's-head smile.

As the final numerals printed out, their leader, Mennon, without turning his tiger's-gaze from the set, indicated the door with a curt forefinger, like a weapons master cueing his bowmen. Without a sound, the albino known as Mouse and his Krail counterpart slipped out into the night and were gone, while Mennon sat watching his prey, a smile of grim satisfaction touching his lips and missing his eyes completely.

Marik tugged himself away from the painful memories of Mennon and Mishli and loss, even as he released the "record" stud. "How may I help you, chom-Sofyan?" he offered courteously.

The woman did something strange then. Searching his eyes individually for a sober moment, she enunciated distinctly, "Plus 7–538, negative 9L." *The number Marik had placed and replaced from the cabin of Oriana. The universal search code for a specific Stored-Unborn.*

"Only Mishli and I had that code," Marik retorted crisply. "How did you—"

"Answers require credentials, sir," she replied, cutting him off. "For your information, the search code is obsolete for this child. She has already been born."

"But Mishli—"

"Her grandfather," she demanded, interrupting again. "What was his name? Quickly now!"

"Hanshilobahr *Domne* Dao Marik. The emperor."

"He was your own ancestor—if indeed you are whom you claim to be! Sitting in that chair proves nothing! I warn you, try no tricks with me!"

Marik leaned back into the chair in question. "No tricks, I assure you. Mishli was of the Royal House of Imran, the daughter of Imran the Younger. We were cousins." Then, smiling a bit, he leaned toward the set and confided boyishly, "And I really *am* Dao Marik."

"Then you'll know her grandfather's name!" she persisted. "The other grandfather. And be quick about it!" She seemed very determined, Marik thought, and not a little frightened. He wondered why.

"Oman Shari-Mnenoplan," he answered softly. She could not know what memories the dear old man's name evoked. "Priyam Oman Shari-Mnenoplan. Her grandfather. My master."

Her face started to light up, but she tried to remain stern, without much effect. "What is One and One and One?"

And Marik quoted, "One and One and One make One, the multiplicity of Congruence—"

"Enough!" she beamed. "Enough, my lord. You are, truly, Dao Marik, and I am your servant, as I was servant to my Sister Life-Bearer, Lady Hennem-mishli. Ask, and I will answer you."

It was Marik's turn to study her face, her eyes. "What do you know of Mishli?"

"I am the Shimshen who was entrusted with my lady's child," she told him proudly. "I bore her, along with my other two, according to my vows."

"And my child?" he demanded huskily.

"She is with me."

CHAPTER

II

THEY LEFT BEFORE dawn.

Having discovered his child's whereabouts last night, the customarily impassive Marik had astounded them all by striding through the hallowed corridors, slamming doors, shouting orders, rummaging happily through storage bins, upsetting tack rooms, and generally creating a monumental uproar among the servants.

They were to travel by horseback, for the terrain leading to the isolated mountain village of Bends-Over-The-River was rough and dangerous and provided no purchase for cruiser treads, and Riker, who was to accompany Marik on his journey, was not familiar enough with gryphon flight to risk efforts in that direction. There was not even level terrain enough to accommodate a skimmer. It would have to be horses.

Nor was the trip their only consideration. Things would be changed at the Palace now. They would never be the same again. Not only would there be one child—and the Han heir at that!—but three! Three children to chase their echoing laughter down the tessellated halls, three to race their ponies across the broad lawns, and sport like small green-gold dolphins in the commodious pool. Three! Not only his one, but three! Marik was ecstatic.

Preparations had to be made. Even now, women servants were making up the room that had been Mishli's retreat, laying out fresh linen for the big bed where another, childish head would pillow its dark curls by tomorrow, and the old *amah* had brought out playthings she had carefully stored away since Mishli's childhood and arranged them critically around the room.

31

Others prepared an adjoining suite for Sofyan and her additional two charges, for she would be expected to remain at the Palace to attend the little *Ka*. Marik even ordered a large parlor to be redecorated as a playroom, sent off a servant to Pal-alden-Shali-Rho for the biggest stuffed toy he could find, and positioned it so the child would see it first upon her arrival at her father's house.

After a while it became evident that no one was likely to get much sleep that night, so around midnight, the steward, Shang, ordered a cold supper of fresh fruit, wine, and a variety of meats to be laid out so that the *Dom* and his guest might refresh themselves. It was served in the study on antique silver service that had come down through the family for many generations.

Marik, temporarily distracted from his furious preparations by the dinner summons, found Riker already serving his plate and joined him with high spirits too intense for small talk. They sat down near the fire, for the wind off the sea was chill even for spring, freshening unexpectedly out of the north—and for a while there was no sound but the snapping of the logs, the far clatter of an occasional plate, and, of course, the measured booming of the surf on the Reef at Bru-Riga.

"I feel a little guilty enjoying this," Riker confided, indicating his plate. There was the platter of small rain against the windows.

"Guilt doesn't seem to affect your appetite," Marik drawled, spearing a louvi with his fork. "Why should you feel guilty? You're my guest."

Riker tipped his head toward the door. "Your people out there. Here we sit, feeding our faces, and they're out there—"

"Slaving away," Marik finished for him. "With 'slave' the operative concept." He shook his head in exasperation. "You can't let that go, can you? Liberal gentility, saving the galaxy. Would it make you feel any better to know that there's an identical repast provided for them in the kitchens? That any one of them, seated here—by invitation!—with us, would feel ill at ease after the first five minutes, and wish with both his hearts that he were back there with his friends, enjoying the kind of companionship he is accustomed to?

"Paul, the kindest thing you can do for a man is to allow him to seek his own level—to find his identity himself, and fulfill it! And then to accept him that way."

"Even if he wants to be a mere servant all his life," Riker scoffed, not bothering to hide his distaste.

"Why not?" There was nothing ironic in Marik's tone. "There is nothing 'mere' about a good servant, just as there is nothing 'mere' about a good starship captain. Paul—" he invaded Riker's eyes earnestly "—not one of those very good people out there has ever aspired to be anything but a good and faithful servant."

"How do you know what they aspire to?" Riker challenged.

"Because," Marik said, smiling, "not one of them—who is still here—has ever made the slightest effort, by word or deed, to be anything else! If they had, I would have done everything in my power to assist them—as I did those who've moved on!" He lounged back in the sumptuous leather chair, tipped back his head, and regarded the fire pensively. He was clearly deep in thought; when he spoke, it was so quietly that he might have been speaking to himself. "Perhaps there is more true charity in permitting a man to be a very good ditch digger—and be proud of it! —than it is to rail at him for not using a robotrak. Worse yet to tell him that the robotrak can do the job faster, better, and for less money! He cannot use a robotrak! Perhaps he cannot afford one, perhaps the learning is beyond his ability, but now you have made him unable to be proud of his sweat and his shovel! You have gained him nothing—and yourself nothing—but you have robbed him of the dignity of his calling! You have ruined him in his own eyes, and no one has the right to do that to anyone!" He turned the full weight of that remarkable alien gaze on Riker. "No one," he repeated, "no matter how well intentioned."

"Maybe not," Riker growled. "And maybe your happy ditch digger—and your contented servants our there—simply haven't had the chance to be anything better."

"That's possible," Marik allowed, getting up and crossing to the table, where half the supper lay untouched. "As you know, we do not have compulsory education here on Eisernon, even though our literacy level is second highest in the galaxy, because we believe that the destiny of children is the direct responsibility of the parents to whom Tadae gave them. If they wish them educated, there is abundant opportunity to be had for the asking. But''—he selected a mushroom—''they have to ask.''

''So if the parents choose to ignore the education of their children,'' Riker said incredulously, tapping the chair arm with the edge of his hand, ''society is stuck with a bunch of dependent illiterates!''

''Illiterates, yes.'' Marik quartered a pij with a razor-sharp little fruit knife, laid it on his plate, and flipped the knife smartly into the cutting board, where it stuck quivering, stinging the air. ''Dependent, no.''

''Not bad,'' Riker admired offhandedly, and Marik thanked him with an inclination of the head. ''Unlike you Erthlikli,'' he continued, ''we Einai do not subsidize those who choose not to work. There is employment aplenty on this planet, Paul. Even for the unlettered.''

''And I suppose your government doesn't subsidize the poor, either!'' He knew better than to mention the elderly. In Eisernon's family-oriented culture, the old were secure.

''No, that sort of sharing is the privilege of those men born more fortunate,'' Marik told him. ''And, of course, the churches.''

''Must be hell on the atheists,'' Riker muttered, and his host gave him a quizzical stare.

''Of course not.''

Riker stared back. ''Why not?''

Marik smiled complacently. ''Atheists don't have a hell, Paul. They don't believe in it.''

Riker, more than a little annoyed, drained his glass and, joining Marik at the table, dropped two ice wheels into his glass with some force, widening Marik's smile a bit.

''So they're not *dependent* illiterates, they're *atheistic* illiterates! That's begging the question, Dao! The fact remains, you have unlettered laborers on your hands! And you can't build a planet on stupidity!''

''Erth did,'' Marik interjected amusedly and, as Riker wheeled on him, laughed aloud. ''I'm sorry, Paul, bad joke. Just . . . slipped out.'' But it was clear that Riker considered the issue no laughing matter and, sighing resignedly, the alien continued: "We do have illiterates scattered here and there—those few who, realizing that their low standard of living is directly proportionate to their low standard of education, choose not to seek an education as adults—but for one generation only. When their children are grown, seeing their peers succeed and realizing what their lack of education has deprived them of, they tend to overcompensate in the education of their own offspring. Statistics—and we keep very good statistics here, Paul—run about ninety-two percent in favor of those children becoming overachievers."

He selected a raw carrot, bit off a section, and munched it thoughtfully. "I'll give you an example: My steward, Shang, comes from what the Erthlikli would term a disadvantaged home: nineteen children, overworked mother, father indulgent and kind, but couldn't hold a job. Played the chukuri rather well, though; used to sit around strumming while the wife and daughters took in laundry.

"By the time he was twelve, Shang—who was fourteenth in line—began to see what was in store for him unless he took matters into his own hands. He wasn't interested in farming or aquaculture like most of his older brothers, nor did he care for any of the trades—smithing, glassblowing, or the like. So he had his father apprentice him to a merchant in return for his room and board. No pay, just room and board."

"The word for that in Ertheng is *exploitation*," Riker informed him.

"It was all he was worth—and all the merchant could afford. Even then, Shang's father had to throw playing his chukuri at the wedding of the merchant's son into the bargain. But the man needed Shang's help, and Shang needed the work to build his character—and his life. Also, the merchant taught the boy to read and write." At Riker's disbelieving glance, he pursued, "He knew how and the boy didn't. Of course he taught him. It's only natural."

At Riker's dry observation that what was natural among Einai wasn't necessarily so among other species, he countered, "But we're talking about Einai here, aren't we?

"Be that as it may, Shang appreciated it. He attended night

classes, worked his way up from sweeping floors and dusting stock to clerking and then to purchasing and keeping accounts, and finally to running his employer's business. He made him rich several times over, and himself into the bargain. And he was the soul of honesty.

"By this time he'd met and married a young girl of similar circumstances who'd been keeping house for the Shimshenli. They were a couple of such competence and piety that they were an example to the whole village, and they came to the notice of the Crown.

"One day, my father sent Shang a message that he wished to see him. It was a great honor," he interrupted himself to explain, "to be invited to the Summer Palace. Not many people got inside the gates in those days. And everyone knew that this was no official or member of one of the royal houses, but the son of Asiya, the local ne'er-do-well.

"After they had conferred together—in this room—for several hours, they emerged together, my honored father looking very pleased, and Shang looking proud but stunned, wearing the medallion of his new office: steward of the Imperial House.

"And, Paul, such was his filial piety," Marik continued impressively, "that the first thing he did was to go back to the village where he'd been loved and brought up—to the hovel where the two old people still lived so as not to outclass their neighbors—and he kissed his parents' hands and thanked them for the gift of Life."

"Then he went back to his plush new quarters and his high social position feeling smug and justified," Riker assisted sardonically.

"No," Marik corrected quietly, "then he rebuilt the village at his own expense, starting with his parents' house. They renamed it after him for that: The Village That Shang Rebuilt. In Eisernai, Shang Ri La." Beyond the fitful patter of the rain, the surf *boomed* against the Reef.

"Shang has five sons and three daughters," he continued briskly, ticking them off on his fingers as he spoke. "Two are physicians, one administers the law, one girl is a Shimshen and worked under fire rescuing children from the war zone, a son was killed and decorated posthumously by the High Council for gallantry in the face of overwhelming odds, and the last three are children.

"Asiya, named for his grandfather, is a superb stableboy and will probably never be anything else, nor should he be—horses are his life. Jol is mechanically inclined and has just accepted an offer from a skimmer-manufacturing firm on Krau, who'll send him to the university, with pay, in return for an option on his services. The last is a suckling babe." He paused for breath. "Not bad for a 'mere' servant, wouldn't you say?"

"Not bad at all," Riker retorted, flushing, "but probably an isolated success story." Marik courteously withheld his contradiction and Riker's flush deepened.

"On Earth—and on Zerev, my colony planet—we believe in the equality of Man. No one's any better than anyone else! By law!"

"But, Paul, be reasonable," Marik persisted. "No two people in the universe have ever been truly equal, except in the sight of Tadae! The mere concept abrogates individuality and free will!"

"They're equal on Earth," Riker expostulated, "and they're equal on our colonies, too!"

"All the same, eh?" Marik persisted, baiting him amusedly.

"That's right!" Riker snapped.

"Exactly alike. No difference."

"None!"

"Like ants."

Realizing that he had painted himself into a corner, and failing to find a graceful way out of it, Riker fell back on his original premise. "We believe in equality." He stood glaring at Marik for a long moment, during which the inscrutable alien's face broke into a slow, wide, white smile, probably at his, Riker's, expense, he surmised correctly.

"Not us Einai," Marik assured him, refilling his wineglass for him. "We believe in *freedom*, which we define as the right to be all you can be, and in *tolerance*, which we define as the sacred obligation to respect people as they are.

"You known what else we believe? We believe in all that bad stuff—like midnight suppers"—he lifted the bottle in salute—"and in emperors"—he made a slight, mocking bow and refilled his own glass—"and in Summer Palaces, so the

very equal Erthlikli have someplace interesting to go on shore
leave." He lifted his glass to Riker. "Prosit."

Riker's reluctant grin had grown beyond his control. "You
go straight to hell," he advised Marik cheerfully, and the alien
gave the suggestion a moment's sham consideration.

"No," he decided at last, putting down his glass, "I don't
think Tadae would like that. I don't think I'd like it, either. I
think I'll opt for a shower instead. We'll be leaving presently.
If you'll excuse me?" He made a courtly inclination of the
head and was gone, limping silently across the marble flooring,
before Riker could formulate a reply.

At last, when the eastern horizon was a dark band of sea and
sky set apart only by the brooding outline of the island of
Tagan, all was in readiness. Marik and Riker had changed to
sturdy riding clothes, with hooded cloaks to ward off the
mountain chill and the cold drizzle falling from the low sky.
Their mounts danced impatiently in the cobbled wet confines
of the stable yard, whickering excitedly and tossing their
heads.

The pony, which was to be led by Asiya, had been outfitted
with a soft red leather pad and a gay little belled harness that
jingled when he moved.

The mules were packed and saddled.

The servants were outside, some with torches, some in their
nightclothes, with blankets or shawls hastily wrapped about
their shoulders, to see the *Dom* off. Marik leaned down from
the saddle and clasped Shang's hand. "Be my eyes," he
commanded in the time-honored ritual. "Be my hands." And
the steward bowed his obedience.

"Go swiftly, my lord, and bring back Eisernon-to-come,"
he ordered reverently. Marik gripped his hand for another
impressive moment, then wheeled his mount, flung them a
joyful salute, and set off at an easy lope for the mountain
village where a child waited who would be called Eisernon-
to-come.

By the time it was light enough to distinguish clearly objects
along the road, the three riders had made considerable progress.

Leaving the extensive, well-manicured grounds of the Palace proper and the dripping primeval majesty of the Royal Preserve (where, Marik confided, some of the best hunting in the world was to be had), they emerged with the dawn onto the highway that led through one of the villages that had sprung up like toadstools during the Federation Occupation.

Marik was utterly silent and withdrawn as they rode through, and looked neither left nor right. Quite unlike his attitude four days ago, Riker reflected, when they'd driven through the nasty place on the way to the Palace. Then he had been voluble—and vehement.

The pity of it, Marik had explained coldly, was that this particular social malignancy had completely cannibalized the lovely little settlement that had once guarded the emperor's gates. Had it grown to be an ordinary village, Marik had muttered, eyes narrowed, hands tight on the wheel, it would have been a pleasure to see it expand. Healthy growth was to be commended, but this untidy cluster of filthy hovels and ramshackle dives, outfitted with neon and billboards, had completely obliterated the tranquil village.

And raucous Federation tourists, with cameras on their stomachs and the inevitable tri-D sets slung blaring over their shoulders, eagerly crowded the curio shops and bars, carrying away gaudy trinkets and impudently tossing litter into the streets and beer cans into the ancient fountains.

There was even a supposed museum, he continued bitterly, run by two ex-servicemen, that boasted an odd assortment of badly preserved flora (available for an exorbitant fee from the management for the making of plastex lamp shades back home); a few one-of-a-kind "antiques" bought firsthand from the locals who, having wept piteously over parting with their last relic of great-grandma and accepted small fortunes for the consideration, promptly went home and turned out another half dozen that afternoon; bits of rock chipped from boulders right down the road and displayed on dusty velvet; and, incredibly, a desiccated corpse, propped up and flaking away in a corner, that purported to be a stuffed Han.

The fee was half a credit. For the other half, you could get a bowl of ersatz tarangi and sit in on a nonstop concert, notable chiefly for the fact that you could hear its vocalist clearly (though not, of course, understand what he was saying, an impediment shared even by patrons sitting in the first row, center) three full blocks away.

This sterling establishment, Marik had finished grimly, was located on a road where once there had been only a street of booksellers and the quiet music of the chukuri.

The village was silent this morning as they rode through. Its denizens, presumably up late enjoying its tawdry fascinations, had not yet put in an appearance. But the litter was in evidence—and plenty of it! That, and the stench. Even the horses picked up their feet smartly, as if disdaining contact with the grimy refuse, and snorted vexedly through wide, fluttering nostrils.

It was with relief that they turned westward out of the offensive settlement, abandoning the spattered, sticky glasphalt for a dusty, unpaved road that led between fields green with sweet clover and wet with the night's rain. They rode through a clean, thatched-roofed farming community that smelled deliciously of fresh-baked bread, where sleepy bos lowed and cocks were increasingly optimistic about the possibility of a sunrise, and turned sharply just beyond the foothills to escort a babbling and delirious young river back up the mountain it had fallen from.

The sky, which had been a blush of tender and indescribable color, a mackerel sky, banded with red rows of small, fleecy clouds, burgeoned into light so clear and pure that Riker was reminded of the quality of light in the countryside bordering Earth's Aegean Sea, which he had seen only once and never forgotten. Newly budded leaves and fresh grasses alike picked up the gold tinge of the sun, and for more than an hour the men rode along in companionable silence, watching the play of broken sunlight on rock and tree and patch of sheltered snow.

After a while, however, the comfortable feel, as of a warm hand laid against his back, seemed more like the heat of an increasingly warm engine. He saw that Marik, too, had flung back his cloak and was guiding his mount into the scant shade offered by the trees along the way. Riker, who until now had been content to ride single file between Marik's big bay gelding and Asiya's mule, spurred his mount ahead until he matched pace with his host.

"How much farther to the mountain?" he wanted to know.

"You're on it. But to the village? An hour, maybe an hour and a half if we take it easy on the horses," Marik estimated. "Why? Getting tired?"

"Getting thirsty. The wind may be cool, but that sun is hot!"

"We'll stop up here. There's a place a little farther on." There was a long pause while Marik rode along silently beside him, apparently warring with himself as to whether to continue. At length he drew a deep breath and admitted, "Paul, something's been troubling me. Maybe you have an answer."

"Try me."

Marik chose his words with great care. "Why would Barren have gone to the trouble of calling us under a scrambler key—as if it were an official message—unless he had something much more important to say than 'May several of my friends come to dinner?' That doesn't ring true."

Riker scowled, considering this. "You're right. It doesn't." He turned in the saddle to stare into Marik's eyes. "You think something's going on."

"Right. I'm betting it has something to do with the interference that had to be cleared up before the call could come through. Could happen we had an audience."

"Wouldn't the ensign have been aware of that?"

"He'd have had to. Couldn't compensate otherwise. And he'd have alerted Barren to watch his step." He shook his head in dissatisfaction. "Whatever Edwin Barren called to say last night is still unsaid. I sense patterns there I don't like."

Riker stretched his cramped muscles. "What you're probably sensing," he drawled, "is an overdue breakfast."

"That, too." Marik reined up in a grassy glen near the water, where the boisterous stream tumbled down a series of small cascades, bumbled together again, and plunged on to its rendezvous with the peaceful valley below. He pushed his way through a willow thicket that screened the glen from the stream and its tumult and led his horse to the edge of the water to drink, while Riker followed with his fretful black. Behind them, Asiya began pulling supplies from the mule's pack and seeing to his master's service.

"I'll tell you one thing, though," Marik shouted over the noise of the water.

"What's that?" Riker yelled.

"When we get back, I'm going to take apart that telecom in my study and go through it piece by piece."

"What for?"

"I think the place is bugged—and I want to know why!"

It was midmorning when they reached Bends-Over-The-River, pausing under the somber shadows of the evergreens at the narrow pass leading into the town.

"Here it is," Marik announced, his voice for once betraying his excitement, and Riker, who, except for the Summer Palace, had only seen the tourist's Eisernon, made an involuntary exclamation of admiration.

It was a picturesque little village, perched precariously on terraces around gushing, noisy freshets that sprang from seemingly endless sources on the summit and surged wildly together among rocks and rapids to form the headwaters of the strong young river they had followed up the mountain. The water was ice cold, light, and delicious.

"Tastes too good to be water!" Riker exclaimed, wiping his hands on his trousers. "Where does it come from?" Melting snow, Marik told him, and added that the villagers had ordered an extra-heavy snowpack this year so that the rapids would be impressive for tourists—especially for the very equal Erthlikli, he added as an afterthought.

They dismounted and gave the horses to Asiya, who would lead them a longer, safer way, for the direct route Marik had chosen was so steep that, Riker discovered, there were places where the road became stone steps hewn out of the solid rock itself. It made Riker's knees ache. He could only surmise what it was doing to Marik, who had been seriously injured during the war.

The alien seemed not to notice. He was gazing about with the attitude of a returning prodigal. Nor could Riker blame him. The place was beautiful. The houses, clinging to their rocky perches, had sharply pointed roofs layered with weathered split shakes, and hand-painted lintels decorated with folk-art designs. The flower boxes under their mullioned windows were full of bright blossoms that, mingled with the pines, gave off a clean, sweet fragrance. The road was cobbled with ironwood bricks, and rustic bridges of heavy timbers spanned the waters in a kind of a ponderous wooden lacework.

A few people were coming and going on various errands, but none so urgent as to prevent their sharing a smile and a greeting with the strangers. Riker was becoming accustomed to the healthy yellow-green complexions of the Einai country folk and fond of the stiff black skirts and twisted topknots of the women. The fresh soft green of a child's cheeks made him want to pinch them gently, as he might an early peach. The air was heady and the sun felt warm and fine.

"I *like* this place," he announced as they waded through a flock of sheep being driven out to pasture on the mountain. "What do they call it—in Eisernai?"

"Kan-chuli La," Marik provided promptly. "It carries the connotation of someone bending over the river to admire his own beauty."

"Narcissus," augmented Riker, who was an admirer of the old classic myths. "Like the Greek of the old story." But before Marik could reply the shepherd passed them by, a handsome youth, golden eyed and green, playing a canticle on his panpipes. He scarcely paused as he made eye contact with Marik, but a peculiar expression—and then a mischievous grin—crossed his face, and he bowed deeply and walked away backward, still watching them, playing a new refrain: one musical phrase, over and over, and variations on the theme, for as long as they could hear him, until his music faded into the secret glens.

"The 'Lei alden Han,'" Marik smiled. "The 'Lay of the Han.'"

Riker shot him a hooded glance. "I didn't know you people went for hot little numbers like that. The 'Lay of the Han,' huh?"

"Very well, 'the Song of the Han,' 'the Poem of the Han,' if you will." He snicked impatience between tongue and teeth. "One of the most disconcerting habits of you Erthlikli is your uncanny ability to find a sexual reference in the most innocuous places."

"Hey, what do I know about you aborigines?" Riker laughed defensively. "I've heard tell that some of these native

ditties are pretty, uh, *whew*!'' Marik, matching his mood of
playful banter, picked up the gauntlet.

"Actually not," he informed him professorially. "It's a
matter of cultures, I think. Heritage. As you know, we Einai
descended from nocturnal hunting cats. Let me emphasize the
word *cats* as opposed to, say, the word *apes*. By their nature,"
he went on didactically, ticking off points on his fingers, "apes
are destructive, disorderly, lazy, and while rather bright, are
grossly ineffectual.

"Whereas on the other hand, cats are inquisitive, careful,
independent, clean, regal, and—while they do not make much
noise about their intentions, as apes are wont to do—they carry
out their plans in a tremendously effective manner."

Riker paused for breath on a flight of stone steps. "If you're
saying what I think you're saying"—he smiled fraternally—"I
may just deck you."

Marik spread both hands in an amused gesture of innocence.
"Look at it this way, Paul," he explained. "There are sports-
men who talk incessantly about hunting, and there are sports-
men who eat venison. There are fishermen who can bend your
ear for four hours about their new reel and their great
technique, and then there are fishermen who bring home fish.
No talk, no fanfare, no tales of conquest; but they know how to
catch what they're after, and what to do with it once they have
it.

"Now, you take your average Erthlik," he went on merci-
lessly, their footsteps echoing on a wooden bridge, "endlessly
talking about sex, making his little joke, finding off-color
references in everything from the screwdriver at the factory to
the fruit bowl on the dining-room table . . . well, we cat-folk
have to feel a little sorry for him. It's like listening to a starving
man talk about food."

"Keep it up," Riker warned, "and you're going to end up
demonstrating how well you cat-folk can swim."

A second flock of sheep was flowing down around them,
accompanied by their middle-aged guardian and his dog. This
shepherd, too, lifted his panpipes and began to play the "Lei
alden Han." Marik inclined his head graciously and the man,
bowing deeply over his pipes, played them away.

"The emperor's theme again. I'm afraid they know we're here—and who we are, Paul."

"Well," Riker amended, "he knows who one of us is! More than that, I think your fan club's throwing us a party!" He indicated a sheltered spot along the river's edge where a line of moss-thick rocks edged into the flood above a series of white-water rapids. There was the sound of shouting and the bustle of a small crowd that grew even as they watched. Several townsmen ran through the alley between two buildings, carrying a coil of rope. Someone at the river was waving his cap and shouting their way, but his voice was lost in distance and water sound. Marik looked back over his shoulder and shook his head in obvious relief as a villager overtook them and ran past.

"No, that's not for us, thank T'ath. There's some kind of excitement down by the Knot, where the Five Rivers join." He began walking faster, studying the signposts along the hilly road. "It's along here somewhere, I think. Everything looks familiar, but it's been a long time." There was a gust of chilly wind, and a thickening of the earlier bands of cloud briefly obscured the sun.

"You've been here before, then." Riker glanced at the sky.

"Oh, yes." He smiled. "Yes, I studied here, under the master, Oman Shari-Mnenoplan, for many years. This was his home. He had a sumptuous pavilion at Allam-Paila, a gift of the Crown—but Kan-chuli La was home."

Another man ran past them, headed for the river, and Riker turned back concernedly. "Something must really be going *on* down—" but Marik's breathy exclamation cut him off.

In one stroke he caught the gray blaze of excitement in the alien's eyes, heard the slap of Marik's palm against the signpost, and, before he could close his mouth on a surprised "Hey!" he found himself alone on the corner, watching Marik stride quickly along the downslope under the faint green tracery of the raintrees, hurrying toward his past, and his future. At the foot of the street, the river flashed and foamed and beckoned.

By the time Riker had caught up to him, Marik had stopped dead in his tracks, his expression concerned and wary. "Some-

thing's wrong!'' he whispered hoarsely. ''Oh T'ath! Paul!
Something's wrong here!''

Riker saw nothing amiss. Only the house, wood shingled and
low, set well back from the street behind a homely garden. A
rough stone wall overgrown with star jasmine. Only a house.

''What do you mean 'something's wrong'?'' he demanded.
''What could be—''

Marik brushed roughly past him, through the gate that stood
ajar, and ran to the door. ''Sofyan?'' he shouted. ''Sofyan!
Misi!'' *Misi: the pet name for Misao, the name he and Mishli
had chosen for a daughter.*

The door slammed open on clear, spare rooms that echoed
their footfalls emptily. A few toys were strewn on a matting in
one room, including a rag doll whose lower face had been
painted the clear and delicate blue of a Shimshen's caste mark.
But the rooms were empty. No one was there, and that was
strange, for Sofyan had promised to be there with the children.
Unless she had lied. Unless something had happened. Unless
and unless and unless. ''*Sofyan!*''

A pungent stench led them through a closed door into a small
kitchen, where a pot reddened ominously on the stove, its
contents a thick black char. The air was heavy with acrid
smoke, and while Marik threw open windows, Riker seized a
towel and flung pot and all into the backyard.

It was then that he saw the shed. A small building, backed up
against the face of the mountain looming above, it stood open,
its door askew on its hinges, flowerpots dumped and broken.
And there was something else.

Riker gripped Marik's arm hard and jerked his head mutely
toward the shed, his entire demeanor warning to silence; unnec-
essary in this case, for Marik, too, could see the limp, outflung
hand that lay on the strewn tiles. There was low, mindless
whimpering, and the muffled intermittent crashes of pottery
hitting the floor, as though someone were still moving about
inside.

Marik leaned down to ease a wicked-looking dagger out of
a boot scabbard Riker had never suspected, and slipped past
him like the shadow of a cat. By the time Riker had snatched
a knife from the kitchen rack and gone after him, Marik had
gained the shed, and Riker found him kneeling beside Sofyan's

inert body, carefully examining a nasty wound at her temple. It seemed deep and depressed, but there was not much blood, which Riker mistakenly thought was a good sign.

A big, shaggy jat, clearly the Shimshen's pet, kept nudging in close and getting in Marik's way, crunching shards of flowerpot under its hooves and knocking things off shelves. Riker got it out into the yard with some difficulty and returned to squat on his heels beside them.

"Is she dead?"

Marik made no reply, preoccupied as he was with continuing his examination of her neck (stiff), her eyes (pupils fixed and dilated), and the wound itself. He winced and muttered, "Quel!" in a disgusted voice, and concluded his survey of the temple wound.

"No, Paul," he answered at last, carefully easing her head down to the tiles, "she's not dead—yet—but not because they didn't try." He picked up a nearby section of heavy ceramic jardiniere and gingerly fitted a bloody angle of it to the side of her head without quite touching it. Without question, this was the weapon her assailant had used.

"Whether they broke it against her head or merely used a piece of it is anybody's guess. Not that it makes much difference." He looked up at Riker. "See if you can get hold of *Hope*. She's in orbit above Pal-alden-Shali-Rho. Have them beam Sofyan up, stat. They've got the best surgical facilities in the galaxy. If we can pull her out of this anywhere, it'll be on *Hope*."

"Got you." Riker ran for the house, and Marik, his fingers on Sofyan's thready pulse, idly toyed with the stained pieces of ceramic someone had used to crush the skull of a gentle, middle-aged lady whose worst vice had been the scolding of naughty little children.

He came to his feet with a smothered exclamation. *Children!* Where were the children? Where was Misi?

He listened, ears and mind alike, focusing his attention on the sound that had been there—he realized belatedly—all the time. He turned his head slowly, seeking its source, every nerve singing, the individual hairs prickling his neck. There! There.

It was a soft, monotonous whimpering, low and sobbing, and he followed it like a creature stalking prey; tracked it into the underbrush behind the shed, a heavy tangle of scrub wedged under the high, brooding pines. There was a faint rustle, a glimpse of pale flesh, and Marik's grip tightened on the dagger haft. Whoever it was had better have answers, he told himself, preferably the right ones.

He came to a half crouch, eased back the branches, and with a lightning pounce, captured his struggling prey and dragged it shrieking into the sunlight, just as Riker came trotting up to help. A moment later, he had sheathed his dagger and was comforting his erstwhile prey—a terrified little boy perhaps two years of age—while Riker pulled out a pocket handkerchief and tidied up the child's eyes, nose, and mouth, which were sloppy from prolonged weeping. "*Botta tannich,*" the child wailed heartbrokenly. "*Botta tannich.*"

"It's all right," Marik soothed. "It's all right now, it was only a game, you see? Only a game. It's all right. . . ."

"One of Sofyan's charges, I gather," Riker remarked, with a grimace of distaste at his soggy handkerchief.

Marik nodded without comment, merely continued to soothe the child verbally, thinking security, tranquillity, friendliness at him. Gradually the child subsided into intermittent sobs, leaned a silky dark head against Marik's chest, and heaved a long, shuddering sigh. One of Sofyan's charges, Riker had said; neither of them mentioned the absence of the other two, the little girls. But the thought was there, just the same, like the broken sunlight or the sound of the river at the foot of the street.

The boy stirred slightly. "*Botta tannich?*" he asked hopefully. Riker frowned quizzically and the alien shook his head.

"Not Eisernai," he said. Riker shrugged it off as inconsequential and confided, "*Hope* just beamed Sofyan up. Sharobi himself took charge of the case."

Marik twitched a brief smile of thanks and returned his attention to the boy. "Do other children live here, too?" he asked gently, and the boy drew away a bit, studied Marik from under his stubby lashes, sucking his thumb, and then nodded reluctantly. "*Botta tannich?*" he ventured shyly.

Marik looked for help at Riker, who shrugged off any knowledge of this strange new word. "Don't ask me. Languages were never my strong point.'' Nor were children, he reflected. Both were constant enigmas, requiring a sort of patience Riker lacked.

"And do you play together?'' Marik was asking.

Another nod. "Play,'' he mumbled around the thumb. "Uh-huh.''

"Now we're getting somewhere,'' Riker jibed. "They play. *Ask him*, will you, where the others are!''

"Patience, son of Darwin,'' Marik murmured, and then, to the boy: "Well, then, who do you play with? Misi and the other girl?'' The boy ducked his head against Marik's chest to hide a smile of recognition at the name, and nodded again, feeling that here must be a friend indeed, if the tall stranger could come up with names. His free hand toyed with the cloak cords knotted at Marik's throat. "And where are they now?'' Marik's even voice persisted. "Where are the little girls?''

The child straightened and looked alertly from Marik's face to Riker's, and took his chubby fist out of his mouth. "Man,'' he said decidedly. "Man bye-bye.''

"Right,'' Riker interposed, his patience having reached the end of its short tether. "Mr. Marik's a man, I'm a man. Right. But where are the other children?'' The boy considered this for a moment, chewing thoughtfully on his fist and drooling a little, and then gave them a suddenly brightened smile and waved an arm toward the open gate.

"Water,'' he chortled, nodding enthusiastically. "Water. Fwim.''

"Swim?'' The sound of rushing water came to them faintly up the street and grew in their consciousness until it was a roaring cacophony, drowning every other sound or thought. The men stared at the gate and then at each other in dawning horror, and Marik went white to the lips.

"Oh, great T'ath!'' he whispered. "The river!''

The river was actually a collection of rivers, a gathering of wild, bouldery freshets that pounded through the brief uplands at breakneck speed and roared together at Kan-chuli La in a deep, dangerous conflux known as the Knot. It was just below the Knot, where the torrent was most deadly beautiful as it surged among the jagged rocks of the rapids, that Marik found

clusters of townspeople milling about excitedly. Some of them
were weeping, others shouting advice or encouragement to a
pair of men balanced precariously on the bole of a fallen tree
that jutted swaying into the flood, anchored sketchily only by
its dry branches to the pebbly bank. They had a long rope and
kept trying unsuccessfully to throw it to—Marik followed their
ineffectual efforts with keen eyes and pounding hearts, and
made out a fluttering wet scrap of red cloth and dark curls that
clung to a smooth rock in the middle of the concourse.

A child.

A little girl.

As they watched, she stood up unsteadily, raising a cry of
fear and alarm from the townsfolk, and tottered uncertainly
toward the near edge. People began yelling and waving her
back, and one woman screamed thinly over the noise of the
water.

Marik's hearts squeezed painfully even as he ripped off his
cloak and shed his boots. A little child, out there. His child. Just
stay there, stay where you are. I'm coming. *Oh, T'ath*, he
prayed as he climbed onto the tree bole and took the rope from
the unprotesting peasants, *please, she's only a baby, she's all I
have, oh, good T'ath, please . . . Stay right there, little one,
stay there.* He would have tied the rope around his body and
swum for her, but before he could knot it, a great cry rose from
the spectators as the scrap of bright cloth and humanity slipped
into the foam, and spinning, submerging and reappearing,
washed downstream with the flood. Marik flung the rope aside
and dove after her.

The current was savage and paralyzingly cold, and it
whipped him downstream precipitously, jerking him under
and tossing him end over end under the foam and fine debris,
until he managed to get his face above water for a few
desperate breaths. The clean air gave him fresh strength, and he
got his bearings as best he could—for the shorelines were only
fleeting blurs of color—and he began to work with the icy
green flow, adding his strength to the monstrous strength of
the river.

The rescue was going to be harder than he had anticipated,
he realized, for there was no chance of fighting the immense
brute force of the frigid concourse. It was all he could do to get

his head above water occasionally and avoid the rocks half-hidden in his way. Catching his first glimpse of the baby as quickly as he did was a small miracle, and he rejoiced in it even as he went under yet again and emerged panicked that he might have lost sight of her.

He found her once more, could see the red dress flash a little distance ahead of him, but she was being carried so swiftly along, as he was, by the torrent that it was going to be impossible to reach her in time. He saw that now. There was one chance and one chance only: he would have to deliberately risk the fastest, most dangerous chutes and get past her. He had to let the river bring the baby to him. In the meantime, if he could somehow catch her up, so much the better.

He pulled for the surging center current, feeling his hearts pound painfully in his chest, and still she eluded him. The river whirled her dizzily, like a limp doll, now seen, now submerged, spun tantalizingly just out of his reach. Between watching for his baby and keeping his distance from the foam-shrouded boulders that kept appearing unexpectedly, Marik missed the greater danger.

Right before him boiled the worst of the rapids, frothing and churning and kicking up against boulders as it plunged down rocky cataract after stony plummet, and as he saw it and began to pull for it, the current had already sluiced him between the rocks and into the chute and over the edge.

He slipped over the first sickening fall and, even as he tried to avoid the worst of it, some part of his mind saw the beauty of the glassy, clear sheeting of water over the falls, even as it carried him crashing down the cascade and into a natural brattice of submerged rocks. He involuntarily inhaled icy water.

He fought his way to the rushing surface, fighting desperately to stay afloat, gagging and coughing and searching for his child. He missed the second, higher cascade that bounced him roughly off the rocky bottom and threw him back up, strangling and clawing for air, into a tangle of weeds and branches that were caught against a tumble of granite.

Bones scraped whitely, bitterly, against the merciless stone, and he held onto it for one moment only, his breath whooping and whistling through his clenched teeth, his vision clearing, tasting blood from a bitten tongue, and vaguely hearing the shouts from the shore over the noise of the water.

Villagers were urging him on, pointing and waving and yelling silently against the voice of the river. There! Something!

He plunged back into the mainstream after a scrap of humanity seen from the corner of his eye, a red feather caught in an eddy, a trick of the imagination. No, there! Right in front of him, a flash of bright dress! He made out a cheek, her mouth open, white lipped in the icy water, a hand! He pulled for her with strength he didn't know he possessed and almost caught her when a torrent tore her away, but not before she made a weak, gargling cry and reached for him.

Alive! She was alive! And she had reached out for him! She knew he was coming for her. *Hang on*, he thought savagely, and the thought was half a prayer. *Live! Live! Oh, good T'ath—*

The thought gave him new courage and he swam harder, using the last of his reserve, ignoring the dull heaviness of his limbs and chest in the snow-fed deluge and the deafening pounding of his hearts in his ears.

The current sluiced him away from the baby, pulling her upstream into a backwater, and he pulled hard against it, stroking powerfully. He dodged a massive hornbeam tree that came spinning between him and the child; missed the tearing branches that threatened to drag them both under; freed her dress with scant seconds to spare as the tree rolled languidly, pulling a shred of fabric under with it and holding it there; and caught the force of the swung bole smartly against the side of the head. There was a gush of blood down the side of his face, strangely hot in the cold current, and his wooden fingers lost their grip on the bright fabric. She spun away as he floundered for a stroke or two, swallowing large quantities of icy water, gasping and gagging. He grabbed the slick trunk weakly for support while lights danced crazily before his eyes, but it slammed into a brace of rocky outcrops flanking yet another cascade, pitching him off and over.

In that instant, as he turned with rattling throat and blurred vision to look for her, the baby slid over the bole and went under in a wicked eddy, and he dove for her, caught the edge of her dress, lost it, smashed against an enormous boulder, and was tumbled half-conscious to the surface, head ringing, relaxed at last in the strong surge of the current. Blood and water bubbled gently in his nose and mouth.

Misi. Reaching for him. Hang on, little one. *Misi*. An eddy swung him in a lazy arc, foam sizzling at his lips and ears. He swallowed water, breathed it. Went under, floated loosely back. *Misi*.

The thought stirred him, brought him back, though he was too weak, too tired to move. He was past any feeling in his hands and feet. His arms and legs were cramped and kept trying to drag him down. Even his body had no feeling of cold anymore. He felt the overpowering need to sleep.

Misi, he said to himself doggedly. *Misi. Misi.* It was in the nature of a rallying cry to his battered consciousness, and he began to make a feeble attempt at staying afloat, moving his leaden arms and shaking his head dazedly to clear it even as the race swamped him, pulled him along, snatched him under. *Misi*. He fought clear. *Misi*.

He summoned the last of his will then, called upon an inner strength, a secret and dangerous reserve to tamper with, since he had gone beyond exhaustion to the brink of collapse. What he drew upon now was not his reserve, but his own essence. What he asked of himself now was a loan against the length of his life.

He flung himself like a spent fish into the center current again, the swiftest race that, he prayed dimly, would pull him downstream, past the point where his baby might be. *Oh, T'ath, oh, good T'ath, spare my daughter—*

He plunged down a bruising cascade, scraped the stony bottom with his shoulder, and fetched up against a stand of exposed boulders with a bone-shaking jar, the river surging and foaming around his chest and chin. But the rocks provided enough purchase for a brief handhold, no matter how precarious, and the people on shore who, he realized vaguely, had scrambled full tilt along the banks, keeping pace with him, were shouting and pointing upstream of him, then closer—and closer—

He caught her, felt the soggy fabric in his clumsy fingers, felt the chill little body slip from the dress and caught her to his chest with his free hand, surfaced, his lungs exploding, and on the third try caught the rope they threw him and, careful to keep her face out of the water, let them drag him in. He felt his knees bump rocks, slip against moss. There were pebbles under him, then sand, then sun-warmed grass.

He toppled onto it and lay there, shaking and bleeding, half-conscious as solicitous hands took the limp baby from his arms and began pressing the water from her lungs, half-aware of Riker talking earnestly to him, chafing his numb limbs. He had a bad spasm of coughing, and after a little while he was violently sick and brought up the water he had swallowed. Somebody blotted the gash over his ear. Somebody wrapped his cloak warmly around his shoulders. Somebody covered the baby's face with a blanket.

"*No!*" His voice was a hoarse croak, and he tried to leap to his feet, but made it only to his knees, snatched away the blanket from the still, sweet little face, and rasped again, "No!" He leaned down and, lifting her into his arms, began mouth-to-mouth resuscitation, forcing his own scant breath into her baby lungs and letting it puff away.

Nothing happened. He tried again with no result: breathe, release; breathe, release; that was the way it was done. How many children had he resuscitated this way and given them back whole to their parents? Breathe, release; breathe, release. Too soon to know, it's only been a minute. Three at the most. *Oh, T'ath, she's such a little chap, oh, good T'ath—*

Breathe, release. There was no logical reason why his child shouldn't do as well as any other: twitch, stir, wail, and be alive. It's really too soon to tell. People give up much too easily, much too soon. *Oh, good T'ath, she's so little—* Breathe, release; breathe, release. Riker's hand gripped Marik's shoulder.

"Dao . . ."

Marik shook him off furiously. Breathe, release. *Oh, T'ath, please.* Any minute now there would be a stir, a breath, a heartbeat. Heartbeat. He put the baby flat on the grass and gave her external heart massage, still breathing for her, still trying. Blackness kept dimming his vision, and blood kept dripping into the baby's face, diluted with river water. Probably the blood that keeps your from seeing her breath, Dao. Breathe, release. If only he could stop coughing. It broke the breathing pattern, and breathing was everything just now. Breathe, release. *Oh, T'ath, I've never asked you for much—*

Riker's hand again. Riker had gripped his shoulder that way when the world where Mishli stood had vaporized, with Marik watching. When his world had disintegrated the first time. *But this is a baby, don't you understand? She's only a baby!*

"Dao. She's dead. Stop, now. She's dead."

Marik swung with everything he had, hitting his friend full in the mouth and lacerating the back of his hand. As blows go, it was nothing, coming as he got to his feet, exhausted. But it knocked Riker backward onto a soft turf, and he lay there with his lip puffing up, just looking at him. There was a compassion in him, and for an instant, Marik hated him.

"Okay," Riker said softly, blotting his mouth with the back of his thumb. "Okay."

Marik wheeled on the still body lying in the grass, and seeing her there, his training told him what his hearts refused to admit. There was a loose, rag-doll quality about her, an unmistakable emptiness, echoed in the sympathetic eyes of the village women who stood mutely watching. The child was, indeed, dead.

Gone.

No hope.

He knelt down and carefully smoothed her hair; drying, it had begun to curl softly in little ringlets at her temples and forehead. He toyed with one of them, almost smiling to himself. Tenderly wiped his blood from her face with the corner of his cloak. Covered her gently with the blanket. Tucked her in against the cold wind.

He got up and stood gazing at her for an interminable while, standing in his own shadow, his own darkness, in the troubled noonday sun. Then, as if waking from some strange and ominous dream, he looked around him at the sorrowful faces of the townspeople as they came up to proffer comfort, or weep, or press his hands. Asiya was there among them with the little boy they had found, and he thought he should know some of the older faces, but somehow he had difficulty in placing them.

Strange. He waited for some sort of devastating grief, but he felt merely numb. Numb and weak. He leaned down and gave Riker a hand up, but it was Riker who supported him, all the long way back up the mountain, and through the murmuring villagers, and back to the empty house.

CHAPTER

III

DONOVAN HAD NEVER been aboard *Skipjack*, and because he was to be the Control/Identity for her upcoming Timeslide, he welcomed the opportunity to familiarize himself with the only sub in the Fleet whose every mission made headlines.

It was a heady new sensation, being the first Controller ever to manage a Timeslide, and he found himself enjoying the respectful attitude his fellow controllers had taken toward him, of late. It was a surprise to find that *Skipjack*'s personnel regarded him as an ordinary citizen, until he realized that if he, who was merely the Controller, was a man destined for the history books, *Skipjack*'s staff and crew were living legend. After that, the tour got easier.

Simon Mbenga, the big black first officer who had elected to show him around (a matter of courtesy on Mbenga's part, he understood; the job could have been done as well by any lowly ensign) stopped the lift on the Power Deck. "You'll want to meet our Black Gang," he suggested, "and, of course, you'll want to take a look at the Egg."

"Oh, yes, to be sure, the Egg," Donovan agreed quickly. In his notebook, he scribbled *Egg* and drew a heavy square around it.

A group of engineers in comfortable white fatigues approached and introduced themselves around—the day watch: Hayashi, the chief; Jackson; Gerffert; Caulkins; Monteleone; and Pollack—and with proprietorial pride took Donovan on a tour of the ship's massive McIvor engines, which would be Donovan's life source during his Control/Identity as *Skipjack*. He went over them carefully, centimeter by centimeter, checking fuel, coolant, the complex new automatic mechanisms that fed fuel or damped

57

reactors, inspected cladding, pipe joints, switches, ran through the software he had written that would program the ship to accept his cerebellar override during the voyage, and at last was satisfied.

He had quite forgotten the Egg until someone mentioned it to him in the most prosaic of terms. They were skirting the auxiliary helm, Donovan busy with his notes, when Hayashi yelped, "Hey, watch it!" and swatted him across the chest broadside with an arm swung at full length. "You nearly stepped on the Egg!"

"Yeah, man, you gotta watch out for that Egg," Jackson confirmed, and the other, laughing a little, formed a loose circle around the object in question as Donovan, rubbing his chest absently, got his first good, hard look at the Elluvon Egg.

It was a solid, gray-green ovoid, some twenty by twenty-five centimeters in size, and darkly speckled over the surface like granite, but unlike granite, it seemed porous, like a fine sieve or minute coral. The men stood watching Donovan expectantly.

"Well—" Hayashi queried with a twinkle, "what do you think?"

Donovan, not knowing what was expected of him, shrugged noncommittally and smiled. "Ah, well, it certainly is an *egg*." It wasn't what they wanted, he knew. Not enough. He continued, "And, ah, it's the biggest damned egg I've ever laid eyes upon, that's a fact! To be sure!" he finished, in what he hoped was a tone of conviction.

They kept watching him stand there with his stiff smile plastered all over his face, waiting for him to say the right thing. He leaned down and patted it gingerly. "And it's *green*," he beamed. "It certainly is *green*, you see." He gave it a harder pat, hoping to rock it away somewhat, but it did not move. He frowned. Odd. "My favorite color," he added lamely, more and more concerned with the Egg's insistence on staying put.

Nobody said anything. They just stood around watching while Donovan tried to be subtle about why the wretched dollop refused to stir. His smile felt as if it had been painted on and was drying tight. He squatted down next to the annoying Egg and patted it in friendly fashion, casually leaning on it with one hand. "It's all right, isn't it, boys," he inquired politely, giving it a subtle (futile) push, "for me to put a little weight on it?"

Oh, yes, they assured him, smiling broadly, all the weight you want. Feel free.

Feeling free, he gave the idiot Egg a shove with the flat of his hand, grunting involuntarily, but to no avail. It did not budge. He was beginning to feel warm, and it did him no good at all that Mbenga chose that moment to chuckle and wag his head. Dropping any pretense at subtlety, he drew back and gave the beast a mighty bash with the side of his fist, and succeeded only in raising on that fist an angry welt no redder than his face had become.

By now the men, First Officer Mbenga included, were howling with laughter, and Donovan got slowly to his feet, wearing an angelic smile that went badly with the color of his face. He brought that face into close proximity to Hayashi's "laughing Buddha" imitation.

"I don't suppose," he suggested between his teeth, in a confidential tone, "you'd like to tell me why you nailed the bloody bastart to the deck in the first place, now, would you?"

Hayashi, holding his sides with glee, choked, "It's not nailed down, Donovan, I swear!"

"Not nailed down!" Donovan roared, swinging his foot back to give it a mighty kick. "By Cavanaugh's dog, I'll show you whether it's nailed down or not!" With that, he swung his foot and kicked the Egg with his full strength. There was a peculiar sound as foot met Egg, a sort of muffled cracking, and everyone bent forward anxiously to see whether the Egg had cracked; but it had remained true to its nature, as immovable an object as ever withstood the almost irresistible force of an angry Irishman. It was the Irishman who had cracked.

Said Irishman, meanwhile, sank slowly to the deck, his face pale, holding his foot with both hands. He smiled tightly, trying to be as good a sport as possible. "I may have hurt myself, just then," he whispered confidentially, and Hayashi nodded ruefully.

"Sounds like."

"Perhaps three or four places, you see. Five at the most. Only the *little* bones."

"I understand, believe me."

Donovan nodded toward the Egg. "Let's have it, then," he continued in a whisper. "The truth and all. I mean, I know you call it an Egg, but what is it *really*?"

Hayashi whispered back, "Classified, right?" The others stifled their grins.

"Mum's the word."

"It's a *time machine*." Donovan's expression changed as a terrible thought occurred too him.

"You don't suppose I injured it, giving it a prod like that, and you'll pardon the expression?"

Hayashi shook his head solemnly, helping Mbenga unlace Donovan's boot. "Not a chance."

"Ah, that's good news. I've a bit of a temper, you see. At least no damage was done. Still—*aha!*"—he jerked involuntarily as Mbenga felt of his foot and signaled for the men to bring the tube sled—"I'd like you to answer a question, if you would."

"Shoot."

"First, it may be a time device, you know, but is it really an Egg?" Hayashi and Monteleone lifted him between them and helped him to a wall hatch that had been opened down in the bulkhead. Inside, he could see a sled big enough to hold two men of his own modest size.

"Yes," Hayashi told him, their banter over, "seriously now, yes, it is. It was a gift from the Elluvon Gestalt."

"Oh, yes, the rescue you people pulled off! Whitman, my chief, was speaking of it. Extragalactic aliens and the whole lot." He sat down gingerly on the edge of the tube sled.

"Right! That's how we can manage a Timeslide at all—the Elluvon unborn powers it. See, when the Elluvon female, Muse, delivered it, it glued itself to the floor plates with some sort of impervious colloid. We tried everything but a jackhammer to get it up, and we were thinking about that when Mister Marik found out what it really was."

"Marik. He's the onboard gook, now, isn't he?" Donovan put in, and Hayashi gave him a quick, analytical glance. There was a look on Donovan's face that he had seen, once or twice, directed at himself.

"He's the second officer, if that's what you mean, and a

damn good one at that.'' Hayashi seemed disinclined to continue his story, so Monteleone picked up the narrative.

"See, Mister Marik walked right in and made some kind of telepathy link with the Elluvon Egg, and it showed him this one spot by the after helm where it had to be for the Timeslide to work. So we eventually had to cut out a section of floor plate and haul it down here by main force.''

They had been helping Donovan into the tube sled and securing the straps. His foot ached abominably, but his curiosity itched even worse. "Now there's another—'' he interrupted, but no one heard him.

"Anyway,'' Pollack provided, "Anderson, our top surgeon, kept tripping over it and cussing a blue streak, so we had to get it out of his way anyhow.''

"Yeah, remember that time he fell over it and grabbed onto Ensign Mendez, and she kept hitting the man and hollering at him in Spanish, and he kept apologizing so polite?'' Jackson chortled.

"Excuse me, I have another—'' Donovan pleaded, but no one was listening.

"Yeah, and after she left he was crawling around on his hands and knees, man, looking for the rest of his pipe? With that little bitty piece sticking out of his mouth?'' Gerffert shook his head. "That was a comical day. That was the day he made us take the Egg out of sick—''

Mbenga laid a massive hand on his shoulder. "The man was asking a question,'' he said mildly, and Donovan gestured at the Egg.

"Just the one question, boys, and I'll be off. Tell me—what are those little wiggly creatures that come out of the Egg?'' They exchanged puzzled glances.

"There aren't any wiggly things,'' Hayashi told him, and Pollack added that nothing, but *nothing*, came out of the Egg. Nothing came out and nothing went in. Period.

"You must be mistaken, Mister Donovan.'' Mbenga smiled. "After all, we did have you going for a moment there. But rest assured: to the best of our knowledge the Egg is static, rigid, and featureless, except for those pinpoint holes in its surface. It does not now, and nor has it ever, moved.'' He started to shut the hatch, and Donovan grabbed his arm.

''Well, it moved just now, boyo, and if I'm not a wee bit off the line, it's moving again.'' He pointed to the gray-green surface, and there at random points in the minute pockmarks, several delicate flowerlike extrusions appeared, waved about faintly, and withdrew.

''Well, I'll be damned!'' Hayashi expostulated. ''Look at that!'' They crowded around for a better view, forgetting Donovan completely, and Mbenga gave him a thoughtful look and then a grave nod.

''Thank you, Mister Donovan. You've been very helpful. I'm sending you down to sick bay now. They'll take care of your foot for you.'' The hatch swung shut and Donovan, for the first time in his life, was whisked away through the tubes on a cushion of compressed air, caroling like a banshee.

Mbenga hit the com stud. It piped shrilly, in counterpoint to Donovan's fading yodel, and Mbenga suppressed a stubborn chuckle.

''Sick bay. Anderson.''

''Mbenga here, Neal. I've got a singing landlubber for you, good voice, bad foot. Coming in on Tube Two.''

''Thanks, Simon,'' Anderson replied metallically. ''Who is he?''

''Our Controller for the Timeslide, so treat him nice.'' He paused. ''And, Neal—pull his psych file, will you? I want you to run a check on his interspecies relationships. Something he said down here didn't hit me right.''

''Will do.''

''Mbenga out.'' He rang off and leaned against the bulkhead, deep in thought, absently watching the Black Gang at the Egg. One of the men had produced a stylus with an extra-fine tip and was gingerly tickling one of the coral-like polyps into appearing again. Mbenga compressed his lips thoughtfully and tapped the communicator panel with the side of his fist, eyes half-closed. Something Marik had told him . . . Coral polyps beginning to appear. Coral polyps. Coral.

He thumbed the stud again. It piped metallically.

''Bridge. Casaletti.''

''Mbenga. Raise the captain for me. We've got a situation he needs to know about. And, Joe: I want the crew on standby and the ship on yellow alert. Cancel all leaves as of now, recall the enlisted personnel, and put me through to the captain as soon as you reach him. I'm on my way up.''

Mbenga caught up with him there. Casaletti spun his chair and said quickly, ''I have the captain, sir. Patched in from a land line. Place called Kan-chuli La.''

The main screen polarized, lit up, and the image of Paul Riker appeared. He was in a country house of some kind, crowded with people. They could hear voices in the background.

''Riker,'' the image said, and Mbenga opened the switch.

''Mbenga here, Captain,'' he rumbled. ''We've got a problem that may require your presence aboard, sir.'' Someone scraped a chair across the floor, and behind Riker, a pair of peasant women were gossiping loudly. One of them drowned out Mbenga's next words with, ''This never would have happened if those men had closed the gate behind them! It always had a tricky latch.'' They caught sight of the image on the telecom screen and peered around Riker in order to see better.

''Can you speak up, Mister Mbenga?'' Riker asked tersely. ''The noise level here makes it a one-by read.''

''Yes, sir, I said we have a situation—''

''But this fellow *did* close the gate,'' the second woman, laying a hand on Riker's shoulder, murmured into the telecom pickup. ''I saw him.'' Riker scowled and bent his ear toward the screen.

''Say again?''

Mbenga raised his voice and the bridge personnel turned to stare. ''I said, we have a situation here that—''

''Oh, not *him* here,'' pursued the first woman. ''The other men. The ones who took the little girl away with them from Sofyan's house. *They* left the gate open.'' She peered closely at Mbenga's image. ''What do you suppose that fellow has on his face, to make it black like that?''

Riker turned to the women and said irascibly, ''This call is Federation business, ladies and gentlemen. I must have privacy for the next half hour, or I will be forced to declare martial law!''

They fell back, wide-eyed and silent, and in a remarkably short time, by twos and threes, the peasants had cleared the

room—and presumably the house—and Mbenga saw Marik
standing at the window, his clothing ripped and torn, holding a
child's rag doll absently in his hands. He seemed uninterested
in the call. Riker watched the last of the villagers leave and
turned back to his first officer with some satisfaction.

"Martial law, sir?" Mbenga inquired politely, and Riker
grinned sourly.

"I had to tell them *something*. Man can't even think with all
that chatter going on. Now, where were we?"

"In deep trouble. Polyps are beginning to show on the
Elluvon Egg. Does that mean what I think it means?" Riker
winced.

"I'm afraid so—but only Marik can tell us for sure." He
looked at the alien officer with some perplexity. "I hate like
hell to do this to you," he said sincerely. And then, to Mbenga,
"Beam us up."

Mbenga was a good officer, Riker thought, stepping down
from the transport grid with Marik behind him, for his staff's
call lights were glowing on the panel, indicating their presence
aboard ship, and Neal Anderson, the ship's senior surgeon, was
standing by. Evidently, Mbenga had caught sight of Marik on
the telecom. Good man.

As Marik stepped down, Anderson intercepted him. "Just a
minute, Mister Marik, let's have a look at you."

"Later." Not so much abrupt as remote. Alien. "Later,
Doctor." If not for the torn clothing and the shocking pallor, no
one would have noticed anything amiss. There was not much
blood, and what there was had mostly dried.

"Now." Anderson smiled affably around the pipe stem
clamped in his teeth and stepped into Marik's path, bringing
him up short. "Right now. Here or in sick bay, you have your
choice."

"Sick bay," Riker interposed and, at Marik's quick glance,
"That's an order, Mister. I want you patched up and in the
briefing room in"—he checked his ticket, which read 12:58—
"half an hour. I need you at your best."

"Aye, sir," replied the emperor of Eisernon distantly,
starting for the lift, and Anderson hung back just long enough
to give Riker a quizzical scowl regarding Marik, behind the

alien's back. Riker shook his head fractionally—*I'll tell you later*—and the good doctor trailed reluctantly after his patient into the lift, which hummed them away. Mbenga let go an explosion of held breath.

"Let me guess. He tried to rescue the big old Minsonai dowager-empress single-handedly from a pack of rabid d'injit. And did it. Before breakfast. Or, no, better than that: he took on the Imperial Krail Army, armed only with a pair of chopsticks. And won."

Riker glanced up through his brows and licked his puffy lip. "How about, he tried to save his baby daughter from drowning in the Kan-chuli La rapids—and lost?" he suggested grimly.

Mbenga was shocked. "Oh, God, Paul, no!"

"'Oh, God, Paul,' yes, I'm afraid. Not an hour ago. And now this, not even time for decent grief. How does the man stand it?" He heaved a weary sigh, blotted his cut lip with the ball of his thumb, and started for the briefing room. "Come on, let's get on it. We've got to know for sure whether those polyps mean the Egg is getting ready to hatch. Marik or no, the Federation has too much at stake for us to blow the Timeslide now."

Marik was on the Power Deck. He had spent a bad fifteen minutes in sick bay and was unhappy about having broken one of his own ethical standards in the process; but it had been unavoidable. The examination had gone well at the start. Anderson grinned around his cold pipe at Marik's various abrasions and rainbow contusions and remarked happily (after Marik divulged the fact he had, in his words, "gotten somewhat involved in a mountain stream"), "Well, fella, you look fine and fit for a guy who's been swimming down waterfalls!"

His fingers probed ribs and Marik jerked involuntarily while Anderson counted, under his breath, ". . . three, four, no, five. You cracked five ribs up pretty good there, old son. Sore, eh?"

"Not much," Marik lied blandly.

"The hell you yell!" Anderson grinned good-humoredly, and made as if to thumb him in the side. The alien jerked again, at once guarding his ribs with his near arm and laying the opposite hand carefully flat against the dark purple-green bruises. "Not much, eh?" Anderson jibed, glancing up from his WP pad, where he was entering Marik's workup. "That in itself should keep you quiet for a few days. Let's have a look at your head."

He examined Marik's scalp gash, swabbed it, and sutured it with a few bursts from his electronic suture. Marik rubbed his eyes. They were burning from the actinic light of the suture gun, and the glare from the overhead lamps made his head throb.

"Eyes sensitive, are they?" Anderson asked conversationally, and before he realized the import of the question, Marik answered tiredly, "Just a bit. Light makes them ache."

Anderson gave him a speculative stare, doused the lights, and, over Marik's protests, did a brief but thorough neurological workup. That completed, he brought the lights up to a muted glow and regarded Marik soberly. "I think you know you have a pretty serious concussion there, Dao. I'd like to admit you for a couple of days, maybe a week, and have you followed by a friend of mine. Neurologist. Very competent man."

"I'm afraid I can't do that, Neal," Marik told him wearily. "It's a question of time. I'm needed for the Timeslide."

"This injury could kill you," Anderson pursued. "You get hit on the head just right, or take a bad fall—any one of a hundred things—and you could go out like a light! A lot of good you'd be to the Timeslide then!"

Marik fixed him with that level gray gaze. "I can't spare the time, Neal. If the Egg is active, we'll have to Jump now. And *Skipjack* can't make the Timeslide without me. I'm the only liaison we have with the Elluvon Gestalt."

"All the more reason to make sure you're in good shape! Besides, we have almost thirty days till we Jump. You should be out and fine by then." Marik hesitated and Anderson pressed his advantage. "The ship needs you at your best, Marik. The captain said it himself."

"Let me examine the Egg," Marik hedged, "and we'll be in a better position to decide issues."

"Take your time," Anderson said by way of a farewell as Marik slipped into his tattered civvy shirt and left. Then he crossed to the intercom and punched the series for the briefing room.

On the Power Deck, several members of the Black Gang were down on their knees, amusing themselves by trying to tickle the Egg's polyps into making an appearance. As Marik limped toward them, they got to their feet, exchanging puzzled glances regarding his unorthodox gear and his more than usually preoccupied demeanor. Gerffert gave him a quizzical smile, but Marik remained composed and remote, as always.

"Mister Marik, sir."

"Mister Gerffert. See to it that the Egg is placed off limits to all personnel, until the Timeslide is complete. I want two security men stationed at the lift, and the Power Deck programmed to reject transportation from both ship and planetside sources. Only the captain, Mister Hayashi, Mister Donovan, and myself are to have access to the after helm area until further notice. Understood?"

"Aye, sir."

Marik nodded. "Dismissed, gentlemen."

As the mystified crewmen hurried away to implement his orders, Marik squatted on his heel beside the Egg and examined it minutely. There were no fracture lines, no nearly invisible sutures beginning to pull apart, as well there might have been. Not many polyps active yet, either. That was all to the good. The longer they delayed, the more time it bought *Skipjack.*

Muse, its mother, had said there were only two times when the Egg would be fully polyp-active: first, immediately after it was laid, when it still reached for the prenatal MotherChild link; then, as those polyps desiccated, and it entered a period of dormancy, it would be safe for motivating a Timeslide. But be careful, she had warned, when the second-growth polyps start to show in earnest; within seventy-two hours of their appearance, the Egg will begin to hatch. And once it hatches, your ship and its crew will remain in Time WhenEver they happen to be. There would be no chance of rescue. Once the Egg hatched, they were caught fast, a fly in amber. Forever.

Good traveling, she wished them, puffing away as a blue mist. Good luck.

Marik assumed that the unusual rapidity of its hatching was probably due to prenatal stress. Temperature shock, too, perhaps. Little creatures were so easily affected by temperature. Especially by cold. Again, he felt the icy water of the rapids, again his hands closed on emptiness. He saw the still, doll-like form lying on the early-spring grass. He shut his eyes tight and, resting his arm against the Egg, laid his forehead upon it for the space of one long, shuddering breath. *Oh, T'ath, I freely accept all that you send me, grief as well as joy; for who am I to count myself deserving of joy, but exempt from grief?*

Footsteps echoed as Jackson crossed the companionway, and Marik lifted his head and continued his examination of the Egg. He laid his hands on either side of it, letting his mind flow into the consciousness of the slumbering infant, their link to the Past and to the Future. He opened his mind flat and featureless and unending, letting it flow into every crack and facet of the fetus's perceptions. Was there a stir, a waking, a *moment*?

It still slept. There was time yet for the mission, he knew, though admittedly not much time. Under its slumber, he could feel the same sensation as was to be sensed in trees about to bud, in a certain flavor of the wind shifting from winter to tentative spring, in the half-seen movement of cloud shadow that touched the grass and was gone. Birth was burgeoning upward in the little creature like well water, springing fresh from hidden sources.

He broke contact. He had his answer. There were only two alternatives: mount the Timeslide immediately, or scrub the mission indefinitely. He had no doubt as to which of the two avenues ComFleet would recommend, not to mention Paul Riker's choice. Marik made his way to sick bay, prepared to serve his ship and the Federation to the best of his ability. He only hoped it wasn't going to cost him his life.

Riker tapped the edge of his hand against the examining table. "Now, let me get this straight, Neal. You're telling me that Marik's got a 'significant concussion.'"

"Right."

"And just what does that mean?"

"A lot of things, none of them good. I'd feel a lot better if we could admit him. He needs a few days' close watching, preferably in a good hospital somewhere.'' Anderson shifted his weight and rolled his empty pipe to the opposite corner of his mouth, talking around the stem and pausing, from time to time, to knock out nonexistent tobacco particles against his heel, as he always did when he was agitated. "Look, Paul, I'm sure that, under the circumstances, ComFleet'll give you another second for the Timeslide.''

Riker, restlessly pacing, shot him a withering glance. "It's Marik or nothing. How many other telepaths have we got in Fleet, not to mention telepathic second officers?" He leaned his hands on the end of the examining table and rotated his head on a stiff neck. Massaged his shoulder with an absent hand. "What happens if he just goes about his business?"

Anderson shrugged. "Maybe nothing much. Headaches, nausea, vertigo. A good deal of atypical behavior. Some of it can get rather bizarre in the Einai, defenses go down and so on. Or maybe a subdural clot forms and he loses function. Or breathing. Or one or both of his hearts stop beating. Maybe the clot dislodges and he has a massive stroke. Or . . . maybe nothing at all.''

"So it's a gamble.''

"True, but we can rig it on Marik's side—*if* we can keep him quiet and watch him for a while.''

Riker thought about the Timeslide, about the hopes and dreams of mankind that could be brought to fruition through this one mission. About the Smithsonian scientists who had been chosen to explore and categorize the biological and geological features of the ancient worlds; of the Cousteau Institute scientists who would have recorded Earth's Mediterranean Landmass when it was still (incredibly) a sea; of the historians, the linguists, and all the other military and civilian personnel who had rearranged their obligations and their careers, not to mention their personal lives, to join this incredible expedition.

He tried not to think of the alien Elluvon Armada, which might not understand what they could only construe as his spurning of their priceless Gift, or what his superiors would have to say about his judgment and, ultimately, his ability to command *Skipjack*. For, whatever he might tell himself, he was

well aware that should he ask for another second officer at this
late date, ComFleet would scrub the mission and he, as captain,
would bear the burden of responsibility.

He forced himself to think only of the situation immediately
at hand, and of the good of the individual. *I'm not responsible
for what anyone else does*, he reminded himself. *I'm responsible for what* I *do. Free will. God's terrible gift.*

"No question about it, Neal. If Marik's in any danger, you'll
have to put him in the hospital. I'll just request another second,
that's all."

Marik, who had a disconcerting habit of appearing soundlessly when he was least expected, was there at the door. He
ignored Neal Anderson and addressed Riker directly. "I have
a question, sir." Riker nodded shortly. "Assuming ComFleet
allows the mission to proceed, with so basic a key personnel
change, and considering that I am the only second who has
experience with the Elluvon in general, what are the mathematical
odds in favor of *Skipjack* getting back without me?"

Riker flushed deeply. "That has no bearing on your situation, Mister. *I'm* responsible for the safety of my crew—"

"I think I have my answer," Marik interjected quietly.
"And now, I'm going to do something that goes cross-
purposes to my ethics. I do it for good cause, in the Name of
Tadae, and for the good of the ship: Paul. Neal."

They looked at him and Riker felt a momentary shock as he
found himself caught and held powerless by those steady gray
eyes. Marik's voice became a susurrant murmur that filled their
common universe, although his lips did not move, nor did his
expression vary from quiet compassion.

"I was unaccountably unhurt by the rapids, Doctor,"
Marik's voice told them, and they believed it. "I was not
seriously injured in any way. The Timeslide will go off as
planned, with no disturbance of the Elluvon, nor of ComFleet,
nor of the ship. And you, Paul, will not have to sacrifice your
career for me." There was a thoughtful pause. "However, you,
Doctor, will order a MAX brought aboard, where it will
remain. Should I require emergency medical help, the ban I
now impose on both your memories will become null and void,
and you will remember all this. If I do not require help, the
memory will become obliterated. Understood?" They nodded,

bemused, and Marik continued, vocally, in a conversational tone, "Neal? Paul? What were you saying?"

The two men roused as if from a daydream, and Anderson took the pipe out of his mouth and pointed its stem at Marik. "I was just telling the captain," he said, as if continuing a long narrative, "that I can't understand how you could slip down a mountain rapids and come off with not much more than a cut on the scalp!" Riker in the background, was frowning to himself, his eyes narrowed thoughtfully.

"Neither can I," he said, absently. Something was troubling him, but he was having a hard time trying to place it.

Marik smiled. "We're a tough breed of cat, Doctor." He hesitated just inside the door. "I'm checked through, then?"

"Oh, yes," Anderson assured him cheerfully. "Healthy as a horse. Good to go."

"Captain?" Marik indicated the wall chrono. "I think we're due in the briefing room just about now."

They sat around the table together, the five of them: Riker, of course, and Marik; Mbenga; Donovan; and a man whom Riker introduced as Dr. Charles Lassiter, a pleasant sandy-haired man who might have taught history or classical languages in some venerable old university.

It surprised them to discover that besides his being a medical doctor, Lassiter was an officer in Interpol, the intragalactic police organization that employed the finest espionage agents in existence. Naturally, the Federation would have notified Interpol of the upcoming Timeslide. As in every history-making event, there was bound to be that element of the population who wanted it stopped, who was out to share it or spoil it, who would commit any violent act for the sake of getting its name—however ignominiously recorded—in the history books and its face on the tri-D.

It was curiously comforting to have Lassiter's lackadaisical presence grace the briefing room.

The sixth man, Engineering Chief Hayashi, was expected momentarily.

"While we're waiting," Riker proposed, "let's recap what we have, for the edification of Dr. Lassiter and Mister Donovan. You want to hit that medlog, Simon?" Mbenga obliged with an unusually fine study of an Elluvon autopsy, done by Marik on their last voyage. Camera moved close on an Elluvon cadaver recumbent on a slab and Marik's voice came in clearly, over:

"Dao Marik, examining Elluvon cadaver number one, sixteen thirty-two hours (the computer added parenthetically, in its pleasant metal voice, notations concerning date, grid, and ambient system). Begin:

"Physically, the subject most resembles an Erthlik trilobite, with biramous limbs and setae absent, and the noticeable presence of overlapping scutes, several of which—"

"Skip it down," Riker ordered. "This concerns the adult. Get to the Egg." The tape and audio whipped past in hysterical gibberish, stopping for breath at ". . . the subject's evolutionary ascent. There is no indica——" and plunging on to ". . . agglomeration of polyps are heavily vascularized by deteriorating arteries, and the amoebalike corpuscles—"

"That's not it, either." Riker turned to Marik. "Got any idea where it is?"

"Farther on, I think," Marik reached for the controls. "About here." A skittering, a flicker, and a clear close-up of an Elluvon Egg appeared on the screen, with Neal Anderson's voice-over:

"Fine," Anderson was saying, on filter. "It's, ah . . . about twenty to twenty-five centimeters—you know that, Marik, you found it yourself!"

The exchange had been recorded by servoCams, automated devices which recorded the details of every surgery, sterile procedure, and autopsy aboardship. The MediComp then selected the clearest, most informative shots for input into permanent records and downloaded the remainder of the information into spangs, which stored easily and took no core memory. As they watched, Camera pulled back to include Marik, shooting past him for the Egg, as: "Neal. Please, if you would."

"Oh, hell. And it's gray-green, sort of, and it's pocked all over the surface, like granite, in a way, and it's hard. It used to give when you touched it, but no more. It's like hard coral, but it looks like granite. And I think it's porous to some extent."

Still holding on the Egg, Camera moved left of Marik for a profile and continued to truck as Marik asked, "Why so?"

"Because I could swear I saw a couple of little flowers growing out of it, but they died off. And nobody'll believe me." Donovan grunted under his breath.

Camera held on a medium shot of Marik with the Elluvon cadaver centered on the table before him. The light was good and the audio pickup clear, as Marik stretched and laughed aloud, locking his hands over his head and regarding the cadaver like a recumbent antagonist. "I believe you, Neal." He grinned. "I believe every word."

"I don't believe you," Anderson's voice argued on filter. "What do you mean 'you believe me'? Why should you believe me? That's crazy! Maybe *I'm* crazy! Did that ever occur to you? Maybe I've cracked up!"

"I doubt it," Marik informed him, sobering. "But—now, listen, Neal, this is important: no one is to come near that object until I give the word! Is that clear? No one is to hit it, touch it, approach it, until I say so. All right?"

"Okay, but why? Is it dangerous? Poison or something?"

"No," Marik said quietly, "it's an egg." Camera zoomed in for a close-up of the Egg. The shot froze as Riker signaled Mbenga to stop the tape.

"That's as good a description as anyone is likely to provide you, gentlemen. I understand that Mister Donovan has already examined the Egg, and we have him to thank for noticing that it has become polyp-active." He gave Donovan a nod. "If either of you wants to view the entire autopsy to familiarize yourselves with the Elluvon as a race, please feel free to ask; Mister Mbenga will set you up.

"Now Mister Marik has a few pertinent details that ought to cover the rest of our situation, and by that time, the chief ought to be here. Dao?"

With a few deft strokes Marik outlined the time frame for their Jump—roughly twenty-four to forty-eight hours—the opportunities and possible dangers inherent in their mission, and the inestimable value of having Muse, their Elluvon contact and the Egg's mother, accompany them. He had almost finished speaking when Hayashi slipped into his seat, smiling apologetically, and wagged his head in a rueful gesture Marik had come to regret recognizing.

"Engines?" he interrupted himself to ask, and Hayashi's unhappy smile widened a bit.

"Worse," he muttered. "Muon-flow problems."

"Bad enough to hang us up?" the captain asked. "I'm requesting a new Jumpslot. We've got to be ready to Jump when the time comes. No snags, Mister Hayashi, no glitches."

"Don't worry, Captain, we'll have it straightened out in no time flat."

"I'm counting on it." He thumbed the stud at his right. "How's that call to ComFleet, Joe?" he asked the pickup, and Casaletti, at his communications station on the bridge, made contact at last. The wall screen flared to life.

"Channel open, Captain," Casaletti's voice stated briskly as he rang off. In his stead, a middle-aged Kraun officer in winter blues appeared on the screen, streaks of white scoring the glossy russet mane that swept from his forehead to well past his collar at the back. He said his name was Wrangtau.

"Captain Paul W. Riker, USS *Skipjack*," Riker said crisply. "Put me through to Vice-Admiral Hastings, please."

"The vice-admiral is a Level-7 officer, Captain. Please state the nature of your business." The enormously patient, leonine visage was carefully uncommunicative.

"I have an emergency regarding Project Timeslide," Riker told him, and the Kraun inclined his head courteously, making the luxuriant mane ripple beautifully in the diffuse light. "Stand by one, sir," he said briskly. "Timeslide has priority clearance." *Snick, snick,* went the switches. "Go ahead, Captain Riker."

The screen shifted to an imposing view of a high-echelon military office, its appointments impeccable, its hardware all of the latest design. Beyond broad windows overlooking a bleak, rocky landscape, a blizzard was raging, but the office, hushed and decorous, appeared eminently comfortable.

At center screen, Vice-Admiral Josiah Hastings, a white-haired, florid-faced old man, sat with his hands folded before him on the desk. One side of his face seemed unusually peaceful, so calm it sagged, and there was a distinct droop to the eyelid that, along with his sour expression, gave him a most malevolent aspect. Stroke, Marik decided disinterestedly, even though that eventuality was rare these days. The man must have had a stroke at some time or another.

Incredibly—for he had been sitting so still as to be mistaken for a wax image placed a trifle too near the fire—the white head slowly lifted and the thick lips pursed arrogantly. After a long pause, the faded eyes stared directly into the screen.

"Riker," he growled. "The Fleet's resident rebel. You again."

"Vice-Admiral Hastings, sir." Riker's eyes went steely, but his tone was respectful. If there seemed arrogance in the perfection of his salute, it might have been Hastings' imagination.

Hastings returned a perfunctory salute, a mere gesture, and busied himself about some paperwork on his desk. Without glancing up, he muttered, "Well, what is it this time? Dug up another bogey for Fleet to deal with, have you? More nonofficial business?" He kept writing, deliberately slow. Riker stood watching him without making an answer, and for a long, tense while, the only sound in either of the rooms was the occasional crackle of the quiet fire Hastings had kindled. At last he looked up sharply, sourly. "Well?" he demanded, and Riker wet his lip.

"It concerns the Elluvon, sir," he confided blandly, and waited for the reaction.

He got it. Hastings jerked up as if someone had jabbed him with a marlinspike and threw down his stylus, ignoring it as it rattled to the floor. "The Elluvon?" he repeated irascibly, with some heat. "What about it, what went wrong? Going to tell me you had another problem with that damned bug? Eh? Eh?" He glared into the screen with the strange yin-yang contrasts of his face.

"I would refer to it rather as a premature opportunity, sir," Riker interpolated smoothly, and his staff smiled at that. "We have reason to believe that our Timeslide motiver, the Elluvon Egg, will be hatching within the next two or three days. Even allowing for the necessary twenty-four hours' hatching time it will require, while still slide-effective, this new data forces us to request an adjustment in Fleet's timetable."

"I trust you have sufficient data to back up this—this

harebrained contention!'' Hastings ground out. ''It would be to
your very great advantage not to be mistaken in this matter!''

"We are not mistaken, sir. If you like, Mister Marik here
can—'' Hastings made a disclaiming overhand gesture.

"I'm not interested in his opinion,'' he said bluntly. ''The
fact is, Riker,'' he continued heavily, ''you've already been
assigned a Jumpslot. Do you know how much trouble the
Fleet!—and the FSA! and commercial shipping as well, not to
mention civilian space carriers!—have gone to, to indulge you
with this''—he swallowed uncomfortably—''this *time toy*
these creatures have provided you with?''

"Yes, sir, I'm aware of the efforts of all the agencies
involved. And I appreciate the time, labor, and money spent to
indulge me and my time toy.'' He rose slowly to his feet,
leaning forward over the desk braced on his clenched fists, and
he spoke low and soft and distinctly, biting off each word as he
said it. ''It is only that I hesitate, sir, to offend the *entire—
Elluvon—Armada* by snubbing its emissary and spurning its
Gift through sheer attrition!

"However''—he straightened and his tone became more
conciliatory—''that matter is best left to the discretion of my
superiors. After all, sir, it is not I who will have to answer to the
Elluvon Gestalt. It is you there, at ComFleet.'' He bowed
slightly. ''Whatever you decide, sir. *Skipjack* is at your
disposal.''

The old man swallowed convulsively several times and
heaved a few deep, steadying breaths. Riker felt it would be
impolitic, just then, to mention that he had done his homework
on Vice-Admiral Hastings, and in the course of it had discovered an entry in the medlog that Hastings had a nearly
uncontrollable fear of the insubstantial Elluvon adults. Impolitic and uncivil ever to mention it, Riker mused, but true just
the same. Usable.

Hastings forced his features into the travesty of a smile and
cleared his throat. ''Taken all in all, I suppose, your proposal
sounds reasonable enough.'' He cleared his throat again and
ran his fingers through his disheveled hair. ''Very well, then,
have your data patched through to my people here, and we'll
try to get you an amended Jumpslot. Where can we locate
you?''

"I'll be on standby, sir. Fleet band."

The old man grunted assent and peered into the screen. "Is that your man from the FSA?"

"Yes, sir," said Donovan, getting to his feet. "Martin Michael Donovan, at your service."

"And you, there," the old man pursued, lifting his chin at Lassiter. "Who are you, his relief?" Charles Lassiter rose lazily to his feet.

"I'm Dr. Charles Snow Lassiter, inspector, Interpol, sir," he explained courteously. His *sir* came across as *suh*, marking him as a colonial, probably from New Georgia. "I'm just here to keep things peaceful." He squinted his pale blue eyes and smiled through thick, fair lashes; a disarming smile, and a deadly one. It was not difficult to imagine him phasing someone out, wearing just such a smile.

"I don't have a relief, Vice-Admiral," came Donovan's pleasant brogue. "I'll be controlling the whole expedition myself." The old man indicated the transparent cast on Donovan's foot.

"What happened to your foot, Mister Donovan? No accident, I hope, nothing to keep you from doing a good job for these men."

"Oh, no, sir," Donovan assured him benignly, while Hayashi shifted his position uncomfortably. "I'm a very careful sort of a man. Accustomed to walking on Eggs, in a manner of speaking." He struck a fist into his palm and Hayashi's unhappy grin widened a bit.

Hastings nodded like a surly owl and toyed restlessly with the papers on his desk, moving them about and reshuffling them. "Very well, very well, you've got the bug and we have to go by what you tell us—after we recheck your data, of course. Always a chance you could be mistaken! But remember this, Riker! We've got that damned Elluvon Armada sitting here at Central!" A muscle began to twitch in his cheek. "Sitting here on our necks," he continued unsteadily, "and I don't want anything to go wrong, understand? Nothing! You got off easy last time!—but try me again and there'll be hell to pay!" His face was a dull plum red. *"Is that clear?"* If the old man hadn't been so vicious, Riker mused, he might have been almost pathetic. The old man slapped the desk hard. "Riker!"

"Yes, sir. Abundantly clear. We expect the mission to go off without a hitch."

"If that's all, then." Hastings' hand loomed toward the cutoff switch. "Dismissed."

"*Sir!*"

The hand paused, withdrew, and Hastings' face came into focus again. His scowl echoed his tone. "Well?"

Riker was on his feet again. "Sir, I have a request to make of you." He looked as uncomfortable as he felt. "Of a personal nature."

"Highly irregular, Riker! Bad form, you know! Well—get it out!"

Riker stammered, "Um, Vice-Admiral, sir, I would like to speak to you privately, if I may. It's a delicate matter." His staff was watching interestedly, and he could feel his face grow warm.

"I sincerely hope, Riker," Hastings said, heavily confidential, "that this doesn't concern some, ah, episode with an eye-eye native woman of some kind." *Eye-eye*, the epithet for the Einai. *Eye-eye, dago, spik, polack.*

"No, sir, it does not." He took a deep breath through his clenched teeth and plunged in. "What it concerns, Admiral, is a certain dinner party that my second officer has been ordered to host at his home tonight—"

"Sir!" They ignored Marik's abortive protest.

"—and because of extenuating circumstances, I respectfully request Fleet to find some other way of pampering its pet bigwigs!"

"Dinner parties don't interest me, young man," Hastings said, conversationally. "What interests me is what sort of extenuating circumstances could be so important as to make you keep jeopardizing your career the way you do. You have no prudence, Riker, no respect!"

Riker, who had been standing in that tough, eager stance, leaning on his braced hands, shut his eyes and dropped his head like a defeated combatant. "I asked you—this enormous favor, sir"—his head flashed up—"because Mister Marik lost his only child, an infant daughter, today! By drowning! And, as it happens, sir, we very nearly lost Mister Marik into the bargain!'' He wet his lip and straightened. ''Under the circumstances, I respectfully submit that he should be relieved of what can only be an onerous obligation and a breach of human decency.''

Hastings laughed. Thinking about it afterward, Riker decided that he could have borne any other reaction; but Hastings laughed. It was a superior and supercilious laugh, and it demeaned both Riker, with his request, and Marik, with his grief made public. Marik himself sat like stone, his face impassive. The intensity of his restraint was eloquent comment upon the depth of his grief and humiliation.

''Come, *come*, now, Riker. *Human* decency? Who do you think you're dealing with?'' Hastings asked sarcastically. ''I've handled these people for the last half century, ever since we beat their pants off at Pal-alden-Shali-Rho. And you know something?'' He leaned forward and smirked. ''They're *not human*! They're not you and me, boy! They bleed *green*! Some of them read minds, Captain! Their cubs are frequently born in multiples, and when they lose one, here and there, they don't *feel* it like we do!''

He sat back with a good deal of satisfaction, feeling he had put Riker in his place, and his Einai second officer with him. Not entertain, indeed! ''They don't feel it like we do,'' he repeated smugly. ''One of God's little mercies, Riker, my boy. Of course your Mister Marik will entertain Fleet's guests tonight—won't you, Marik?''

Marik turned blind, opaque gray eyes toward the screen as Hastings continued, ''Because the Fleet has been good to Mister Marik, Einai! And because the Federation has been *very* good to *Mister* Marik! I'd like you men to know that *Palace* he occupies is by courtesy of the Galactic Federation, who very kindly didn't turn him and his penny-ante parents out of it and onto a gallows, like they deserved! Should have hung 'em all, like the war criminals they were!''

Marik rose to his feet in a fluid, catlike motion of perfect balance, and his eyes were no longer empty. They glittered blackly, and were frightening, and his voice was low and venomous.

''That will be all, now,'' he said softly. ''I will entertain

Fleet's guests, as I agreed, and we will cease discussing my honored parents.'' Hastings hooked an arm over the back of his chair and sneered.

"Well, well, well, I believe I struck a nerve. What's the matter, *Mister* Marik, references to the late and unlamented Han royalty bother you? Don't like to remember the eye-eyes lost, do you?''

"You are making a serious mistake, Vice-Admiral,'' Marik cautioned in the same even tone. "I would advise you to be careful of what you say.'' Hastings straightened haughtily and sat stiffly erect in his chair.

"And I would advise you to remember just what you are!—and just who you are talking to! And I caution you, *Mister* Marik, to mind your manners when you're speaking to your betters.'' Marik made no response and he got bolder. "As I was saying, we would've done better to put the whole damn bunch of Han to the sword when we had the chance! Oh, he's a Han, Riker, don't let him fool you, he's no ordinary gook! We've had our eyes on him since the beginning! Dossier that thick!'' He measured a considerable space with his thumb and forefinger.

"I'm well aware of Marik's racial background,'' Riker snapped, feeling that things had gotten far out of hand, but Hastings was hearing none of it, and rambled on almost incoherently.

"Let me make it plain, Marik, you filthy Han, and *your parents* in particular, were the dirtiest bunch of—''

"Stop now.'' Marik's voice was scarcely above a whisper, but his presence in the room seemed to have increased tenfold, so that every one turned his way. If he had never been alien before, he was absolutely alien at that moment. "Not another word.''

Hastings forced an uneasy chuckle and sat back a little farther in his chair. The muscle in his cheek was twitching again. *It's not just the Elluvon he's afraid of,* Riker realized suddenly, *it's aliens in general. The poor old curmudgeon is afraid of Marik!*

"Hurts, eh?'' Hastings pursued desperately, viciously. "You don't like to remember that we, uh, we beat you eye-eyes to your knees! It's . . . it's unpleasant, isn't it? To know that you owe us! It's by . . . by the goodwill of, uh, the Federation, uh, that you have any place to go at all! And as far as that brat of yours''—Riker caught his breath involuntarily, thinking, *Oh, no, don't touch on that, for your own sake!*—''as far as I'm concerned, that's just one less Han for us to worry about! Good riddance!''

Something changed in Marik. He did not move, neither did he alter his countenance; but something changed, and Hastings saw it change and was terrified by it. He leaned back hard in his chair and fumbled his collar open, stretching his neck as if the room had suddenly become too hot for him. ''You'd better be careful, Marik,'' he threatened, his voice rising a notch in volume and in pitch. ''You'd better not do anything you'll be sorry for!''

A series of brilliant sparkles of light ran experimentally up his uniform sleeve and down again, danced across the front of his tunic, and coruscated in the palms of his hands. He flung them away wildly, like a scarecrow in the wind. The speckles of light remained, hesitant as the initial volley of a war, or the first tentative notes of a concerto, played by a virtuoso pianist.

Hastings grasped his throat, tearing his tunic away from his neck, pushing himself slowly and inexorably against the back of his chair. His breath was coming hoarse and loud and his eyes seemed twice their size. Sparkles foamed over his shoulders from his spine and poured down the front of his tunic, pooling in his lap. Brilliant pinpoints of luminescence flared at the end of each hair of his head, and he tore himself away and floundered to the window, tearing it open and inhaling great, inhuman gulps of air. Snow melted under his glowing hands. Icicles nearby began to drip.

Riker, fighting a sudden violent headache, grabbed Marik by the arm. ''Dao, *no*! You're throwing your career away! He's not worth it!'' The sparkles increased in depth and intensity, moving more quickly, haloing Hastings' head and body. The tips of his hair singed. His face ran with sweat. His tunic cuffs began to smoke and smolder.

Riker grabbed Marik's shoulders and shook him, to no avail. It was like wrestling with a mountain; like reasoning with a river. He could neither divert Marik nor stop what was happening to Hastings. The old man's breath was whistling through his teeth now, his face contorted, his eyes starting from their sockets, and still Marik had not moved. The staff men were on their feet, confused and noisy, holding their pounding heads with both hands. Even Lassiter had a fist pressed against his temple, but he was observing the proceedings with the keen professionalism of a crack Interpol agent, and Riker felt they could hardly have had a more dangerous witness. Something had to be done, not so much as to save Hastings as to spare Marik. And it had to be done now.

As a last resort, Riker grabbed a heavy glass water carafe from the table and, reversing it in his hand, brought it down with everything he had upon Marik's unprotected head.

It never hit.

The alien whirled on him and caught it on the downswing, gripping Riker's wrist in fingers that felt they would crush his bones. By degrees, Riker's hand let go of the carafe of its own accord, and Marik stood, still holding the wrist, glaring at him from inches away out of those terrible, pained, glittering eyes. Then he tore his gaze away and focused his attention on a blank space in the crowded room, where a tiny point of dazzling light bloomed and burst with a shattering sound like fine crystal breaking. Marik slumped into a chair, totally exhausted, his anger spent, his forehead resting on his interlocked fists.

"Oh T'ath, Paul," he whispered, "I almost killed him. *I almost killed him!*" Riker clutched his shoulder, massaging it a bit, and heaved a welcome sigh. It seemed he had been holding his breath for half an hour. Charles Lassiter, who was picking up pieces of the broken water carafe off the floor, squinted at him thoughtfully.

"You were doing so well, Mister Marik," he drawled admiringly, "that I'm just a *tad* disappointed you didn't keep it up. At least till he learned his lesson." He indicated the screen, where Hastings was pulling himself into some semblance of dignity. The surly image pointed a finger at Marik.

"I'm going to get you for this," he threatened hoarsely. "I'm going to have your hide, Marik! I'm going to bring charges that will—"

"Ah, I *do* hate to interrupt an officer and a gentlemen, sir," Lassiter interjected mildly, "but I hope you aren't planning to take any rash measures against Mister Marik here, who is, by the way, legal heir to the planet of Eisernon.''

''Rot!'' Hastings expostulated. ''He insulted—attacked!—a superior officer, and he's going to pay for it—in spades! This dirty eye-eye—''

''Ah, as a senior inspector for Interpol,'' Lassiter interrupted, smiling apologetically, ''I would have to testify, sir, that Mister Marik had ample justification of a varied assortment of violent acts upon your person.'' He folded his arms. ''And you are providing him more.''

''You'd stand there and say that in front of this—this alien felon?'' Hastings shouted indignantly. His face was flushing heatedly again. ''You'd take up for the man? Assaulting me, his superior officer?'' Evidently the thought was inconceivable. He had a lot to learn, Riker thought, vice-admiral's ranking or no.

''Not only would I defend him,'' Lassiter mused aloud, speaking slowly and deliberately, ''I think I would go so far as to hold his coat while he chastised you, sir.'' He nodded pensively. ''Yes. Yes, I think I would. I would certainly hold his coat.'' He turned to Marik, who had his face buried in his hands. ''That is, if he were wearing a coat. As it is, Mister Marik, I hope you won't take offense at my suggesting you get along home now. If you have some entertaining to do, you'll likely want a little rest time, won't you?'' Marik lifted his head and drew a ragged breath, grateful that Lassiter had spared him the anguish of condolences.

''I'm afraid I owe the vice-admiral an apology,'' he began, but Lassiter shook his head.

''There's an apology due here, my friend,'' he told him, ''but you're not the man who ought to make it. You go along now and, ah''—his craggy face broke into a genial smile— ''Mrs. Lassiter and I will see you for dinner with the rest of the . . . what was that word you used, Captain?''

''Bigwigs,'' Riker mumbled, clearing his throat.

''Bigwigs, that's right,'' Lassiter agreed jovially. He squinted benevolently at them both and offered his hand to each in turn. His grip was firm and brief. ''See you tonight, then. Looking forward to it.'' He returned his attention to the screen.

''Now, as we were saying, Vice-Admiral, sir, (and please

remember that this interview is being recorded), you *do* want to assist the captain and crew of *Skipjack* in any way you can, especially on this historic occasion. Is that correct?''

As Marik and Riker left the room on the heels of the staff, they heard Hastings choke on his reply; but Lassiter had him repeat it for the recorder, and this time it came loud and clear:

''Certainly we do, Inspector, certainly. Nothing is too good for our brave men in the Star Service!''

''That's what I thought you said,'' assisted the honeyed drawl that followed them down the corridor. ''And thank you very kindly, sir.''

''And thank *you* very kindly, sir,'' Marik repeated pensively, as if to himself.

To which Riker replied, ''Amen.''

CHAPTER

IV

Saturday—2:17 P.M.

THEY HAD PLANNED to beam down, but they were not prepared for the scene that greeted them at the Transport Sector. The main transporter room was cordoned off, and Hansen, one of the men on night watch, out of Engineering, had partially dismantled the main console—had eviscerated it, as a matter of fact—and he and two technicians were busily engaged in what appeared to be an electronic postmortem. Metal and glass components were strewn in disorderly piles all over the deck. Riker impatiently waved away their salutes.

"What's the trouble, Hansen?" Hansen pulled his head out from under the console and made an apologetic grimace, wagging his head.

"We got a buncha bugs, Captain. Looks like the whole synthesizer is shot. We're gonna have to replace her." Riker exchanged a concerned glance with Marik, who squatted on his heels beside Hansen and examined the unit himself.

"How long do you figure it?" Riker demanded, and Hansen shook his head again. "Maybe six hours, maybe all night, I don't know, Skipper. Depends on how soon we can get a new unit out here from Central. Those guys planetside tend to sit on it."

Marik got to his feet, dusting his hands. Nodded to Riker, confirming Hansen's option. "Unusable in its present state, Paul. Even discounting reassembly. And we're going to need it." He turned to Hansen. "If Central Supply can't get us a unit in two to three hours, try Mister Kazarian, on *Bowfin*. He had a spare synthesizer in Stores last time I spoke with him, about a week ago. I believe it's a Ward IV. Perhaps he can help us."

Hansen shuffled his feet. "Yes, sir. Thank you, Mister

85

Marik, uh . . .'' With a clumsy gesture, indicating Marik's
tattered and orthodox clothing, he wondered aloud, ''Anything
we can get for you, sir? You, uh, excuse me, but you look like
maybe you had a accident. Anything I can do?'' His sincerity
was unmistakable, and Marik regarded him with his customary
grave courtesy.

''Thank you, Hansen,'' he replied pensively. ''No, there's
nothing you can do.''

''Come on,'' Riker urged gruffly, ''we're going to be late as
it is. We'll take one of the boats.''

It was easier said than done. Because *Skipjack* was in dry
dock, undergoing repairs to damage sustained during her last
mission, she was on standby power only. Her Environmental
Control was operative, and her Communications, and her other
absolutely vital functions (including, until half an hour ago, her
Transport Sector), but such niceties as automatic davits had
been shut down on the theory that, with the ship in synchronous
orbit with one of the most diverting cities in the galaxy, there
would be no one, except the obligatory onboard skeleton crew,
who was going to be in need of ship-to-surface transportation
after the first twelve hours.

As they stepped out of the lift on the hangar deck, Riker
could see through the observation blister the repair crews
covering the new plating with stark white paint and carefully
stenciling bold black numerals on her spanking fresh hull. The
sight affected him like the sound of sharp salt air slapping wet
canvas, and he wondered if Dao Marik shared his sudden sense
of excitement and impending adventure; then, in a more coldly
sober vein, he realized that if Marik were feeling anything at
all, just about now, the emotion would hardly be one of
excitement.

He watched the alien hit the manual override stud for Boat
Nine's davits, thinking how glad he was that Mbenga had
called him about the Egg. Another XO might have let it slip by
him, passed it off as just another strange alien anomaly. They
might have forfeited the whole Timeslide by sheer default. Lot
of good the fresh white paint would have done them then, he
thought wryly. But Riker was lucky. Simon Mbenga was his
XO, and Simon had checked it out, made sure. Called him.

Very good man, Mbenga. The boat still hung suspended, and they stood waiting for it to decide to come down.

"You know," Riker offered casually, indicating with a lift of the chin that Marik should try the stud again, "it's a good thing Mbenga let us know about the Egg; with all that noise, though, it's a wonder I could hear him at all." Marik pushed the stud again. Nothing.

"Noise?" Marik asked disinterestedly. "I wasn't aware of any noise." The boat remained suspended, and Marik pressed the stud more firmly and gazed up at the rigging to make sure that nothing was fouled that should be free.

"Of course there was noise," Riker argued pleasantly, stepping past him to try the stud himself. "Especially those two women with their talk, talk, talk about the gate—" He stopped dead, his face blank as his mind completed what his voice refused to repeat: *the gate being left open,* his mind repeated, *left open by those men.* But I was careful to close the gate, even the second woman saw that. *Not this fellow here*, she had said, *the other men*—oh, sweet God, had she really said what he thought he remembered, had she really said, *The men who took the little girl away with them—from Sofyan's house*? Had she really said that? And if so, if *so*! For who else would they have taken but Marik's child, the Han heir? Whoever the kidnappers were! *Who else would they take?*

"Captain? Is something wrong?" Riker wet his lip and tapped the bulkhead with the edge of his hand. Don't let on, Paulo, don't raise false hopes until you *know*.

"Look, I've just thought of something I've got to take care of. Get a couple of the men to help you crank the boat down manually, will you? I'll be back in ten minutes."

When he returned, the boat, designation SJK-9, was down and locked into the runners that led through lens-aperture hatches into tube-shaped air locks. Marik was waiting.

"I'll drive," Riker told him, and slipped into the cockpit as Marik slid into the passenger's side. Ignition, the swift run, boosted by the air exploding outward, and they emerged beyond the boundaries of the great riveted metal plates into the clean, open space outside.

The planet was, for their purposes at least, at late dayside, with the orbiting ship approaching the terminator, and the

reflected light made a silvery chiaroscuro of the cabin. A giant
crane floated by, her tubes glowing hot blue with power, and
over the back of her huge ten-man cab there was a big sign
reading, "Tjaden Drydock Services," and under that, in
flowing script and pinstriping, "Jump Safe with Tjaden." One
of her crew, a thick mug of steaming liquid in his hand, waved
at them through the visiplate as the skimmer darted past, and
Riker lifted a hand in salute.

They could see in the middle distance the mammoth white
bulk of USS *Hope*, Priyam Mykar Sharobi's cruiser-sized
hospital ship, which had been damaged in the mission along
with *Skipjack*. She, too, was being repaired, and they could see
construction men and little skittering orange servos, like so
many orange insects, crawling all over her hull and hovering
about her broad, gleaming flanks. From welders on half a
dozen hull plates, languorous fountains of golden light spilled
in incandescent sparkles against the steady stars.

A big, streamlined commercial carrier, appearing to move
slowly only by reason of her size, sailed past them, and they
could see her ports begin the automatic closing sequencing to
protect passengers' eyes and psyches from the red glare of
reentry; a thousand little eyes, like the Little-Eyes of the
legend, shutting simultaneously at the end of a long, long
journey.

Riker yawned involuntarily and began to follow her down,
carefully keeping the legal separation, but evidently it was not
enough, for his communicator crackled: "Navy Skimmer
SJK-Nine, this is the Control/Identity for MSS *Inverness*. You
are point oh seven degrees off your drop pattern and are
following too closely in my wake. Will you fall back, please?"
Riker touched his throatset.

"*Inverness*, this is SJK-Nine. Sorry for the intrusion. This is
our off-ramp, anyway. Luck!" He banked the skimmer gracefully and veered off, flaring out neatly in the stratosphere, and
hearing *Inverness* wish him luck in return. To the left, over the
Single Sea, they made out the contours of a tropical storm
system, looking deceptively soft and fleecy from their privi-
leged vantage point.

"Coming up on some weather," Riker commented, breaking

a long silence. "Looks like she's coming in right over Bru-Riga. Think she'll blow the pavilion away?"

He turned a friendly grin on Marik, who blinked, stirred, and murmured, "What? Oh . . . no, no, that's a small, fast one. More rain than wind. It would take more than that to blow us away." He resumed his introspective silence and Riker, busy with reentry, hit atmosphere with scarcely a shudder, and the cabin breathed and burned like an ember, evoking memories— for Riker, at least—of autumn and bonfires.

Marik spoke only once more before they landed, as they circled in at the pavilion's spacious skimmerport. It had been raining, the first squall lines of the approaching storm, and the glasphalt was a wet mirror, with puddles of silver and lemon reflecting the sky. Marik was gazing down at the varied craft, presumably those of his guests, parked neatly in slips along the taxiway. When he spoke, it was so low, so unexpected, that Riker had to strain to hear what was said.

" 'Good riddance,' he said, Paul. She was such a little chap. How can a man say such a thing—even to one of us, whom he hates?" Riker shot him a startled glance, but Marik's countenance was as sincere as his tone had been. "How could he say such a thing?" he repeated, but Riker had no answer, even for himself, and then they were down, taxiing to a stop on the runway, the engines dopplering down to nothing. Riker switched down and would have spoken to Marik then, but the Einai's attention was held by a group of people—some of his servants, Riker saw—standing at the edge of the field. Presumably they had been told about Misi's death, for it was evident that many of them had been weeping.

Marik alighted from the skimmer and stood silently watching his people as they came across the wet glasphalt toward him and stooped one by one to lay a hand on the instep of his boot. Some of them made the Infinity Sign as they did so, but no one spoke. It was eerie, Riker thought, such an abundance of sympathy, even of mute tears, but not one of them made a sound.

As each of his retainers stooped to touch his boot in what seemed to be a customary gesture of compassion, Marik laid a gentle hand briefly upon his or her head. Otherwise he stood remote, even regal, in his tattered peasant's clothing in the soft, wet, buffeting wind that blew now warm, now cold, from the heavy cloud bank gathering to the southeast. There was no sound but the scuffing of the women's sandals and the muffled flutter of Marik's tunic against his arms and throat.

Shang was the last to approach. He dropped to both knees in the wet, pressing his forehead to Marik's boots, and the Einai leaned down and lifted him up tenderly, as if he were an old, old man, making eye contact, a silent shake of the head that was so singular that Riker felt he had unwittingly intruded into some private family conversation. The steward handed Marik a rose, barely budded, his face contorted with grief.

"She is with your ancestors," he choked, and Marik took the rose in a steady hand and nodded once, trying to ignore the throbbing in his head, the ache in his hearts.

"The boy?"

"Inside, *Domne*. The *amah* bathed him and put him to bed." His face twisted again and he covered it with his palm for a long moment, while Marik studied the sea, patiently waiting for him to regain his control.

Shang breathed a deep sign and added, in a more even tone, "Forgive me, *Domne*. Your guests have been shown their quarters and I have taken the liberty of making your apologies—"

"Not—"

"No, no, sire! Only that you were called away on Federation business and will return presently. Wine has been served on the East Terrace and your guests are comfortable."

Marik rapped the side of his head with his knuckles in a brief, feline gesture of platonic affection. "Good Shang. As always, you have served me well." He traced the Infinity Sign on his steward's forehead with a quick thumb, and Riker caught the pleased surprise on Shang's face as he bowed low.

"'Like the rain,'" Marik quoted, and his servant bowed himself away. Neither of them saw the rose that had fallen to the ground, and Riker asked, as he stooped to pick it up, "'Like the rain'?"

"His blessings, Paul. I wished him blessings as numerous as the rainfall." He paused. "He buried her in the family crypt, with my parents. He spared me that, at least."

Riker, handing the rose up to him, saw that the remarkable

gray cat eyes were swimming with tears, and upon one of those strange impulses that men sometimes get and follow and can never explain afterward, he laid a hand in compassion upon Marik's boot for a moment, his head bent, his throat tight, and was surprised, and yet not surprised, when Marik's hand fell lightly upon his head and rested there, in genuine understanding and in blessing, for what seemed to be a long, long time.

Because of their various preoccupations, neither Marik nor Riker had seen, on their descent, the figure of a farmer trudging along the path that led between the deepest, most mysterious part of the Royal Preserve and the thinning individual groves along the drive up to the Summer Palace. His clothing was muddy, torn, and drenched from the heavy rains that had been falling intermittently all day. There were bites and abrasions on his arms and face, and his feet, swollen, blistered, and bleeding, wore shoes tied together by vagrant bits of twine and rag. He was a mess.

But he was a happy mess.

His name was Arbat.

He had been on the road for three days, days reckoned by the disasters that had befallen him since he left his farm.

He shook his head and placed his sore feet gingerly on the uneven path. Of course, he reflected, many people might say—indeed, many people had said—that he was a fool, walking a hundred kilometers to the Summer Palace pushing a barrow with a cheese in it. But those people had never had a dream. When you had a dream, Arbat told himself, nothing was too much to dare.

And Arbat had a dream.

Arbat and his wife and their nine children owned a small dairy farm and a herd of native m'lis and m'lis-Holstein crosses, and produced the richest milk in all the village. In fact, he amended mentally, being honest with himself, they produced the only milk in the village, since they owned the only kine. He negotiated a rickety bridge, balancing his barrow as carefully as his thoughts.

Because they had had an abundance of creamy, salmon-colored milk last season, Arbat and his wife had gone back to cheese making, just as they did before every Firstgreen; but this

time they went at it with a grand disregard of the usual
necessary economy. This time, they could get creative, for
there was milk to spare. Bucket after bucket of thick, fragrant
milk was sloshed into the great copper vats, heated to the
perfect temperature, and inoculated with exactly one *kimi*
gourd full of an extract his wife made from purple thistles.
Then it was heated again, stroked down, carefully cut to extract
the whey (which his children relished as a drink, with honey),
and after further processing in the back chisei, was pressed by
the hundredweight into round kalaree-fiber hoops, so that it
emerged months later as thick wheels of aromatic, almost-
translucent red cheese and melted in the mouth and tugged
sweetly at the angles of the jaw.

Arbat had been making cheese, and loving it, since he was a
small boy in his father's house. He recalled a vivid memory: a
sultry noon with his father and his cronies eating their lunch
under the village pipal tree. He was still very small and had
amused them enormously by stating categorically that one day,
T'ath willing, he would make a cheese good enough for the
emperor himself. And the emperor, he further declared, over
their good-natured chuckling, would be so pleased that he
would invite him, Arbat of Keri La, to stay to dinner! With the
cheese for dessert!

When the laughter had died down (but never out—people
had been shaking their heads after him ever since) they asked
him questions: How did he plan to go about meeting the
emperor? And how could he get past the guards at the gates?
And most basic of all, what made a little boy like Arbat think
he could ever make a cheese good enough for the emperor?
Arbat had leaned his head on his father's chest and smiled. "I
am the son of Penj," he told them, which was the answer to
everything, for him.

No one could gainsay him, and the dream grew. With the
memory of his father's blessing hand on his head, Arbat's
dream grew, louder than the scoffing of his neighbors, longer
than the memories of the now-old men who had laughed under
the pipal tree, even stronger than the arguments of his practical
wife, who was content merely to make the best cheese in the
province, and raise the best children.

But it would happen one day, Arbat knew. It had to happen. It was his destiny.

This Firstgreen, it *had* happened. The winter milk had been exactly right; the kine had been fed the freshest grass from sheltered glens, and gopher leaves, which emerged first after the snow. Even the copper pots seemed to cooperate, and the kalaree-fiber hoops stayed only as moist as they should. Everything, *everything* had come out right. The eighth wheel of cheese was so superior that even when it was first undressed and buttered, Arbat knew that it was the cheese he had waited for all his life.

Ignoring his grinning neighbors standing with their elbows hooked over the half doors, and the tittering of the women at the village well, he horsed the great yellow-waxed wheel into his wooden barrow, tucked a packet of cold hennem-cakes into the pocket of his smock, and slung a flask of flat *bia* at his belt, and, embracing his wife and each child in turn, he was off. The shouts and catcalls followed him from field and gate until he was well beyond his village.

What Arbat went through in his journey to the Summer Palace, only he and his God knew, but by the time he saw the glittering white star, the shining dart (which he regarded as a good omen) loop lazily downward from the sky over the Summer Palace, he had only one fat wedge of cheese left. A full nine-tenths of his big, beautiful wheel was gone. It was foolish to keep trundling the remainder along in an empty barrow, he knew, but he could not leave the barrow by the wayside for someone to steal, and he could think of nothing else to do with it, so he kept pushing it along before him, setting down his bruised, sore feet, one after another, on either side of the line the wheel drew in the mud.

He was bedraggled and tattered and very, very weary when he reached the dense woods just short of the Summer Palace. It had taken him the better part of four hours before he could catch glimpses of the Palace pavilion once in a while through gaps in the timber. The shining dart looped down. Somewhere a bird called.

The forest was called the Royal Preserve, Arbat knew, and it was the titular property of the Han emperor, but in actual practice (and at the emperor's insistence) even tourists, within

reason, could hunt and fish there, provided they paid the
exorbitant license fee to the warden. The license fees provided
the local fishing fleet and outlying villages with a well-
appointed, professionally staffed clinic and surgical complex.
Of the fees, Marik's cut was exactly nothing.

There were, naturally, those poachers and outlaws who paid
no fees and respected no laws, men who lived by their wits and
their weapons, robbing innocent passersby. They seldom killed
anyone, on the premise that a dead goose lays few eggs;
instead, they set their victims free, knowing that tradesmen
returned to the selfsame markets every week, no matter the
peril of occasional thievery. There was even a rumor that a
certain tinker had been robbed so often by a certain thief that
they became fast friends and eventually went into business
together, though no one could remember which of their
separate businesses they had chosen.

The trouble was, the thieves were right, Arbat thought,
trundling his barrow over a log that spanned a clear, pebbly
brook. People did tend to follow the same habits, the same
routes. That made it all the more uncertain. You never knew
when a brigand would turn up right in front of your nose.

He was startled, then, but not surprised, when three formi-
dable shapes resolved themselves out of the long blue shadows
among the trees. They were dressed like jungle bushmen, with
well-worn *viith* hung in leather sleeves, like archery quivers, at
their shoulders. The one Arbat noticed first was a stout giant of
a man who stopped Arbat dead in his tracks merely by
clamping a huge hand firmly over the entire top of his head.
Arbat stopped short, fearing for his bones, and eyed the other
two men warily out of the corners of his eyes. There was a
small man with a smooth-shaven head, who frisked Arbat
quickly and professionally, and shrugged at the third member
of the group, clearly their leader. "Not even fleas," he said.

The leader was tall and rangy, with bushy dark hair and a
well-trimmed beard. His tiger yellow eyes narrowed speculatively as he scrutinized the farmer. Arbat tried to keep his chin
from jumping by clenching his teeth. This maneuver had the
added advantage of stopping the teeth from rattling. He did not
consider himself a coward, but it was not every day that a man

met brigands. The bandit chief casually walked around and around him, viewing him from every direction.

"Let me see . . . what have we here, Ilai?" he asked, in a surprisingly cultured voice. The bald man shrugged in lieu of a comment, and the leader answered his own question. "I do believe we have a farmer, a tiller of the soil, a"—he spotted the cheese and lifted his brows, pulling a wry smile—"a *cheese maker*, no less!" He picked up the cheese and Arbat, forgetting himself, lunged for it. They juggled it between them for an anxious moment, but the bandit emerged victorious and Arbat's hearts sank.

"Oh, no," he begged, "you have to leave that alone, good sir, you have to let that be! It's for the *Domne*, you understand, I made it especially for him!" The bandit held it out of his reach and gestured to the big man, who gripped Arbat's head again. He stood there, whimpering, while the leader sniffed the cheese appreciatively and weighed it in his hand.

"No." Blunt and cold. "No, he doesn't get this. This is one lovely thing that Priyam . . . Hanshilobahr—*Dom*—Dao—Marik"—he bit off the words and spat them out— "will have to live without!" He tossed the wedge of the emperor's wonderful cheese to his man and, in taking it, he took the dream, and Arbat's life, and much of the reason for his existence.

It was too much. Along with his blistered and bloody feet, and the fighting he had done to keep it safe, the dam broke, the wellspring overflowed: the little farmer sank down to the forest floor and began to cry openly, big, sluicing sobs that came unbidden from chest and belly, and were as much beyond his control as the impending storm. The leader put his fists on his hips and regarded Arbat with ill-concealed contempt.

"Come, now, fellow," he scoffed. "It's only a cheese, after all. Why the fuss? You can always make another cheese."

"You don't understand, sir," Arbat mumbled thickly. "You just wouldn't understand." His own village, his own wife, didn't understand. The bandit nodded, neatly catching the tossed-back cheese which was now thinner by two healthy slices.

"You're right! I don't understand. It's hard to stomach a man who'd snivel over a bit of cheese. What a churl you are,

fellow!'' There was scorn in his voice and Arbat wiped his
nose on his muddy sleeve and got to his feet; trembling and
afraid, but on his feet.

"No, I'm not!'' he retorted hotly, throwing caution to the
winds. "I'm an honest man, which is better than you three!
And that's *my* cheese! *I* made it for the *Domne*, *I* walked over
a hundred kilometers through the cold rain and hot sun, *I'm* the
one who fought off a whole pack of d'injit to keep it, even
though they ate a good half! And I had to give some to a
crooked innkeeper to let me sleep in his bos-barn, like T'ath!
And I lost more to a band of tramps—to a *different* band of
tramps!—who beat me and left me only that little bit! And that
little bit goes to the *Domne*! And that's that!'' His chin was
jumping and he clenched his fists at his side to keep his hands
from shaking and stuck out his chin pugnaciously. He felt sick
to his stomach. "I mean it!'' he threatened unsteadily.

"Listen to the cricket!'' exclaimed the man Ilai. "He's
found his voice at last!''

"And what a song!'' laughed the chief. He leaned against a
tree, carving a thin, ruddy slice of cheese for himself with his
viith, and gestured encouragingly. "Say on, fellow, you amuse
me.''

"I will, oh, I certainly will!'' Arbat drew himself up. "Now,
you have called me churl, and there are three of you and only
one of me, and three of us here are thieves and lowlifes and I
am not one of them!''

"Mennon,'' the big man rumbled, but the leader waved him
to silence. "Say on, little man,'' he smiled charmingly,
chewing appreciatively. "Say on.''

"You have stolen the dream I had since I was seven years
old,'' Arbat railed at them, gathering momentum. "You have
stolen my hearts and my wife's hearts, and the work of my
children and my cattle! Only a piece of cheese, you say? Only
the honor of my family! And my ancestors! And my village!''

"You forgot 'my province,''' the leader suggested casually,
cutting himself another slice. "Excellent cheese, by the way,''
he said around the wad in his cheek. "My compliments. You
were saying? 'My province'?''

"That, too!'' amended Arbat belligerently, sticking out his
chin and chest in what he believed to be a defensive posture.

"You'll have to fight me for it!" he shouted, and started dancing around as lightly as possible for a man of his fatigue and short, rounded stature. He went so far as to land a few ineffectual blows before Mennon's tipped-up beard summoned the giant, who picked Arbat up by the scruff of his smock, where he hung free, eyes shut, still swinging wildly. The bandit leader detached himself from the tree he had leaned against and crossed lazily to him, speaking softly.

"Now, pay attention, cheese maker," he told him. "Your story has amused and enlightened me, and because I have been amused and enlightened, I am not going to cut out your tongue for your rash words"—Arbat stopped swinging his fists—"nor am I going to lop off your arms for striking my person." Arbat opened his eyes and paled visibly, but stubbornly thrust out his hand.

"I want my cheese back," he squeaked faintly. "Please."

The bandit laughed shortly, half-admiringly, holding the farmer with his eyes, and carved a narrow crescent of the ruby stuff. He handed the thin wedge to Arbat and threw the rest to Ilai, who shoved it into a rucksack lying behind the tree.

"Now, listen well, cheese maker," Mennon warned as the big man put Arbat down, not ungently. "You are to bring this cheese to the *Domne*"—he spat out the word as if it were poison—"and carry on your business as if nothing had happened here. But you are not to say anything to him about our being here in the Preserve, do you understand? Nothing. For if you do"—he lifted Arbat's chin with the razor-sharp tip of his *viith*—"we will know it. And we will come for you, no matter how far you run."

With this warning ringing in his ears, and clutching his precious remnant of cheese in both his hands, Arbat left his barrow where it was and ran on his poor, blistered feet through the remainder of the Royal Preserve and across the broad, impassive lawns, and up the drive to the Summer Palace as fast as his legs could carry him.

Not once did he ever look back.

Therefore, he did not see the dog until it was too late.

It was not an ordinary animal; not some stray cur prowling the Palace grounds for a vagrant bone or an open trash receptacle. No, this was a winner of prize and cup, a dog among dogs, with a wall full of blue ribbons and a diamond collar: a purebred Desert Linja, its pedigree harking back through fifteen hundred years of Sauvagi history. It was also undoubtedly the most badly spoiled animal in the known universe, and consumed enough meat at each meal to sustain several starving children in the poorer regions of Minsoner. However, the children had no known pedigrees, nor was there any record of any of them having won a blue ribbon at anything.

It was a large clean creature, this Linja, its glistening yellow-white coat standing rigidly on end with excitement at the smells of fresh grass and new freedom. It had spent seven cramped hours in a surface-to-surface private craft and was fairly bursting with pent-up energy. Neither had it eaten during that time.

It was not surprising, then, that when this canine paragon sighted a running figure dashing across the lawn, smock fluttering, shoes flapping, and smelled the ripe, delicious odor streaming from the cheese in its hand, it broke free of its ornamental restraint and, tongue lolling wetly, jeweled collar twinkling in the setting sun, it made the distance to Arbat's side in precisely eleven long, loping strides. One snap, and the precious remnant of cheese was snatched out of Arbat's hands and gulped down a purple gullet. The one abortive defensive move Arbat made was met with an impressive array of two-inch fangs and a warning snarl. Arbat subsided, empty-handed and weary, and the dog sniffed at him disinterestedly, trotted away across the lawn, and saluted one of the ancient trees, while its owner picked her way across the damp, fresh grass making worried little clucking sounds. She glared at Arbat.

"What was that he ate?" she demanded.

"Only a piece of cheese," he replied humbly. "Just cheese."

"Cheese!" she bridled. "Cheese, indeed! Cheese isn't good for Desert Linjas!" She trip-trapped behind the strolling dog, gingerly trying to catch him. "I certainly hope eating that cheese isn't going to do him any harm!"

"No," Arbat mumbled. "It won't hurt him." And then he added darkly, under his breath, "But it would if I were a bigger man!'' He turned away dejectedly and met the quizzical stares and murmured conversations of some of the *Domne*'s guests, there at the broad, shallow main-entrance stairs. Most of them tactfully pretended to have missed the byplay, and he backed his way around the corner of the building, bobbing and smiling uncomfortably.

Once safe around the sheltering edge of the building, he leaned for support against the damp wall and blew out a long breath. Stared at his empty hands. His ridiculous flapping-open shoes. His torn smock. He was dirty, too, he knew. What a sight he must make, he thought ruefully. Just as well the *Domne* hadn't seen him like this.

He looked around for the first time, trying to get his bearings. He was on the south side of the building, with a low western sun slanting against the mosaic walk with a peculiar brassy light that picked up the colors of the tiles. He was a few meters from a pergola that stretched along the Palace wall and covered a side entrance. Across the tessellated pavement from him was a long stone bench set into the wall of a garden. He could smell the heady scent of rained-upon roses in the air, which had grown strangely warm, still, and humid. There was a prolonged mutter of thunder from over the sea, where a thick, dark cloud bank was building up ominously. Not a leaf nor a grass blade moved.

Arbat hobbled over to the bench and sat himself down, his hands hanging limply between his knees. He felt unbelievably weary and sore and disheartened. It would be nice, he thought wistfully, if he could just stretch out here on the damp old stone bench outside the emperor's rosary, close his eyes in the thin warm sun, and sleep.

The smell of food cooking mingled deliciously with the spicy perfume of the roses, and Arbat's stomach writhed emptily. He'd had nothing to eat that day but a few wild onions and copious amounts of cold water from an occasional brook. It had never occurred to him to touch the *Domne*'s cheese. He wished now that he had. Better himself than the dog, he thought. Nasty beast. Arbat had never liked dogs much anyway. His feet throbbed and smarted inside his pieced-together shoes. He should have worn his klompen, he mused sadly, the hand-carved wooden footgear made of willow that could withstand hard wear and exposure to water; but the idea of clumping around in wooden shoes down the emperor's stoneglass halls had been insupportable.

Instead, succumbing to vanity and a good sales pitch, he had bought a pair of Erthlik-style shoes. No stockings, merely the too-large brown leatherette wingtip shoes that rubbed big, moist, open blisters on his feet before the first day's sundown. They had not held up well, either, and that was a shame, for the peddler had said they would hold up even in water. Had charged him extra for them, because of it. He unbound the rags and vines and let the shoes drop piecemeal to the mosaic walk, wiggling his swollen toes luxuriously.

As he was doing so, a side gate opened in the rosary wall, and a young man stepped out from under the weeping-cherry trees that flanked the gate. The blossoms sent down a shower of petals, a pink rain, on his dark head. One of the servants, Arbat decided, for the man's clothing was torn and he looked tired and sad. He caught sight of Arbat picking up the pieces of his shoes and approached him with a kind expression, giving him a quick, keen scrutiny.

"Can I help you? Are you looking for someone?"

Arbat started to speak, but what could he have said to this kindly servant? He shook his head dejectedly. "No. Not anymore." He didn't know what to do with his hands, or with the smelly pieces of leatherette he held in them.

"Here, let me have that," the servant offered. He took the bits without apparent disgust and disposed of them, and then: "Tell me, what are you doing out here? Are you waiting for someone?"

"N-no. But . . . look, do you think they would let me sleep here? Just for tonight? If I wasn't any trouble?" he added hurriedly.

"Here? At the Palace, you mean?"

"Oh, goodness, no," stammered Arbat, flustered. "Here on the *bench*. I won't be any trouble, really I won't, and I'll leave early, before sunup. Before the emperor knows I'm here, I won't be." He nodded encouragingly, hopefully.

The man studied him more closely. "You're a farmer, aren't you? From the Chil Keri region, by the look of you."

Arbat nodded again. "Keri La is my village. And I'm a dairy farmer. A cheese maker, as a matter of fact. That's the problem." His chin started jumping again and he supported it on his palm, elbows on his knees, staring down at the beautiful patterns of the tiles. The gray-eyed man sat down beside him companionably on the stone bench.

"Why don't you tell me about it?" he suggested.

So Arbat told him about it. Every mundane detail, every drop of sweat, every tear. Even the name of the bandit chief.

"*Mennon*, you say," the man repeated, his eyes narrowed.

"Yes, but whatever you do, don't tell the *Domne*. He promised to cut my throat from here"—he pointed—"to here if the *Domne* found out they were there."

"Not a word," the gray-eyed man promised. "But you were telling me about your trip."

"There was a funny thing," Arbat mused aloud, assisting his slow words with fingers drawn expressively on the air, "the way people acted about it. Not in my village, you understand, but . . . well, sir, in other villages I came through, at first they were surprised to see a man wheeling a cheese along in a barrow.

"But then, after a while, people began to ask, 'Are you the man who's bringing the cheese to the emperor?' And some of them said, 'I am a carpenter' (or a tinsmith, or a silverworker, or whatever)," he interrupted himself to add, " 'and I, too, will bring a gift to the *Domne*.' I was so proud of my beautiful cheese. . . ." He sighed, looked up at the gray-eyed man who was listening so respectfully, and felt a little better. He put his hand near his new friend's face. "This is what it smelled like," he said proudly, "when I still had it."

The servant inhaled deeply. "Wonderful," he praised, sincerely.

"Do you know what else?" Arbat confided. "I thought—I actually thought, it's silly, I see that now—but I thought the emperor would be so pleased when he tasted my wonderful cheese, you know that"—he grinned shamefacedly, his eyes welling—"that he would ask me to stay for dinner. With the cheese, you know, for dessert," he finished in a whisper.

"That's not such a big wish," the man said softly, "especially for such loyalty as you have for the *Domne*. Wait here a moment.'' He crossed to the side door and spoke quietly to someone just inside, who had been standing there, Arbat realized, for quite some time. There was a bit of murmured conversation Arbat couldn't make out, and then his patron came back.

"What is your name, friend?" he asked him, and when Arbat told him, he confided, "Well, Arbat of Keri La, you're in luck. It seems there is an empty place at table for dinner tonight, and the *Domne* asked my friend Shang to fill it for him. So you see, you get to have dinner with the *Domne*, after all."

"But—but, my clothes . . . my feet, I have no shoes! I'm *dirty!*" Arbat was aghast, and the gray-eyed man smiled. He had, Arbat thought, a beautiful and appealing smile for a man.

"Shang will take care of that. You may trust him completely. And I'll see you at dinner." Arbat ran after him, plucking at his torn sleeve, and the man stopped and looked at him.

"Excuse me, sir, and thank you, but . . . what do I say to him? How do I *act?* I don't know how to act!"

"Just be yourself, Arbat. You'll be fine just as you are." Arbat's chin was jumping again, with fear and excitement and joy.

"Suppose he doesn't like me, though? What will I say to him? I don't even know what kind of a man he is."

The gray eyes narrowed again. "He's an ordinary man, Arbat; like anyone else who's ever loved his wife . . . or his child"—he trailed off for a moment; then he brightened and continued—"or needed a friend or enjoyed a good cheese. What will you say to him? Tell him 'I brought you a cheese, but it was too good to last.' ''

"And he'll understand?" Hopefully, biting his stubby nails. The gray eyes warmed. "He'll understand."

In the west hall of the Summer Palace were several interesting architectural features. Two matching alcoves, formed in the webs of the soaring fan vaults, were lined with neriosh in a clear cerulean color, and held a pair of priceless Ming vases imported from Old Earth. Then there were the leaded crystal windows, cut in intricate patterns, that admitted whatever light the corridor claimed, and lastly, the stonework itself, in design and execution a sculptor's masterwork.

Riker was tired of looking at them. Having admired the architecture and the artwork (the vases; a sculpture from a planet whose name, for the life of him, he couldn't remember; a *bun* tapestry, diagramming the emperor's theme), he checked his ticket for the hundredth time. It read 17:35, three minutes later than the last time he'd checked. He began pacing up and down in the long shadows that lay somberly on the stoneglass corridors, nervously tossing in his hand the cassette he had brought from *Skipjack*'s bridge.

He had been waiting here in the west hall since just after touchdown, debating with himself whether to show Marik the cassette concerning Misi, and he was seriously uncomfortable about it.

On the one hand, he was loath to raise false hopes in his friend; more than the loss of his child this afternoon, Riker knew, the death of the beautiful young Hennem-mishli, Misi's mother, was still a deep and lasting wound for Marik. This double loss was too painful for Riker to intensify it with fantasies.

On the other hand, he rationalized, what right does any man have to withhold information of this sort?—no matter whom it hurts!—when the greater good may be served, and with it a man he was proud to count his friend.

He decided to go with it, snicking impatience between tongue and teeth. He only hoped he was not doing more harm than good. His collar felt tight. The air was still and oppressive.

The sunlight had given way to a dull gray illumination that made the floors gleam wetly. A deep, sustained roll of thunder sounded over the sea, and at last a cool gust of damp air eddied down the hall. He could hear the wind beginning to rise, a soughing in the trees. Marik's uneven footsteps padded toward him and he turned abruptly out of the alcove, bringing the Einai up short, like a cat startled on the prowl.

"Paul! What—?"

"Got a minute? It's important."

Marik consulted the ticket at his wrist. "Most of the guests have already arrived. Can it wait?"

"I think Misi's alive," Riker told him. "Still want to wait?"

Marik pulled him into the study, shutting the doors firmly behind them. "Explain," he commanded.

For answer, Riker held up the cassette he had brought from *Skipjack*'s bridge. Marik weighed it in his hand and met his eyes, saying nothing; then he crossed to the telecom and ran the tape, standing motionless with his forearm braced against the top of the set.

The screen blazed on. Marik watched without comment the crowded room, Riker's impatience with the noise, and most important, heard the two peasant women discuss the broken latch on the gate, the child who had drowned, and, oh, sweet and merciful T'ath, *the child the men had taken away with them from Sofyan's house*. But of course, idiot, Sofyan had gestated three children, Misi and two more, and which of the three would be in danger of being kidnapped? Only Misi, certainly, only the Han heir! Hard on the heels of *How could they have known where she was?* came the answer, the squiggle, the electronic bug he suspected in this very telecom. Oh, T'ath, she's alive, she's alive.

He forced himself to remain calm, to control the hope and joy that were trying to claim him. Only a possibility, only a chance. *But a chance, a chance!* Marik froze the frame, reversed the tape, and replayed it again and again, a dozen times, searching for flaws, for a defense against the hope and joy that made his hearts thud painfully.

There were no flaws, no errors. There is a certain quality about the truth when it is heard, a spontaneity and thrust that renders the listener defenseless. So it was with Marik. He knew for a certainty, *he knew*, that Misi (*his* Misi, not the pathetic little child he had nearly died for today) had been kidnapped, and he knew the name of her abductor. The cheese maker, in all innocence, had told him: Mennon, his old friend, his new enemy. Kles Mennon.

And she would be safe with him. Having loved the mother, Kles would never harm the child. Would he?

But Misi had not drowned. Misi was alive. Alive, alive, alive. It made a singing in his ears, and the hope and the joy welled from his chest into his throat and squeezed out from under his tightly shut eyelids, until finally he let the tape play itself out and simply stood there with his forehead resting against his arm, making no move, no sound at all.

He did not stir as Riker slipped quietly out of the study, shutting the door gently behind him, and made his way to his luxurious quarters to dress for dinner.

CHAPTER

V

Saturday—7:13 P.M.

THE VIEW OF the impending storm was magnificent from the
East Terrace, and the guests were suitably impressed. The long,
slow, glassy ground swell of early morning had given way to a
shorter, more restless sea, and to an unnaturally high, rising
tide that had already engulfed the rocky jetty as it flung itself
against the Reef, booming majestically.

A bank of surprisingly fast-moving clouds that had been a
picturesque brushstroke when the guests arrived was quickly
becoming a low, ominous overcast, against which the dark
outline of the island of Tagan was barely a blur on the horizon.
Daylight had dimmed to a strange, gray-green illumination, and
the wind, which had been light and changeable since the earlier
heavier rains, was beginning to freshen smartly under yet
another rapidly approaching squall line.

Audrey Lassiter, her hands gripping the splendid marble
balustrade at the lookout the steward had called "the Promontory," stood watching the panorama with shining eyes and
parted lips, the soft, wet wind lifting the dark fall of her hair
from her neck and pressing her gown closer against her. At the
first lance of lightning, she gave a delicious little shiver and her
husband, Charles, turned to her solicitously.

"Are you cold, Miss Audrey?" He never called her simply
Audrey, unless he was displeased. She flung him an absent
smile.

"Oh, no. No, Charles, it isn't that. It's just so . . ." She
lifted a shoulder in a helpless shrug. There were no words to
describe the sensation, seen through the eyes of an artist, of
standing vulnerable to an approaching storm on an alien planet.
Even the smell of the wind was different and exciting. A cock

107

standi flew past them over the sea at eye level, his dull plumage barely discernible from the gray and heaving sea below, and a moment later, his smaller mate, glistening white, followed after him, calling against the wind.

A dark fishing-*byela* was patrolling the waters near the island of Tagan, doggedly breasting waves that looked too rough to be truly safe. Audrey thought its presence, considering the oncoming storm, a bit of a curiosity.

The island itself was a curiosity as well. Protected from tourists by governmental decree and tales of ghosts and smugglers (and more practically, by Einai ecologists, for Tagan was part of the rampers' breeding grounds) Tagan sat like an enigma on the horizon. Audrey had seen a paragraph or two about it in her Baedeker's.

Early explorers had seen the shape of Tagan as resembling the head of a ramper. A protected harbor, opening to the west and looking from the air like a long, open mouth, nestled between the main body of the island and its southern wing, which was known as "the Jaw." At the hinge of the Jaw was a meandering passage called the Narrows, and it was a brave boat and a foolish one that would try to navigate it. Each attempt further clogged the channel with wreckage. West of Tagan was a second tiny island, just beyond the open mouth, called I'a, the Einai word for "one," or, more correctly, "one fish," after the rampers' customary prey.

It had surprised Audrey to read that the Einai counted everything, from apples to *zoris*, by numbers of fish, as in "one fish," "two fish," and so on; but taking into account the fact of their being cat derived, their system made more sense.

The name of the isle at the mouth of Tagan could just as easily be translated "Isle One" as "The Fish," except that local usage made it clear which of the two meanings was applicable.

The fishing-*byela* was still churning back and forth in front of the harbor entrance, its wake luminous in the dying light. Some needy Einai fishermen risking the storm for a last load of fish, she supposed. Probably family men, willing to risk their lives to feed their children. At the thought of children, an old familiar sadness weighed on her heart. At least they have children to worry about, she thought. At least they have them.

"Look, Miss Audrey." Charles pointed and the sight made her catch her breath. Scores of fishing smacks, smaller and more graceful than the unwieldy *byela,* their brilliant orange, gaff-rigged sails almost fluorescent under the lowering sky, were running before the wind, making for the snug harbor in the lee of the Point. She could see the inlet if she leaned out a bit: safe inside the jetty, a curved slice of sea strand overgrown with cozy fisher shacks and deserted shrimp platforms.

A fine, thin rain had begun to fall, hardly more than a veil, haloing the watery points of lamplight below, and there was a mutter of thunder over the water. Across the cove, on the Point, a snubbed headland nosing into the sea, stood the Eyries, where the famous Imperial Racing Gryphons were bred and trained. The lights had been lit there, too, earlier than usual because of the storm, and they looked cheery and warm across the misty twilight.

Audrey felt a pang of nostalgia, a sense of loneliness not entirely brought on by the scenery or the weather, but by the circumstances of her own life. She felt a need to reach across and touch Charles' hand, but Charles was not given to public displays of affection, and that knowledge kept her hands clasped composedly in front of her. Thunder rolled away over the sea.

The fishing smacks were right under the Point now, escorted by close ranks of whitecaps that marched into shore only to be dashed to pieces on the submerged rocks. The boats, evidently fearing the same fate, were converging at the apex of the Point, maneuvering through the pass a few at a time, and tying up to mooring buoys in the sheltered cove.

Little dinghies had put out from shore to pick up the crews, bobbing and dipping precariously in the tossing waters, and watching them, Audrey forgot to breathe. They would make it, of course. They were fishermen, after all. They knew the sea. But when one overloaded dinghy heeled over hard and began to take on water, she caught her breath and reached instinctively for Charles, only to find that he was gone. She was alone on the wet Promontory with the dark sky, and lights being lit all through the Summer Palace, and the guests gone inside. More Federation business, she supposed. She had learned never to ask.

There was a sound, as of a distant trumpet, from out across the water, rising for an instant above the booming surf and the thunder, and she whirled to find its source, but it had grown too dark to see. Even the dinghies were lost to view. And, hair damp and curling from the mizzle, gown snapping at her ankles, she hurried into the shelter of the Palace, looking for a quiet place to repair her appearance and her emotions, in order to meet the man her husband had referred to as His Excellency: Priyam Hanshilobahr *Dom* Dao Marik, the emperor of Eisernon.

Earlier, Paul Riker, freshly showered, shaven, and resplendent in dress whites, strolled casually around the East Terrace, nodding to acquaintances, declining a glass of champagne in favor of a bowl of tarangi, and studying the architecture. He saw Charles Lassiter standing at the lookout on the Promontory and would have gone over to speak to him, but there seemed to be some tension between him and the young woman who was with him, so he decided to leave well enough alone.

Along with everything else, he was keeping a weather eye on the sea and sky. He noticed, as the others probably did not, that the ceiling was dropping along with the temperature. Over the past eighteen hours or so, according to *Skipjack*'s tracking system, this small fast tropical storm had been working its way toward the coast. Now its arrival was imminent.

Give it another couple of hours, he thought, sidestepping a puddle of rainwater, and the really heavy squall lines would be moving in. He felt a twinge of pleasant anticipation at the thought of burrowing comfortably into the deep, soft bed his host had provided him, with a good book at his elbow and the banked embers glowing in the grate, drowsily listening to the storm *whumpf* away at the Palace with all the wind and rain and fireworks at its command, while he lay safe and sleepy inside.

There was another, closer rumble of thunder, echoed by the roaring breakers, and he lifted his tarangi bowl slightly in salute to it and drank, feeling pleased with himself and with the world. The wind smelled of storm and mystery.

''Sounds like we're in for some bad weather, eh, Captain?'' The owner of the voice, a short, blocky, khaki-clad officer with a chest full of ribbons (mostly ordinary stuff, Riker noted) and a glass in his hand, crossed toward him out of a chatting group of expensively clad Earthlings. The officer came up, extended his hand, which Riker shook perfunctorily, and clapped him on the back. "Riker, isn't it?"

"Paul Riker, yes, sir." He tried to place the face, with no result. "I'm afraid you have me at a disadvantage." The blocky man laughed shortly.

"Harve Jessen, colonel, Federation Armed Forces. No, you don't know me, Paulo boy. But I know you. Recognized you from the tri-D. Read all the reports." He wagged his head admiringly. "That Oolivon mission—great job, son, great job. Opened up another whole galaxy for us, do you realize that? Another whole galaxy!"

"Yes, sir, that thought did occur to us at the time. By the way, it's, ah, Elluvon, Colonel." Riker smiled uncomfortably, being drawn by the still-clasped hand into the group. "Like in 'Ell-loo-vohn.'" He jerked his hand free as politely as possible and adjusted his collar with it.

"Oolivon, *right*," the colonel repeated, not really listening to him. "I want you to meet some of our party, Paulo," he continued. "Dr. Kei Matsushita. He's not a doctor that does anybody any good, you understand, he's an oceanographer." They shook hands. "Dr. Marlowe Dunn, xenobiology." The handshake, the murmured pleasantry. "And Frederick Simes. Good old Fred's in steel, out on Birmingham IV, practically runs the planet, eh, Fred?" Good old Fred permitted a grimace to rearrange briefly his craggy features, and gripped Riker's hand in what felt like a metal vise.

"What 'practically,' Harve?" he demanded of Jessen, dropping Riker's crushed hand. "Bing IV turned out duralloy for seven starships over quota for these guys"—he rapped Riker's chest with the back of his knuckles—"and that's peacetime production schedules—this past ten quarters, because yours truly runs the place. No 'practically' about it!" He gestured disinterestedly at Riker. "So who's the Navy?" The Earthling group, with boredom freezing their faces, had turned away to chat coolly among themselves about other subjects.

"The Navy," Jessen informed him blandly, "is only Captain Paul T. Riker—it is Paul *T*, isn't it, Paulo?" he interrupted himself to ask, and Riker, remembering his conversation yesterday with Marik about these people's unique ability to help Marik's war-torn planet, stifled everything he might have said and several things he wanted very much to say, and said, instead, "No, sir, it's Paul *W.* Paul *Whitfield* Riker." *Little snobbery, there, Riker,* he thought. *Bit old for that sort of thing, aren't you?*

The mocking, sophisticated faces swung his way like balloons on a common string. Evidently he had said the magic word.

"Fine old name, Whitfield," someone remarked at the back of the group. Riker smiled tightly, making no response, and someone else added, "Yes, but . . . well, I don't suppose the good captain would be from Zerev, after all."

"As it happens," Riker informed them brightly, "I am from Zerev. Born there, as a matter of fact. My parents own a little land, you see."

And then they asked him questions, and he was forced to admit that yes, indeed, his ancestors had been among the settlers from the starship *Mayflower,* and that the 'little land' his parents owned provided a respectable percentage of the fuel for the ships Fred Simes was so proud of turning out.

Jessen cleared his throat. "As I was saying," he continued in a slightly louder tone, "Captain Paul Whitfield Riker, who captains the USS *Skipjack,* was recently decorated by the High Council for the famous Oolivon mission. I know you people are familiar with it, it was all over the tri-D." He turned to Simes. "How does that grab you, Fred?"

"That grabs me right here," Simes growled happily, clutching his heart, "and I want to shake your hand, Captain Whitfield—"

"That's 'Riker,' sir," Riker informed him pleasantly, while Simes wrung the few remaining bones in his hand and slapped him on the back fraternally. It was like being back-slapped fraternally by a tyrannosaurus.

So then there were more questions, this time about how *Skipjack* had managed to find an Elluvon, way out in the middle of nowhere, and how it looked and what it wanted and how they had gotten it out of being stuck in the tubes system, and about how starships worked in the first place, questions that Riker sidestepped with a palpably rising blood pressure and all the courtesy he could muster. Fred Simes laid a leaden hand on his shoulder and leaned on it.

"The only thing I can't understand," he confided in his gravelly bellow, "is how a man of your caliber got stuck with that eye-eye gook on board. What's his name, Marrick? Any relationship to, uh . . ." He gestured around him at the Summer Palace. Riker nodded conspiratorially and, picking up Simes' hand from his shoulder, dropped it like a rock.

"As a matter of fact," Riker informed him, *sotto voce*, "he's the same man. And the way I got him is, I asked for him." Which was not quite the truth, he reflected, for Marik had been assigned to him as an unknown quantity; but had he been given a say in the matter, Marik would have been his first and only choice, which he felt amounted to the same thing.

Simes grimaced wryly and shook his head, speaking now in a normal tone, oblivious to the Einai waiter who was removing their empty glasses. "Bad idea, fraternizing with the eye-eyes, friend. I know what I'm talking about. I've got 'em on Bing IV, and take it from me, they aren't worth the powder to blow 'em to hell. Give 'em a job and they screw it up every time. Not that they don't get the right results! Oh, they get the right results, all right, but the way they go *about* it! Some offbeat idea you'd never think up in a million years! And there's no way to check up on 'em, if you see what I mean. I mean, if they use their own ideas, who knows what they could be putting past us, huh? And try to teach 'em right—they just stare at you." He made a wry face. "They just can't hack it. Face it, it's in the blood; they're inferior."

He took a fresh glass from the stony-faced waiter's tray and handed a second to Riker. "Here, have some good Earthling booze, leave the green stuff to the native help." He saw Riker's face then, and slapped him companionably on the back again. "Hey, look, no problem, huh? It's not like they can *help* it, you know!"

Riker's irritation surged to the surface, but before he could formulate a properly controlled response, the gangly Dunn had come up and was pumping his hand again as if he expected a momentary oil strike.

"I can't tell you what a terrific honor this is, Captain! We certainly were delighted to hear that the hero of the You-la-von mission was going to be here tonight! Only thing that made the trip worthwhile!'' he enthused, with such heartfelt sincerity that Riker felt perspiration begin to trickle agonizingly down his spine. He mumbled some nonsense about duty and team effort and the ship's being more than the crew, and finished uncomfortably with, ''By the way, it's pronounced Elluvon, as in Ell-loo—''

''And I don't think you've met Madame Louise Bechtel,'' Colonel Jessen interposed, walking him along while Dunn kept pumping his hand. He retrieved it deftly and made a brief bow to Madame Bechtel, a scrawny old harridan in a shockingly decolleté dress whose diamonds almost covered the tan freckles on her bony chest. She inclined her head slightly in answer to his bow and a wicked light glittered in her eyes.

''Tiens, tiens!'' she exclaimed, offering her hand mockingly. Riker took the proffered fingertips to touch his lips to them in the appropriate gesture, when she took his firmly by the jaw, turning his head quickly from side to side with dispassionate intensity, as she might a biological specimen. *''C'est vous le célèbre Captain Riker? La soirèe va finir par être amusante,''* she remarked to the others, as Riker jerked sharply away from her hand. ''This should liven up the project considerably.''

''Vous me faites trop d'honneur, Madame,'' Riker protested sarcastically, feeling that enough was enough. Then, dropping into Ertheng, ''As far as I can see, you people are lively enough without my help. I only hope you find what you're looking for.''

''Hoity-toity!'' she exclaimed, laughing. ''Yes, we have, as a matter of fact. I think we have.''

''Wonderful,'' Riker said. ''Now, if you'll excuse me.'' He bowed stiffly to the assembly. ''Ladies.'' Nodded curtly to the men. Made off down the hall with as much dignity as he could muster, fuming inwardly. The old woman motioned to someone in the crowd.

''Where's Cynthia? Ah! There you are. Make yourself useful, girl, go after that young man and keep him company. He's headed for the rose gardens, if I have my directions right. Keep him away from us old dodderers, we've a lot to discuss. There's a good girl!''

Riker walked quickly, trying to reason with himself. It was

not that important. Madame Bechtel was an old woman, and elderly people often had their peculiarities. She was from Earth itself, and sometimes Earthlings forgot that colonists and aliens had rights, too. But the source of his indignation was not simply the passing rudeness of an elder. That would have been easy to overlook. It was the whole sad situation, wherein Marik had lost his wife, his child, and even the privacy of his own home.

And to top it off, if the unvarnished bigotry of Marik's guests were not enough to bear, this imperious old cadaver had provided the last straw to Riker's staggering camel, examining his face like that of an errant schoolboy, and commenting upon him in French, no less! Just who the hell, he wondered politely, did Madame Louise Bechtel think she was? The only saving grace in the whole business was that he, Riker, had to endure that nonsense, rather than Marik, who would have his hands full enough of it by dinnertime.

He shoved his way through the double doors that led off the board overhang of the south veranda, heard feminine heels tap-tapping behind him, and out of common courtesy, disinterestedly caught and held the closing door to avoid its slamming in her face.

"Do you always walk so fast?" asked the bored, amused voice at his elbow. "I almost couldn't catch you."

"Sorry," he began ruefully, over his shoulder as he let go the door. "I didn't know you were trying to get my atten——"

She presented a cigarette in an ivory holder. "Got a light, Ace?" She was standing very close beside him, and the long lashes lifted and revealed startling ice blue eyes, ringed with green, so like Madame Bechtel's that he was struck, first by the resemblance, and then by the cynical amusement in them. He took the cigarette, struck it on a stoneglass column for her, sheltering it from the wind with a cupped hand, and returned it while the eerie pale eyes laughed up at him.

"I'm sorry," he repeated, with a good deal less warmth.

"Don't be," she advised him succinctly. "I'm used to walking fast. She takes those incredible liberties with everyone." She blew smoke and watched as the wind pulled it now this way, now that. "Has to do with being a councilor adviser, I suppose. Goes to their heads."

Aha, Riker thought. *That* Louise Bechtel. "Relative of yours?" he asked.

"Aunt. I conned her and Daddykins into wangling an invitation for me. It's so damn boring at Patton Base I was ready to jump out of my skin. So when the greenie headman here," she gestured negligently at the Palace, "asked if I would 'honor him by acting as his hostess,' no less, I jumped at the chance to get the hell out. Naturally," she hastened to add, "I have no intention of hostessing for the greenies, but I certainly wasn't going to tell Daddy about it—not till later, at any rate. No use spoiling a holiday if you can help it, don't you agree?" She traced the pattern of his tunic weave with one long, carefully manicured fingernail. "I'll bet my aunt is right, Captain. I'll bet those *are* rose gardens behind that wall. Nice and quiet, and . . . romantic, do you think?"

As she was speaking, Riker really looked at her for the first time: tall and fashionably thin, with carefully coifed, honey-colored hair, she was wearing a long blue thing that draped gracefully and was caught at one shoulder by a diamond pin that fairly screamed money. Her earrings said the same thing, but not quite as loudly. She had had several drinks. Spoiled, indulged, and bored stiff, he assessed.

As if hearing his thoughts, she added, "All that—but rich, Ace, very, very rich. And that makes up for all the rest." She dragged on the cigarette again. "Want to walk me through the rose gardens now, Captain?" she offered sweetly, toying carelessly with his medals. "'A pleasant walk, a pleasant talk, along the briny beach'?" He spared her the ghost of a smile, which she misunderstood, and reflected that he might as well go along with the farce. At least she wasn't after his enormous military paycheck, he thought wryly.

"'The Walrus and the Carpenter,'" he mused aloud, taking her elbow and steering her down the shallow steps into the fine, innocuous mist of the rain. "Let's see, now . . . you're not the walrus, are you? That's a seagoing creature."

"Hardly," she laughed scornfully, heels clicking on the exquisite mosaic walk.

"So you must be the carpenter." She dragged again at her cigarette, wincing at its dampness, and crushed it out on the intricately worked tiles. They paused under the pair of weeping cherry trees that flanked the entrance to the rosary, and Riker braced a hand against the bronze-strapped wood of the gate, blocking her path.

"And if you're the carpenter of your cute little quote, lady," he continued, regarding her speculatively, "just what is it you're building—or building up to?"

Her cheeks flushed a bit, hard to see in the gathering darkness, and she lifted a bare shoulder; but she did not drop her eyes, or turn her face aside, or do any of the other modest, charming female things that made women so attractive to Riker. Instead, she kept staring insolently at him, and passed her tongue around her lips in a gesture that would have been cunning in a kitten. Unfortunately, Cynthia was not a kitten.

"Maybe livening up a dull native dinner party where I'm going to have to put up with their little greenie 'emperor' all evening—with a handsome Earthling partner." She laughed mirthlessly. "Life among the savages. Survival among the bores." She placed an index finger against his restraining arm and he dropped it, allowing her to pass through the gate and into the rose garden. He shut it behind them, and she turned to speak over her shoulder, still walking away from him. "Or maybe I'm just a horticulturist, Ace, you never can tell."

"Sure I can." Riker plucked a rose and handed it to her. "Peace?" he asked gently, and she stopped and retraced several steps, reaching for it triumphantly.

"Apologizing, are you, Captain?" She buried her face in the rose and inhaled deeply. "Mending fence?"

He pursed his lips in a brooding smile, frowned pleasantly, and shook his head. "Oh, no, nothing like that. That's the name of the rose: Peace. I didn't *think* you recognized it."

She smiled bitterly and crushed the flower in her fist, dropping the shreds to the ground. "You're very irritating, do you know that?" she said tightly, and Riker grinned.

"I know," he admitted. "I know something else, too."

She glared at him poisonously and he leaned toward her confidentially, as if sharing a secret.

"You're definitely not a horticulturist." He did not wait to see whether she would share his smile, but picked another rose and strolled slowly along the old-brick walk, enjoying the flowers, for here in the garden, subtle lighting bloomed up

among the shrubbery and misted down from the trees, making
it light as day. The wind was fresh from the north now,
promising more squalls, and showers of rose leaves pattered on
the walks with a sound as of rain. In the center of the garden,
half-obscured by trees and flowering bushes, there stood a
small white marble pavilion, open on all sides and facing a
reflecting pool that mirrored the one piece of statuary it
sheltered.

He walked closer, vaguely aware of the girl beside him, and
saw that it was the statue of a lovely young woman, wearing a
flowing robe and crowned with wreaths of coreliae. She was
imminently pregnant, though the abundant folds of her robe
masked her condition with a certain amiable grace.

"Not bad," Cynthia decided reluctantly. "Trite, of course,
but not badly done. In fact"—she turned her head critically to
one side—"here where they've shaved the marble thin, you
can actually see light through it. I wonder what kind of laser
does that fine a job?"

"The Einai don't use lasers for sculpture, Miss . . ."

"Jessen. Cynthia Jessen," she provided. "The colonel's
brat. My, my, Ace, you take a girl for a walk in the garden and
you don't even know her name. Tsk, tsk. You sailors are all
alike."

"Miss Jessen," he pursued, sticking to the subject, "they
work with a mallet and chisel. It's all done by hand."

"Fascinating." She patted a fake yawn and moved closer;
walked all the way around him dragging her empty cigarette
holder along his shoulder, his back, his near shoulder, like a
child pulling a stick along a picket fence. "Why don't you tell
me what all these medals are for, Ace?" she suggested huskily,
flipping them with the holder. "I'll bet I'm just dying to
know."

For answer, he reached out and caught her by the shoulders,
drawing her to him strongly, and slipped his hands up to her
throat, her face, cradling her head in his hands. Her breathing
speeded and he saw her mouth go soft. Her pale eyes glistened
wetly silver in the lamplight, and there was the smell of roses,
and of rain. He brought his face closer until their lips almost
touched, and whispered, "Too bad I'm not just dying to tell
you, isn't it?"

It was worth the slap.

He laughed, rubbing his cheek, and strode away alone down a long, secluded path, feeling better than he had all evening. Lightning flashed with a sudden clap of thunder, very close, and he heard the tapping of heels coming behind him almost at a run. So the lady was afraid of bad weather, eh? Well, she would have more than enough of it before the evening was out. The storm was moving in fast. The heels tapped closer, and Riker smiled to himself but did not acknowledge her presence, but simply kept walking; and, as they neared him, the footsteps slowed. Obviously Miss Cynthia Jessen, the colonel's brat, was waging mighty battle with her pride, and Riker had no intention of upsetting the balance of power. Besides, something else had caught his attention.

There was a dark *presence,* a tall *something,* faintly lit, down the way, and his curiosity was caught by it. He approached it purposefully, scarcely hearing her mutter, "I'm sorry—about the slap. I suppose I deserved all that."

"Hm? Oh, yes, yes, you did." He stopped before it, pleased and mystified. Someone had erected a bluestone plinth among the roses. Set in a quiet, out-of-the-way corner, it was not so much incongruous as enigmatic. Scarcely over a meter and a half high, it was perhaps twelve centimeters in depth and twenty wide. Its only claim to significance was the ideograph carved one-third the way down the facing surface of the stone.

"I *simply* don't believe it!"

Riker, trying to puzzle out the ideograph, frowned absently at Cynthia's comment. "I beg your pardon?"

"I said, I can't believe it, Captain. You'd think the greenies would know better than to spoil this . . . this perfect symmetry"—she swept an encompassing hand vaguely at the rosary—"with a slab of old stone stuck into the ground. If it's supposed to be some sort of abstract art, it falls far short." She broke off to strike another cigarette on the stone, and Riker, intrigued, traced the ideograph with his fingers. Then he had it. Of course.

Life.

Strange, that, he thought. The plinth was new. It had had no time to weather. It lacked the velvet cover of green moss that rimmed the edges of the other garden stones, and no creepers or other small plants had grown up to soften its edges. Even the soil around it was freshly disturbed. Without a doubt the plinth was newly installed. He tried to think what was just that height.

An insistent gust of wind blew a scattering of rose leaves and rain at them, and Cynthia drew her wrap close but made no move toward leaving. Instead, she leaned over for a closer look at the smooth stone below the plinth, half-hidden by freshly planted jasmines. "Maybe it's one of their quaint little native gods," she suggested, half in jest. "It seems to have had a devotee or two, of late."

He followed her pointing cigarette holder and saw the limp bouquet lying at the foot of the plinth. Mystified, he pushed the low branches aside for a better look and found three more, in various stages of deterioration. Four, he thought. One for each day Marik and I have been here. But—bouquets? For a slab of stone, an unfeeling monument? The Einai built no idols.

Then it hit him. Then he knew. All of a sudden, it came to him precisely what—or, rather, who—had been just so tall, just so slender. And he knew why the ideograph read *Life*. Marik, with nothing to bury, no place to weep, had needed a place to lay his roses.

He shut his eyes painfully. "Ah, Marik," he breathed softly between locked teeth.

"Marik?" Her voice was shrill, astounded, mocking. "*Marik?* The, ah, deposed monarch in there? *He* did this? Oh, this is priceless! *In*-credible!" She shook her glossy coiffure in dismay and gave that damnable chuckle. "Natives at heart, posturing like gentry. I think that's funny, don't you, Captain?" Riker took a deep breath and made no answer, and she persisted, "How about it, Ace? Don't you agree? Don't you think the Einai are a very funny bunch?"

Riker replaced the dying bouquet at the foot of the plinth and stood up, his eyes smarting. "Yes," he said quietly, past the lump in his throat. He gave her a tight smile, quickly gone. "Oh, yes, they're a very funny bunch."

A baby was crying. Payina Tasa Bournt, gliding along the corridor in search of a ladies' retreat, paused for a moment and listened. Herself the mother of a large family, she anticipated the pattern of a baby's crying: the initial wail, the building outrage, the change in the cry when the child received what he needed, and the sweet murmuring decline into silence.

But there was no change this time, no quieting. This child would not be comforted, and her heart went out to it. Following her instincts and the sound, she found the child's room and opened the door just as the wind flung a handful of rain and wet leaves against the window, making the child sitting on the floor jump nervously and scream all the louder.

Dao Marik, flawlessly turned out in dress whites with ribbons slantwise across his chest, was kneeling beside him, trying to soothe the child, who was clearly having none of it.

"There, now, you see?" he explained reasonably, while the pretty little boy sat there verging on hysterics, "it was only the rain. We're going to have a storm in just a bit." He gingerly offered him a toy. "Look here, it's a skimmercraft for you to play with, just like a real—" The boy shoved one fist into his mouth and with the other hand snatched up the toy and flung it across the room. Marik sighed, ran his fingers through his close-cropped dark hair, and got to his feet just as Tasa Bournt, still smiling, shut the door behind her.

"I think it's terrible how the *Domne* mistreats little children," she said in mock sternness, and Marik recognized her with a mixture of relief and welcome.

"Tasa! It was good of you to come!" He gave her a brotherly hug. "I wasn't sure you could make it on such short notice, but of course, I had high hopes."

She patted his cheek with a velvet palm and slid him a knowing look out of the corners of her emerald eyes. "Oh, we wouldn't have missed it! Dodol heard from his aide how you came to give this dinner—it's all over Parliament!" She turned her eyes away delicately and murmured, "And tonight of all nights!"

Feeling she had said too much, she scooped the screaming child off the floor, and carried him to a bentwood chair from Erth that rocked when you sat in it. She adjusted the cushions. She sat.

"Enough," she told the child, gently but firmly. "Enough." He stared up at the great, soft feline face, the gentle emerald eyes, and thrust a thumb into his mouth, hiccupping raggedly. Knuckled tears out of his eyes. Yawned prodigiously.

Rocking softly, cradling him on her pillowy left arm, she traced the outlines of his face—eyebrows, cheeks, chin—with a furry forefinger while Marik waited patiently and the baby stared, blinked his heavy eyelids, and stared again.

"We thought you might need your friends," she finished at last. She kept her head bent, softly stroking the little boy's face, while he began to drowse.

"I always have need of my friends, Tasa, you know that," Marik smiled. "But it's especially good to have you here right now." He brushed back the damp tightly-curled ringlets from the baby's forehead, hesitating involuntarily as a quirk of memory *knelt him on the grass beside the baby, toying with the ringlets in her drying hair, and Riker saying—*

But Misi's alive. I saw the tape. She's alive! She has to be!

He looked up with a guilty start into the compassion in Tasa's face, and he bridged the silence with a quick smile, tousling the boy's silky curls. "He's a noisy little fellow, isn't he?" Tasa grinned back at him, her eyeteeth lapping her full lower lip only slightly, like those of a well-fed tabby.

"They all are, believe me! When the quints were born, Dodol threatened to sign up for Rim duty, poor dear, to protect his ears."

"Dodol came with you tonight, didn't he?" Marik was glad to have the conversation back on safer ground. Tasa nodded once, careful not to disturb the boy, whose eyelids snapped open intermittently, to be sure he hadn't been put to bed.

"He's in the Great Hall, talking to your guests."

"Ah, yes," Marik breathed. "My guests." There was a long silence while the rain beat at the windows and the baby's breathing became soft and even.

Tasa bit her lip, then murmured, "I saw some of *Fleet's guests,* Dao. And they saw me, too. I'd venture to say that half of them never saw a real live Kraun before. They tend to edge past you in a corridor, smiling a lot." She smiled her slow, mischievous smile. "I was tempted to hiss and spit at them," she confessed in a whisper, "just to see them jump. Poor little things." Marik crossed quickly to her side from the window.

"You weren't snubbed, I hope," he asked in a worried tone, and she shook her luxurious auburn mane girlishly, making the clusters of tiny glass ornaments in it jingle merrily.

"Not out loud, at any rate. But they do forget—or perhaps they don't realize—what good hearing we humans have. Even a whisper . . ." She half closed her eyes. "Don't even worry about it, *Domne*," she purred in an elder-sister tone. "Dodol and I can take care of ourselves."

Marik frowned, biting his lip. "That's another thing, Tasa. You have to remember that the empire doesn't exist anymore. This '*Domne*' talk—" But the Payina jerked bolt upright in her chair, her eyes suddenly snapping green fire at him. The baby, waking abruptly, began to scream again, and she patted him vexedly.

"Now, let me tell you something, Dao Marik!" she interrupted him hotly. "My husband and I had the privilege of knowing your honored parents when you were not much bigger than this *cubbin* here. My parents—and Dodol's!—were members of the old *Domne*'s court, before the One-Day War. And we know something these stupid Erthlikli—and you!—seem to have forgotten! You *are* the Han heir, the true and rightful ruler, before God, of Eisernon! And Krau! And Minsoner! And Sauvage! And all the smaller worlds! Like it or not, Dao, you are the emperor! That may not mean much to the Federation—or to those rabid bigots out there—but it means a great deal to us, Priyam Hanshilobahr *Dom* Dao Marik!"

The emerald eyes sparkled with angry wetness, and Marik put an arm around her silken shoulders and held her close. "Why, Tasa," he chided gently, "I don't see tears, do I? Not at the emperor's dinner party!" She sniffed into a scrap of lace handkerchief, patted his cheek, half laughing in spite of herself, and shook her head, the glass ornaments chiming faintly in her hair.

"Go away, *Domne*," she ordered thickly, "go talk to your company while I rock this baby!"

"Alai, Payina." Marik made a courtly bow and chom-ala that started out to be an affectionate jest, but the Payina returned the gesture so gravely that he was in a sober mood as he limped down the corridor toward the Great Hall, and his guests.

Though, in reality, they were not his guests, but Fleet's guests. Tasa was right about that. In another, far part of the house, he could hear the orchestra playing a few bars of an old

Einai folk song that tugged at his hearts-strings. Had he been asked, half the people sharing his table tonight would never have gotten within two lights of the Imperial Coast, much less the Summer Palace. Erthlikli, mostly, and, as he had explained to Paul Riker, trying to help Eisernon get back on its feet. He had to try to be grateful for that, at least. Although, he amended, if Erth had left them alone to begin with, there would have been no need for reconstruction. Eisernon would be whole.

And he? What would he be? He slowed his pace. All right, conceding the fact that he had never been formally crowned emperor—no ceremony, no royal guests, no dancing in the streets—he was still the heir apparent. Crown prince, to be exact. The people of the now-defunct empire still looked to him as their leader. To his embarrassment, there had been too many letters, telecom calls, demonstrations, for the Federation to ignore. Which was why, he reflected bitterly, he was permitted to live in his own house instead of some BOQ, or the WMCA downtown.

The orchestra was playing the "Lei alden Han," the emperor's theme, and Marik paused midway in the corridor, listening. Time to get his emotions under control, he told himself, time to stop living in the past. It worried him, this recent preoccupation with empire, and it would do no good. The empire was dead and gone; it was nothing, it could come to nothing. Better to leave it alone, see to his job as science officer of a very good ship, and have done with it. Tasa Bournt was wrong. She had to be wrong. It was the only way Marik could accept his painful situation with any degree of resignation at all.

He dragged himself back from his dark reflections, and in the silence of the deserted corridor, he could hear the storm worsening. The heavy squall lines were coming in hard now, and rain hit the broad expanses of window like volleys of shot. He paused again. There were several original paintings near vulnerable windows; they really should be removed for safe-keeping until the storm abated. He thought a summons at Shang and after a patient moment of waiting, his steward appeared.

"Here I am, *Domne*. You called me."

Marik absently rubbed the side of his aching head with his

fingertips and dropped the hand abruptly as Shang followed the gesture with concerned eyes. "Yes. The paintings in the north corridor . . . have they been removed?"

"The servants are busy at it now, sire. I should be happy to see to the Scroll if my lord wishes."

"No, I'll attend to that myself, thank you. Is Captain Riker about?"

"I believe he has just lately come in from the rosary, sire—with a lady." The pause was barely perceptible, and delivered with the utmost gravity, which drew a reluctant smile from Marik.

"Then it's safe to assume he is otherwise engaged. I have a guest, Charles Lassiter by name." Shang inclined his head. "Bring him my compliments and ask him to examine the telecom unit in the study. He'll know what to look for. No one else need be bothered with this."

"As you wish, my lord." Marik started to walk away and hesitated, glancing at his ticket. 18:42 hours. Dinner was to be served promptly at 20:00. He had time, and to spare, to check on the Scroll.

"Oh, and, Shang," he decided, "you might ask the orchestra to play several more selections while the guests are being seated. I'll be along directly."

"Very good, sire." The steward bowed and hurried away while Marik, enjoying his last few moments of solitude, strode down the silent corridor where the servants were padding away with the last of the carefully covered paintings, and into one of the Palace's many drawing rooms (this one facing due north and receiving the full brunt of the storm) where long ago he had caused one of his chief treasures to be displayed.

It was a Wedding Scroll, done on whitebark in the Old Way and painstakingly illuminated by Mishli herself in a fifteen-centimeter band all the way around it. She had incorporated tiny flecks of neriosh, gold leaf, and lapis lazuli into the illumination as birds' wings, unicorn hooves, scales, or flowers, a process she had learned during her life at the monastery, and the result was exquisite and invaluable. It had been her wedding gift to him, and he prized it above every other possession.

The verse, written by her grandfather, the venerable Oman

Shari-Mnenoplan, was copied thereon in his own hand, which made the Scroll doubly precious. To imagine this tender memento exposed to the elements was more than Marik could bear. Indeed, it had rarely been so much as viewed by other than Marik, except for Mishli herself, a few close friends, and the servants who kept the room in order.

Therefore it came as no little surprise to Marik, as he entered the room, to find that he was not alone. An arrestingly lovely young Erthlik woman was standing rapt before the Scroll, puzzling out a few Eisernai words, and Marik, nettled and resolved to retain his privacy in this matter at least, started across the room toward her. Somewhere, in another part of the house, the orchestra began an old Einai love song, Mishli's favorite, called "The Stars of Shali-Rho." The music masked his presence and the visitor, still unaware of Marik as he sauntered up behind her, was reading to herself:

" ' . . . unsinging song' . . . I think . . ." He reached past her to touch the glass over the Scroll.

" 'Un*sung* song,' " he corrected coolly. "Here, the accent, you see."

She looked up at him pleasantly, not much surprised, making a pretty picture with her ivory skin and thick dark chestnut hair, and the lights deep in her eyes. The white lace dress that fell from her throat to her feet, leaving her arms bare, had evidently been designed by an artisan who appreciated the handiwork of his Creator, and molded the fabric accordingly. There was nothing coy about her attitude. Instead, she searched his face and eyes with a serene candor that left no room for duplicity.

"Thank you." Her voice was low pitched and gentle. "I'm not very good at Eisernai yet, I'm afraid." Marik made no comment to that and she continued hesitantly, "I wonder . . . would you mind helping me read this? You do read Eisernai, don't you?" She accented the question with a childish little shake of her head as if anticipating an affirmative reply.

"Like a native."

"Oh—good!" she breathed. "It's awfully important—to Eisernon as well as to me." Her eyes were shining softly. "I think it's an authentic Wedding Scroll, the kind the Han emperors used to have made for them."

He walked around to the front of the framed Scroll and ran a distasteful finger over a few flecks of dust on the lower edge of the frame. "It is a Wedding Scroll," he said curtly. "A private Wedding Scroll, in a private room, in what was once a private home. You have no business here."

Her reflection in the glass was startled and chagrined. She quickly picked up the reflection of her evening bag from the reflection of a chair upholstered in striped silk, and murmured, "I had no idea. Please excuse me." She started for the door and he wheeled about.

"'Important to Eisernon,' you said?" he demanded quietly of her retreating back, and she paused. Turned. Studied his face.

"Yes."

"How?"

"I'm an artist. Specializing at the moment in the restoration of Eisernon's planetary treasures. I believe this Scroll might be one of them."

"The Scroll is not in need of restoration. It has been very well kept. Your solicitude is commendable, but in this case—"

She took a few steps toward him, her expression very serious. "I'm afraid you misunderstand me, sir. I was not browsing through the Palace to amuse myself with the *Domne*'s personal memorabilia; I came in out of the rain, lost my way, and found myself here. And when I saw the Scroll . . ." She moistened her lips and began again.

"You must understand, I've heard about Wedding Scrolls at the university, and at the galleries, but this is the first I've ever seen. You cannot blame me for my interest. I assure you, it was a professional one. I had no idea I was intruding."

The man in the white uniform studied her face in his turn, pulled a long, deep breath, and smiled a most appealing smile. "No," he agreed reluctantly, "I can't blame you for your interest." He indicated a chair. "Won't you sit down?"

He took the chair opposite her and, resting his elbows on the arms of it, clasped his hands and pressed his thumbs against his lips. After an interminable time, during which she dropped her eyes away from that even gray gaze that seemed to probe her very thoughts, he stirred and asked courteously, "What have you heard—about Han Wedding Scrolls?"

She carefully refolded her gloves in her lap, smoothing the creases with her fingers as she spoke. "According to my professors, when a Han *Domne* was married, a Scroll was made for him by his subjects, or a close member of the court, or some relative. They say the artists vied with one another to produce the most perfect Scroll."

"'They say' correctly so far, except to mention that the Scrolls recorded the emperor's deepest emotions, as sung by his closest friend. Which is why," he added, "our Wedding Scrolls were never publicly displayed. We are, by and large, a very private people."

"That explains it, then," she murmured, her cheeks flushing. "There are only two fragments of Wedding Scrolls extant at the university. One is very beautiful, very poetic. We have no idea of the author or the *Domne*. And the other is"—her flush deepened and she hesitated, fumbling for words to describe it.

"That would be the Scroll of Hanshilobahr *Dom* Timujin Kesh, am I correct?" Marik inquired drily. She nodded, and they shared comradely laughter.

"I am familiar with the Scroll of Timujin Kesh," Marik confided, "and I, for one, think assassination was much too good for him. He was a ruler back in the bad old days who thought honor less important than conquest, and went around proving it with a vengeance. And now," he finished owlishly, "all we have left of him is a fragment of his Wedding Scroll. *Sic transit gloria Einai.*"

"But that's the point, isn't it?" she wondered, sitting forward eagerly. "All the Scrolls were supposed to have been lost in the One-Day War, except the bits we have at the university; so this one"—indicating the framed masterpiece—"must be a copy, mustn't it? But somehow I don't believe that." She stood up, straight and slender as a candle, her chin firm with determination. "I don't know how, but *I know this simply isn't a copy.* It's an authentic Scroll." She paused. "Only one thing bothers me about it."

Marik, who had risen to his feet when she stood up, clasped his hands behind him, watching her mobile lips and thinking his own thoughts. "Go on."

She chose her words carefully, feeling her way. "Well . . .

if all the Han Wedding Scrolls were lost in the war, you see, then"—she shook her dark head in perplexity—"which emperor could this Scroll belong to?"

Marik regarded her broodingly over his cheekbones. "This one," he said. Her eyes widened slowly, and the smile touched them before it curved the perfect lips.

"How fortunate you are," she breathed, "to have this sort of evidence that someone loves you. How I envy you!"

A shadow passed over her face and she looked away quickly at the windows, where the rain streamed down like tears, but not before Marik had glimpsed the abyss of sadness that lay behind her smile. He, too, was struggling with a private sorrow, and he felt an immediate kinship with the lovely young woman. He wondered if she could sense it, and then discarded the thought. Hardly likely. They were perfect strangers. His imagination was working overtime. Emotional stress. Shock. The weather. By tomorrow he wouldn't even remember her name. It struck him that he didn't know her name, nor could he think of a valid excuse for finding it out. Unimportant, really.

She looked up at him, not quite smiling, and he regarded her with brooding interest. Vulnerable as a child. Someone ought to be watching out for her. Someone who loved her a great deal. She looked as if she would be easy to love. Innocent little alien.

There was a strange silence in the room, even though the storm beat at the windows desperately, like something lost that was trying to find its way home again. Marik was grateful for the sturdy glazing. It was acceptable being close enough to see this sort of a storm, as long as you were insulated from it in a calm spot of your own making; it would have been quite another thing to have had to deal with it firsthand. He couldn't handle a storm firsthand just now, he thought. Any kind of a storm. What *was* wrong with his imagination?

He took a deep breath. It was a good time to break the silence, he felt, a good time to tell her about the Scroll, as she had asked. Music drifted in on a damp breeze, a sad Einai folk song from the villages along the rain forest, faintly over the rain.

"The man who wrote the verse for me," he began quietly, "was my mentor, my master, Priyam Oman Shari-Mnenoplan.

This is his own hand. He made the ink himself, out of *ponpolo* leaves.'' His voice dropped to a drawl. "He was killed at Sum ChiT'ath, during an Erthlik rocket strike.'' He put away the memory of fire and screams, and the muffled roar of thunder overhead sounded for an instant like the rumble of roofing beams, or tunnels collapsing, or of mountain rapids.

"But . . . how can that be?'' she wondered. "You were on our side, weren't you? How could Earth bomb you?''

His lips twitched in a brief, bitter smile. "A tactical error. An accident of friendly fire. After all,'' he finished drily, "they *did* apologize.'' She glanced at him quickly over her shoulder, met and held his eyes with the sincerity in her own.

"Bitterness doesn't become you, my friend,'' she confided, and there was a long, uncomfortable pause. As much to fill the quiet as anything else, she ran a finger lightly down the border of the Scroll through the glass.

"Who did the illumination?'' she asked. "It's wonderful.''

"My wife.'' He was looking at the Scroll now, through the Scroll and into the past, speaking almost to himself. "My *late* wife. Her name was Hennem-mishli, 'Wheat-in-the-Wind.' You'd have liked her, I think. Everyone did. She was full of life—and funny. She loved children . . .''

"Children,'' the young woman echoed in a lonely whisper, but he did not hear.

"—and she was small—and gray eyed—and very, very beautiful. Oh!—she was so beautiful!'' After a moment, he continued, less steadily. "The verse reads something like this:

> "A bowl of carved charis-wood,
> 　　filled to the brim
> With leaves of tarangi, floating,
> 　　is she.
> Ah, pity him who has never laid
> 　　eyes upon,
> Laid mind upon
> My love.
> Rain to the hennem, web to
> 　　memlikti,
> Is she to me.
> Touches my hearts, makes me

                    complete.
        I go to her pavilion: gray eyes,
                unsung song,
        Garments drop like petals at her
                feet.
        She lifts her hand and so our
                fingers meet.

        (None else can lay a finger on my
                mind
        And leave its imprint there)
        Scent lingers in her hair, black
                wind from the Sea,
        Light from the dark stars,
                intoxicating me . . .

        More than tarangi, fragrant in
                charis-wood
        Is she.''

He read the last few lines in a husky whisper and fell silent,
his throat tight. Impulsively, she laid a light hand on his arm,
pressing it gently. Her eyes were swimming.

"Oh—I'm so sorry," she murmured sincerely, shaking her
head in a childish gesture of negation, and Marik took a
steadying breath and laid a hand reassuringly atop hers.

"So am I," he confided in a whisper. He touched his pocket
handkerchief to her eyes and they shared a tender smile like
longtime friends. "I've never read that—to anyone—except
Mishli," he muttered. "And I find I don't even know your
name." She was standing very close. Very conscious of her
presence. You're behaving very badly, aren't you, *Domne*?

"My name is Audrey," she said, and he tucked her hand
through his arm as they moved slowly toward the door to rejoin
the others.

"Owdri?" he repeated, his faint accent making her smile yet
again. "What a strange, beautiful name. I've never heard it
before. Owdri." She started to reply, but as he opened the
doors, a gust of brisk, damp air flowed into the room, carrying
with it the lively, inviting strains of a Strauss waltz. Marik

stopped dead in the doorway, causing her to lift her brows in unspoken question.

"Do you waltz, Owdri?" he asked abruptly, and her laugh gurgled deliciously.

"Do I what?" she repeated incredulously.

"Waltz. You're an Erthlik, now, tell me, do you waltz?" She laughed again and he joined her, pursuing obstinately, "You do, don't you?"

"Why . . . yes," she replied in bewilderment, "why do you—"

But before she could say another word, Marik caught her impetuously around the waist with his gloved hand and began waltzing her commandingly in huge circles around the deserted drawing room, skirting the priceless tables and barely missing the staid, erect armchairs that stood properly at attention, both of them laughing in astonishment and sheer enjoyment until their laughter died in the symmetry of the motion. The swinging circles lifted her hair back from the slender neck and whispered sibilantly in the lace of her skirts.

Marik sobered, watching her, and the smile faded from her face and was replaced by an unself-conscious expression of utter abandon to the music, speeding his pulse. Then, as she met his eyes, it changed first to one of relaxed friendliness, and then to puzzlement, and then to a certain wariness, like that of one who has wandered far into an afternoon forest only to find herself lost by night. She tried to pull back a bit against his unyielding arm, but he danced all the harder, sweeping her almost off her feet, making her head swim.

The rain slammed against the pane, the music sang on and on, and Marik, his hearts pounding, whirled the reluctant young woman in tighter and tighter spirals, until finally they drew abruptly to a halt, breathing unevenly. High color bloomed in her cheeks and she moistened her dry lips with the tip of a pink tongue.

Searching his face with troubled eyes, she started to back away when, with a shattering crash, a blown branch exploded the window inward, scattering glass and admitting the storm. She made a sharp, half-audible intake of breath and pressed close to him, and Marik's arm tightened reflexively about her waist. Slim waist. Acutely conscious of her warmth. Her hand lying lightly on his chest. Rain pouring in, whipping at them, slapping his flat cheeks. Those big, apprehensive dark eyes looking up at him. Her softness.

A *moment* passed between them, an understanding, a frightening realization in which Marik found that, try as he might, he could not evoke Mishli's face. The storm had caught up to him at last, and without quite knowing what he was about, Marik swung her forcefully against him and found her mouth, kissing her fervently, with all the pent-up passion he had so long denied.

She made a breathy little sound of surprise, struggling softly in his arms like a captive dove; then, slowly, she melted against him, offering no resistance to his kiss. He even imagined that there was a response, a tilt of the head, a tightening of the small, cool fingers behind his neck, when a shocked voice from the doorway stammered: "Forgive me, *Domne*! We heard the crash—" Shang tactfully kept his eyes on the broken window. Marik, distracted by Shang's untimely arrival, was caught off guard, still holding the girl in the circle of one arm. She turned her head away from him, face pale, laying unsteady fingers over her trembling lips.

"You had no right to do that!" she whispered brokenly. "Emperor or no—*you had no right*!" Gathering up her full skirts with both hands, she broke free of his encircling arm and ran from the room, past the beautifully trained servants, who went about their work as if the room were empty, and away from Marik himself, who followed her anxiously, as far as the doorway, spanning the frame with both hands as he gazed down the hallway after her.

Shang, busily picking up soggy leaves and pieces of broken glass from the wet marble floor, was appalled to discover that the Wedding Scroll was not in its usual place.

Still intact in its protective frame, it had been blown off the wall by the force of the storm and was resting, safe but entirely forgotten, on the small, ornate table that had stood beneath it.

CHAPTER

VI

Saturday—7:43 P.M.

AUDREY FLED. SHE ran down the hushed corridors, pursued by the music, listening for his footsteps but hearing only the pounding of her heart. She risked a glance behind her and blundered into a large, soft, furry mass that resolved itself through her misty eyes into a Kraun female, who cried happily, "Audrey! What a delight!"

"Oh, Tasa," she whispered brokenly, clinging to her. "Oh, Tasa, I'm so glad it's you!" Tasa Bournt drew her into a dimly lit room where a baby was sleeping in a crib, and gently shut the door behind her. Audrey leaned wearily against a wall, hands over her mouth, tears cold on her cheeks, and Tasa took both her icy hands, concern drawing her features down.

"Audrey! Child! What's happened?" Audrey shook her head, tears starting afresh.

"I can't tell you, Tasa. I can't talk about it! I'm so ashamed!"

"Nonsense!" the Payina announced briskly. "Now, you sit here by the fire and tell me what happened, and don't give me any foolishness about 'can't talk about it,' either! We're women together and there's nothing we can't talk about, and you know it!" Audrey twisted the handkerchief in her hands, biting her lip. "Is it Charles?" Tasa persisted gently. "About children again?"

"No. No, I've given up asking him for children, Tasa. He has Heck, and for him, that's enough." Her eyes brimmed over. "This is ever so much worse. I've been unfaithful in my heart."

135

Tasa folded her arms across her bosom, sighed compassionately, and waited.

Audrey whispered, "Well, I had been outside, you see, watching the storm come in—and Charles left—so I went in to see if I could freshen up—because of the wind."

"And . . . ?"

"And I got lost. So I started looking for the way back to the terrace, and I found this lovely drawing room, with an authentic Wedding Scroll on the wall! Oh, Tasa," she interrupted herself, "do you realize the artistic significance of that? It's just priceless. And . . . I had started to puzzle it out, when before I knew it, *he* was standing there."

"*He* who?" She read her face. "Not Dao. The *Domne*?" She brightened, and Audrey's eyes brimmed over again.

"I don't see anything to smile about. It was awful! I just cannot understand myself, Tasa!"

The Payina took her hands again with the same tenderness she afforded her own children. "What happened, child? What did Dao say to upset you so?"

She turned her head from side to side in an agony of mortification, tears flowing once more. "He didn't say anything wrong, Tasa. That's the trouble. He was the soul of courtesy. He was sensitive—and gallant—and handsome"— she dropped her hands hopelessly in her lap, a gesture pathetically young and vulnerable—"and he danced with me, Tasa. We danced and we danced—"

"Well," chirped Tasa brightly, "that doesn't seem bad enough to cry over, dear. Lots of people dance with handsome men. Not as handsome as our Dao, perhaps, but—"

Audrey averted her eyes. "And then we stopped dancing."

"Ah," breathed Tasa, "I see."

"He kissed me, Tasa, as if he meant it! And, oh, Tasa, I kissed him back! I wanted him to kiss me, and hold me, and never let me go! I felt so safe, so loved!" Her hands wrung the handkerchief miserably. "What must he think of me? And, oh, what I think of myself! I've been unfaithful in my heart. I'm a married woman. How could I?"

"Oh, Audrey, I thought you had done murder, no less!" She fetched a damp cloth from the ivory basin. "Here, wash your face, child, and listen to reason." She sank down boneless as a cat on the floor beside her.

"I'm the last person on Krau who'd advise you to play fast and loose with your marriage, Audrey. But you know as well as I, yours was a marriage of convenience. Did your marvelous relatives ever bother to ask if you loved Charles? Or *wanted* to marry him? Did they once stop counting credits long enough to ask?"

Audrey studied her hands. "Charles is a fine man, Tasa," she said. "And he is my husband."

"That's true," Tasa admitted. "And because he *is* your husband, you had no right to be in Dao Marik's arms. There's no doubt about that."

"I know," whispered Audrey miserably.

"And yet, you didn't plan the rendezvous, did you?" Tasa inquired judiciously. Audrey's head flashed up.

"Oh, no! Tasa, I never met him before tonight. It was all a dreadful mistake!"

"Exactly!" Tasa was triumphant. "And when Dao thinks about it, he'll probably be very apologetic."

"Dear God! I hope not! Charles"—she altered what she had been about to say—"would be embarrassed. After all, he is my husband."

"Is he?" Tasa purred discreetly. "Husbands produce children, where I come from." Audrey turned her face away.

"Only if they want them, Tasa. Only then." And, trying to smooth it over, she added: "He's very busy, you know. He hardly has time even to come home and visit with Heck and me, and there are only two of us. If we had more children, why—" The tears welled again. "Why, why, why?" she asked softly, not really asking at all. "Why me? And why Dao Marik?"

"Audrey, child, listen to me," Tasa soothed. "What happened is over and done with. Forgive yourself and don't fret about what Dao might think. He's the finest man I've ever known, except my Dodol, of course. There is no possible way he could think ill of you. Now, here, dry your tears, there's a good girl."

Audrey patted her face with the towel and repaired her

disheveled appearance. "You're treating me like a baby, you know," she accused mildly, and Tasa nodded.

"But only because you need it right now," she sympathized. "And speaking of babies, let me give you a treat." She padded over and brought the sleeping baby from his crib, handing him into Audrey's eager arms. "Dao's going to name him Kalan Vath, after Kalandan Vath, who's a guest tonight. Isn't he precious?"

"Oh, yes," Audrey murmured, sitting in the rocking chair and holding him close. "Tasa, he's so beautiful!" In the half light, with the curly-haired little boy on her lap, Audrey resembled a painting Tasa had bought on impulse one Christmas, of the Lady Eisernon holding the infant T'ath. It hung even now over the fireplace in the castle-keep at Shallan. Tasa felt very pleased with herself; but then the door swung open sharply and Charles Lassiter stepped in. He took in the whole room at a glance and smiled his charming smile.

"Audrey," he said aloud, waking the baby, who started crying again, "I suggest you put down that child and come along now. The entertainment is about to begin." He nodded to Tasa, who ignored him. "Payina."

Audrey handed the baby back helplessly and quietly shut the door behind her. Tasa jiggled the baby agitatedly, sat down hard, and began to rock. "Enough, enough, *cubbin*," she soothed, and then muttered to herself: "Enough, indeed! Too much!—that's what it is! Too, too much!"

The evening's entertainment was long overdue by the time Marik, with Tasa on his arm, entered the Great Hall. According to protocol, everyone rose (although he caught the distinct mental image of a snicker or two), making it impossible for him to locate the beautiful Owdri among them, in his cursory sweep of his guests. He made a brief chom-ala, seated Tasa and himself, and indicated to the conductor that the program should begin.

It promised to be profoundly satisfactory. At Administrator Barren's suggestion that he invite "a little local color, a few natives," Marik had chosen his "natives" with the same discrimination he employed when purchasing art objects, with an eye to the finer points of Erthlik education.

Sunimal Haron, prima donna of Eisernon's Metropolitan Opera, had been his first choice. She was an effortless coloratura soprano of astounding range and flexibility, whose portrayal of Jacqueline in Giacomo Bellini's opera *November in Dallas* had been the high point of her luminous career. She was to perform the aria, "Mio Amore, Quando Accende la Fiamma Eterna . . ." ("My love, when lighting the eternal flame"), which was one of Marik's especial favorites.

A Chopin étude followed, performed by the Einai piano virtuoso Tyho Brahovin. Brahovin was well known to Erthlik audiences, Marik knew, having trained under Rolfe Cliburn and attended the Conservatory of Berlin, USE, Old Earth, before finishing at the prestigious Academy of Concert Music on the planet Monastery. As an encore, Brahovin played selections from *The Trumpet Suite* by the noted composer Kalandan Vath, who was also a guest.

Rounding out the evening was the erudite and witty actor/historian Sir Joshua Baksavi, who had been knighted for his comedic genius by the dowager-empress of Minsoner. He was the first non-Minsonai knight ever to have been dubbed, and the break with tradition provided the media several weeks of comment. Baksavi, whose humor relied heavily on Erthlik history for material, did the "I am not a crook" scene from Tolwin's satire, *What Tapes?* As in the original, his nonsense tonight was eminently successful.

By the time the appreciative applause rang out for the final time, to a standing ovation, the rich aromas of an authentic *festa* began to waft into the Great Hall, and dinner was announced.

Marik, standing with Sir Joshua, Miss Haron, Vath, and Brahovin in the receiving line, greeted his guests one by one, speaking a few courteous words to each. He was, in fact, genuinely happy to see only a few of them. One of them, the archbishop of Bru-Riga, was especially welcome; another was *Tchum* Anthon Tersa of Xhole, a thin blue agronomist involved in crossbreeding new strains of hennem to feed Eisernon's hungry millions.

The cheese maker, Arbat of Keri La, came next, fairly sparkling in his new finery. He kept passing a reverent hand down the front of his tunic, just to feel the smoothness of it, and stood self-consciously erect until he saw Marik. His face cleared and he relaxed.

"*There* you are! I've been looking everywhere for you. I thought I saw you working in the kitchen, just before the music started, but everybody stood up for some reason."

"I've been awfully busy," Marik apologized, sotto voce. "The guests, you know." They shared a few knowledgeable nods, and then Arbat looked Marik up and down, from the high collar of his stark white uniform, past the colorful ribbons slantwise across his chest, down to the white shoes and back again.

"You look pretty good," he complimented, and regarded his own clothing with innocent conceit. "Want to feel my jacket?" he invited. "Go ahead—it's so *smooth*." Riker who, with Cynthia Jessen on his arm, was next in line, hid a chuckle under a convenient cough and saw the twinkle Marik was earnestly trying to hide.

"Thank you, no," the alien demurred. "The guests." He nodded fractionally, confidentially, toward Riker, and Arbat jumped.

"Oh, my goodness! *Hei*, I'm sorry I made you wait, chom-shan!" He asked Marik in a stage whisper: "What do I do now?" Marik indicated a potted palm just outside the dining salon.

"Wait for me over there and I'll show you where to sit," he assisted, and Arbat obediently trundled over to stand next to the plant, rocking contentedly, heel to toe, and wishing his wife could be there to see him.

Riker came next. There was the formal handshake and Riker muttered, "Feeling better?" He did not add "now that you've seen the cassette," but Marik knew what he meant, and replied quietly, "Hope is always a change for the better, Paul." He turned to Cynthia, cocking a quizzical brow, and Riker tardily remembered his manners.

"Priyam Hanshilobahr *Dom* Dao Marik, may I present Miss Cynthia Jessen, daughter of the colonel." Cynthia's jaw went a trifle slack, Riker thought, with a good deal of satisfaction, and Marik bowed over her hand as she stared.

"Delighted, Miss Jessen," he lied gallantly, and Riker led her away babbling, "That's not really him, I mean, the native, the posturing little greenie, is it? I mean, he looks just like us, almost, I mean, omigod, he's gorgeous! If I'd known, I would've been *happy* to be his hostess!" Riker grinned from ear to ear and patted her shoulder. "Tough bananas, Ace," he sympathized.

Charles Lassiter, last in line, shook Marik's hand warmly and said, "Beautiful, Priyam Marik, beautiful. The entertainment was superb, sir. It's a privilege to be here." He bent forward a bit, and said pleasantly, for Marik's ears alone, "Ten o'clock, the study." Marik scarcely nodded. "About that other matter, we took care of it." He straightened. "You were right," he chuckled, as if enjoying a good joke, and Marik inclined his head, joining in the act.

"*Very* good to have you here, Dr. Lassiter."

"Charles! Please!" Lassiter insisted in his easy colonial drawl. "After all, we are going to be working the Timeslide together, aren't we? And now, may I present my wife. My dear, the emperor of Eisernon, Priyam Dao Marik."

Still looking at Charles, Marik had taken her hand and begun to bow over it when he glimpsed the white lace of her skirts and lifted his head sharply, startled and unguarded. She was pale, her dark eyes wide and apprehensive. Her fingers felt cold even through his glove.

"Priyam Marik," she whispered formally, breaking the tension, and he remembered himself.

"Mrs. Lassiter. *Mrs.* Lassiter?" he murmured, and bent to kiss her fingertips. Retaining her hand for a moment, he met her eyes briefly once again. "*Mrs.* Lassiter," he repeated unbelievingly, and pulled his attention away to address her husband, his tone as casual as he could make it.

"You are to be congratulated, Charles, on your good taste. Your lady takes my breath quite away." Lassiter smiled, too, his eyes, behind the pale, thick lashes, flicking from Audrey's pallor to Marik's easy courtesy.

"I noticed that, Priyam," he said affably. "And I think my Audrey's kind of taken with you, too, aren't you, Miss

Audrey?'' A smile sketched itself across her lips and quickly
disappeared.

"Yes, of course," she agreed, saying nothing. She avoided
Marik's eyes, and Lassiter's.

"Her first trip to Eisernon," Charles explained, and Marik
had no opportunity to comment, for Arbat had got tired of
waiting. He crossed to Marik and tugged at his uniform sleeve.
"I'm hungry," he announced innocently. "When does he get
here, so we can eat?"

And Marik glanced at his ticket—19:52—and answered
kindly, "We can go in now, if you like. He'll be at table
presently."

"Oh, all right," Arbat agreed, and marched himself past the
waiting guests, the astounded servants, and Shang himself, who
looked on in horror, as Arbat preceded everyone else into the
dining salon.

"Who's the gentleman waiting for, Priyam? Or should I say,
who isn't he waiting for?" Lassiter ventured.

"He's waiting for the *Domne*," Marik replied, chagrined.
"He thinks I'm a servant."

"Aren't you going to tell him—before he makes a fool of
himself?" Audrey asked distantly.

"As soon as I can, yes. I'd hoped he would realize the
situation, but . . . it can't be helped. I suppose everyone is
ready for dinner. We'd better go in." He offered his arm.
"Mrs. Lassiter?"

She would rather have entered alone than on his arm, but she
was a thoroughbred. She hesitated only an instant, then placed
her hand on his arm as if it were a bannister. Charles patted the
hand, squinting through those pale lashes. "My Audrey's a
little bit shy," he apologized, "but she's charming when you
get to know her." The mute appeal in her face touched Marik's
hearts, but Lassiter was made of sterner stuff; he nodded
encouragingly and urged, "Go on, now, Miss Audrey. Priyam
Marik doesn't bite." As the others fell in behind them, chatting
and laughing, Marik found time to observe that no apology
could remedy their awkward situation.

"But you must believe," he insisted ruefully, stammering
just a bit, "that I had no idea you were a married woman. That
is to say, even if you were not, I—" He began again: "You

must understand, Mrs. Lassiter, it's not my custom to . . . to impose unwanted attentions upon guests in my home. I hope you'll forgive me. I am not myself tonight."

She shook her head in embarrassment, averting her eyes. She had the feeling that everyone knew, and was watching. "Please," she begged in an undertone, "no apologies. Could we just . . . not talk about it?" She looked up at him. "Can't we just forget it ever happened?"

Can we, Marik wondered, but he replied, "A truce, then?" He seated her at his right hand and entreated, still holding the back of her chair, "Can we be friends?" After a moment the glossy head made an almost imperceptible nod, and Marik looked up into the veiled gaze of her husband.

"I told you she'd grow on you, didn't I?" he asked, and Marik allowed him his illusions.

When everyone was comfortable, Marik embarrassed the Earthlings by having the archbishop ask a blessing, and then the retinue of waiters began serving the *lentamente*, to begin the meal. It was so attractively prepared and served as to cause comment even among the Erthlikli. The archbishop, Preston Marquette, seated at Marik's immediate left, was especially complimentary. "This reminds me of the old days, Dao, when you and Mishli used to give those wonderful dinners."

"Good days, Your Excellency," Marik agreed, "and long gone." The archbishop sobered.

"So much is gone. Especially back at Allam-Paila"—he addressed the other guests, who were patiently listening—"my archdiocese before the war was the region around Allam-Paila."

"Mostly fern forest down there, isn't it?" Lassiter asked, and the archbishop nodded.

"Oh, yes. From Allam-Paila south and west, past Sum ChiT'ath and almost to Bex-Elakli. It's all fern forest, gopherwood, and some good stands of *mahagani*. And very good people . . ."

"It got pretty bad down there, during the end," commented Dodol Bournt, Tasa's white-maned husband. "We sent millions in aid, but we were never sure how much good it did."

The archbishop began nodding vehemently halfway through Bournt's speech.

"Yes, I remember. News of it filtered into the outback, but we never saw food or medicines. Even the jungle outposts at Needles and Sum ChiT'ath were destroyed, so we had no help at all." He smiled reminiscently. "Fellow named Paige ran the one at Needles. Fine young man, fine doctor. I often wonder what became of him." Marik leaned forward interestedly.

"*Tom* Paige? Thomas M.? Sandy hair, about my age?"

"Yes, yes, the same man. Do you know him?"

"He was on USS *Hope* during the Elluvon mission, so we had the chance to work together. He's stationed there now, you know."

"Good. Good." The waiters served the next course, a fragrant soup with edible blossoms floating in it. "Let's see, Needles was destroyed . . ."

"Three years, five months ago," Marik provided. "The day after Sum ChiT'ath was hit."

"That's right," the archbishop agreed, "because that was the year of the big night moths." He paused. "And the man Laj."

"Tell us," Audrey prompted softly, and the archbishop, gazing down into the past, wagged his head and muttered, "Strange fellow, that Laj. Strange year.

"We always had the moths, you understand, but that year there was a plague of them. They blundered into travelers on the road, and thumped the windows of those lucky enough to have windows, and roosted by day in trees whose branches broke with the weight of them. To us, they were a nuisance; they say it was worse in the outback.

"I was dealing mung then. There were a lot of orchards gone wild when the houses were burned, or abandoned when their owners fled the Krail. Technically, it was illegal, but it was wartime, the government was in chaos, and we had to feed a hundred and forty-six orphans that three Shimshenli and I were hiding from the Krail. I felt I had nothing to fear: Krail military don't conscript priests, especially men my age, and their slave-masters wouldn't have touched me with gloves. The orphans were a different matter. And the Shimshenli. We kept hoping the Earthlings would come and rescue us. So far they hadn't, but there was always tomorrow. That, and the mung fruit.

"I met the man Laj in a clearing some distance from the caves. He was an Einai, clearly a farmer in peacetime, one of the volunteers who joined one side or the other for the sake of their families, or for the adventure, or to punish—or identify with—the Earthlings for conquering Eisernon fifty years ago.

"He came trudging up the hill with a sack over his shoulder, his eyes on the ground before his bare feet. He was wearing a loincloth on his lower half, but on top he wore a secondhand Krail tunic, without the ebony buttons. He was upon me before he came to himself with a start and, seeing me, made as if to run away.

"'Chom-ala,' I greeted him. 'Peace to you.' His eyes cleared, and he came back cautiously, never easing his hold on the sack he carried.

"'Chom,' he said. 'You are a priest?'

"'How did you know?' He made the Infinity Sign over his forehead and breast, and I had to smile. I *had* made the Sign; I do it automatically in times of stress. Perhaps I am getting old.

"We squatted down a few feet apart on the grass to make talk, each putting our burden behind us; but I noticed that he kept one hand on his burlap bag, as if he were inextricably bound up with it. He fumbled at the band of his tunic and brought out two battered *cigarek*.

"'Tabac?' he offered politely. His hands were shaking. I shook my head.

"'Child of Tadae,' I said to him, 'your hearts are heavy.'

"He didn't answer, just smoked quietly for a while in the peaceful glen, with the uala calling in the fern trees, and aun hives droning in the bush, until his pupils contracted to slits under the strong narcotic. I took the opportunity of such rare peace to chant the Divine Praises, and I'd almost completed my second chanting when he pulled a clean human skull out of the sack, set it ceremoniously before him on a rock, and idly began to blow smoke into its teeth.

"I thought about running away, because if I became his next trophy, what would the orphans and the Shimshenli do? I was

their only provider. While I considered this, the man said to
me, 'My name is Laj. I want to tell you a story.' As you know,
custom forbids leaving a story, and so I was held. This is his
story:

" 'I was a scout for the Erthlikli (he said) before the
destruction of Sum ChiT'ath. It was a terrible massacre. A
terrible thing.' He shook his head. 'I ran away. The squad
leader, Garrett, looked for me, but I hid. He knew where I hid.
I think he knew. But he let me go. I do not know why. I did not
ask and he did not say.' He blew smoke at the skull. 'Later,
when I ran out of *cigarek*, I came back. He did not speak. He
only handed me my food, in a tin plate, like always.

" 'The squad was headed for Bex-Elakli. The way was
supposed to have been cleared for them, there should have been
air support and artillery walking in; but the fern forest became
nasty open woods, and there was no air support, no artillery.
All there was were Krail, sitting in the treetops with their
inhuman patience, waiting for hours, sometimes days, to pick
off Earthlings.'

"There were six men in the squad, besides Laj: Garrett, their
leader; LaFarge, Connors, Ross, Sanders, and Doc, their medic.
Six men who had fought together on Krau, on Sauvage, on
Canopus Five. Now they were on Eisernon. Same play,
slightly different setting: fern forest instead of barren
scree, tropical rain instead of sleet, lush vegetation blending
into open woods, tall deciduous trees. There were deep silken
grasses under the trees, gleaming in the sun, and jats barking in
the distance. Somewhere a bird twittered. Even the occasional
spatting of small-arms fire could not disturb the essential
quiet. There should have been picnic baskets and long-haired
girls.

"Garrett thumbed back his helmet and wiped his sweating
forehead with a single gesture, and opened his map. The men
gathered around the small square of plastex and Garrett pointed
to a row of hills that mounded up of their own accord in the
heat of the sun. Laj had thought it magic, but the Erthlik only
said, 'Plastex remembers.'

" 'Village just the other side of these hills,' Garrett told
them. 'Name of Keri La. If we can make it by nightfall, SurCon
can pick us up.' He got to his feet, his needler loose and easy

in the crook of his arm, dragged at his cigarette, handed the butt to Laj, and pulled down his faceplate. 'Sanders, you've got the point. Take the eye-eye with you. Let's move out.'

"The dark Erthlik started off, Laj trotting beside him, and the rest of them scattered, filtering into the woods. Laj carefully spit into his hand, drowning the ember, and tucked the precious cigarette into his waistband. The sun was warm on his bare shoulders and his smooth green skin blended with the surrounding greenery, so that after a while it seemed to the men that Sanders was walking alone through the watered silk of the grass.

"They were far ahead of the others when the whisper came. One minute they were moving along quietly, and the next, Sanders was lying still in the shimmering grass, with the birds twittering and the sleepy murmur of aun hives and the flat chatter of a skirmish off in the distance.

"Laj, protected by his natural camouflage, slipped over and touched Sanders' face. The Erthlik did not move. Sanders might not be dead, but then again, he might, and here was this military tunic to consider, stained from the wound in Sanders' chest. The blood would wash out. There was hardly any hole at all. The Erthlikli were always wasting perfectly good clothing, burying it with the dead. Laj stooped beside the Erthlik's supine body, considering the situation.

"Fifteen minutes later, Garrett's men found Sanders lying there in the silken peace of the forest, with the sun making dappled shadows on his bare chest. Neither Laj's nor Sanders' uniform tunic was anywhere to be seen.

"Laj ran.

"He fled the Erthlikli and the Krail and the war itself that had nothing to do with Eisernon, his planet; nor with Bru-Riga, his province; nor with Laj himself; but which dealt with idealogies he could never comprehend, even had he been aware of their existence. He ran back into the fern forest and the jungled hills, toward familiar territory and people he could understand.

"By sundown he reached the clearing, and the water in the paddies stood hot and still. The sky was a certain color, like the water, as if the edge of the world was on fire, and had charred

the cypresses black at the horizon. The huts were deserted and
Laj, fearing disease or ghosts, ran on.

"It was the moths that finally forced him to stop. They
buffeted him dully with their pale, powdery wings and clung to
him with their minutely clawed legs, reminding him of the tales
the headman told about their being the souls of the dead.
Sometimes they were the souls of your own ancestors. If
enough of them grabbed you at the same time, people said, they
could carry you off. It was not a pleasant thought.

"The air was full of them, thumping, blundering, pow-
dering his nose and mouth and making him sneeze helplessly.
He ran blindly, slapping at talcum ghosts, fleeing his past,
and stumbled into the clearing that was to determine his
destiny.

"There was a tiny fire, big, overhanging trees, and a man
there, wearing a Krail jacket, a *viith* sleeved at his shoulder. He
rose cautiously to his feet as Laj approached, but returned his
chom-ala. He was of medium height, young, and did not seem
hostile.

" 'My name is Arv,' he offered, and Laj nodded warily.

" 'I am Laj. This is my province.'

" 'Mine, too. We are neighbors?' They smiled, and Arv
pointed to the ground next to the fire.

"Laj sat gratefully, feeling the weariness settle in his bones,
and Arv continued, 'There is a stream that way'—he tipped his
head—'and that way is the war.'

" 'I do not want the war,' Laj told him.

"Arv squatted by the fire and stirred up the coals with a
stick, sending up a shower of sparks. 'Have you been away
long?'

"For a while there was only the crackle of the flames and the
humid night wind rustling the leaves. Laj wanted to say that
one day away was another world entirely, that with all he'd
seen, the man who had left was not the man who would be
coming home. But there was no way to tell him. There was
nothing to say. He looked up.

" 'I am thirsty, neighbor,' he said, and reaching for a
leaf, twisted it cleverly and pinned it with a thorn. And Arv,
too, twisted a leaf and followed him to the edge of the creek

where they drank their fill. A little animal skittered into the bushes and Laj muttered, 'Are you hungry?'

"Arv made a rueful shrug. 'If only we had a net,' but Laj signed him to silence. He gathered a handful of pebbles from the streambed, selected a stout branch from the streamside debris, and hid himself. Everything grew quiet. From the underbrush where the animal was hidden there came a faint rustle, and then nothing.

"A tiny movement caught Arv's eye. Another. And another. Then he realized what was happening. Laj was flipping pebbles out into the open, one by one, to attract the furry scavenger. He was about to tell him it would never work when a twitching nose stuck itself out of the leaves, and then a paw, making cautious swipes at the pebbles, and finally the little creature— the *fat* little creature—was pouncing upon them playfully, rolling over them and batting them with its velvet paws. It never saw the branch, or felt it. Holding out his hand silently for Arv's *viith*, Laj skinned and gutted the scavenger beside the stream.

"'That was clever, neighbor,' Arv admired. 'Did the Erthlikli teach you this?' Laj glanced at him in surprise and he indicated the stolen tunic. 'Your uniform,' he apologized. Laj flipped the viscera into the stream and ignored the violent agitation as the *lashri* devoured it and were gone.

"'No,' he said, 'hunger taught me.' He lifted his chin at Arv's jacket. 'And you, neighbor Arv. Why did you join the Krail?'

"'Ah, well.' Arv shrugged as they started back toward the fire. 'We had a farm of mung. Pretty good as farms go, but dull, eh? And there was a woman. A good woman, a clean woman. Her hearts are good. But the Krail came, in their black uniforms. With their white skins and their guns. They looked important. And I, too, wanted to be important.'

"Laj nodded as they came up to the fire, the raw carcass swinging from his hand. He knew. The Erthlikli had seemed important, too, with their dusty elegance, their sense of belonging to places he could only dream of. Laj had been in love with the Erthlikli. He had spent a whole day, once, memorizing the imprint of a tank tread in the soft mud, until the rains washed it away. How beautiful, the symmetry, the order.

He traced the pattern of it now, in the moist earth, while Arv stuck a green branch through the carcass and suspended it above the fire on two crotched sticks.

" 'They were good days,' Laj said, 'before the war. There was hennem-*riis* in those days.'

" 'There is *riis* now,' Arv confided. He pulled a leather pouch out of his bulging jacket and spilled some of the dirty, grayed grains into his palm. The meat was beginning to sizzle and smell and Laj's stomach writhed hungrily.

" 'I will get the water,' he offered, and they shared a neighborly smile. It was just like in the old days, Laj mused, when neighbors met by chance and shared a meal; except, of course, for the jackets. The off-world jackets, that made them enemies. He wondered for a fleeting instant why they shouldn't just take them off, but then he dismissed the thought. In doing so, they would become merely Einai again, and unimportant.

"They put the hennem-*riis* in a twisted leaf along with the water and suspended the leaf over the fire, where it spit and fumed but did not burn. Arv kept looking at the stars, even as he squatted down and pulled a joint off the carcass. 'We should be fighting,' he said with his mouth full of meat. Laj tore off a leg and commenced his meal, too.

" 'Why? I am not angry with you.' The *riis* was beginning to boil.

"Arv pointed to the stars, big and bright above the treetops. 'When the stars of "the Huntsman" disappear over the mountain,' he said solemnly, 'the truce time will be over. We will fight.'

"Laj shrugged wearily, thinking of Sanders lying in the long green grass. He had seen enough of fighting. 'Maybe I will go away.'

" 'No. There is a bounty on heads, you understand,' Arv explained patiently. 'More meat? No?' He helped himself to another joint from the sizzling carcass. 'The Krail buy heads, for money. I am a poor man, but if I bring enough heads, I can go back and take the woman for wife. Even now, she is making me a son.'

"Laj looked up from the *riis* with interest. 'Ah. We should drink to his health, this son of yours. For you see'—he gestured at the moths—'*they* come and take the strength of the little ones.

" 'My own sister had a child, who was found with moths in her little-boat-of-the-air, and she died of smothering.' He finished his *riis* and threw away the soiled leaf, seeing again in his mind's eye the soft wings fluttering, fluttering away from the child's hanging crib.

" 'Some say the powder on the moth wings smothers the infants,' Arv suggested. Laj shook his head. 'Our headman says the moths drew her soul away and flew off with it.' Arv shuddered.

" 'Our medicine chief tells a story,' he said, lowering his voice and drawing closer to the fire, 'that the moths are the souls of the dead, trying to find their way home. What think you, neighbor?' The orange firelight lapped his face with shadow and made his eyes twin embers glowing with lambent fire. Laj frowned.

" 'That would explain why there are so many this year,' he mused. 'The souls of all the soldiers are trying to find their way home in the dark.'

" 'I would not like to be lost in the dark,' Arv confided.

" 'Nor would I,' Laj agreed, 'so I will not fight you. I will go away and plant my *riis*. You will go back to your woman. And we two, at least, will have peace.'

" 'Too late.' Arv had turned away to study the stars. Now he turned back, regretfully. The firelight flashed on the double-bladed *viith* in his hand. ' "The Huntsman" has gone beyond the mountain.' He shrugged apologetically, half smiling. 'Now one of us must die.'

" 'There is no other way?' Laj asked for the last time.

" 'No. I'm sorry it has to be like this, but it's the war, you understand.'

" 'A war,' said Laj, getting to his feet and deliberately picking up the skewer, 'is an evil thing.'

" 'So . . . you fought.'

"He came to himself from a great distance, turned the skull thoughtfully in his hands, and blew the last of his smoke into its teeth. 'Oh, yes,' he said at last, 'we fought, all right.'

"Hoping to lighten his mood, I made a poor jest. 'And who won?' He did not smile.

"'I am not sure, priest. I am not sure.' He sighed. 'I held him with the wood still in his chest. He said, 'Now I will never be important.'

"'You have made a son,' I told him. 'And he will make a son, who will make many generations of sons. What can be more important than this?'

"He did not speak again—but he smiled. 'I buried my Erthlik jacket with him.' He studied the skull a moment more, tucked it into the sack, and began gathering up his belongings like a man in a dream.

"'Where will you go, child of Tadae?'

"'I promised I would bring the woman his bones.' He met my eyes soberly. 'Happen I will be lucky and get through.'

"I gave him my blessing and half my sack of mung fruit and warned him about the Krail patrols. I didn't want to discourage him in his brave and probably futile hope. After he left, staggering under his added burden, I prayed that he would find the one village, the one woman, and the son she had made for Arv. Then I started back for the mung orchards, batting the moths aside as I went, and wondering if somehow, one of them was the soul of Arv.

"It was late when I got back to the caves, and the Shimshenli told me that another child had died. We had no help, except for God, and no way out; but like Laj, we bore our precious burden and did not give up hope. We kept thinking that, perhaps tomorrow, the Earthlings would come."

The archbishop fell silent at last and everyone began to stir slowly, as if waking from a dream.

"How long was it," Tasa Bournt asked gently, "before help reached you?"

The servants quietly removed the soup dishes and replaced them with individual porcelain bowls containing one crisp-fried item that smelled deliciously of shrimp, pecans, and mushrooms, and was none of them. The archbishop pondered Tasa's question.

"Almost a year," he reckoned. "By then we had only seventeen children left, and two Shimshenli had died."

"But *you* are still *alive*, Bishop," Louise Bechtel observed. "How convenient for you."

The archbishop smiled introspectively. "Yes, it was, wasn't it?" he answered, and attacked his hors d'oeuvre with evident relish. At the other end of the table, finger bowls of rose water were being passed. Audrey's was placed, and Marik's. Arbat regarded his own with a novice's interest.

"As it happens, Madame Bechtel," Marik commented smoothly, "His Excellency—"

A quickly stifled intake of breath called his attention to Arbat, who in his ignorance was drinking great gulps from his finger bowl. In the instant of silence, as he set it down empty, he realized suddenly something was amiss. He peeked around him guiltily, his cheeks deepening green, and turned a spaniel's eyes on Marik.

"As I was saying," Marik continued evenly, lifting his finger bowl to his lips and sipping from it, "His Excellency is not alive because he spared himself at the expense of his charges, Madame. He is alive because the Krail do not permit their political prisoners to die."

As he spoke, Sir Joshua raised his finger bowl to his lips, Audrey sipped delicately from her own, and Tasa and Dodol, exchanging warm glances, drank from theirs. Arbat blew a relieved breath and sat back limply.

"I stand corrected, Mister Marik," Madame Bechtel conceded. "I'm sure the archbishop went through all sorts of *dreadful* things for his people." She dipped one hand, then the other, in her finger bowl, drying them on the napkin provided for that purpose. "That's the standard, isn't it?"

"No." Marik answered crisply. "No, *dying* was standard for religious on this planet, during the war, Madame. Merely living was extraordinary; helping others live was heroic. And becoming a prisoner of the Krail—"

"Please, Dao!" the archbishop begged.

"—to prevent their finding helpless women and children was martyrdom in its most exquisite form." He shut his eyes briefly. "Personally, I'd rather be thrown to a hungry ramper."

"Did you see that woman washing her hands in her flower soup?" Arbat asked, in a loud, indignant whisper, and people seated nearby laughed. Arbat joined them, for all the wrong reasons.

Marlowe Dunn sat forward interestedly. "Then you *do* have rampers here at Bru-Riga!"

"I'll say they have rampers!" Riker assisted, chuckling.

Dunn scanned the faces at the table. "Have any of you ever seen a live one?"

"You might ask Mister Vath," Marik suggested. "Kalandan?" This last to Vath himself.

Vath steepled his fingers. "Many times. Before I composed *The Trumpet Suite,* the *Domne* graciously permitted me the use of the Summer Palace for over two years, so that I might study rampers in their natural habitat, off Tagan Island. I was particularly interested in the trumpets, rather than the females, because of the pitch of their vocalizations."

"You keep referring to 'trumpets,' Mr. Vath," Colonel Jessen remarked. "Isn't a trumpet a musical instrument?"

"So it is. Named, I believe, for its resemblance to the call of a trumpet ramper." He leaned back to facilitate the waiter's placing his entree before him. "The females are called strumpets, but their call is more subtle." Fred Simes choked on his wine, and Kei Matsushita pounded him solicitously on the back until the spasm passed.

"Are you all right, Mister Simes?" Marik inquired, and Simes nodded roughly.

"Yeah, yeah, I'm just fine. He"—gesturing at Vath—"just caught me off guard, that's all."

"I'm afraid I don't understand." Vath frowned, as Simes took a healthy bite of food.

"Well," he chuckled, his mouth full, "I just never heard the word *strumpet* applied to an animal, that's all. Sounds kind of funny, y'know?" He gestured at the meat on his plate. "Say, this is pretty good. What do you call it?" He took another prodigious bite.

"Jat, Mister Simes. A special breed of jat. Payin Bournt"—Dodol inclined his head—"raises it for us on his barony at Shallan, Pike, on Krau."

"Ah, you are the baron of Shallan, the ecologist!" Kei Matsushita interjected. "I have read all of your books." Dodol bowed slightly, showing long canines.

"You should visit our great forests and lakes, Dr. Matsush-

ita," Tasa interposed. "Then you'd see just how brilliant an
ecologist Dodol is." Dodol laid his hand atop hers.

"Now, Tasa," he said indulgently. They exchanged a look
meant for the two of them alone, and she dropped her eyes and
murmured, "Oh, very well." She slid her emerald eyes back to
Kei Matsushita and confided, "But it's true, all the same," and
gave her full attention to her dinner, while Dodol regarded her
with affectionate exasperation.

"What *I* can't get over," Fred Simes announced to the table
in general, "—is this guy calling that fish a strumpet. Can you
beat that?"

"They're not fish," Dunn corrected, but Riker, at the foot of
the table, countered Simes with:

"I can't beat it, Mister Simes, but I may be able to explain
it. Unfortunately, it's always been an Earthling habit to
compare immoral women to females of animal species." He
ticked the names off on his fingers. "Cow, pig, vixen,
dragon—" He caught Cynthia's baleful eyes, his smile widening a fraction.

"Bitch," he said. Glaring at him, she reached angrily for her
wineglass and tipped it over, causing a small furor among
waiters and guests, while Marik shot Riker a fishy stare. He
spread his hands innocently. "So I imagine," he continued,
"that the use of the word *strumpet* in referring to certain
behavorial patterns among human females would be culturally,
if not semantically, correct." He made a truncated bow, hardly
more than a curt inclination of the head, to Marik, who
responded in kind.

"Yeah, maybe you're right at that," answered Simes, who
had missed the byplay. "It just sounds funny, that's all." He
chuckled again. "Wait till I tell the guys back on Bing IV about
this."

Thunder crashed immensely right above them, dimming the
lights momentarily before they resumed. They could hear
the torrential rains, heavy even for Eisernon, which was
known for its rains, sluicing the house and pounding on the
terraces.

"Mr. Dunn," Marik invited, to distract them, "you
seem to covet our rampers. How did you come by this
interest?"

Marlowe Dunn replied loftily, "It's 'Doctor' Dunn, *Mister* Marik. I am a xenobiologist. My specialty is Einai fauna, and as associate to the curator of the Galactic Museum, Old Earth, I intend to bring a skein of live ramper young back with me."

"Do you mean to say," Marik asked slowly, "that you expect to take a skein—Quel, even a single brat!—away from its dam—and live to tell about it?" Several of the Einai guests smiled broadly and Dunn remarked that as a scholar with a Ph.D. in xenobiology, he expected to do exactly that. Marik grinned boyishly and suggested that it might be safer to go around biting lions. Everyone laughed in a friendly manner, and Dunn smiled stiffly.

"We shall see what we shall see," he said cryptically, and Marik wished him well.

Dodol Bournt got to his feet, a bowl of tarangi in his hand. He cut an impressive figure with his splendid mane of luxurious white fur from brows to shoulders, and the sashed formal attire that civilized his seven feet, twenty stone of brute bulk.

"A toast," he proposed, and the gentlemen—and Cynthia—rose to their feet. Dunn, standing beside her, muttered that the ritual was intended for gentlemen only, and was promptly invited to go straight to hell.

Dodol Bournt lifted his bowl and rumbled, "To our Lady Eisernon!" and all but the Earthlings echoed, "To our lady!" They drank, and Anthan Tersa extended his bowl toward Marik.

"And to the emperor!" Again the echo, while Marik simply stood there. Arbat was livid. He jerked on Marik's sleeve urgently, and Marik bent toward him as the others drank. "Why—*you're* the emperor!" he expostulated in a stage whisper. "You lied to me!"

"You lost my cheese!" Marik returned, mock defensive and much amused. "It would serve you right if I changed my mind about making you Cheese Maker to the Royal House!" He straightened as Arbat, starry eyed, subsided weakly.

Around the table, everyone was watching Paul Riker, who

extended his bowl toward Marik and said quietly, meaningfully, ''To Life.''

Their eyes met and Marik echoed his toast, and drank the
thin, green, alcoholic liquid whose fumes filled his head with a
scent reminiscent of roses.

CHAPTER

VII

THE STREETS OF the dingy village outside the emperor's gate were deserted, the storm whipping the rain into horizontal needles, snapping tree branches and flinging sopping wet debris against buildings and the rare pedestrian alike.

Mouse, the albino, made his way unobtrusively through the crowds at the skimmerport, squeezing between well-fed tourists who were milling about, waiting to board. The heavy squalls had dampened their enthusiasm for sight-seeing, and their only thought was of getting home. Ordinarily a light-fingered swamplander like Mouse would have found this preoccupied group easy picking, but tonight Mouse had other things on his mind.

He slipped along the back streets until he came to a low door in a graffiti-spoiled wall, opened it, and ducked inside.

The men were gathered around a small table, holding down the edges of a map Mennon had spread out, for the old jatskin had a tendency to curl. As he entered, Mouse said, without preamble, "They found the bug." Mennon looked up sharply.

"You saw them find it?"

The albino nodded, sweeping his hair out of his eyes impatiently. "The Erthlik Lassita," he assented. "He went straight to it. Marik must have known. We are in trouble, Mennon?"

Mennon toyed with the white scar line at his throat. "No, Mouse, no trouble. Inconvenience, perhaps, but no trouble. What were they doing? Was there a lot of excitement?"

Mouse shook his head no. "There was music," he remembered. "They had not eaten."

"But they were making preparations to eat," Mennon

159

pursued, and Mouse nodded. "Then they were not unduly disturbed. All right, then. This steps up our timetable. Guests or not—storm or not—it has to be tonight." His tiger's gaze rested intently on each of them in turn. "Tonight. You know what you have to do." He gestured shortly. "Go."

A few at a time, the men filtered out into the stormy night, leaving Mennon alone. He traced the outline of the Palace with one finger as the edges of the map slowly curled, and paused at the drawing of the East Terrace. He tapped it thoughtfully for a space and then, lips compressed, struck the map with his clenched fist.

"Mishli," he muttered, shutting his eyes as if in pain. "*Mishli!*"

Saturday—10:34 P.M.

Marik's guests were leaving. That they should pilot their various craft through a tropical storm was so unremarkable as not to be mentioned, an ordinary occurrence. With craft outfitted with the new Cole-15 stabilizers and weather shields from General Electric, hurricane skimming had become relatively safe. Indeed, in some quarters, it had been refined to an exhilarating, if heart-stopping, sport. On the pleasure world Disni, artificial indoor storms were fabricated on a child-sized scale, creating an incredible ride requiring two R tickets and a duralloy stomach.

No tickets were required for the storm that was bullying its way into Bru-Riga, but then, no one was going to pull a switch and make it stop, either. The residents of the entire province were in for a bad night, and all they could do, short of skimming away from it, was to stand fast and pray.

Marik, well aware of the situation, was relieved to see some of his guests off. According to the local weather watch, this lessening of the pounding rains and howling winds was merely a prelude to worsening conditions. The squall lines, with the progressively shorter intervals between them, had been getting closer and closer, worse and worse, all evening. Now the wall cloud was approaching.

Before midnight, the eye would pass.

Several of the evening's guests still remained: Cynthia

Jessen, who launched such pointedly arch comments in Riker's direction that he struck up a lively conversation with Kalandan Vath, just to keep her at bay; Fred Simes; Kei Matsushita, who volunteered to drive the tipsy Simes back to Birmingham IV, if someone could help pry him away from the brandy; Marlowe Dunn, who bent Marik's ear interminably about what a skein of live ramper brats would do for his career; Charles and Audrey Lassiter; and lastly Nom-pau Alain, the taciturn young Krail historian.

Alain had been noticeably silent throughout dinner, even for a Krail, and he was silent yet, gazing out through the library window at the storm raging just beyond it. He was standing much too close to the glass. Marik, pouring brandy into the blown crystal snifters, hoped it would bear up under the savage pressure of the wind. Some windows gave way when the going got rough, and people could get badly hurt. He was grateful that (leaving personalities out of it) when the drawing-room window had blown in, he had been in a position to protect one of his guests from harm. In this case, it had been Mrs. Lassiter, but it might have been anyone. Certainly wouldn't want a guest to come to harm in his own house. Merely a chance circumstance that it had been Mrs. Lassiter. Owdri. No. How did she say it—Awdry? That sounded almost right. Audrey.

He certainly wasn't proud to have romanced another man's wife (even though there was no way to tell she was married, not even a ring, such as married Erthlikli generally wore) but his arms around her must have been some protection from flying debris. In all probability, he told himself gravely, he had protected Mrs. Lassiter from serious injury. Nice to have protected his guest, Mrs. Lassiter. Audrey. Sweet little alien name. Audrey.

He glanced up from pouring the brandies, and caught her looking at him, seeing in the instant while their gaze held, the soft shine of her eyes, the white line of her teeth behind her parted lips, the vulnerability of her expression, as when he held her close, just the two of them, and the storm.

She dropped her eyes. High color bloomed under her cheekbones as she crossed to the warmly banked fire, where some of the remaining guests were gathered around the archbishop, sipping their brandy and chatting. She curled up in

Marik's favorite chair like a kitten, her feet under her, and sat watching the embers breathe and burn. She did not look at him again.

"Awfully good brandy to pour on a table," reproached the mocking voice at his elbow, and he startled guiltily and righted the decanter while Cynthia Jessen leaned down to sip from the glass he had overfilled. A servant moved in to clean up the spill and, as Cynthia started to twine her arm possessively through his elbow, Marik pressed a glass into the operative hand and gave her a brotherly pat on the shoulder.

"The archbishop is telling some of his best stories, Miss Jessen," he told her. "You won't want to miss them." He excused himself and went to the double doors, where people were saying their good-byes, leaving Cynthia standing there with a glass in each hand. Recovering quickly, she sidled up to Riker, who was standing nearby.

"I seem to find myself with an extra glass," she began, and Riker smiled.

"You certainly do. Excuse me, won't you?" He caught a fractional nod from Lassiter, there in the shadowed hallway. On the way out, he coughed discreetly and saw from Marik's sharp glance that his summons had been noted.

The drivers brought the skimmercraft to the porte-cochere, and the gentlemen of Earth gripped Marik's hand warmly and said what a fantastic evening it had been, and how they hoped to come back one of these fine days. Last to leave were the Bournts, and Tasa hugged him and patted his cheek with her soft palm, the wind making her russet fur iridescent.

"Now, you be careful on these silly missions, Dao. Don't go risking your life unless it's absolutely necessary."

Dodol took her arm, smiling indulgently. "Say good-bye, Tasa darling."

"Good-bye, Dao, dear—" and as Dodol led her firmly toward their craft "—Oh, and let us hear from you sometime, too," she called over her shoulder, against a force of wind considerable even in this sheltered place. "What's the use of having a barony if you never come and visit it?"

Dodol closed the hatch firmly and came back to crush Marik's bones in a one-armed bear hug. "The last of anything is invaluable, Dao," he rumbled. "Take care of yourself."

"And you take care of Tasa—and all seventeen of those children."

Dodol Bournt, baron of Shallan, smiled his self-satisfied smile, slid into the driver's seat, waved a huge hand by way of salute, and they were gone in a breath of blue flame, the sound of their engines lost in the larger sound of the storm.

Marik's study faced to the south and west, and its position in the house muted the sound of the storm; only the crackling fire disturbed the quiet. Riker was sitting on the edge of Marik's desk, thumbing disinterestedly through a book, and Charles stood gazing pensively at the fire. He was checking the ticket on his wrist yet again when at last Marik entered the study. "Sorry. It took a little longer than I'd thought."

"No problem, Priyam. We'll be leaving, too, in a minute. Just wanted to tie up a few loose ends." He took a small monitoring device out of his pocket and handed it to Marik. "You were right about the bug in your telecom. You can read it right there on the monitor. Somebody's been doing a lot of listening.

"We don't know what it's all about, of course. Could be related to your homecoming, or to the Purist Klan, or even the Timeslide. We're not sure. I'll leave a man here for a few days, just in case. We don't expect any problems, but you never know.

"What we do know is, this room's clean now, so I'm free to give you your new orders. ComFleet cut new paper an hour after you went planetside. They're very willing to cooperate, Captain. Not all Brass is Vice-Admiral Hastings' ilk. You cast off at oh nine hundred tomorrow morning, gentlemen."

Riker wet his lip in the familiar, abstracted gesture and gave Marik a triumphant glance. "Thank you, Dr. Lassiter," he said fervently.

Lassiter resumed his place at the fire, holding out his hands to the warmth. "I have your new orders with me," he told them. "I assume you have the old ones on your person, Captain?"

"Right here, sir," Riker said, reaching inside his tunic for them. But he never pulled them free, for there was an urgent knocking, and Marik opened the door to a sopping and sober

Fred Simes, who stepped quickly into the room and shut the door behind him. There was no sign of inebriation about him, only a tough professionalism, and Riker stood up slowly, sensing trouble.

"Bad luck, Charlie," Simes growled. "Your skimmer snapped a cable and flipped over. Looks like you're stuck for the duration."

"Did you look around?" Lassiter wanted to know, and Simes, hunched at the fire, jerked his head yes and rubbed his cold hands vigorously. "I checked outside, but with this storm, there could be an army out there, and I'd miss it. Kei's scouting the house. He thinks one of the guests is an operative."

"Could be," Lassiter admitted. "What about the Krail, what's his name, Nom-pau Alain?"

"We thought about that, but it's pretty obvious," growled Simes. "Besides, he's with the others in the library, so if we wanted to make a covert seizure, we'd be hard put to carry it off. Maybe we'd better send somebody out to keep an eye on him."

Riker felt the fool. "Wait a minute," he interjected. "All the time out there on the terrace—!"

"I really had you going, didn't I—*Whitfield*?" Simes needled him, and Lassiter squinted at him pleasantly.

"Mr. Simes is one of our senior non-official covers, Captain. Interpol sent him along with me and Kei to make sure you people would be protected, in case anybody got funny ideas. And it seems," he added ruefully, "like somebody has.

"Priyam," he proposed, "why don't you go on down to the library, as if nothing had happened, and mingle with your guests while we have a look around? That way if Alain is our man, and he starts something, you'd be in a position to stop him."

"That's agreeable with me," Marik assented, rubbing his aching temple with his fingertips. At the door, he paused. "I'll notify the servants, so you won't be disturbed."

"We don't want any intercom messages," Simes worried. "The enemy could pick up on it."

"Don't worry, Mr. Simes," said the Han Einai at the door. "Your enemy operative isn't likely to pick up on any communication we Einai might have. Good luck."

The archbishop was, indeed, telling some of his stories. As Marik came back into the library, he beckoned to him. "Come sit down, Dao," he invited, and as Marik pulled up a chair, "I have a story even you haven't heard, because I've never told it to anyone till now.

"Some years ago," (the archbishop began) "when I was teaching in the seminary, I went to a bookstore one day to pick up a reference book I'd ordered. One of the old sort of stores—you know the kind I mean: stacks of old tomes, the dusty smell of leather and time past. . . ." He sipped thoughtfully, smiling a bit.

"Well, to get on with it, I was digging through the stacks, picking up a Thomas Aquinas here and a Thomas Merton there, when my eye fell on a volume, near the bottom of the stack, entitled *How to Hug*." His audience responded with an anticipatory chuckle and the archbishop smiled and settled his glasses more firmly on his nose.

"Now, let me make it clear," he provided, "that I was interested in the book. I felt that since my education in such matters had been somewhat neglected, I owed it to myself to become more fully rounded in, let us say, social awareness. We are extensively trained," he interrupted himself to say, "in medicine, sociology, history, psychology, even psychiatry; but there is another dimension, that of the, um, hug, in which some of us might be deficient in personal experience." He chuckled again and added confidentially: "Besides, I was eaten up by curiosity.

"So I dug it out, carried it to the desk between the other books, and surreptitiously handed it to the clerk. 'A plain brown wrapper, if you please,' I recall asking. It was the custom in my day to wrap such things in plain brown paper. The clerk looked at me strangely, but I was too overcome with curiosity to give it a thought.

"I paid for my package and hurried home with it. It was a late-fall evening, October, I think, with wet leaves all over the sidewalk and a thin, cold drizzle of rain falling. 'What a fine evening for a long, hearty read,' I told myself.

"I could hardly get through dinner, thinking of the package I had left on my dresser upstairs. Why call a book *How to Hug*?

I knew of one way to hug: the simple, straightforward hug my
father used to give my mother back in my youth. Were there
more kinds of hugs? What kind? And what were the moral
implications thereof? In short, what did they know that I
didn't? I'm sure some of the other men thought I had snubbed
them. Old Pinky Scarlatto especially was very annoyed by the
time dessert rolled round. Poor old Pinky. He was always
annoyed if people wouldn't talk football.

"Anyway, after dinner I made my way out of the common
room as quickly as civility would permit, rushed up to my
room, showered and dressed for bed in jig time, hopped under
the covers, and—at last!—unwrapped *How to Hug*. I leaned
back luxuriously against my propped pillows, opened the
book"—he paused with a wry grimace, peering at them
whimsically over the tops of his glasses—"and found I had
bought volume eight of an encyclopedia!"

There was a burst of spontaneous laughter, which the
archbishop joined at his own expense. Even Alain permitted
himself a dry chuckle as he turned back to the window. Behind
him, Marik was offering brandy around again, and a silver
service on the sideboard steamed fragrantly of coffee.

Alain considered getting himself a cup—coffee was one of
the Erthlik tastes he had developed since joining Mennon—but
just then, out there in the dark, a light flashed and was quickly
gone. He waited tensely. Again, the brief flash; gone; and
again. Three lights. Mennon's signal. He struck the red tip of a
cigarette against the emery band at the end of the package, let
it flare for the slow count of three, and, placing it in his mouth,
inhaled lightly before crushing it out. *All clear*.

He was unpleasantly surprised to see a woman standing next
to the window only a few feet from him. By some freak of bad
luck, she had been standing on the opposite side from him of a
small container-grown tree, and he had missed seeing her. He
started to contrive some sort of covering conversation, when
his attention—and hers—was drawn by three long, rain-
drenched strokes, quickly gone.

The face she turned so quickly to the room was composed
and pleasant, but Alain had seen the realization, the quick
startled look that gave him—and Mennon's plan—away. No
chance now to employ the element of surprise, unless—

"Mrs. Lassiter?" She pretended not to hear him, but he stepped in front of her. "I'd like to talk to you, if you have no objection." He moved aside the front of his tunic and revealed the butt of a pulser.

"I'm rather tired just now," she replied politely. "If you'll excuse me?"

"I beg you to reconsider." He laid a hand on the weapon. She met his eyes squarely.

"If that's meant as a threat, Mr. Alain, you're wasting your time. I find threats unbearably boring." She stepped around him and started for the fireplace.

"Not you," he warned softly. "The Priyam." It stopped her short and he felt a wave of triumph. "That *is* whom your husband is here to guard, is it not? What a pity for him to have failed, for want of a little cooperation." She turned back with white lips and clenched fists. Her obvious anger was well, if coldly, controlled.

"What do you want?" she demanded.

"I don't want anything, actually," he assured her, drawing her by the wrist into the protection of the potted tree. "But unfortunately, you were in the wrong place when the signal came. Now we're going to have to decide with to do with you."

"I don't know what you're talking about," she retorted, "but it you don't let go my wrist, I intend to do a good deal of very unpleasant screaming."

He ignored her outburst. "You are to act as if nothing is amiss. You will accompany me to the fire and behave normally. Unless, of course, you want to be responsible for the loss of a great many innocent lives." She made no reply, but he slowly squeezed the wrist until at last, catching her lower lip between her teeth, she barely nodded her agreement. He let go of her wrist and, making an exaggerated "after you" gesture, escorted her to the fireside.

Kei Matsushita padded silently down the corridor, accompanied only by the sounds of the rising storm and his own sober thoughts. This part of the Palace was unoccupied, and had the feel of a museum at night or of a house waiting for its owner to return. It was strange to be looking for an enemy operative in a place like this, he thought.

He examined every drawing room, every bedchamber, searching closets, anterooms, baths. He found nothing. No one. Despite his training, he began to relax. Perhaps there had been no breach of the Palace as yet. One could only hope. Matsushita was a master of martial arts, an expert with the *viith* and the glaive; but he had grown sick of killing, tired of intrigue. He was, he thought, probably getting old.

He'd had four more years to go in the government service before he was tapped for the Timeslide. Now things were changed. Now he had only to complete this one last, historic mission, and then—his service ended, his future secure—he could retire. It would be good to get back to Earth, to the mid-oceanic island he and eight million others called home, and resume his love affair with the sea. It would be good to tend his irises and to drink soup Takako would make for him. He could spend a pleasant hour watching umbrellas go past his door in the soft gray rains of spring. He could meditate upon the colors of the drifted autumn leaves. Perhaps he could write haiku.

He heard the footstep at the same instant the *viith* hit him, with some force, a little below and to the right of the left shoulder blade. He made a last sharp inhalation of breath, and the intruder lowered his body to the floor, dragged it into an adjacent room, and, shutting the door behind him, regained the corridor without making a sound.

Charles Lassiter found his way into the deserted kitchens, where the cooks had heard Marik's mental warning, laid down their utensils, and gone to their quarters. He prowled the darkened alleys between the prep tables with their high-piled containers, left unwashed and stacked haphazardly. He inspected the extensive pantry, snatched open harmless cabinets, peered into the bins.

Nothing.

Turning, he saw that the cellar door was standing ajar. Not far, the merest crack, but open. The hackles rose on the back of his neck. He crossed the room on cat's feet, watching it. Probably nothing. Some servant had given it a push, expecting it to close, and it didn't quite make it. Closer now. He could see the darkness beyond. Natural. Cellars were never lit without good cause. Wasteful. He eased the pulser from its holster at the center of his spine and flattened against the wall beside the door. Flipped it open abruptly with his foot, sweeping the yawning entryway with his weapon.

Nothing.

Moved out cautiously onto the first step, peering down into the gloom below. Pulled the door silently shut behind him. No need to silhouette himself, aiding the enemy's aim. Now they were in the dark together. He paused for a long moment, listening for the faintest sound, the barest breath that would indicate another presence.

He heard nothing, felt nothing. But the merest cool breeze stirred the air. An exit, escape route, entryway? He slipped down the steps and made his way slowly down the narrow, cask-lined aisles, past open arched passageways leading off into dead-end rooms, lined with wine bottles that glistened like dark jewels in the light of his hand torch.

A sudden faint skitter, the sound of a shoe scraping stone, made his heart thud; but then the perpetrator, a mouse (*Mus eisernonica*, the rabbit-tailed speckled miniature rodent that plagued the households of Eisernon) ran suddenly across his foot, startling him to a half-audible expletive, and he flashed his torch around the cave, with its scores of fragrant cheeses stacked to cool in the salty wet air.

This, then, was the source of the breeze he had followed. No open exit hatch, no mysterious passageway for bogeys to escape through, but merely an aristocrat's wine-and-cheese cellar, kept at optimum temperature and humidity by natural air currents bleeding in from the sea. But for *Mus*, there was nothing alive in the cellar except himself.

Lassiter gained the steps, the kitchen, switched on the light, put away his torch. As an afterthought, he decided to investigate the huge refrigerator-freezer.

He crossed to the heavy, insulated door of the refrigerator and flipped the lever, but it was stuck fast. He tried again, to no avail, and finally he used both hands to wrench at it.

It opened suddenly, slamming him against the wall, and with it came the giant bushman who had been holding it from the other side. Charles stumbled awkwardly, and the huge intruder backhanded him, knocking him against the wall, where he hit hard and lay still. The giant leaned down and felt for the throat

pulses and, satisfied that he was still alive, carefully lifted him
in his arms, placed him on the floor of the walk-in freezer, and
closed the door quietly behind him.

Then, as he had been instructed, he went to find Dao Marik.

The guests began to retire. The storm pounding at the roof,
combined with the good meal, warm fire, and—in many
cases—a fair amount of brandy, were inducement enough. The
archbishop, too, got to his feet, smothering a yawn. "Dao, my
boy," he said affably, "in accordance with my age, infirmities,
and your wonderful cognac, I'm going to bed." Marik smiled.

"Good sleep, Your Excellency. And, by the way," he
confided, "I've ordered an entire encyclopedia sent to your
suite, in case you'd like to do some reading." The archbishop
murmured something no one else heard, but the two of them
enjoyed it enormously. "Ah! There's Wim now," Marik said.
"He'll show you to your rooms." Each guest said a few words
by way of gratitude for Marik's hospitality, and then they were
gone. At last there were only Dunn, Vath, Alain, and Audrey
left with him in the library. Marik heaved a satisfied sigh.

"The room seems so much bigger now," he commented
boyishly, and Vath answered warmly, "What a fine evening,
Domne. It was like old times."

"It was, wasn't it?" Marik agreed, and Dunn smirked, but
neither the Krail nor the tense, white-faced young woman
ventured a reply. Marik regarded Audrey soberly. I hope
nothing is the matter, he thought.

"Did you manage to enjoy the evening, Mrs. Lassiter?" he
wondered, and she replied distantly, "Yes, thank you." I was
right, Marik thought. Something *is* wrong. I only hope that
episode earlier isn't still bothering her. She didn't look at all
well. He leaned down solicitously.

"Aren't you feeling well, Mrs. Lassiter? Perhaps we
should—" He had started to say, "Perhaps we should call your
husband," but all at once warning lights went up inside his
head, and he caught the edge of a fleeting thought: of signal
lights in the rain, and threats, and the pulser in Alain's jacket,
and changed his sentence to "Perhaps we should let you get
some rest."

"She's fine, just as she is," the Krail whispered. Marik

turned slowly to look right into the muzzle of the pulser. "I like her sitting right there in the pretty chair. I think I'd like you sitting beside her, Priyam. Mr. Dunn. Mr. Vath. Over there, please. That way I can watch all of you.

"Sit, please. I quite insist," he repeated, his face growing chill and nasty as Marik stood staring at him. "And no Han tricks, *Priyam*, or I'll be forced to stop the nice lady's heart. You wouldn't want that, would you? No? I thought not."

Marik sat slowly on the arm of Audrey's chair, the same way, she thought, as tigers settled at the snap of the trainer's whip. It probably would be unwise for Alain to turn his back. Evidently Alain shared her thoughts on the matter, for he edged his way to the window, holding the pulser steadily on them and, taking a lamp, swung it in a wide arc, once, twice—

An abrupt crackling burst of thunder directly overhead, accompanied by a lurid coruscation of lightning that put out the house lights and illumined the grounds, jerked Alain's head around in reflex. In that instant, before Marik could intervene, Vath leaped up and grappled with the Krail, who struck him across the face with the lamp. The episode would have ended there, but Vath clung to his arm, immobilizing it, even as he slumped to the floor. Alain started to train the weapon on him, but Marik sprang to a flying tackle, bringing him down in a crash of lamp, outflung pulser, and thudding limbs. They fought savagely for leverage. Alain got a hand over Marik's face and thumbed the orbit of his right eye, even as Marik's free hand shoved his chin back and back as he struggled to get out from under the thin man's surprising weight. Alain made a strangled sound and went over backward, and Marik dragged Alain to his feet and let go with a short, powerful right to the midsection that buckled the Krail's knees, followed by a left to the head that floored him and sent him rolling slowly, hugging his middle and wheezing through his teeth for breath.

Marik straightened just in time to sidestep the first lunge as the giant bushman, appearing unexpectedly from the corridor, launched himself in his direction. He prepared to do battle yet again. The giant waded in like a bear, and Marik stepped back nimbly out of his way. Those powerful arms looked as if they could crush him without visible effort.

Out of the tail of his eye, he saw Dunn cowered on the divan and Vath, his face bleeding, standing guard beside the kneeling Alain, holding the fireplace poker threateningly over his shoulder like an Erthlik *beisbol* bat. So distracted, he was almost caught in the bushman's death grip, and barely dodged away in time. In doing so, he saw his chance.

There on the sideboard stood the steaming coffee urn, its two ornamental handles making it easy to grip. Not necessarily his first choice as weapons went, but infinitely better than nothing.

Planning his moves carefully, Marik kept backing, guiding the giant bushman where he wanted him. Dodging swipes, avoiding sudden lunges, and constantly shoving pieces of furniture between them, he gained the sideboard and, seizing the coffee urn, splashed its scalding contents across the giant's face. The giant roared and grabbed for his eyes, and Marik shoved him backward over a chair. He hit hard and came up furious.

"Careful, *Domne*!" Vath, watching anxiously, turned his attention from Alain for a single moment. It was a fatal mistake. In one swift move, Alain wrenched the poker from Vath's hand and struck him down with it; then he came after Marik.

Audrey darted out and picked up the pulser, turning it on Alain. "Stop it!" she commanded. "Stop now! Right where you are."

Alain froze, poker in hand, glaring venomously at her. Jek, the big man, only paused an instant, but that instant bought Marik time for a skillful feint that avoided the giant's next murderous blow.

Audrey held the Krail at bay, warning him back with a lift of the pulser when he made an abortive move to take it from her. She watched his face, thinking it a trick when his expression changed from anger to smug victory. She wavered; was someone behind her?

The blow was quick. One moment she was holding the pulser on Alain; in the next, she had made an involuntary outcry, the weapon leaped away, and her wrist was swelling from the sharp downward stroke of the poker in the Krail's deceptively swift hand. She reached out weakly to support herself on the back of a chair, for the pain in her wrist made her sick and dizzy.

Marik glanced up, startled at her cry, and the giant grabbed him in a bear hug. He got in a couple of vicious lefts to the belly, but it was like hitting a cliff face; there was no response. The giant simply lifted him off his feet and began to squeeze, his knuckles forming a pressure point against Marik's spine. Marik tried to fight his way free, but the inexorable pressure kept building. His spine felt as if it was about to shatter. He got one good solid right at the bushman's mouth, cutting his knuckles on freshly broken teeth, before the giant ducked his head and squeezed harder. Marik's vision blacked over and his breath was a desperate gasping. In a final all-out effort, he extended his arms and brought both thumbs to bear, striking them simultaneously just below the giant's ears.

With a yelp of pain, the giant dropped him and grabbed his ears with both hands. Marik bounced off the floor, expecting to resume the battle.

He did not see Alain behind him. The poker hit him above and behind the ear, opening the gash he had got earlier in the day, and he crumpled to the floor. Alain, breathing hard, opened the doors onto the terrace, admitting four bushmen, among them the drenched Mouse, who hurried over to the fire, shaking with chill. "You took long to answer," Mouse complained. "The rain is cold."

"You want warm rain," Alain replied sullenly, kneeling to bind Marik's wrists behind him, "go back to your marshes, swamplander."

Audrey was aghast. Marik lay so still he might have been killed, and she was alone with a coward, the dead Vath, and a roomful of rough bushmen.

For the first time, she knew fear.

Had Charles been killed, too? And, oh, said part of her mind she couldn't control, what if they've killed the Priyam? I've got to get help, she thought. Perhaps he's still alive.

The pulser was on the floor under the end table. If only she could only get to the pulser—

The bushmen were muttering among themselves, checking the Priyam's pulses, examining Vath's obviously dead body, which had bled greenly all over the lush carpet. She sank faintly to the floor, the edge of her full skirts covering the weapon. God knew she was grateful for the solidity, for her

knees were decidedly wobbly. Her swollen hand was beginning
to turn a nasty shade of blue, and she pulled the cocktail ring
off her index finger and dropped it, giving her an excuse to
reach under the table. Her fingers found the ring, passed it by,
touched the edge of the pulser.

For the moment, it was enough. She rested her head against
the leg of the table and dully surveyed her captors. Alain was
busily going through Vath's papers. The giant had found a
handful of tea towels and was mopping his blistered face
gingerly with them. Dunn was watching her, but Dunn was in
as bad a fix as she. He was on her side, or, at least, not against
her. The Priyam had not moved.

She palmed the weapon. Slid it carefully inside the elbow
she then cradled in her left hand. Slowly pulled herself upright,
while her wrist throbbed, making her feel weak and sick. By
sheer force of will, she got to her feet, supporting herself
against the back of the chair. It took a moment to regain her
balance. The muzzle of a second pulser pressed firmly against
the small of her back, and she froze and let go a shaky breath.

"The pulser, please," said the small, shaven-headed man
who held out an imperative hand for it. She handed it to him
reluctantly.

"Thank you. Now go, lady, and sit down. I mean you no
harm, but I will have to kill you if you do not obey." Against
her will, she sat.

"Where is the captain?" the small man demanded, and
Alain shrugged and indicated Marik with a jerk of the head.

"My job was to keep *him* occupied."

Mouse brushed his hair out of his eyes. "Riker is already on
the boat, Ilai. We go now?"

The shaven-headed man looked at Audrey, at Dunn, and at
his men. "We go," he agreed.

Cynthia Jessen, the colonel's brat, was having a hard night.

Not that her quarters were uncomfortable. Far from it.
Seldom in her well-traveled young life had she enjoyed such
luxurious accommodations. The fire was cozy, her sumptuous
bed had been turned back for her, and the Einai maid assigned
to her room was flawless in anticipating her every whim. The
storm should have lent the final touch to a night of deep and

uninterrupted slumber; but Cynthia Jessen was having a hard
night.

She rolled over in bed and scowled tipsily at the ceiling.
Some indefinable noise had roused her from a fitful doze, some
sound distinct from the far-off torrent of the rain, the rush of
wind. There it was again, a noise as of a heavy object thudding
against a wall. Then everything was silent. She sat up unsteadily, brushing her disheveled hair off her puffy face, and
rehashed the evening for the hundredth time.

Things had started off nicely. She had met the dashing
captain of USS *Skipjack*, exactly as planned. Auntie had played
her part to perfection (even though there really *was* some sort
of councilor errand the High Council wanted Paul Riker for, at
some later date; Cynthia knew nothing about it and could not
have cared less). The important thing was, she had met Paul
Riker.

Everyone at Patton Base knew about him, envied her going
to a party—even an Einai party—where she could catch a
glimpse of him. Her college chums were positively green with
envy. And here she had managed to play the sophisticate, had
gotten him alone in a rose garden, no less, and had almost
gotten him to kiss her, until, damn the luck, something had
gone wrong. She couldn't think what.

To make matters worse, Riker had been there when, instead
of a fat, sweaty little green alien in a grass skirt and paper
crown (which had been her mental caricature, though not her
actual image, of Dao Marik), here stood this young Greek god
in the receiving line, resplendent in sashed white uniform and
saber, and she had made a positive fool of herself, babbling
away like that.

And Riker, damn him, had loved every minute of it.

Her efforts to make up and be friendly later had fallen flat.
The Priyam was as cool as he was attractive, and was
obviously, courteously, not interested. Left with a brandy glass
in either hand by both of the handsome Navy men, Cynthia had
retaliated by downing both glasses and going back for numerous refills. By the time Marik was getting his guests off, she
was feeling no pain whatsoever.

Several retaliations later, during the archbishop's story, she
wandered out in a dizzy euphoria, tooled down the halls

humming a space chantey, and, upon reaching her quarters, changed her cocktail gown for black silk pajamas. Thus attired, she paced the room unsteadily, mentally rewriting the evening for her girlfriends. After a while the discrepancy between the truth and the rewrite became so marked that even Cynthia could stand it no longer, and, bursting into a torrent of maudlin self-pity, she flung herself across the bed and wept herself into a troubled stupor.

She might have been able to sleep then, but there were loud reverberations from the library just beneath her room, of metal falling and rolling to a stop, of running footsteps and of heavy objects forcefully striking the floor. She tried for a while to ignore the noise, but it persisted and, muttering vehemently, indignation rising, she thrust her arms into the sleeves of her matching robe, jammed her feet into high-heeled slippers, and clattered down the stairs in high dudgeon.

"What'sa matter with you people?" she demanded thickly of the austere and empty corridor, crossing to a drawing-room door and throwing it open with a satisfying crash. "Can't you k-keep the party within reason'ble lim-limits?" She opened a door to an empty room. "Keep it down!" she ordered the room. "People're tryin'a sleep, you know!"

No one was there, but it was rather nice, getting the feelings out, so she slammed the door with all her might and swaggered down the deserted halls to the next closed door, her voice increasing in volume and heat with every crash. "How dare you mess up my sleep?" *Slam!* "You don't wanna play, fine!" *Crash!* "Okay! Well, you just shut up, you hear?" *Bang! "Just you shut up!"*

Crossing the hall, she flung open yet another door and shouted, "Anybody here doesn't keep it down, out he goes! Complaints in triplicate may be sent to the adj'tant's office, where they will be prom-promptly discarded!"

A self-satisfied smile touched her face as she marched up to the carved double doors of the library and, kicking it open with an irreverent foot, yelled, at the top of her lungs, *"So just you shut up, you stupid bunch of greenies!"*

But this time, she found herself face-to-face with an imposing group of jungle bushmen, all of them green but one, whose very white hand held a pulser aimed directly between her eyes.

What appeared to be a dead body lay on the floor beyond, and an enormous bushman had the unconscious Priyam slung limply over one shoulder. She backed away a step or two, trying an unsuccessful smile.

"Wrong room?" she suggested softly, without much conviction.

The very white man shook his head slowly in the negative, and she sighed.

"The whole day's been a bitch," she mumbled miserably.

The sloop *Oriana* lay moored in a natural grotto in the massive rock below the Promontory. This convenient quay was reached, Audrey discovered, by means of a spiral stairway, carved through the rock itself, which led downward from a room inside the Summer Palace. Doubtless, she surmised, some royal scoundrel had made his escape from justice in that way centuries before. Perhaps the fabled Timujin Kesh had stolen out of his father's Palace by this very means when he set out to win the heart of his enemy's daughter. Then the passage must have been mysterious and full of secrets.

Tonight it was frightening and fraught with danger. The bushmen, whoever they were, seemed familiar with these steep, wet stones, pushing and jostling each other and their captives as they hurried down to the grotto. Audrey was shoved into line behind the giant, so close to Marik's head that she could see little beads of sweat on his temples and catch a whiff of the blood drying behind his ear and in a smear on Jek's fatigues. She controlled an impulse to brush back his hair from his forehead and concentrated instead on negotiating the slippery steps.

At the bottom of the flight was an open area, part of the grotto itself, lit by electronic torches, that stepped down progressively to the sea. A trim runabout rode on a long painter secured to a mooring cleat driven into the rock. *Oriana*, riding far out in the heaving black water, was a measure of the excessive height of the seas, for she generally lay alongside the quay. There was a bushman on deck, speaking into a throatset like the one Ilai wore, and after a few minutes' exchange, Ilai motioned them into the runabout.

Dunn was terrified. The gangly xenobiologist watched in

horror as they pulled the boat close, and the seas washing the shingle blackly, the hiss of rain and the dull pounding of the surf devouring all other sound. When it was his turn to board, he folded up his long legs, clutched the gunwales, and kept his eyes tightly shut. The giant dumped Marik in unceremoniously and gently swung Cynthia and Audrey aboard. The remaining bushmen clambered on deck and the craft purred off, its sound quickly lost in the rush of the storm. Marik made what looked like a voluntary motion, and Audrey leaned down to see if she could revive him.

She knelt in the bottom of the boat, lifted his head with her bad arm, and clumsily dabbed at the Priyam's face with her handkerchief. It startled her to realize, in the dim light and the press of the group, that he was watching them through his lashes.

"You're alive!" she breathed, in relief so great it brought tears smarting to her eyes.

"They mustn't know," he whispered, his lips barely moving. "They have to think I'm dying, understand?"

"But why?"

His eyes closed and his head became immensely heavy against her arm. "Priyam Marik? Priyam?" She felt, rather than saw, Alain leaning over them.

"He cannot hear you, Mrs. Lassiter," Alain gloated over the sound of the storm. "He'll be out for some time, I think."

She touched Marik's face with her handkerchief again. "You might have killed him!" she accused. Alain shrugged and reached for the rail of *Oriana*'s accommodation ladder. Lines snaked down from *Oriana*'s deck, and bushmen held the runabout steady.

"Now or later," he asked coldly, "what's the difference? Get aboard."

Paul Riker sat on the edge of the bunk in *Oriana*'s cabin, his hands bound behind him, trying to figure a way out of his predicament. He had been apprehended while checking out the broken skimmer cable Simes had mentioned, finding that rather than having snapped from the force of the storm, it had been neatly, purposely cut by parties unknown.

On his way back to the house with this bit of news, he had encountered several dark figures who subdued him—not without considerable difficulty—bound him, and hurried him onto *Oriana*. One of them had frisked him and removed the sealed packet of orders from his inner pocket. Then they threw him into the cabin of the sloop to await further developments.

As soon as the hatch was shut behind them, he had made a thorough search of the cabin, looking for a weapon, a cutting tool to free his hands, anything that would help even the odds between one man and a boatload of pirates. He found nothing. Even the telecom had been smashed into bent metal and pieces of glass too small to be of any help.

There was an outside chance he could break the glass in the deadlight and cut his bonds with that, but before he could test this theory, the hatch swung open, admitting Marlowe Dunn, Cynthia Jessen, and Audrey Lassiter in quick stumbling succession. Two of the pirates shoved Marik down the companionway into the cabin, and then slammed the hatch and secured it from the outside.

Marik fell loosely against Dunn, who sidestepped him, and measured his length on the deck. Audrey and Riker were instantly on their knees beside him.

"Marik!" Riker commanded. "Marik, wake up!" To Cynthia, "Here, help me with these ropes!" She worked at the knots as Audrey lifted Marik's head onto her lap, and finally freed him. Riker patted Marik's face roughly. "Come on, man, here you go!"

Marik turned his head and pulled a ragged breath. He curled on his side and lay still again. Blood had dried on the side of his face and neck and stained the shoulder of his white uniform. "What happened?" Riker demanded of Audrey.

She briefed him on the scuffle in the library, including Vath's murder, and described the bushmen as best she could, ending with, "One of them was the biggest man I have ever seen."

"I met him," Riker winced, remembering. He leaned down again. "Marik! Wake up, man! Come out of it." Somewhere below, they could feel the muted throb of the engines starting.

Marik slowly rolled over on his back, opened his eyes, and moistened his dry lips with a wooden tongue. He lay there for a long minute, coming to his senses. "We're at sea . . . aren't we?" He frowned. "Mrs. Lassiter?"

"Right here. Safe and sound. And Miss Jessen and Dunn as well. Here, let's get you off the deck." He helped Marik onto the bunk, where he seemed to black out again. "Marik? You all right?" There was no answer.

Dunn leaped to his feet. "Do you hear that?" he exclaimed. "Do you feel it? The boat is moving!" They stood very still, listening.

Oriana was definitely moving, the engines not merely idling but working at a task. They were moving out of the protection of the grotto, and into the teeth of the storm.

"They can't take us out into that weather," Dunn protested fearfully. "We'll be sunk in no time!" He climbed up the narrow companionway and beat on the hatch with his fist.

"Here! You up there! You can't take us into that storm, do you hear? You'll kill us all!" He clenched his fists together and beat on the hatch with them, lost his balance and slipped on the wet steps, barking his shins, climbed up and started hammering at the hatch again. "Let us out, do you hear? Murderers! Incompetents!"

Audrey crossed to him, supporting her balance with her good hand against the bulkhead. "Mr. Dunn, they can't hear you," she coaxed, "and they wouldn't care if they could. Let them be. Come down here with the rest of us!"

"You don't understand, young woman!" he snapped. "If they sail us out in a hurricane, we'll sink in a minute!"

"Well, they're not going to sail any better with you beating on the door, Ace, that's a sure cinch," Cynthia informed him. "Why don't you keep quiet and let them do what they can?"

"They'll do what they can, yes, for themselves," Dunn expostulated. "If we start to sink, you don't think they'll let us out, do you? We know too much. We'll drown like rats in a trap!" He began beating on the hatch again. "Felons! Murderers! You can't do this to me! *Do you know who I am?*"

As they tried to reason with the shouting Dunn, Marik grabbed Riker's arm in a firm grip and said clearly in a low voice, "Paul, I want them to think I'm badly hurt. Don't give me away."

Riker stifled his amazement and resumed watching Dunn and Audrey at the hatch. "You have a plan." It was barely more than a whisper.

"Several."

"How do you propose to keep us afloat?"

"There's no wind to speak of." And Riker became aware that the wind had abated, that the rain was no longer drumming on the cabin top and hissing in the sea outside. "We're in the eye of the hurricane. The calm spot. The only danger is the sea, and the stabilizers can handle some of that. With any luck at all, we'll make it to Tagan."

"And we want to get to Tagan," Riker said in a sardonic mutter. "I don't know why, but we want to get to Tagan."

"Of course you know why," Marik told him quietly. "That's where Misi is."

CHAPTER

VIII

THE ISLAND OF Tagan was the site of a long-unused medieval fortress, and its heavily forested slopes, rock shelves, and blue-sand beaches sheltered the remnants of earthworks and barricades, deserted blockhouses, stone jetties, and, high on the crest overlooking the open sea, the old Citadel itself. Long flights of steps had been carved, like the Citadel, out of the living rock, and the island was honeycombed with subterranean chambers and secret passageways.

The stone cell wherein Riker, Marik, and the others found themselves was part of the Citadel's prison complex, and was fitted with a stout door made of weathered timbers and boasting a small open grille. Across the room, a barred window afforded a view of dark, rain-drenched forest. The air inside the cell was damp and cool and smelled of hay, of mildew, and of mice.

Marik lay motionless on the bare planks of the prison bunk, and Riker wondered how much of his injury was subterfuge and how much actual wound. Several times, when he had tried to get Marik's attention, he had actually seemed unconscious, and the word *concussion* kept coming to Riker's head. He knew very little about such things, so he decided to turn his attention to more immediate concerns.

Escape was first on the list.

He began to investigate his surroundings. The bars of the window were laser-drilled into stone, not likely to be easily removed. He pried at them anyway and proved himself correct.

"What are you doing, Captain?" Dunn was standing too close behind him, right in his way.

"Just having a look around, Mr. Dunn. Trying to find a way out of here." He ran his hands over the door, letting touch tell

183

him what he had not the light to see, while Dunn craned myopically over his shoulder.

The door was solidly made, with a large metal lock responding to a key rather than a touch code. Perhaps there was some hope there. He rifled his pockets for a tool, but came up empty. Anything he might have used to jimmy a lock was lying on the dresser in Marik's guest room.

"Do you have anything I could use as a pry bar, or a tool of any sort? Something metal or plastex."

"Of course not!" Dunn replied irritably. "And besides, even if you got us out of here, what then? We'd still be in the middle of the Citadel. How could you get us off this godforsaken island? You're the famous hero, Captain, why don't you do something?"

Riker eyed him speculatively. "I'm trying to do something, Mr. Dunn. I'm giving it my best shot. Miss Jessen?"

"Sorry. All I've got is a smoke. Anybody interested?" No one was. She reached into the pocket of her black silk robe and fished out a package of cigarettes, struck one, and inhaled, shivering, for the cell was cold. Riker wished for the jacket they had taken from him aboard *Oriana*. He looked at Audrey Lassiter, but the wet white lace had no pockets, or even sleeves, in which a tool might be concealed. He didn't even bother to ask. He gave her what he hoped was a reassuring smile and continued his examination of the cell.

The hinges of the door, perhaps. Hung with the flanges set into stone, they, too, were impregnable. He hit the door beside the hinges with an experimental shoulder block, but there was no give, not even a quiver, in the heavy metal-strapped barrier.

"That isn't going to work, you know," Dunn informed him, stepping up closely to criticize and scraping Riker's ankle with a misplaced step. "Nothing you're doing is going to help at all."

Riker inhaled deeply, counted down backward from five to null, and replied quietly, "Let's wait and see, shall we?" He looked around the cell as much to stem his own annoyance as to find a tool. Perhaps the bunk would offer an answer.

Marik's eyes were open, the wet gleam of them barely discernible in the half-light reflected from the bunker off among the trees. He'd been awake and watching all the time, then. Riker envied him his night-sight, a gift from his feline ancestors, for the cell was very dark. At first it had seemed pitch-black, but as the eyes grew accustomed to the darkness, the faint reflected light loomed brighter by contrast. That was something to be grateful for, at least.

Riker looked at the window and then at the bunk, and decided to make his own tool. He planted a foot against the wall and after several vigorous tries, jerked off a sturdy plank from the edge of the bunk, making it even narrower than before.

"What are you going to do with that?" Dunn wanted to know, and Riker lowered one end of the plank to the floor and favored him with the last of his patience.

"I haven't decided yet, Mr. Dunn," he replied evenly. "But I've got it narrowed down to two choices: either I'm going to pry out the window bars with it, or I'm going to ram it down somebody's throat." There was no reply from Dunn's corner of the cell. "All right," he told them, "take cover, now, because things will probably be flying around."

Riker thrust the thick board between two of the stout bars, adjusted it so that it could not slip free, and pulled back with everything he had, expecting momentarily to hear the satisfying *spang* of bars breaking loose from stone.

The board flipped with all its considerable resiliency, but instead of the bars breaking, Riker himself was catapulted abruptly into an impromptu aerial somersault and landed in a bruised heap against the far wall, with the board stuck fast and still humming between the bars. He lay there for a disassociated moment, trying to figure out what had happened. Nothing came to mind.

Dunn piped up with: "It didn't work, did it, Captain? It didn't work, right?"

Cynthia laughed aloud, and Riker thought he heard a chuckle from Marik's direction. Audrey said nothing, but he was sure she must be laughing, too. He got up carefully, unraveling arms and legs that felt as if they had one too many joints in them, trying to figure what had gone wrong.

"No, Mr. Dunn," he said ominously. "It didn't work." He made his way to Marik's bunk and sat down heavily on the edge of it, nursing a contusion on his elbow. "Shut up," he said under his breath, and the chuckle became more pronounced.

"That was beautiful," Mark whispered, laughing. "You should have seen yourself. Flighted man. It was one for the history books. You monkeys certainly are talented."

Riker was spared the necessity of a reply, for the door was noisily unbolted, unlocked, and swung open, and under the needlers of two outsized bushmen, a woman entered the cell carrying a bucket of presumably fresh water. She carried a hand torch, and in its reflected light, Riker got a close look at her.

She was dark, with long, thick black hair held out of her eyes by a multicolored bandeau, and she showed the feline ancestry of the Einai more than did most. Her yellow eyes were wide-spaced and slit-pupiled, and her nose broad and snubbed. She had a short upper lip and slightly longer canines, and she moved with an effortless grace. Her peasant skirt and loose blouse hung limp on a lean, tough, athletic frame, and she wore a *viith* sleeved at her shoulder. There was no doubt in any of their minds that she was capable of using it.

"I am Jana," she said curtly, putting down the pail. She flashed the light into their faces. Riker squinted past it at her.

"You would be the captain. Mennon wants to see you."

"I want to see him, too," Riker said meaningfully. She swung the light into Dunn's face. "And Dunn." He put up his hands against the glare and looked away.

The light passed right over Cynthia as if she were not there and jumped to Audrey, who was standing quietly beside her. "Who is this?" she demanded.

"My name is Audrey Lassiter, Jana," Audrey told her, and the discrepancy between the two of them was so apparent as to make the native woman uncomfortable. She took refuge in ridicule.

"Well, Missis Owdri Lassita," she observed acidly, "you look very foolish, wearing a rich-woman dress in prison. I hope you know how foolish you look." Audrey said nothing, and after a pause, the light from the hand torch leapt to Marik's face. He appeared unconscious again, and Riker had time to reflect that either Marik was a very good actor, or he was more seriously injured than any of them suspected.

"This would be the Marik." Jana walked closer, peering at his face. "What is wrong with him?"

Riker's tone was solemn. "Your men overdid their persuasion. I think he is badly hurt."

She studied his face in the torchlight. "Bad? How bad?"

Riker feigned knowledge ill-concealed. "Oh, I don't know. I'm not a doctor, you know. I'm a ship's captain."

"But you have an idea, ship's-captain-Riker." Her face grew sly. "You are not telling me all you know, Brau," she said to one of the guards, "the captain knows more than he wishes to tell me. Do you think he will maybe tell you?"

Riker put up both his hands in a disclaiming gesture. "I wouldn't do anything rash, Jana," he advised, giving her a charming smile. "Mennon probably wouldn't like to lose *both* of us."

"Both of you?" She pounced on the phrase. "Are we then losing the Marik?" The light leapt to the bunk and back to Riker in unspoken agitation. "Brau! Maing! Bring Mennon!"

"What about us?" Dunn demanded. "You can't just leave us here in this damp cell! We'll catch our death! You—"

"If you are not quiet, Erthlik," Jana warned, "you will catch worse than death!"

"I demand to see Mennon!" Dunn declared hotly. "I want some results. I don't intend to sit here and be incarcerated like a criminal. I'm not part of this crowd, I've been a great help to—"

"Enough! Take him!" Jana ordered, and he was hustled out into the corridor before he could sputter another furious word.

Audrey was trying to reestablish her bearings when a presence loomed behind her. A gentle hand fell across her mouth and Marik whispered, close beside her ear, "Say nothing." She nodded slightly. "My daughter Misi is a prisoner on this island. She's only two years old. I have to find her and get all of us off the island before the second wall cloud hits. Will you help me?" She nodded again. Was he really there or was it a daydream, a mirage? His hand was warm against her mouth but when she tried to touch it, she felt nothing but her own face. His voice continued: "From the guard room down the passageway, a set of stairs leads down to the quay. *Stay well away from them* until you hear *Oriana* blow. When you hear the explosion, count ten, take the stairs, and run for the *byela*—the fishing boat. Remember! Ah!''

Suddenly the phantom hand over her mouth was gone. There were footsteps in the corridor, and the door opened, admitting the guards and a lean, bearded Einai Audrey knew could only be Mennon. He stalked over to the bunk and said nothing, simply stood looking down at his recumbent foe, and Marik smiled up at him faintly.

"We meet again, Kles."

"Different now. Now I have the upper hand; I am the master." Marik said nothing, and Mennon continued: "I have the child. She is here, and safe. I offer you a trade."

Marik waited.

"We found your orders in the captain's tunic. You are scheduled to Jump in just over three weeks. And so you will; but if you want the child alive, you will have *Skipjack* prepare for a different voyage than ComFleet has planned." He glanced at Riker with his yellow tiger's-eyes. "I want the Elluvon. We're going back in time to NGC-5850. Back to the nova. Back for Mishli."

"Back? You don't understand, Mennon," Riker cut in. "It's already happened! You can't go back there and snatch her out! Don't you think we would have saved her if we could? Three went down—four can't come back!"

"Four won't come back," Marik breathed, understanding. "One of us stays. Isn't that right, Kles? One of us dies in her place."

"The right one, this time," Mennon agreed coldly. "The coward who left her there on a vaporizing planet to—" He shut his eyes briefly in the darkened cell against the glare of a sun gone nova. "And with you gone, *Domne*," he continued, "it will be my arms she runs to, my hands that bring her her child. Mine, her gratitude."

"And you think you loved her," Marik told him compassionately. "Ah, Kles. You didn't even know her."

"Of course I knew her! We three were raised together, weren't we?" Mennon expostulated. "The accident of birth that made my mother a slave—and yours an empress—didn't keep me from wanting Mishli—and loving her! I loved her then; I still love her!" He missed hearing the sharp, pained intake of breath from Jana, standing at the door.

"You didn't even know her," Marik repeated, so softly they almost couldn't hear him. Mennon ignored him and addressed Riker instead.

"I suggest you turn the ship, the crew, and the Elluvon over to me if you expect to see the child alive again."

But Riker was not listening. His attention was focused on Marik, who had lapsed again into that drifting unconsciousness. Riker felt he should remember something about it, but it kept slipping off the edge of his mind. He touched Marik's shoulder. "Marik?" No response. He shook him, calling his name again. Nothing.

Mennon was suddenly beside them. He slapped Marik's face, none too gently. "*Temteg, t'umbin!*" he commanded, to no avail. To Riker, "How long has he been like this?"

"Since one of your men waylaid him with a fireplace poker," he retorted crisply. Surprisingly, the word brought associations. Fireplace poker. Poker deck. Poker face. Control, that's the key. Poker-faced control. He wet his lip and tapped the edge of his hand on the bunk. He was getting an idea, and it was a good one. It was also a dangerous one. He decided to go with it.

"What if I call your bluff, Mennon?" He gestured carelessly, smiling. "Lay it out for me."

"It's very simple, Captain," Mennon stated coldly. "If you cooperate, Marik's child goes to the arms of her mother. If not"—he smiled—"the rampers are always hungry. The choice is yours."

Riker spread his hands and inhaled deeply, prepared to gamble. "We seem to have a misunderstanding here, Mr. Mennon," he ventured, "and I'd like to clear it up. This child you keep talking about—she belongs to Marik, not to me. Think about it: viewed logically, what is she to me? We're not even the same *race*—or social level."

"I don't think the *social level* of the Han Einai is under question anywhere in the galaxy," Mennon interjected stiffly.

Riker smiled condescendingly. "Oh sure, I understand, and I agree with you. Every aboriginal tribe has its head honcho, I'm not denying that. But look at it from my point of view: you want me to risk my career and my ship for one of a million native kids who all look alike to me—when *my* ancestors came from Old Earth; and she's just an eye-eye native; *I'm* descended from the Whitfields—and she's a—a *greenie*! No offense intended, of course.'' It was wonderful to see Mennon's reaction to that one. It's working, Paulo boy, he told himself. He laid it on a bit thicker.

''Naturally, I hate to see people die as much as the next man, but face facts, this has been a long, messy war, and a good many civilians have zilched out, children included. I mean, it's a shame, but war is hell, don't you agree?'' He shrugged, trying to ignore the knot in his belly, and played his final card. ''You want to throw one more native kid to the lions, that's your affair; but what makes you think it has anything to do with me—and my ship?''

Mennon blinked several times, looking more off balance than Riker had seen him yet. ''Are . . . are you telling me,'' he asked slowly, ''that you would let this child *die* rather than turn *Skipjack* over to me?'' Riker cleared his throat.

''It's a *very* expensive ship,'' he began, when an explosion of indignation rocked the cell.

''Why, you *miserable* creep! That is the most vicious, rotten thing I ever heard anybody say!'' Cynthia expostulated, storming up and hitting him in the chest with both fists as hard as she could. ''Are you going to stand there and let this maniac throw that poor baby to the lions and not do anything about it? I might have known! You sailors are all alike, you don't have the slightest—''

''Maing!'' Mennon commanded angrily, and the bushman wrapped a restraining arm around Cynthia and put a hand across her mouth, where it promptly got bitten. He swore and dropped her, shaking his hand violently, and she fled to the opposite side of the cell. He started after her, but Mennon's gesture stopped him in his tracks and directed him outside.

Riker felt sick. Cynthia's outburst had lost him any advantage he might have gained, for Mennon was coldly in command again. So much for the first round of poker with Kles Mennon. He wondered wryly who would win the second.

''I warn you, for the safety of your party, control that—*lady*, and get Marik functioning again. The Han heir may mean nothing to you Erthlikli, but I suspect he may feel differently!"

"Assuming I can get him functioning. Assuming I can keep him alive."

Again Mennon seemed to waver. "I can see him breathing from here. Of course he is alive."

Riker pressed his advantage. "For how long? I've seen men die of this kind of injury before, Mr. Mennon. For all I know he could have a fractured skull. That would really scotch your plans, now, wouldn't it?"

Mennon turned slowly to face him. "In what way, Captain?"

"Well, you just may have done yourself out of a Timeslide. I can't Jump without my SO, and there's not another second in the Fleet qualified to take over for him. It's Marik or nothing. If your men have put him out of commission, you've lost your leverage, haven't you? Then you're in real difficulty."

"Not like you are, Captain," Mennon smiled. "You had better pray that Marik lives. With him dead, what use do I have for any of you?" He paused beside Jana at the door and turned back to Riker. "I suggest you spend a few moments considering that. I will return later for your decision."

"And in my spare time," Riker amended, with a disrespectful survey of Jana, "I could always contemplate your undying love for Marik's late wife." Jana colored darkly, and Mennon put an arm almost protectively around her neck, pulling her close. His eyes were yellow slits in the gloom.

"She's not Mishli by a light-year," he muttered, "but she has her uses." She gave him a venomous glare, jerked away from him, and slipped out the door. Mennon, watching her exit with a puzzled expression, added absently, "Also, I would waste no thought on escape. It's impossible."

"Hearsay evidence," Riker retorted, and Mennon answered his grin with a brief one of his own. But if he could get out, Riker thought, get to a weapon, he could even the odds a bit. He would be willing to bet there were a few weapons lying around the Citadel. If he could keep Mennon's attention focused on Marik, there was a slim chance— "If you expect me to do anything for Marik," he ordered, "get me some light. I can't help him if I can't see him."

Mennon eyed him speculatively. "Bring him along. There's

light out here." Riker hoisted Marik to his feet and half-led, half-carried him out of the cell, which Mennon locked securely behind them.

The door clashed shut and the sound and the light disappeared together, leaving Audrey and Cynthia alone in the chill darkness of the cell.

Audrey whispered, "We have to get out of here and help them."

"Oh, right." Cynthia struck another cigarette on the emery strip of the package and dragged deeply on it. "Would you like to go out together? Or shall we go one by one? Who's first?"

"First," Audrey told her firmly, unfastening her white lace gown clumsily with her bad hand, "help me get out of these clothes. Then I have a plan. . . ."

As Mennon turned to lock the door, Riker grabbed his chance. He let Marik slump down the wall and took off like a sprinter, racing down the corridor, around the bend of it, and directly into the swung barrel of a needler in the hands of the small bald bushman called Ilai. He took the full impact on his left cheekbone, and the force of it knocked him off his feet. He hit the flagging and sat there stunned as Mennon sauntered up and stood looking down at him with grim amusement. Ilai's needler was aimed at his throat, and beside him Brau and Maing were poised for action. Riker felt his rapidly swelling cheekbone. It hurt like bloody blue blazes. This was, he felt, definitely not going to be one of his better days.

"Shall we try it again, Captain?" Mennon asked, gesturing gracefully toward the doorway. Riker looked at him and blew out a long breath. Okay, so he was zero for two playing poker with Mennon. There was always the next deal. He spread his hands, capitulating for the moment. The needler dropped harmlessly away and the bushmen helped Riker regain his feet.

"Take them into the office," Mennon ordered, and Brau stared.

"*Them?*" He frowned. "He dropped the Marik back there."

Mennon met Ilai's eyes and indicated the bend of the corridor with a tilt of this head. The bald man padded silently to the curve and stopped short, disbelieving the testimony of his own eyes. The corridor was empty.

Marik was gone.

"Mennon," Ilai reported from where he stood. "The Marik is not here."

Riker laughed aloud in surprise, and Mennon turned on him like a tiger. "Oh, clever, clever Erthlik," he hissed, "you have just killed yourself! Maing, Brau! Keep him here! Ilai!"

He raced off down the corridor, Ilai at his heels, and Riker followed his guards into the office and spread his hands innocently as he sat slowly into a chair. Maing took up a position behind him, with the cold muzzle of the needler resting uncomfortably against the base of his neck. Brau stood at the doorway, where he had full view of both room and corridor, *viith* at the ready.

It was Brau who noticed the fire first. In the darkened corridor it started as merely a rosy glow, a pale warmth, and blossomed quickly into a crackling yellow roar, interspersed with the screams of the women inside. Swearing softly under his breath, he ran to the cell, unlocking the door even as he peered through the barred peephole, sleeved his *viith,* and swung the door wide. The woman in black silk flung herself at him, clutching his tunic wildly, and he fought her off and shunted her into the corridor, out of his way.

"Help her," she shrieked, beating on his back and shoulders and pushing him toward the fire with both hands, "Mrs. Lassiter is caught in there! She hurt her leg! Quick, she's burning to death!"

Brau, choking on acrid smoke, waded through the smoldering straw of the floor toward a sobbing figure in white huddled on the prison bunk. He kicked away burning hay, scooped her up unceremoniously, and staggered out into the corridor again, choking and gagging, and carried her into the brightly lit room where Maing was detaining Riker.

"There was a fire," he said by way of explanation. "I got Mrs. Lassiter out." Riker's face was a nice mix of emotions, and he said casually to the blonde woman in the soot-smudged white dress, "I'm glad to see you safe, *Mrs. Lassiter.*" She gave him a pixie's smile and dried those startling ice-blue eyes with the backs of her hands.

"Thanks, Ace," she replied softly.

Maing stepped away from Riker far enough to cover both of them with his needler. "Where is your *viith*?" he asked Brau silkily. "And where is the other woman?"

Brau fumbled at the emptiness of his weapons sleeve. "Uh . . ." It was obvious he had totally forgotten about the second woman, and kept reaching again and again for his *viith* as if it might magically appear where it belonged. "I . . . uh . . ."

"No matter." Maing sat down behind the desk, still keeping the needler handy, reached into the bottom drawer, and pulled out a stoneglass tarangi flask that must have belonged to Mennon, for Riker noted that Brau seemed shocked. "She won't get far. Storms always drive rampers onto the Reef and around the leeward side of the island. It will be crawling with them out there tonight." He put up his feet and took a long pull at Mennon's flask. "She doesn't have a chance."

"There's always the other side of the island," Riker pointed out.

Maing smiled coldly. "Not even patrol boats come close. We've had a fishing boat seeding these waters for weeks, getting ready for this. Bait's easy enough to come by. Rampers will come miles for the slightest trace of blood." He smiled, showing his long canines. "And we can always find something to kill."

"When Mennon finds out," Brau suggested humbly, "it might be *us*. He wanted them *here*." Maing looked uncomfortable, uncrossed his legs and took a last long pull at the heavy flask while Brau swallowed hard.

"All right, I'll have a look around, see if I can spot her before the second wall cloud hits. You watch these two and don't lose any more prisoners, understand? I'll be right back."

Riker stood up slowly and crossed to Cynthia, pretending to examine her hands. "Are you badly burned, *Mrs. Lassiter*?" he asked, then muttered quickly, "We're getting out of here. You with me?"

"You got it," she shot back, under her breath, "but not in this rag. Where the hell's Wardrobe?"

"Looking at us."

For Brau, who had resumed his place at the door, was wearing dark, rugged bushman's clothing.

The walking wardrobe scowled at them fiercely. "No talking!" he commanded. "You! Move away from her!"

Riker complied by sauntering toward his chair, changing course for the desk while Cynthia fixed Brau with her insolent stare, deliberately reached down the front of her dress, and slowly and insinuatingly extracted a pack of cigarettes.

"Cigarette?" she offered Brau, and pantomimed a kiss.

Riker snorted disgustedly to himself, but nobody heard him. He continued his slow progress toward the desk.

Brau scowled even more fiercely. "Don't try tricks with me, woman!" he commanded. "I am immune to Erthlik females— and Erthlik tricks!" She shrugged and struck a cigarette for herself, took a puff, and strolled over to him while he watched warily.

"Stay away from that door!" he ordered, and she smiled.

"With you here? I can't think of one reason why I'd ever want to be anywhere else." She laid a cool hand on his dark, gold-green arm and took the cigarette away from her lips with a little *moue* and offered it to him, filter first. "You sure you don't want—one puff?" She sounded as if she had suddenly developed laryngitis.

Hearing that from across the room, Riker winced. She must see an awful—and he did mean *awful*—lot of old flix, way out there at Patton Base, he thought. Poor kid.

His hands closed firmly around the flask and he turned and leaned on the desk, the bottle behind him, waiting his chance. Brau was completely engrossed in Cynthia. "I don't know," he growled quietly. "I'm supposed to guard you two."

Cynthia stepped very close, lifted her brows, and half closed her eyes. "I can't think of any reason to leave," she murmured huskily, hamming it up to the hilt, "as long as . . . *you're* here." She blew smoke into his face.

Brau slipped his free arm around her waist and pulled her toward him, bringing his face down fast; but Cynthia, who had developed instant reflexes as an army brat, jammed the cigarette into his mouth instead, nearly burning her own cheek in the process.

At that same instant, Riker brought down the heavy stoneglass flask just behind Brau's ear, and he dropped like a felled beef and lay still. Cynthia leaned over and looked at his face.

"I just thought of a terrific reason," she confided.

Riker was stripping off Brau's dark camouflage clothing almost before he hit, while Cynthia worked at the fastenings of the soot-smudged white dress.

"Give me some of that stuff, will you?" she demanded, and Riker, exchanging his white uniform for the camouflage, tossed the bushman's dark shirt over his shoulder. For himself, he had the trousers, jacket, and soft bush boots that made no sound.

"I feel a little stupid," she ventured.

He looked around at her and cleared his throat. She had rolled the sleeves of the shirt that, clearing her knees by a good six inches, was the longest thing she was wearing. In fact, he realized with a mild shock, it was the only thing she was wearing. Maybe it cleared her knees (slim knees in shapely long legs) by eight lucky inches. More probably ten. Great legs.

"You look nice," he offered lamely.

"You've been at sea a long time, Ace," she commented, with that spoiled-brat grin. She regarded him thoughtfully for a long minute. "We've got to do something about you," she decided. "Come with me."

"Wait!"

She darted across the corridor, and Riker sprinted after her into the burned-out cell, mightily annoyed. There was so little time to get off the island, every instant was crucial. She was not only wasting their time, but risking their lives, and he was about to say so, but at first he couldn't see her at all. Only when she moved was she a blur, black on black, doing something with the hay.

She turned to him as she rose, her face all but invisible in the darkness, and moved very close, reaching for him eagerly, stroking her hands gently over every inch of his face. Her breath was warm on his cheek. Her lips were parted, her eyes a silvery sheen in the gloom.

"There," she murmured, "there . . . and there."

Studiously ignoring the delicious shudder engendered by her cool, quick fingers behind his ears, Riker decided that it was high time he got the situation back under control. He cleared his throat and caught her by the wrists, firmly holding her away from him, and wet his lip.

"Ah, listen, Miss Jessen—Cynthia—dear—believe me, I think I can understand your situation. Uh, how it is, living among all those men stationed at Patton Base, and being a v——" He coughed. "A young girl. And a very pretty one at that." She was staring at him uncomprehendingly and he continued: "And I can even see how you'd be attracted to a starship captain. Impressionable young girls are often attracted to sophisticated older men; but this is no time for roma——"

"Are you nuts?" She stared at him aghast. "I'm trying to blacken your face, you half-wit, so the pirates or smugglers or whatever they are don't see us. See for yourself. It's soot." She opened her hands and displayed black velvet palms. It fact, he noticed belatedly, every exposed inch of her skin was blackened. "I rubbed it off the hay we burned, for camouflage." He dropped her hands abruptly and the pixie grin began again, her teeth startlingly white in her blackened face.

"Impressionable young girl, huh?" she needled him, hand on her hip. "Sophisticated older man? That's pretty good, Ace. Tell me more."

"We don't have time for nonsense," he growled. "We've got to get out of here." He grabbed her hand and started for the door, pulling her behind him, and she laughed softly. "Make up your mind, you want to hold hands or don't you?"

He stopped short so suddenly that she ran into his back and he flattened against the wall, dragging her with him. "On second thought," he whispered urgently, "we're staying right where we are. Don't make a sound."

Casual footsteps were coming down the corridor, and Maing's voice called lazily, "I can't find her out there, she must— Brau!" There was a scramble of motion, the sound of a heavy body being rolled over, and then Maing shouted, "Mennon! Mennon!" They heard his running footsteps grow fainter and fade away.

"I think he's gone." He eased around the doorjamb for a scan of the empty corridor.

"Audrey said," Cynthia whispered, "that Marik wanted us to tell you, 'when *Oriana* blows, run for the *byela*—the fishing boat.'"

Riker turned his head sharply and looked at her. It was the key, the clue, the word he needed to go on, and it gave him a sense of exhilaration. And Cynthia, the brat, was on his side. She was annoying and exasperating, but she was also tough and gutsy and unsinkable, and on impulse he grabbed her by the back of the neck and kissed her quickly, hard, on the mouth. ''Come on,'' he said, ''let's get out of here.''

CHAPTER

IX

MENNON AND ILAI vanished down the corridor at a run, and Maing and Brau shoved Riker into the brightly lit room down the way, their voices muffled and distant. But in the empty hall, the wall resolved itself from the illusion of stones to the figure of Marik, who crossed silently to the prison cell, meeting Audrey's wide eyes. She had seen it all through the little grille in the door. Before she could tell him their plans, he put his finger on her lips. "No time," he whispered. "Forgive me."

She felt subtle mind-touch, and suddenly she *was* Marik, bore the responsibility of their rescue, and ached for his child, just as, the same instant, he *was* Audrey and knew her plan in its totality. But more, in that instant, he *crouched with her in the blackened ruins of the manor, while the invading Krail coldly massacred her family, hearing, beyond their cries, a mockingbird fluting somewhere; fled for days with her through the marshes, avoiding predators and reptiles, and shared her overwhelming gratitude when Charles Lassiter, unexpectedly stepping out of the brush, phased out the pursuing Krail and gently led her to a safe new life. Shared her ache for a child of her own, her child, his child. The ache merged until neither of them could distinguish whose need, whose loss, whose life*—for a moment they were utterly *one*, and he understood the kinship he had felt with her at their initial meeting.

The hay started to smolder under Cynthia's encouraging cigarette, and Marik disengaged the mind-touch and brought himself back to the present. "It's a good plan," he approved. "Yours?" She nodded. "It will get you out, never fear." And then, "Remember. Make for the fishing-*byela* as soon as

199

Oriana blows. Tell the others. If Paul can get some weapons, so much the better. Where's Dunn?"

"They took him away." The barest whisper.

"I'll find him." He touched her face briefly with his palm and faded to nothing before her eyes. "Take care," said his voice, close by. And he was gone.

Moments later, Audrey was free. When the fire started and Brau tore open the cell door, she feigned hysteria, pounding on his back long enough to steal his *viith*; and as he shoved her away toward the corridor and rushed into the acrid smoke of the cells, intent on rescuing Cynthia, she followed him, to hide behind the door until he carried Cynthia out. It was hard to hold her breath so long, but she feared she might cough and give herself away.

As Brau carried Cynthia into the bright room, Audrey, in Cynthia's black pajamas, followed cautiously, the stolen *viith* heavy in her waistband. She waited her chance, and when Maing turned to cover Cynthia and Riker with his needler, she darted past the open door and flattened against a recessed doorway down the hall. They would, she prayed, look for her only in the direction of the exit. She held her breath, her ears and even her skin seeming to tingle with the effort of listening.

Moments later, she heard footsteps emerge from the room and amble down the corridor in the wrong direction. She wondered how they could miss hearing her heart, beating so loudly it surely must give her away. But no one heard. No one came. She waited for the count of fifty, peered out carefully, and, seeing no one, slipped down a side hall and began her search for Marik's child.

It took Marik only ten minutes to search the building. Having used the old Citadel as a playground in his boyhood now stood him in good stead. He knew how many rooms were in the old fort, and what they were; which doors were rusted shut, and what was behind them; where the stones were safe, and where to watch your step.

He knew Mennon's favorite caches, and in one of them, he found what he had been searching for: several coils of rope, complete with grapples; a selection of Erthlik, Krail, and Eisernai weapons (and even a Minsonai glaive or two); and box after box of high-grade explosives. There was a bin full of odd pieces of camouflaged bush clothing, and Marik dug through it and quickly exchanged his stained uniform for the comfortable fatigues and bush boots that Mennon and his men wore. The legend on the boxes read LO! SEDDAJ POLIZ and DANJÉ: SUPÉ-THER-MÍT. Marik traced the stenciling with his fingertips, thinking fast. The Seddaj had had an uprising only a few weeks ago, and had blasted the local FSA Center, the Grand Moritz's palace, and several government buildings into the Hundred Arms of Siv. The arson squad claimed that persons unknown had stolen an entire shipment of police ordnance, including just such explosives. He wondered, even as he pried off the tops of the crates with the blade of a glaive and filled the pockets of the fatigues with the small, sealed packets of timed explosives, what Mennon had to do with the Seddaj uprising. I'll have to ask him that, among other things, he thought. Of the weapons, he chose only a well-honed *viith,* and as an afterthought, an ordinary Earthlik *gon* for Riker and another for Dunn. He shoved these into his belt and sleeved the *viith.* Now he had everything except what he wanted most: his child.

She was nowhere in the Citadel, nor was Dunn. He swept the island with his mind, picking likely hiding places for two such disparate prisoners. He discarded as unlikely the various bunkers and deserted phaser cannon emplacements, for none of them showed any light, and there must be light, if only to keep the child unafraid. A crying child could give them away. There would have to be light. Also, the buildings were too primitive to house prisoners, and too far from both harbor and landing strip, in case of trouble.

The landing strip itself, a flat outcrop on the unforgiving northern rock face, was another matter. There was a converted cave at the strip that could house several people in comfort for weeks. The problem was access. There were two ways to reach the strip: the first was known as the Kesh Tunnel, a natural fault that led directly through the mountain itself. It had only one drawback: the rickety bridge that spanned a deep interior chasm had collapsed when Marik and Kles were children. There was no way to pass.

The only alternative was a shallow natural crevice in the living rock, open on one side to the sea below. Mennon would not likely risk the dangerous passage with a small child in tow, especially if that child was the key to his blackmail.

So, for the moment, at least, he could discount the landing strip, but he filed the idea of skimmercraft for later use. That, and the fact of Mennon's presence in an upper room of the Citadel. He'd not disturb him now, Marik thought. Plenty of time for that later. Right now he had to stick to the job at hand: he had to find Misi and Marlowe Dunn. The sign he would look for was light.

There was only one place they could be: the guardhouse near the harbor, easy to defend, and near escape by sea if something went wrong. He would look for them there—but he would be very careful. He would have to be: if Misi and Dunn were there, they were not alone.

He avoided the stairs. The spiral stairs, leading down through the Citadel proper to the sea, were the only egress from the mountain fort, the way they two had run down to the beach when they played pirate there as children. There was no other way out of the place, unless you counted the parapet passage: the narrow walk, bordered by a low stone wall, that edged the Citadel on the north and west. Giving off of the end of the fort's main corridor, it dead-ended in a two-hundred-foot drop into the open sea. To the left, it became the steep crevice that accessed the landing strip. To the right, the passage climbed steeply over the top of the fort, past the old lookout posts, and abruptly became a path—and then a track—that dove sharply through dense forest down to the harbor, and the guardhouse, and the blue-sand beach.

Mennon knew these things, and would not expect a man with a head injury to chance the crevice or the slope. He would figure that Marik must take the stairs, and would have them heavily guarded. Knowing this, Marik took the other way, up over the roof and down the heavily forested southern slope of the mountain.

He gained the roof. Above him were scudding tatters of cloud and tentative starlight. The wind, here in the storm's eye, was light and variable, but to the north a dark brute bulk of cloud was moving in fast. He estimated twenty minutes before it arrived. If he did not find Misi and Dunn and get everyone off the island before the second, more dangerous, wall cloud hit, they were all in serious trouble. The scuff of a footfall behind him told him that his troubles might already have begun.

"Hey! You, over there!" Marik turned slowly. The watch loomed dark at the parapet, limned against the stormy sky, his weapon held at the ready. "Come here!"

Reluctantly, and keenly aware of the needler pointed at his chest, Marik started toward him.

Riker and Cynthia found themselves in what once must have been the garrison commander's quarters. The rooms were open and spacious, the inevitable fireplace large. Riker began pacing, trying to orient himself to the mainland, talking to himself. Cynthia paid him no attention. Though it was dark, she could mark out where the desk must have stood, and she found lighter areas on the wall where she thought rich tapestries must have hung, and said so.

"Maps, more than likely," Riker corrected. He strolled to the center of the room. "Let's see. We came in from the east, docked, and went up the stairs to the south, so that means—" But he never got the chance to say what it meant, for just as that moment, Cynthia found something interesting.

"What's this funny little button?" she asked, and without waiting for an answer, trod on the floor stud that had once rested beneath the commander's desk. Abruptly, the section of flooring that Riker was standing on fell away, and Riker with it. Cynthia saw him drop down the chute, heard his fading yell for the count of *one, two, three,* and then the floor snapped back to its former solidity as if he had never been there.

"Oh, no, you don't!" she expostulated. "You're not leaving *me* here all by myself! You're not getting away with that!" She stomped the floor stud, ran onto the section just as it dropped open, and slid frighteningly fast down the slippery chute, all the long, long way to the bottom. "A-a-a-ce," she wailed, "wait for meeee!" Then the floor closed up again, and all was still.

Marik started across the flagging toward the armed watchman, thinking fast. There was no time to draw his *viith*. The needler would have him before his hand touched the haft. Both *gons* were tucked safely, awkwardly, at the small of his back.

No chance there, either. It would have to be hand-to-hand combat. Nearer now. The guard grinned unexpectedly.

"Look at that!" One arm shot out and pointed over the sea. "Rampers. Look at 'em! Never saw anything like it! It's a mob!" Dozens of long silver bodies were sporting hungrily in the restless sea. One of them called down the wind, a far music above the surf.

Marik nodded wordlessly. After the initial shock he realized that his face was indistinguishable in the darkness, that only his half-seen bushman's gear was familiar. The watch had mistaken him for his relief. All to the good, he thought.

"You're early," the watch remarked, glancing at the luminous face of his ticket, and back at the rampers. "I got a half a hour to go yet."

"Thought I'd give you a break," Marik said evenly, walking up beside him. "Got a drink?"

"Always." The watchman leaned down to fetch a dark bundle at the base of the wall. Two well-placed blows and the man went down like an empty sack.

Marik touched his skull gently. "I fell, Mennon. I saw no one, and I fell," Marik whispered. The man would remember only that he fell while reaching for his tarangi flask. The inevitable headache would corroborate the illusion.

Headache. He touched the side of his head gingerly. If only his own headache would ease off a bit. Back to the business at hand. He pitched the man's needler into the sea below, crossed to the south side of the roof, vaulted the low parapet, and rolled into the shelter of the underbrush.

He waited, listening: there were no cries of alarm, no running footsteps. He hadn't been seen, he thought. So far, so good. He got to his feet and began making his way down the slope toward the water below.

Mennon, panting, finally slowed to a halt, weapon in hand, his bald lieutenant beside him. Marik was nowhere to be seen. This corridor, like every other, was dark and empty. He shook his head in a passion of frustration.

"Gone! I want guards posted everywhere, Ilai. The boat. The steps. Jana's to stay with the child; make sure she's well armed. Post the others around the Citadel, on every floor!

Wherever he is, find him!'' He showed his teeth in a grimace of mirth. ''*I will not lose him now!*'' Mennon growled, biting off each word. "Not this time!" Ilai ran. Mennon remained where he was, considering the sun, and Mishli.

And Marik.

All she had found was the ring.

Audrey, making her way through the myriad upper rooms of the Citadel, at first had found nothing but . . . rooms. Empty, clean stone rectangles, each with its own corner fireplace, most of them giving no information as to what they had been used for. Occasionally she found a clue: spent ammunition casings, a few papers, a coin, but nothing recent that would help her find the Marik child. She kept at it doggedly, prowling the dark halls in her dark clothing, freezing when the occasional guard passed a crossing corridor, and going on.

At last, quite by accident, she made an important discovery. She was searching through a few old papers on the floor of an empty room, when she heard the haunting two-note music she had heard earlier from the Promontory. Crossing quickly to the window, she leaned out and peered into the darkness. The music came again, and she tilted back her head, listening. Leaned out a bit farther, and felt the *viith* slip out of her waistband and go tumbling into the forest below. She grabbed for it, missed—and saw the tower. Above and behind her to the left, it would not be visible to the casual observer. Had she not leaned out, she, too, would have missed it. Strange, she thought. There was no tower, nor access to a tower, in the room she had just left. It puzzled her. Why would there be a tower with no access? She frowned. Or was there? Would it not be the perfect hiding place for a child?

She retraced her steps with growing excitement. The room she entered was small, square, and bare, with a corner fireplace, like all the others; but this room was different, she knew. Somewhere in this ordinary stone room was the access to the tower, and she was determined to find it.

She viewed the room with an artist's eye: the ceiling, like the floor, was seamless rock. No trapdoors, panels, or the like could pierce such solid barriers. The walls betrayed no asymmetry; no faint line delineated one stone from another, hinting

at secret passages; no stone stood differently aside to provide
the slightest handhold, or foothold, for climbing up to—where?
There would be no climbing through the solid stone of the
ceiling. She completed her circuit of the room and dusted her
hands. There *was* no way out except the door. She blew out a
discouraged breath. There went that theory, up the flue, she
thought. Her eyes widened.

Up the flue!

She ran to the fireplace excitedly—*no charcoal, no soot,
there had never been a fire in it!*—and looked up the chimney.
It was no chimney at all, but a passage, and in the light coming
down it, she could see metal cleats in the sidewall to aid a
climber. She crossed herself and, careful of her bad hand,
began to climb.

Audrey entered the tower, and in this one small circular
room, clearly lit by starlight and set off by itself, her search was
rewarded. Although Misi was not here, she found evidences of
a child's presence: a toy *viith*, lying on the floor as though its
owner had just been called home to bed; several old and
desiccated fruit pits; a broken pair of child-sized *zoris* that had
seen hard use.

Not far off, carefully arranged on a flat rock obviously
brought in for that purpose, was displayed a handful of assorted
treasures: seashells laid in ascending order according to size,
several bright feathers, a small model of a skimmercraft like
the real ones her older brothers used to fly when she was small,
and something round that shone in the faint light.

She picked it up. It was a ring, perfect and probably
valuable, for it was heavy for its size, with an ideograph
worked in high relief on its crest: a ring so small it could belong
only to a child. A little boy, probably, for it was a boy's ring,
just as the toys were boy's toys.

She held it closer to the light, trying to puzzle it out, and
deciphered it more quickly than she thought possible. She
smiled softly, her eyes misting as she took in the toys, the
shells, the bright feathers that had captivated a small boy, once
upon a time. "Marik," she said softly in the silence. "It says
'Marik.'" She had found not Marik's child, but his childhood.

She could hardly leave the ring there. He had probably left
it himself, as a boy, and forgotten where it was, and perhaps

had even been disciplined for losing it. He would surely want it back. She dropped it resolutely into her pocket and then took it out again. It could easily fall out and be more lost than ever. Finally, she slipped it onto her finger for safekeeping and, closing the door behind her, resumed her search.

The trees blotted out the faint starlight, made shadow under shadow, their constant dripping vying with the hoarse surf in masking Marik's stealthy footsteps as he made his way down the side of the mountain. Twice he avoided sentinels stationed along the path by keeping to the deepest thickets and moving only when the wind gusted.

Halfway down the slope, he almost walked into a guard standing beside an ancient oak, his silhouette blending with its irregular trunk. He was within arm's reach when Marik brought himself to a halt, and surely would have heard him if a ramper had not just then given tongue, the familiar two notes ringing clearly across the island. The guard turned casually toward the sound.

And Marik, feeling detached and dispassionate, tried a maneuver he had seen Riker use once in a barroom brawl. He tapped the man's shoulder, and when he whirled, delivered a powerful right to the face that bounced him off the tree. He hit the springy wet turf without a sound and did not move, even when Marik frisked him for weapons, which he dropped down the nearest open rock chimney.

Marik felt remotely amused. The urgency he had felt earlier seemed unimportant, and he felt detached even from the pounding headache, the whiff of nausea he was unable to shake. Some far part of his mind kept nagging at him about Anderson's diagnosis. A significant concussion, it kept repeating, but Marik ignored it.

It was nonsense. He had conceived and executed a plan for his own escape and was now in the process of rescuing his child and the others in his party, including the very beautiful and desirable Owdri. Audrey. He had almost kissed her again, there at the cell, and wondered vaguely why he had not. If only the headache would go away.

He had thoroughly enjoyed decking several of the bushmen

and was now on his way to blow up *Oriana*. Taken in context, it was reasonable enough. Logical.

Does that sound to you like a man with a bruised brain, Doctor? he asked Anderson mentally; and the little voice in his head insisted that just such unaccustomed behavior proved the diagnosis. Marik made a quick, negative shake of his throbbing head, stubbornly dismissing the thought as he made his way down the mountain toward the harbor.

It was pitch-dark in the slide, and after his initial yell, Riker clenched his teeth, shot out of the far end of the chute, and hit the wet, slick stone floor, sliding fast and striking his spine just above the kidneys on something hard. It brought him to a sudden stop, and he lay there for a moment, seeing bright lights inside his head and wheezing for breath. The air was wet and fetid and something ran quickly across his foot. Time to get up, Paulo. He pulled himself gasping to his feet just in time for a screaming projectile to hit him just behind the knees, and he went down again in a tangle of limbs, noise, and stagnant water.

For a nightmare moment they struggled, then: "Ace?" quavered Cynthia's voice in the dark. "Is . . . is that you? Please be you!" Riker let go of her throat and got up wearily.

"It's me," he returned tiredly, pulling her to her feet. "And it certainly is you." He tried to rub the bruise over his kidneys but it was too sensitive to touch. There was the sound as of a piece of furniture moving slightly, and Cynthia cried out sharply, "Ouch! I think I broke my toe! And this floor is all cold and horrible!" He remembered that she was barefoot.

"Stand still, Miss Jessen," he told her. "Let's get our bearings." He thought fast. "You started a fire in the cell up above. Do you have a light?"

"Self-strikes. And only two left."

He tried the first cigarette on the wall, but it collapsed into a soggy mass after the first couple of swipes. "Let me have the other one." He felt around in the dark for the object Cynthia had stubbed her foot against, assured himself that it was some sort of table, reached under it, and struck the cigarette on its relatively dry wooden surface. It flared to life, revealing the dismal room.

"A dungeon!" Cynthia cried. "Omigod, we're in an alien dungeon! This is priceless! The girls are never going to believe this in a million years!"

"The girls are never going to get to hear about it, if we don't get out of here," Riker retorted. "See if you can find something to burn." There was a piece of cloth lying in a corner, ancient and damp, but flammable after a fashion. It lit up the room enough to let Riker find several pieces of wood (table legs, after he upended the table, a wooden box, which he splintered to tinder) and start a lively, warming fire on the table's dry underside. The voice startled them.

"Hey! Stop that! What do you think you're doing?"

There was a rattle at the door and it swung wide to reveal a large and ugly guard with an equally large and ugly needler at the ready. "Put your hands up," he commanded.

Riker rose slowly, ready for anything—except Cynthia's next line.

"Hi, loser. Bring the marshmallows?" she greeted the guard casually, reaching into the fire and moving a stick or two. "Here—catch!" Still smiling, she flipped a burning brand at him with deceptive speed, and he juggled the scorching wood, making his first shot go wild.

At the same moment the brand left Cynthia's hand, Riker catapulted into action, grabbing the needler in an iron grip. The second charge whispered past Riker's ear as he hauled it around by main force, wrenched it out of the man's control (although not out of his hand), and slapped him across the bridge of the nose with the barrel. The man swayed where he stood, his grip relaxing. Cynthia assisted by swatting him over the head with a sizable piece of table leg, and the man crumpled to the floor. Riker gave her an offended scowl. "I was doing just fine."

"You're welcome." She picked up the needler, holding it backward, and started poking at it. "How does this thing work?" Riker made a grab for it, for she was looking down the muzzle.

"Here, don't touch that—!" Her hand closed over the stud and there was the spiteful whisper of the weapon discharging. She startled, then laughed and handed the empty needler to him.

"I guess it's out of ammunition," she apologized. "Good thing, eh?" Riker stared at her for a long, contemplative moment without answering, and she stood glaring with growing indignation.

"That's not funny, Ace. I could have been killed. Just because I'm a good sport—!"

"Keep it down, sport, or we'll both get killed." Riker, busy searching the guard, found no weapons, even the usual *viith*, but he came across a hand torch and thrust it in a thigh pocket of his bush fatigues. Then he tore the man's jacket into strips and bound his hands and feet securely.

Cynthia was standing nearby in the dying firelight and Riker had the opportunity to reflect yet again that she had probably the best pair of legs in this part of the galaxy. Aloud, he said merely, "If you're cold, I can get you his pants." She took an astounded step backward.

"Me? Wear his pants? Are you out of your mind? I could catch something!"

"Pneumonia, if you stay like that," he pointed out, finishing his task and standing up.

"I'll risk it." She eyed his handiwork and approved. "All right. Now what?" He switched on the torch and carefully stamped out the remains of their fire.

"Now we find a way out to the sea."

There was a classic grace about *Oriana*. She rode the slow, deep swells in the brimming harbor with a majestic balance that was beautiful to behold. Just below him, where the trees were beginning to thin out in earnest, Marik could see not only *Oriana*'s clean profile at the jetty, but the black hulk of the *byela* at the far end of the harbor, torches bobbing as guards patrolled the swamped beaches, and the steady warm light pouring from the windows of the guardhouse.

Light. The *lighted* guardhouse. He had found the sign he was looking for.

And Misi.

After the initial flush of satisfaction, Marik realized that he was going to need a diversion to draw attention away from the baby so that he could rescue her. He would get only one chance, and he'd have to make it count, for there was that nasty, open expanse of beach between the shelter of the trees and the harbor, not to mention the well-armed guards on the jetty.

He frowned. Strange. He should have thought of this before. He knew she'd be guarded, didn't he? What was the matter with him? His mind was working in slow motion. The thought troubled him.

He dragged himself back to the problem at hand. The explosives. He had explosives in his fatigue pockets. He could use the explosives, or some of them, to lure the bushmen away. If he set them in sequence, he mused, set them to go off as though they were climbing the mountain *toward* the Citadel, while in reality he made his way to the beach . . .

He began spinning an idea, and it was a good one, but it would involve climbing all the way up to the Citadel. He calculated he had perhaps fifteen minutes to get his people away from the island. In fifteen minutes, the wall cloud would hit, and with it, the wind-blown surge of perilously high water he was counting on to get them out of the Narrows. Otherwise they would be just another wreck and all would be lost. He marked the ominous curved clouds converging upon the island from the north. Time was scarce, and there was still much to do.

He began making his way up the mountainside as fast as he could go.

"You are an imprudent man, my friend." Kles Mennon smiled over his wineglass. He handed a filled glass to his guest, who stirred uncomfortably on the packing crate and did not mention the strange proximity of wineglasses to rough wooden crates. From the look of him, Mennon would probably never be far from crystal and a selection of fine wines, even in a ruin such as the Citadel.

"Imprudent? How so?" he inquired.

"You talk too much, under stress. Several times, you were on the brink of letting Marik's people know our plan. I'm afraid you are a careless man—and a very foolish one."

"I did not, however, spoil your plan." His guest sat back against a smaller crate and regarded Kles Mennon with a superior air. "And presently, sir, I will be a very *rich*, 'very foolish man.' Assuming you pay as well as you promise.'' He finished his wine and, uninvited, poured himself a second glass of burgundy.

Mennon sobered. He held up a leather courier's satchel and let it swing slowly in front of the man's eyes. ''You'll get your pay, when all of my prisoners are safely in a cell again.''

''If your men can find them,'' his guest smirked complacently. ''Are you sure you have enough people to cover the exits?''

''I have men on every level of this Citadel, and men on the shore besides.''

''Then you expected an escape!''

''No,'' Mennon smiled, ''I prepared for the unexpected.'' His eyes clouded as he contemplated Marik. ''I just didn't take my preparations far enough, that's all.''

''Well, that doesn't concern me,'' said the man on the crate. ''I did my part. Now you owe me what's in that satchel, Mr. Mennon, as per our agreement.'' Mennon nodded curtly.

''The money to be deposited in a Xhole bank in a numbered account, just as we agreed.'' He tossed it contemptuously onto the floor. His guest followed it with his eyes.

''That's right. I've already given your man the account number. I wouldn't want to have to explain a big deposit to my associates—or to anyone else, either!'' He took a deep draught of his wine, and Mennon lifted his brows.

''I'd be careful of too much of that. You still have a job to finish before you're home safe.''

''Job?'' the man demanded truculently. ''I did my job! I let your people into the back of the Palace, I rigged the intercom for your bugging device, I even helped you capture Marik and Captain Riker! What more do you want?''

''You misunderstand, my friend,'' Mennon instructed. ''I'm not referring to your, ah, invaluable services to me.'' He poured himself another glass of wine. ''I was referring to your *heroic* intention of capturing a skein of ramper brats for your museum.''

''University,'' the Erthlik corrected sullenly. ''And I don't see it as *heroic*. Perhaps for the layman the adjective applies, but for a man such as myself, it should be a piece of cake.''

Mennon, sipping his wine, reflected that his guest would be

extremely fortunate ever to set foot on the mainland again, but he kept his own counsel.

Someone had seen her. She was sure of it. As she turned the last corner, Audrey could hear footsteps following, not hurrying, but keeping pace with her, as if to see where she went. She had to lose them. She had to get away, to help Priyam Marik find the child he had called Missy. Misi. However you said it, it was sweet. Would she have Marik's steady gray eyes? she wondered, and then dismissed the thought as irrelevant.

There was a distinct scuff in the darkness behind her. There was no mistaking it now. Someone *was* after her. She walked faster, as quietly as she could. Don't run. Don't panic. Keep your wits about you, Audrey, my girl.

Another hall, another quick turn, and there, the faintest of lights shining out from under a door left ajar (by some long-dead soldier, she thought, who had been guarding the emperor's coastline). Probably starlight shining through. That would be good, she thought, making a determined effort to remain calm. She could do with a bit of light.

She hurried through the door and shut it quietly, listening with an ear pressed to it as the footsteps went stealthily past. Heaved a relieved sigh. Turned to the room.

Kles Mennon was sitting relaxed on the corner of a crate, a wineglass in his hand, smiling at her not unkindly. "Why, my dear Mrs. Lassiter," he greeted her sardonically. "How kind of you to join us—isn't it, Mr. Dunn?"

"Without a doubt," smirked Marlowe Dunn. "Without a doubt."

They were near sea level. The sound of heavy waves was close outside and the walls of yet another cell glistened wetly under Riker's steadily weakening torch, revealing a barred black slit of a window, manacles hanging from wall chains (theatrical, Cynthia decided), and an unsavory-looking blanket wadded up on a rude plank bunk. It crumbled to dust as Riker touched it, and Cynthia backed into the shadows, waving her hands to fend off the musty particles. She stumbled and sat down hard on what felt like a pile of kindling. "Ow!"

"*Will* you be quiet!" Riker whispered urgently. "You'll have the whole gang down on us!"

"Sorry!" She flung it at him like a spoiled egg, rubbing her bruised bottom and feeling behind her for purchase to lever herself up. Her hand encountered what felt like a small, bony soccer ball, and she picked it up—and catapulted off the floor and into Riker's arms with a shriek. "A sk—— a head, a human head," she babbled, her fingers splayed against his chest. "That's a . . . a bare *skull* over there and it isn't *with* anybody! It's just standing there, all by itself with those bones! A head!"

He tried to comfort her, between her outbursts, but she would have none of it. "*Shh!* Miss Jessen, be quiet, it's— Cynthia, it's all right, it's not really a head, with hair and everyth——" Riker's patience, never his best resource, gave out. He grabbed her shoulders and shook her sharply. "*Dammit, Cynthia!*" he snapped. "Will *you shut up*!"

He saw the wildness go out of her eyes before she closed them and relaxed against him, still sobbing raggedly. She hugged him close for one long, shuddering breath, and he put his arms around her protectively. "You all right?" She swallowed convulsively and nodded once.

"I'm sorry," she whispered. "I . . . I'm fine, really, I'm— It just scared me for a minute, that's all." She smiled up at Riker, fragrant of soot and Chanel and stagnant water, and he cleared his throat and gave her what he hoped was a brotherly pat on the shoulder.

"No problem," he said gruffly.

She straightened up, smoothed her disheveled hair, and soberly considered the skull, who grinned back. "Poor slob," she sympathized, "I wonder who he was?"

"Probably some tourist who waited too long to get out of here," Riker retorted. "Come on."

He crossed to the door, motioned her to stay close behind him, and eased out into the corridor, carefully checking both directions and marking the incongruous presence of a chair a few feet down the way, which hinted at the recent presence of a guard. He glanced back to say as much to Cynthia, but she was nowhere to be seen. A knot clenched at his belly. If something had happened to her—! "Cynthia!" he whispered hoarsely. "Where are you?"

"Here," came the whispered shout from inside the cell.

Muttering vehemently under his breath, Riker eased back down the corridor and peered into the cell. "What—are—you—doing—in—there?" he hissed exasperatedly.

"I'm putting him back together. It's the least I could do. Hey, you want to shine that light in here? I can't see a thing!"

"No, I don't want—!" His annoyance peaked and he commanded, as if she were one of his crew, "Get out here, Mister! On the double!" After a long pause she emerged reluctantly, wincing as he made a sharp, sudden gesture with his thumb toward the corridor.

"I was only trying to—" she began, but he made the thumb jerk again, warning her to silence with a scowl, and they started off again, this time with Cynthia in the lead. He was feeling a bit better when behind them, Riker heard the distinct sound of someone approaching. Dousing his torch, he grabbed Cynthia around the waist with one hand and the mouth with the other, dragged her back into the cell, and shouldered the door shut, just as the guard appeared.

They could see him through the narrow grille as he sauntered to the slit window at the end of the hall and back again, paused at the cell door, eyed it speculatively, and reached for his *viith*. Cynthia's eyes shone wetly, wildly over Riker's restraining hand, and she gestured excitedly at the guard with both hands, there in the darkness, but Riker shook his head urgently. *Hush. Wait.*

The guard sat down in the chair, tipped it back against the wall, and, resting his needler on his knees, began cleaning his fingernails with the tip of his *viith*, whistling tunelessly to himself.

Cynthia relaxed weakly and Riker slowly, slowly released her mouth, warning her yet again to silence with a gesture. She nodded and whispered immediately, "How are we going to get out of—" He clapped his hand on her mouth again and pointed an imperative finger at a spot some three centimeters from her nose. She shrugged apologetically. Under his hand he could feel her smile. She licked his palm and he jerked his hand away and wiped it on his fatigues.

And, despite himself, he began to laugh. He stifled it as best
he could, but suddenly everything—the abduction, the escape,
even Cynthia, standing there in nothing but a bushman's shirt
and bare feet—was unbearably funny. Try as he might, he
could not prevent a sustained low chuckling escaping him and
echoing eerily around the cell and the corridor beyond.

The guard glanced up and down the hall, frowning. Waited.
Then, as Riker controlled his laughter by a supreme effort of
the will, slowly resumed cleaning his nails. He was not
whistling anymore, but peering out from under his brows, wary
and listening. Riker decided to give him something more to
listen to.

Stationing Cynthia in the corner behind the door, he began to
stalk slowly up and down the cell, bringing his heels down
hard. His steps rang hollowly on the stone, and they heard the
front legs of the chair hit the floor outside.

"Who's there?" demanded the guard. "Advance and be
recognized." They saw him pass the grille to peer down dark
hallways that led off into gloom. He came back. Looked
around uneasily. "Anybody there?" After another long pause,
he sat gingerly. Sleeved his *viith*. Checked the charge on his
needler.

Riker began walking again, a slow measured tread under-
scored by the sound of the sea. The guard jumped up and
squinted into the cell. Riker flattened beside the door as a lance
of light stabbed nervously around the cell, paused at the
skeleton, and swept the cell again before disappearing.

Again, Riker paced in long, slow steps, accompanied this
time by a mournful low moan that echoed repeatedly in a kind
of unearthly fugue. He barely made it to the door before it
slammed open, the bushman filling the frame, and as it swung,
Riker jumped out at him yelling sophomorically, "Boo!"
Cynthia screeched in unison, and the startled guard leapt back
reflexively. Before he could collect himself, Riker followed a
short left to the midsection with a beautiful roundhouse right to
the jaw that dropped him where he stood.

Riker scowled at Cynthia, rubbing his knuckles. "This time
stick with me," he ordered, and again eased out into the
corridor. Probably nobody else around, he decided, or they

would have come when the guard called out. It was reasonable to assume that the coast was clear.

"Get ready to make a run for it," he warned over his shoulder, and gained the side hall. He checked it out in both directions, sprinted across, and resumed his sneak down the long, dark corridor. At least there was something positive about Cynthia: she moved quietly, he had to give her that. He hadn't heard a sound. Maybe she was learning her lesson.

"We're not doing too badly, eh?" he offered in a confidential whisper. There was no answer. He had a horrible thought. He stopped. Whirled. She was not there.

He found her in the cell, kneeling next to the recumbent guard. "Oh, hi, Ace," she chortled, unimpressed by his exasperation.

"Take a look at this." She had snuggled the skeleton up against the guard, its skull resting cozily under his chin, its arm across his chest, hand on his heart. "That ought to get his blood going again."

Ignoring the idea of just how funny the guard's reaction was going to be when he woke up, Riker employed his considerable control and became very military. "Miss Jessen," he told her firmly, pulling her to her feet, "in case you haven't noticed, we are running for our lives. We don't have time for fun and games with a skeleton." She leaned against him, her arm across his chest, hand on his heart exactly as she had arranged the skeleton. Her hand was warm and felt wonderful.

"How about with each other?" she purred. "Little fun? Few games? Hm?" Not dignifying her comment with an answer, Captain Paul W. Riker grabbed her hand off his chest and led her determinedly out of the cell and off toward the steps, the sea, and freedom.

Marik lay very still. The dripping bush barely concealed him as he lay flat against the soggy leaf mold on the mountain, listening to the two guards talking about him.

"I know I saw somebody sneaking around over here," the one insisted, and the other made a snort of derision.

"Probably a tree. Or a shadow."

"Yeah, a shadow of the man I saw." He stepped closer, his boot pinning Marik's sleeve to the forest floor. He shifted his weight, pinching Marik's arm. "I tell you he was right here."

The other man's voice was bored. "Well, he's not here now. I think you're lookin' for that reward, that's what I think."

The bush boot lifted; the guards left. Their voices faded. Marik waited the slow count of fifty before he dared get on his way again. It had been too close, he told himself. He must be more careful. Then again, time was so short.

He reached the great oak, where he had decked the sentinel, in record time after that. The man was just pulling himself to his feet, bracing himself against the tree with one hand and shaking his head groggily, when Marik arrived. With a feeling of calm inevitability, he came up behind the sentinel and tapped his shoulder once more. Again he spun, again Marik let go with a short right to the center of the face, and again the man flopped limply onto the turf.

Marik continued his ascent, positioning a timed packet of explosives every twenty yards, each set to go off fifteen seconds after the preceding charge, until he reached the south parapet. Setting the timer to go off in ten minutes, he flung the sealed packet over the wall and, as fast as he could, sliding on wet pine needles and losing his footing only to regain it hearts-stopping seconds later, retraced his steps down the mountain.

He was nearing the great oak when he became aware of a presence nearby. He halted, listening. Someone else was here. Riker? Audrey? More probably a bushman. There! A footstep! A twig snapped behind him and someone tapped *him* ponderously on the shoulder.

With instant joyful recognition, Marik wheeled and threw the short, vicious punch simultaneously, catching his assailant— the sentinel—dead center on his strangely spongy nose. With a pitiful whimper of defeat, the man struck the sodden turf underfoot for the third time and lay still.

The first explosion stunned the air below. Its fireball revealed armed men running toward it, someone shouting orders, even a couple of sentries running helter-skelter down the mountainside, toward the action. Marik joined them, keeping well to the west and veering sharply away seconds later, when the second explosion went off exactly on time. A bushman appeared behind him, hurrying down the mountain, needler ready. "See anybody?" Marik asked, feigning excitement. "What's going on?"

"It's the Marik! It's got to be! He's coming up the mountain!" he shouted, and Marik yelled back, "I'll head him off!" The man ran into the cover of the trees and Marik headed for the harbor.

Kles Mennon slowly stood up, regarding the lovely young Erthlik at the door with a connoiseur's admiration. "Do come in, Mrs. Lassiter," he invited courteously. "Please don't stand on ceremony." He followed her gaze. "Ah. You've met Professor Dunn, I see."

"Yes."

There was something of the brave child about her, although it was obvious that she was at least cautious. Very possibly frightened. Mennon's hearts warmed, despite himself. Ah, Kles, you fool, he said to himself, you've always been soft on the gentry. His own father. Marik. Mishli. And now this one. This Mrs. Lassiter.

She was carrying it off well. Regal bearing. Natural good breeding. Even in borrowed sleepwear, she might have been holding court. It was always pleasant, dealing with gentry. Civilized.

It was Mennon's custom to miss nothing, and he noticed, even as she stood at the door, an addition to her hand. She had been wearing no jewelry when she arrived, but now a gold hoop glistened on her finger. Interesting. He lifted her unresisting hand and examined the ring, familiar from long ago. Marik's ring. He remembered the day Dao had received it. And the day it had turned up missing. Now it was on Mrs. Lassiter's hand. He met her eyes and she made no explanation, simply withdrew her hand and held his gaze. *Quel*, but she was beautiful for an alien, he thought. He had always been soft on the gentry.

Perhaps Marik felt the same way, he mused, although in Marik's case this affinity for his own sort would be subliminal, rather than a learned art. Kind calling to kind. Marik and Mishli. And now—he lifted his brows at the new idea—Marik and Audrey Lassiter? He smiled slowly to himself. What an extraordinary concept, he thought. What a marvelous discovery.

He crossed to the door and opened it slightly. "Well done, Mouse. She's here and safe. Now find me the Marik." A murmur of assent from the hall, and the footsteps padded away.

Her chin lifted proudly, and her tight little smile was triumphant. "You've caught me, Mr. Mennon, but *he* escaped! Good for him!"

Mennon regarded her through slitted tiger yellow eyes for a thoughtful moment and pursed his lips. "Good for him," he echoed, "yes. But what for you, Mrs. Lassiter? What for you?" He had meant it to frighten her, to establish dominance, if nothing else; but she surprised him by walking confidently into the room and seating herself gracefully on a low crate.

"For me? A glass of wine would be in order, I think," she told him, meeting his eyes steadily. "White, if you have it, please." She utterly ignored Dunn.

Kles Mennon smiled his charming white smile despite himself. "All we have in the white is a Riesling. I trust that will suffice?"

Audrey regarded him cooly. "Thank you, yes." He poured the wine and handed it to her. "Did he tell you he was married?" he taunted softly.

"It wouldn't matter one way or the other. *I* am married." He smiled bitterly.

"He killed her." Her shock was mildly satisfactory, even though she recovered quickly.

"Hardly. A man like Mister Marik—"

"He's a coward! He abandoned his wife to save his own worthless hide. And how did she die? No quick pulser bolt, no *viith* across the throat. No, no. Nothing so merciful as that. He left her alone on a planet that vaporized when its own sun went nova." She studied her wine.

"So you are a liar as well as a thief and a kidnapper, Mr. Mennon." She sipped delicately. "How disappointing. You have no redeeming qualities at all." He reopened the wine bottle.

"May I freshen your glass?" As he returned her glass, their fingertips met. She dropped her eyes, then lifted them and smiled right at him.

At first, he thought the sound was inside his head. A throb of admiration there, like those in his hearts, even though she was merely an alien, and an Erthlik at that. The second and the third *poom!* might have been the pounding of the surf. But each succeeding detonation, thudding its way upward, brought him nearer an awareness that suddenly surfaced.

"Those sound like explosions," he muttered, then, as the realization hit him, he whirled on Audrey. She met his eyes evenly, sipping her wine.

"Marik!" he breathed, astonished.

"Just so," she agreed, and calmly splashed her glassful of wine into his eyes at close range. Mennon grabbed his face with both hands, shouting, "Ilai! Mouse!" Groping for his prisoners, he stumbled clumsily around the room, tripping over crates. A bottle fell and shattered noisily. There was another, closer, explosion. Audrey flew to the door. No one was outside yet. "Hurry, Mr. Dunn! They're waiting for us!"

With a strange expression on his face, Dunn snatched up a leather shoulder bag, such as Einai couriers carried, and followed her down the dark corridors at a run.

Even as Marik boarded *Oriana,* with the sealed, waterproof explosives heavy in the pockets of his fatigues, he regretted what he was about to do. He and Kles had helped the workmen build *Oriana,* and with Mishli, they had sailed her around half the continent, before the war. Destroying her would put the final punctuation at the end of an era. But *Oriana* was of no use as an escape vessel, for the others could never have boarded her unseen, and compared to the slow, unwieldly old *byela*, she would have been too dangerous a pursuit craft.

There was no other way. *Oriana* would have to go.

He made his way below, pulling out the explosives as he went. *Oriana* was a boat, no more, no less. Only a boat, and not even that for much longer. He began setting the timers on the paks.

It had been easy to get aboard. Trot down the shore, cross the beach, jog along the jetty, and climb the ladder. The bush gear made him familiar, and therefore inconspicuous. They saw him, but no one noticed. They were all charging up the hill, needlers primed and ready. The sentinel leaned down to give him a hand up, and Marik said curtly, "Relief."

"But I don't have a re—" A hand jerk on his arm, a mighty splash, and the bushman was a seagoing creature.

"Sorry, friend," Marik called from *Oriana*'s deck. "Need help? No? Well, better get onto the jetty," he advised chummily. "It's crawling with rampers down there."

Even as he spoke, a long, sinuous body rose from the dark depths a few meters away and submerged again, flukes slapping the water smartly, and the man scrambled for the shore, yelling that Marik was here, *here,* but his shouts were lost in the larger sounds of the storm, the excitement, and the strobing chaos of the explosions.

Mennon could hardly see Mouse and Ilai even as he spoke, for his eyes were tearing profusely, and he kept wiping them with his sleeve. "Get the men down to the harbor! Don't let Marik get aboard *Oriana,* Mouse. She's their only way out of here, and he'll try it, if I know Marik! Ilai, you know what to do with the child. Go."

Mouse left immediately, but the shaven-headed man hesitated. "But, Mennon—"

"We knew this was an alternative when we brought her here, Ilai. Now! Before Marik finds her! *Go!*"

Reluctantly, Ilai left.

Marik finished setting the timers, quickly packing *Oriana*'s cabin with explosives timed to go off every ten seconds for two full minutes. Even should they fall into the water, he knew, these new high-grade combustives would go off as planned, sending out shock waves that would panic bushmen and discourage rampers as well.

It would be yet another diversionary tactic, he thought. If all went as planned, he could get his party off the island before the wall cloud hit. *If* Riker could get the others to the *byela* in time. And if he could get to Misi. That would be the next job. Getting to Misi.

Several bushmen had evidently heard the sentinel at last. As he came up on deck, Marik could see them pounding down the jetty, looking back at the explosions as if they could scarcely believe that he was not on the mountain. Keeping the coach top between them, he let himself into the water on the harbor side of *Oriana*. The sea was warm and black and heaving, with deep troughs even here in the sheltered harbor. He could only guess what the open sea would be like. A silver shape arrowed past in the darkness far below, only barely glimpsed before it broke water some distance away, swashing the water with loud trumpeting and the gnashing of teeth. There were yells of alarm from the beach sentinels, and Marik, treading water in the ramper-infested harbor, would like to have gone ashore down the beach from the melee.

But the sentinels were alerted now, and the beach was flat and empty. It would be worth his life to chance crossing it. Marik realized his dilemma: if he tried for the guardhouse, any bushman with half an eye could pick him off. Needlers had incredible range and accuracy, for what they were. And he could never stay where he was, for the explosions from *Oriana* were about to blow her—and everything near her—sky high. Marik, old man, he told himself, you've got a problem.

Riker stopped short in the dark corridor and lifted his head. "Listen!" he hissed, and Cynthia said, "I don't hear any—"

"*Shh!*" A pause. "I heard it before, a couple of—" And they heard it again, a dull *poom!*, closer now, that shook faintly the foundations of the Citadel itself. *Poom! Poom!*

"There it is," Cynthia breathed. "Three . . . four . . ."

Riker grabbed her arm. "The explosion! We've got to get out to the boat! Oh, God, good sweet God, how do we get out of here?"

As if in answer to his question, another explosion went off just outside the wall. The roar was incredible, a thundering cacophony of biblical proportions that knocked them off their feet. Riker fetched up hard, slamming his bruised kidneys against the opposite wall. Cynthia screamed shrilly as she went down. Great stones flew, a spray of mortar and dust stung them sharply, and as they watched, a hole the size of a hangar door rumbled open in the side of the wall. They helped each other to their feet and stared at it. There, only a few yards beyond the veils of floating dust, they could see the forest, and freedom, and the menacing sky.

"Now, that was impressive," Cynthia said in an awestruck

tone. "I mean, I'm really impressed by that one, Ace." She
turned to him, more sincere than he had ever seen her. "That
was practically a religious experience! How'd you *do* that?"

"Oh, *would* you shut up!" Riker ground out, and, grabbing
her wrist, pulled her with him over the tumulus, out of the
opening in the Citadel wall, and into the safety of the midnight
forest.

The ramper itself solved Marik's problem for him. It
beached itself unexpectedly and was thrashing around on the
sand, snapping viciously at anyone who came near. Several of
the bushmen were firing at it, but they succeeded only in
wounding it, which enraged it further. The two guards were
clattering clumsily aboard *Oriana*. Men were climbing up the
mountainside through the darkness of the trees. The sky was
heavy and ominous, with lightning flailing at the stars.

No one was paying attention to the guardhouse.

The trumpet bellowed, slapping the wet sand with its fanned
pectoral fins, and rearing skyward. Watching his chance, Marik
waited until the ramper reared again, then sprinted across the
deserted beach, expecting to hear momentarily the spiteful hiss
of a needler. Someone yelled and he tensed, but the man was
calling someone else. He stumbled in the soft sand, caught
himself, and went on, his footsteps loud and rasping in the
coarse, wet, grit. Any minute someone would hear him. Any
minute a needler would whisper good-bye to Dao Marik. Any
minute he would have Misi in his arms. It seemed an eon
before he reached the guardhouse.

It was a small stone building, solidly made. One side backed
against the mountain; the other, windowed, side, overlooked the jetty. Its door faced the harbor entrance, and he
flattened against the outer wall beside it. Drew his *gon*. Tried
the knob slowly, gingerly. Unlocked. That was peculiar. The
lights were on, but the door was left unlocked. They must be
pretty sure of themselves, he thought.

Two steps took him inside. It was empty. Misi was not there,
but there was evidence on the battered desk that she had been
there: a milk mug, a toy memlikt, a fuzzy pink blanket. Bitterly
disappointed, he picked it up, smelling the sweet baby smell of

it, and almost missed the sense of *presence* that brought him around sharply.

In the doorway stood the giant, his face still raw from the scalding coffee. He slammed the door behind him.

"Where is she?" Marik demanded. The giant shook his head sadly.

"Too late," he said. "You came too late. Baby gone now."

Outside, Marik heard the trumpeting of hungry rampers.

Audrey and Dunn plunged down the spiral stairs at a dead run and hit the beach without breaking stride. From every direction came the confusion of bushmen hurrying to scale the mountain, the explosions going off with frightening regularity, and the trumpeting of rampers over the crashing surf. The water in the harbor was rising visibly as the wall cloud approached.

"Who's waiting—for us?" Dunn panted as they ran awkwardly together through the coarse blue sand. "I can't go dashing off—unless I know what I'm doing!"

"Captain Riker—Priyam Marik—Cynthia," she named them between breaths as she ran, "and—hopefully—his baby! Marik's baby!"

"Where?" he persisted, jerking her to a rough halt. "Where are we supposed to meet?"

"The fishing boat," she panted. "Please—let go of my arm, we have to hurry!"

"The fishing-*byela*," he repeated. "Of course. Let's go then!" She kicked off her shoes for ease in negotiating the deep sand, and they fled toward the *byela* looming at the end of the harbor.

Mennon stumbled onto the rampart, eyes and nose streaming, leaning his hands on the parapet and bowing his head. Even with his burning eyes shut, he could see beach and forest alive with running men, garishly lit by the explosions slowly walking up the mountain toward him. One went off against the west wall of the Citadel, and he could see his men converging on the site. "Not here," he muttered to them. "Not the mountain, you fools! *It's Oriana!* He's after the boat!" He lifted his head and, clenching the air with his fist, roared suddenly at them, *"Not here! Oriana! Oriana!"*

She blew.

The bushmen had forgotten the fishing *byela* moored at the end of the harbor, near the narrow rocky outlet between the island proper and its ancillary arm (known as "the Jaw"), whose forested peaks hid the harbor from the mainland. The outlet gave onto the sea from the back and was clogged to just a few feet under the surface by the wreckage of boats that had failed to negotiate its slim, tortuous passage.

Knowing this, Mennon's men had discounted the possibility of anyone's escape through the Narrows. *Oriana*'s length would prevent her passage, even if her keel would have permitted it; and the wrecks were so near the surface that even the *byela*'s shallow draft would snag. No, they told themselves, there was no possibility of escape. They had no idea that anyone would cross the mountain parallel to the beach, descend at the hinge of 'the Jaw,' board the *byela*, and wait for a hurricane to help them escape.

By the time Riker lifted Cynthia aboard, the fishing boat was rocking hard in the heavy, rising seas, her mast a pendulum against the angry sky. The earlier starlight had disappeared and the darkness was all but tangible. The air felt electric and portentous. Cynthia, peering down the beach, shivered involuntarily. Riker, below, was feeling his way through an engine check. "Looks like she's as ready as she's going to be," he called. "See anything yet?"

"I—I think I hear someone coming." She lowered her voice. "I'm sure of it, Ace. And they're running! I can hear them running!"

"Get below! Come on, I'll give you a hand—"

"But why? I don't want to go down that hole! I'll bet they have bugs down there!"

"Because if it's not one of us, you could get very dead, very fast!" he snapped. *"Move!"*

She tumbled past him into the cramped, stuffy cabin that smelled of old fish, mold, and sweat, while Riker snatched up a gaff, sprang to the deck, and gained the rail. He could just barely see a figure making for the boat at a run. Relieved, he lowered the gaff and called, "Marik! Over here!" The figure veered toward him, but there was something about it not quite right. "It's Marik—right?" he persisted, and the man dropped to one knee and squeezed off a near miss. Riker hit the deck and rolled hard against the gunwale.

"Wrong," he said ruefully to himself. "It's not Marik."

Marik moved around almost casually, keeping the battered old desk between himself and the giant. The anger kept growing, and he felt no need to curb it. It was, he felt, just and justified.

"Has Mennon killed my child?" he asked evenly. The giant made no answer but feinted to one side of the desk and jumped ponderously to the other. Marik vaulted the desk easily and landed with both feet on the chair. His head was now level with that of the giant, and he sank slowly until he was squatting on his heels. "Is she alive?" he persisted. The giant made no answer, but his mind flicked involuntarily to the child, and Marik felt a surge of exultation. The mental impression had been crystal-clear. "The landing strip!" he exclaimed. "He has her at the landing strip!"

The giant blurted, "How did you know? Ilai just moved her there!"

Marik was spared an answer by the violent coruscation at the end of the jetty, as *Oriana* exploded with a shattering roar. The window blew in, showering them with glass, and as the giant startled, Marik picked up the heavy desk chair and hit him with all his strength. He went down on all fours across the doorway, shaking his great head like a dog, and Marik took the only other way out of the room. Backing against the far wall as a second explosion rocked the area, he dove through the open window, rolled, and gained his feet, ready to sprint down the strand; but in the same unlikely moment a section of stout plank, flung spinning from the exploding *Oriana*, glanced off his back and struck him down. He crumpled to the ground, gasping for breath.

Stunned, he was aware only of the iodine stink of the wet sand against his face, the pelting of the rain, and the hollow, burning ache at the small of his back.

For a long while he simply lay there, viewing the activity

around him as if through the wrong end of a telescope. He felt the overpowering need to sleep. Lazy thoughts floated slowly upward and burst leisurely inside his throbbing head; others raced impetuously about in no order at all.

Hard on the heels of *No pursuit* came the thought *Misi is alive! At the landing strip! Alive!* Somewhere, far off, he felt elation, but he was too exhausted to sustain it.

Audrey and Dunn were racing toward the *byela*, but though he wanted terribly to rise and run with them, he could only lay there, even when the giant started toward them across the beach.

Her legs ached, she had a stitch in her side, and Audrey thought she must stop running or die. Yet she kept up desperately with Dunn's long, tireless stride. Explosion after explosion went off, lighting the harbor and the lowering sky, but Dunn pounded on, Audrey racing behind him. The fishing boat, a dark hulk at the end of the water, seemed almost as close as the small stone building backed against the mountain off to her right; but it was as if she were on a stage, with the scenery standing still and she, running madly in place, getting nowhere. Huge drops of warm seawater pelted them from the erupting harbor, soaking them to the skin. The sand was deep and soft and hell to run through. Her lungs felt on fire, her face icy.

In the light and noise and confusion of the explosions, the sudden looming presence of the giant directly in front of them, barring their way, made Audrey gasp, and she tried to shear off, but she stumbled. Dunn stopped short and, as she blundered into his back, he thrust her with all his strength into the giant's grasp.

With the enemy thus encumbered, Dunn darted around him and escaped down the beach, toward the fishing *byela* and safety.

The lurid glare of explosions silhouetted the armed bushman, and Riker decided to try and take him. Odds were about even, he thought, for a Riker with a gaff and anyone else with an automatic weapon. It was worth the try. With Cynthia safely below, he could take the chance.

He flung himself over the side into the rapidly rushing water, wallowing his way to a precarious foothold on the slippery rocks. Another explosion glared against the sky, and as it faded, he thought he heard the report of a gun, but could not be sure. There was so much noise.

"Don't shoot!" cried a familiar voice, presently accompanied by the sound of someone splashing clumsily into the water. "Don't shoot, it's I, Marlowe Dunn!"

Riker stood suddenly, gaff ready. Glanced quickly up and down the beach. "Get down! There's a man out there with a pulser!" Dunn looked fey.

"I didn't see anyone," he said. "Come on! We have to get out of here! Look at the sky!"

Riker had no need to look at the sky. He knew all too well that the wall cloud was upon them. The tons of restless water built up in the harbor had told him as well as any meteorologist might have done. "Where are the others? Marik and Mrs. Lassiter? And the baby?"

Dunn, standing there in the furious rush of the water, turned innocent eyes upon him. "Dead," he said sadly. "All three of them. I saw it myself."

The last explosion, down the beach, was the lesser shock of the two. Riker stared down the beach for a moment; then he said, "I'm going back." Dunn gripped his arm like a bird of prey.

"*No!* No, you can't do that! Mister Marik said you were to get us to safety!" He clutched his courier's pouch as he spoke, too quickly, in a thin falsetto. "It was his dying wish. His last wish: 'Have Captain Riker get you and Miss Jessen to safety,' he said. I swear to you. You're the big hero, Captain, you have to get us out of here! You have to get us to safety!" Riker made a grimace of distaste and, prying Dunn's fingers off his arm, flung his hand away.

"Get aboard," he ordered thickly, and boosted the gangly academician over the side. He vaulted up behind him and, crossing the deck, disappeared into the wheelhouse.

In the space of a breath, the engines roared to life, and they began to move into the Narrows just as the wall cloud struck the island of Tagan.

CHAPTER

X

HE WAS COLD. Even before he opened his eyes, Charles Lassiter was aware of the wracking cold, and imagined he was back on Krailim, hiding from the secret police. Frost crusted his lashes and crunched under him as he moved. Careful, he warned himself dully. Don't want to tip off Krail's finest. It was dark. He hoped they had not brought out the hounds. Frost rimed the metal grid above him. The walls were thick with it. Walls? Grid? He blinked.

The grid was aluminum shelving, supporting wrapped packages. Great frozen sides of meat hung from hooks in the overhead. He found himself staring face-to-face with frozen fish. He sat up, and his perceptions cleared with an all but audible snap.

He was in Marik's freezer. All at once he remembered tugging at the door handle, and the shock of its sudden opening. He had a vague recollection of being picked up bodily and set down in the coldness. Then the world had gone dark.

Charles got to his feet stiffly, in the bone-chilling cold, and clumped to the door. A few healthy shoulder-blocks, the door opened, and Charles was in Marik's blessedly warm kitchen.

Moments later, shaking with hypothermia, he was engaged in a search for a blanket, a pot of hot coffee, a telecom link to headquarters, and Dao Marik, in that order. It had not occurred to him to wonder about Audrey's safety.

The abrupt onset of torrential rain and hurricane winds jerked Marik awake soaked to the skin and urged him to seek shelter. The air was thick with debris, and his skin was raw from windblown sand. The deluge beat down fiercely, making it difficult to breathe. Rapidly rising seas, forced into the already water-gorged harbor by the veering winds, had encroached upon the beach to only a few feet from the guardhouse, and raged frothing there.

It would be impossible to stand against the storm, so Marik combat-crawled around the lee of the stone building, and from there toward the opening in the mountain leading to the spiral steps.

High above, a gigantic tree blew over and came hurtling down the mountain toward him, snapping smaller trees like matchwood. Marik froze momentarily in horror as the tree bounced crazily and balanced above him with a tearing groan. It paused, swayed, and, branches cracking like pistol shots, slipped again, only to tangle with other trees and pause once more, its huge, dangling roots stopping just short of him.

It hung there, teetering precariously and blocking the stair entrance, and Marik waited his chance. When the next blast of wind rocked the massive roots again, he made it past them just as the tree hit the beach like a pile driver and drove itself several feet into the wet sand.

Inside the stairwell, the relative quiet gave him time to collect his thoughts. He hoped the *byela* had gotten away in time. Misi was alive, at the landing strip. His head hurt abominably.

Mrs. Lassiter? And Dunn? He remembered the giant barring their way—*and Dunn protecting himself by sacrificing Audrey!* He felt anger rising in him again.

She was Mennon's prisoner, then. They would have taken her to the landing strip. But how? Had they dared the rock crevice, or had they found a way to use the old Kesh Tunnel? He decided to chance the tunnel.

Take the second landing and face the wall, count four from the right, and push them all. It was the little rhyme they had learned from the Old Master as boys here, playing at pirates and secret passages. More fun if the passages were real. Marik gained the landing, counted the stones, and pushed them all.

The wall segment swung, admitting him to the tunnel. It was a secret panel, fitted centuries ago by Timujin Kesh to conceal an escape route, a natural fracture in the rock of the island itself. The incredible height of the crevice boggled the vision, and the bottom of the chasm, covered by still-warm lava, cut deep into the planet's crust. Timujin Kesh's tunnel was useful, leading, as it did, to the landing strip; it was also extraordinarily beautiful.

Eons ago, mineral-rich solutions of seawater had been forced up through the rock by heat and pressure, its heavier minerals precipitating out over many ages, filling every fault, from the merest crevice to this vast cathedral chamber, with thick massed clusters of exquisite rose quartz crystals. Their smooth facets lined the walls with jeweled buttresses, merging hundreds of feet above in a rough Gothic arch. It was a fugue of millions of rose-tinted mirrors, reflecting reflections. Extrusions of natural silver bloomed in corbels and wires and sprays among the geometric quartz, forming unimaginable crystal flowers.

It had always seemed to Marik a living fantasy, with its luminous fungi hanging in twinkling garlands from the quartz-encrusted stalactites high above and spangling the rock faces and stalagmites below. Reflections mimicked reflections in a thousand jeweled facets, a thousand twinkling lights. Walking through it was like walking into a geode.

Carved by the hand of Tadae Himself, the Old Master had commented solemnly to his two students. The boy Mennon had chuckled derisively. The boy Marik had believed it. Some part of him believed it still. His sort of God would be as interested in beauty as in logic, in mercy as in justice. Perhaps in mercy most of all, he amended, it being so rare a commodity nowadays.

Strange thoughts for a man who was searching for his child, he mused, continuing up the passage as fast as he dared. *Oh, merciful and just Tadae, help me find my baby!*

He hurried on, alone in the silence of the mountain's heart.

The fishing *byela* entered the Narrows with Cynthia at the wheel. It had been a serious concern for Riker, but time was short; all she really had to do, he reasoned, was keep the engine going and steer. She could fly a skimmer, couldn't she? Steering was steering. He knew better but ignored the knowledge. He certainly couldn't expect her to stand out in a hurricane and push the boat off the rocks.

"Remember," he told her hurriedly in the cramped wheelhouse, "when we cast off, there's going to be a surge as she rides the flow. You have to keep her away from the rocks. Keep her in the middle. Can you do that?"

"I'll do my best." Soaking wet, with her streaky makeup, her hair down, and her clothes plastered to her back, she was, with that statement, absolutely beautiful.

Riker rechecked her jury-rigged lifeline. Tested the wheel for excess play. Tapped the dials with his finger. Cleared his throat. "If something happens—it won't, but just in case—stick with the boat, understand? Rescue party can see a boat better than a man in the water." Lightning flashed, followed by more of the same. "Woman," he corrected himself. "Woman in the water." The boat rocked hard and he shifted for better balance.

She nodded. "Got it. You take care, okay?" He touched the latch and the storm slammed open the door. Rain and wind filled the wheelhouse. "Ace?" she called. He turned. "Close the door behind you, will you? It's cold as hell in here!"

"Live with it!" he yelled back, and, turning to fight his way back to the rail, muttered intensely, to her and for her, "*Live!*"

He had stationed himself and Dunn on either side of her bow, armed with stout poles to keep the boat away from the rock walls, and lashed to the rail by lengths of line from the sail locker below. He had fixed further lengths of the same warp to her aft mooring cleats, to stream in her wake and, with luck, stabilize her. He hoped it would work as well on a *byela* as on a sailing vessel.

Dunn yelled something as Riker grappled his way around the gunwales toward him. Riker shook his head and tapped his ear.

"I can't do this," Dunn repeated, screaming shrilly into Riker's face. "My health is bad! Chest problems!" He tapped his chest. "Chest! Chest!" The wind threatened to tear their heads off and Riker, his patience at an end, glared at Dunn in the deluging rain. He pointed toward the Citadel. "Bushmen!" He bellowed. He jabbed Dunn's bony chest with one finger, popping up a spurt of water from his drenched jacket. "Gun!" He pointed to the steep, rough sidewalls they were about to enter. "Rock!" he bellowed further. He pointed at the water below. "Sink!" He pushed his face close to Dunn's face and yelled, "Dead! You got it? Dead!" He snatched up the pole and slammed it sideways against Dunn's chest. "Work!" Dunn, his jaw slack, took the pole.

Riker started toward the mooring lines, pole in hand, leaning against the storm, slipping and falling with disgusting regularity. The rain was so heavy that breathing was a major accomplishment; it was impossible to distinguish rain from windblown spume. The deck was awash; whether from the rain or from the seas, he could not say. The sky blazed with lightning. He glanced up at it and could see, through the window of the wheelhouse, Cynthia bracing herself, hands on the wheel, a very determined glint in her eyes. God help the hurricane, Riker thought admiringly; then, sobering: And God help us.

He reached the lines and cast off.

None of them was prepared for the precipitous rush that shot the *byela* into the Narrows, accompanied by a wail from Dunn that carried even above the storm. The huge outflooding of the built-up water in the harbor was escaping not only through the harbor entrance, but through the flooded channel, widening it, lifting the *byela* swiftly over the rocks and wrecks and—push poles splintering against the sidewalls—catapulting it down the passageway and out into the open sea.

Beyond the cathedral chamber, the path led steeply upward, and there were fewer quartz crystals in the tunnel walls, although glints of other minerals (once, a face of pure neriosh) reflected in the light of the sparkling fungi. Farther yet, the air became warmer and more humid, the twinkling of the fungi was softer, almost misty, and the rock faces glistened with moisture.

Marik knew he was approaching the Crossover.

At the Crossover, the lava floor of the tunnel dipped abruptly to an immeasurable depth, lost in light, steam, and molten rock glowing far, far below. The chasm was not much broader than the width of the tunnel, but it might well have been as many kilometers. It was utterly impassable.

Centuries before, Timujin Kesh had spent scores of slaves and prisoners in building a bridge over the chasm, and it had served him well. By the time the Old Master had brought Marik and Mennon here as boys (to study history at firsthand), the old drawbridge had been in serious disrepair, and they had been strictly forbidden ever to try crossing it. (Naturally, they had gone across the very next time they came out to the island, and Kles had lost a *zori* to the chasm, along with several bridge timbers, coming back.)

Now things had changed. Evidently Mennon had replaced the rickety old drawbridge; in its place was a newly made, sturdily timbered bridge strapped with metal and bolted to the tunnel walls with duralloy. He had made the Crossover as safe as a garden path. After his first elation, however, Marik's hearts sank.

The bridge had been left half-drawn and unusable, cutting off access beyond the chasm. He could see the seared place on the near wall, where the Eye had been blasted by a pulser from the far side, effectively putting the bridge out of commission. Clearly, the giant had ensured his own escape by preventing Marik's use of the tunnel. There was only one way to get to the landing strip now, he knew. Only one hope was left him. If he was to rescue Misi and Audrey, he would have to go up over the mountain and take the dangerous left-hand path.

He would have to go through the crevice. And he would have to do it while the storm still raged.

Charles Lassiter stood warming his hands at the fireplace in Marik's study, waiting for the steward to return. Abundant hot coffee, warm blankets, and a tot of brandy had gone a long way toward restoring his sense of well-being, and now Marik's beautifully trained servants were engaged in a head count of the occupants of the Palace.

Lassiter, a longtime Non-Official Cover for Interpol, knew better than to rush off in several different directions at once. Obviously, there had been a break-in and a move against Marik and/or Riker by agents of unspecified origin. Vath was dead. But beyond that, nothing was known.

As yet, he had not notified the local police. This was very likely an interplanetary matter, coming under the jurisdiction of Interpol. No use shaking up the local gendarmerie as yet. Interpol was prepared for this sort of thing. There were procedures. There were rules. He was to follow them to the letter, and await further orders.

Shang entered the room and made respectful chom-ala. "I am sorry to report, Dr. Lassiter," he announced, "that Priyam Hanshilobahr *Dom* Dao Marik is not to be found."

"Captain Riker?"

The green mask made no change of expression. "Also absent, chom-shan; as are Professor Dunn, Miss Jessen . . . and, regrettably, Mrs. Lassiter."

"Thank you." The servant left without a sound, pulling the door quietly shut behind him. Charles turned back to the fire, which provided the only light in the room. Audrey gone? He kept his feelings under strict control. Discipline, that was the key. He could complicate matters by emotionalism, he reflected. Out of all the things that might have happened, only one had, and he could handle that when the time came. Better to think of other things until he had more data.

He picked up a handful of big brown *luminaria* pods from the copper scuttle on the hearth and began punctuating his thoughts by tossing the pods absently into the fire. Generally, they exploded like popcorn into a silken fluff that burned away quickly; but it was said that once in every ten thousand or so, a *luminaria* pod would detonate into a multicolored miniature fireworks display that lasted for many minutes before it became ash.

Charles smiled and rubbed the furry outer hull with his thumb. He had seen many pods burn without more than ordinary result. Folktales, he thought. Fanciful. Still, it was a pretty story. Despite himself, his thoughts kept coming back to the missing personnel. Five were missing: Marik, Riker, Dunn, Audrey, and Cynthia Jessen. He had taken the news with outward equanimity, though it distressed him more than he cared to admit.

Interesting, the absent personnel, he mused, the thought elaborately casual. One could almost call it a man and two couples. He tossed a pod onto the fire and watched it burst into fluff that shimmered away. Miss Jessen and Dunn? He frowned. No, it had been clear at table that there was no love lost there. Captain Riker and Miss Audrey? The next pod puffed into nothingness. Not likely; Riker may have come from venerable old money, but there was too much of the rugged individualist about him, the self-sufficient borderline rebel, to appeal to Audrey, his girl-wife. Dunn appealed to no one, Charles thought, flipping a pod into a breathing ember and watching it blacken and burn. Riker and Miss Jessen? He scored a bull's-eye into the center of the flame and the pod burst beautifully—into fluff, and singed away. Perhaps one could call them a match, he conceded, but then, you see, that would be impossible, because that would leave only—he weighed the last pod in his hand for a long moment before he tossed it into the fire—Marik and Audrey.

Fireworks.

If Marik had found his journey up the mountainside yet again a bad one, with trees toppling around him and branches lashing in high winds, it did not compare to his difficulty in crossing the flat, open expanse of the Citadel roof.

The watchman he had struck down earlier was no longer lying there and Marik was somehow glad for him. There are enough of us out tonight, friend. Hope you're somewhere comfortable nursing your headache. His own skull throbbed.

It was impossible to stand up. He got down as low as possible to present less wind resistance, and started across the unprotected expanse of the roof. The rain plastered his hair to his head as he made his way crab-wise through the rough freshets of rainwater rushing across the flooded flagging. The wind tore at his drenched fatigues and blinded him with its flung deluge, and he came up hard against what must have been the parapet wall.

Left, now. Left and up the crevice to the landing strip. Lightning flashed garishly, illuminating the roof, the parapet, the crevice.

Less than a meter wide in some places, the crevice was dangerous enough in fair weather, for its north side was open to the sea, hundreds of feet below. In a hurricane, its floor would be slick and perilous. Lightning flashed again, twice, and Marik got to his feet, flattened against the inner wall, facing the full brunt of the storm, and moved out into the open crevice.

Far below, the heavy seas broke hard against the mountain, and broke again, and again.

Seen from the open water, the seas were tremendous. The *byela* shot out of the Narrows with a frightening rush and wallowed clumsily in the meshing currents in the lee of the island. She actually rotated a full circle on her pivot point, rolling and pounding, while Riker slipped his short safety line and clawed and sprawled his way through the driving rain to the wheelhouse. He tore open the door as the vessel rolled, and fell against the wheel, at once conscious of the blessed absence of rain lashing at him, the close, stale air that smelled of fish and sweat and, incredibly, of Chanel, and the warm presence of Cynthia, who hugged him from behind. He grabbed the wheel and righted the *byela* so that she rode a following sea, the water breaking over her starboard quarter. Immediately the rolling became less severe and the boat began to move into the open sea.

Away from the protection of the island, the seas were titanic, crosscurrents wringing the *byela*'s hull with a frightening assortment of creaks and groans, and Riker kept her at full speed and fought the helm to keep her running with the seas, so as to make headway.

Her warps were streaming astern, and he would have liked to perform the maneuver known as "dodging," wherein a motor craft heads into the seas with just enough power to give steerageway, paid off a bit for buoyancy, and lays-to.

But presenting her flat, broad hull to a beam sea to reach a lie-to position would have invited disaster. Riker felt his only hope was to run before the wind, streaming warps and praying.

Mountains of water rose on all sides of them, their crests a phosphorescent white in the blackness of the storm. The boat wallowed and lumbered through the first few dozen seas, and Cynthia motioned through the windscreen for the terrified Dunn to come into the wheelhouse, for each consecutive sea inundated him; but he shook his head violently and indicated his lifeline, evidently fearing to be washed overboard without it. Riker could hardly blame him. The storm was a watery nightmare, and they were lost in the middle of it.

"Awfully big waves," Cynthia ventured as they slid into a

trough, pounded hard, and began climbing up the next steep
sea. Riker nodded shortly. She pointed to port through the
windscreen, where luminous spindrift was being blown off the
top of a particularly large sea.

"Big one there, too."

"Right." Riker wrestled the boat's head around to keep her
on course, for the veering wind was shoving hard and the
rudder had a mind of its own. The engine was laboring and
several dials trembled in the red zone. Riker studiously ignored
them and kept his mind on his steering.

"Wow!" Cynthia exclaimed joyfully. "That's the biggest
one of all!" Riker glanced back and his heart pounded once,
hard. For behind them was an enormous sea, coming faster than
any he had ever seen, a black mountain of water with an eerie
foaming white crest, building and building and seeming to suck
the water up into itself from beneath the very boat.

"That's a bad one," he blurted. "You want to hold on tight.
We'll make it." He shut his eyes tight, opened them. Make it,
he told the boat. Make it.

The sea climbed inexorably, like some gigantic surf, its tip
beginning to bend inward toward them in slow motion respec-
tive to the speed of the sea.

"All right, now, don't panic," Cynthia said quickly. "We
can get out of this. Stay calm and don't panic. Think!"

"Shut up, Cynthia," Riker gritted softly, as the gargantuan
sea rose higher and higher behind them. He brought the *byela*
around to take the sea dead astern, hoping that her duck-shaped
contours would give her enough buoyancy aft to avoid their
being pooped. The idea of a giant sea smashing the *byela*'s
entire stern was not a pretty one.

"I've got it!" she exulted suddenly. "You can say what you
said before! Remember how you got the wall to open up? Try
to remember what it was you said! Uh, let me see, I think it
was, 'Oh, sweet God'—I think . . .'" The seas rose even
higher and the *byela* began to pitch sharply and plane a bit.
"Yes, I'm sure. It was 'oh, sweet God—'"

"Oh, good God," Riker muttered under his breath. The
wave's foaming white tip was beginning to curl over her stern
as she slid quickly into the deep watery trough.

"Right, it was 'oh, *good* God'—and then what?"

"Hold your breath!" Riker shouted as the sea broke. "Hang on!"

"Hold your br——?"

There was a tremendous crash, an inundation of cold water drowning the decks and shattering the windscreen, foaming and boiling into the wheelhouse. The *byela* stood over on her beam-ends, recovered, pitching and yawing crazily; there was a sharp crack, a loud report, somewhere astern; then, amazingly, she righted herself. Water poured out of the wheelhouse and cascaded off the deck as she climbed the next sea, and the tropical downpour pelted them through the broken windscreen. Cynthia picked herself up from the corner, squeezing water out of her stringing hair, gasping and shivering. Lightning glared against wet sea, wet sky, wet boat, and glared again.

"I *knew* those were the wrong words!" she shouted, scared and indignant. "Now I mean it! You try it again, Paul Riker! And this time say it right!" Riker started to laugh in astonishment when his eye fell on the inert figure lying next to the starboard gunwale. "Dunn!"

Handing the wheel to Cynthia with instructions to keep the seas directly behind them— "like a roller coaster," he explained, "make the boat ride up the seas and down again" —and ignoring her insulted scowl, Riker worked his way to starboard, where Dunn was beginning to stir. He leaned over the man's face, protecting it from the elements with his own body. "Dunn! Dunn!" he yelled against the sound of the storm. "You all right?"

Dunn opened his eyes, wheezed, and tapped his chest weakly. Riker leaned close to catch his words. ". . . chest . . . ," he panted. ". . . chest . . ." Riker pointed to the towering seas.

"Drown," he shouted reasonably. "Water. Die." He pointed to Dunn, then to the wheelhouse. "In."

Then, incongruously, he began to laugh in earnest, and could not stop even when he saw the first of the coral heads looming before them among the rain and surf and spindrift.

Marik had scaled almost the entire crevice without incident when it happened. He was carefully edging his way along the open-sided passage when suddenly two skimmercraft whined away from the landing strip just above him and disappeared over the mountain. *Too late! Misi! Audrey!* He made an involuntary start, tried to turn and follow their flight, and his foot slipped on the wet surface. He fell heavily and slid toward the edge, clawing desperately at the rock floor. A leg went over the rim, dangling over nothingness. He pressed himself against the rock, but the cascading rainwater prevented any real friction coefficient. He could feel himself inexorably losing ground and he scrabbled frantically for a handhold, but even that motion pushed him closer to the edge.

A flash of lightning saved him. It glared on the crevice and the water pouring down it, highlighted the uneven purl of water over a rough area next to the inner wall, and Marik, recognizing the meaning of that ripple, grabbed for the unevenness.

It was not much, it was nothing, but it provided the bare finger-hold that stopped his inexorable slide, a purchase by which he could pull himself back up again, centimeter by painful centimeter, and at last lay safely on his chest, resting briefly in the cold, urgent sluice of the crevice.

Long moments later, leaning against the inner wall, he took a deep breath, hearing the surf below and thankful to have escaped a closer look at it. He turned his face, his thoughts, back toward the landing strip.

Even if Misi and Audrey were lost, he told himself, Mennon might still be there. And the possibility of Mennon's presence would be reason enough, after what had passed, to reach the strip alive. He had business to transact with Kles Mennon. It was time, Marik decided, that he taught Mennon what it meant when a Han Einai finally decided that enough was enough. It was worth risking his life to do so. With another deep and satisfied breath, Marik began the last, easiest leg of the ascent.

Riker grabbed Dunn by the jacket and jerked him upright. "She's going to hit!" he yelled. "Get ready to jump! Keep your shoes, we're going onto coral, but get rid of your jacket," he tugged at the courier's pouch slung over Dunn's shoulder— "and this!" Dunn snatched it away from him, wide-eyed.

"No! It's mine!"

Riker, shedding his own jacket, muttered, "I knew I should have stuck to one-syllable words!" He clawed his way to the

wheelhouse just as the *byela* stove in against the coral, swung
wildly, and broached-to in the trough of a high sea. Riker
dragged Cynthia out of the wheelhouse as the boat rose a few
meters in the surf, and dashed herself against the coral yet
again. The shock separated them, and Riker frantically swam
after her, hoping to reach her before she got torn up on the
coral. All she was wearing was that stupid shirt.

The sky lit wildly, and he saw Dunn reach the coral outcrop
and pull himself up, wide abrasions on his legs bleeding freely
and washing clean in the engulfing surf, only to bleed again.
Cynthia was swimming blindly, confusedly, nearby, almost
invisible in the spume and rain and heavy seas. Dunn made no
move to help her, and Riker started toward her, tiring quickly
now. The surf pounded the *byela* repeatedly against the coral,
breaking her up in earnest, and Riker, using a sturdy timber as
a float, managed to drag Cynthia up safe beside him and take
his bearings.

They were outside and at the tip of the long, broad coral arm
that enclosed the lagoon, where Riker had met his first ramper.
If he could reach the calmer water inside the lagoon, he
thought, if he could get them past the cruel surf, they stood a
good chance of surviving. Thus encouraged, he started swimming the timber across the surf, around the main coral head,
and was making way, of sorts, when, over the storm and surf,
he heard skimmercraft approaching from the island of Tagan.

Audrey followed the giant obediently through the Kesh
Tunnel, watched as he destroyed the Eye that would have
permitted her rescue, and emerged with him at the cave near
the landing strip. The giant opened the door for her and ushered
her in, closing it firmly against the weather. Kles Mennon rose,
smiling, from behind a battered desk.

"Mrs. Lassiter," he greeted her. "We meet again." His eyes
were green-rimmed and swollen but his manner was courtly, as
always. "Won't you sit down?" He indicated a comfortable
chair that would be easy to surround.

"Mr. Mennon," she replied. "Thank you, I'd rather— Oh!"
This last was breathed rather than spoken, for Jana emerged
from an anteroom wearing Audrey's white lace gown. It lacked
the air about it that it had when Audrey wore it, but it

transformed the Einai woman into a fairy-tale creature. She looked beautiful, and she knew it.

"How lovely you look, Jana," Audrey said courteously, because it was true. The woman tossed her dark head.

"Yes, I do," she agreed coldly. "It is *your* rich-woman dress. I have taken it from the other woman. I will keep this rich-woman dress and wear it whenever I want."

Audrey looked quickly at Mennon. "The other woman? She isn't . . . ?"

He gave her his brilliant smile. "Miss Jessen seems to have traded it for Brau's bush gear. He . . . was not pleased." He spread his hands. "Fortunes of war."

"If she had not left it, I would have taken it from her!" Jana snapped. "It is the same thing!"

"Call it a gift, then," Audrey offered. "From me."

"No! I took it. And you could not stop me! It is mine, now."

Audrey began to see the pattern of her thinking, and decided to play along. "Very well," she murmured, "but . . . I wish you hadn't taken my favorite dress."

Jana put her hands on her hips and bit the inside of her flat cheek to discipline her triumphant smile. "Well, I did," she replied smugly. Then, relenting, added, "Wait. I will show you what else I have." She left the room and quickly returned, carrying Marik's child on her hip. Audrey's eyes misted and she held out her hands. "May I?" she whispered. Jana shrugged and handed her the child, who made no protest, and Audrey took her and sat in the proffered chair, oblivious to the others in the room.

Misi was a beautiful baby, with soft, dark curls all over a well-shaped head, flyaway brows, and gray, almond-shaped eyes. Her long lashes made little black fans on her cheeks, and her golden skin had the faint jade tinge of the Han Einai. She sat studying Audrey's face intently and then, evidently approving, smiled slowly and pensively, showing very white, even teeth.

"She looks exactly like Mishli," Mennon said huskily, standing beside them. His eyes were wet, but it was probably from the wine she had thrown at him.

"Rather like her father, too, I would imagine," Audrey assisted. Mennon made no reply, and Audrey asked the child confidentially, "Would you like to hear a rhyme?" Misi lifted a hesitant shoulder, and Audrey sang, softly, as she had sung so many times before:

> "Hickaby, heckaby, my dog Trot
> Takes a swim when the weather's
> hot;
> Takes a bath when the weather's
> warm.
> He's the cleanest dog on my
> father's farm."

There was a silence, and then Jana, admiring her image in a small mirror on the wall, sighed. "It is a stupid song, Missis Lassita," she decided solemnly, without rancor, and Audrey laughed.

"It's meant to be. It's a song I made up for my husband's son, Hector. We call him Heck, because he's full of mischief. Sometimes he calls me Heckaby, too, just for fun. A pet name, you see, just between us two."

Jana continued to consult the mirror. "It is still a stupid song," she said. Misi tugged at Audrey's sleeve, and slowly the image of a flower, childish and imperfect, touched her mind shyly. Its fragrance was unmistakable. Roses. Their eyes met. Misi gazed at her with that pure, gentle, unearthly gray stare, and Audrey held her eyes steadily. Suddenly the baby smiled and hid her face against Audrey's breast.

And with an artist's eye for accuracy, she thought of Marik's rose garden, the look, the scent, the feel of it, and about walking with Misi among the flowers. The child was enchanted.

"Very, very *good*, Mrs. Lassiter," Mennon complimented her, surprised. He walked across the room and seated himself at a table, upon which was the inevitable bottle of tarangi, a bowl, and several wineglasses. "One does not expect such imagery in an alien species." He lifted the bottle. "I would offer you a glass of wine, but, ah . . ." He shrugged charmingly. "Well, you understand." He poured himself a glassful, studied the light through it, and smiled at her.

"What shall we drink to, my dear Mrs. Lassiter? Shall we

drink to *Skipjack*? Or to the memory of *Oriana*? There's a thought. To you?" His smile widened. "To me?"

"I've got a better idea," Marik said from the doorway. "Let's drink to me."

The skimmers were almost upon them, rocking a bit in the powerful winds, their searchlights lancing downward at the heaving water. Dunn was nowhere to be seen. Riker, clinging to the timber with Cynthia, risked a glance at the coral heads. Much nearer. They were drifting toward the lagoon, and comparative safety. If he could draw off the skimmers— Cynthia was hanging on to the timber loosely, eyes closed. He shook her, but she seemed numb and dull.

"Cynthia!" he shouted. "I'll be right back! Hang on! Don't let go!" She opened her eyes and he yelled in her ear, "Wait for me and I'll tell you what I said, back there at the wall!" She nodded weakly and took a fresh grip on the waterlogged timber.

Riker flung himself into the circle of skimmer light and floundered around, yelling frantically. It was important that he look as if he were drowning, and yet not drown. He hoped he could survive the ruse; the storm was still severe, and the seas huge.

The pilot of the first craft spoke into his throatset. "I have a target in my beam, Alain. Permission to zilch him?"

"Negative. Negative." The Krail's voice was cool and metallic as the second skimmer approached. "Mennon requests safe return of all hostages. Rig for pickup of all personnel."

Riker waited until he was certain that both pilots had him in their beams, then he hyperventilated as much as he dared and sank beneath the surface. He pretended a struggle, went down several times, and finally remained below.

The current was fierce, the pressure tremendous, but the searchlights illuminated the underwater scene, and he saw a peculiar light shining through several of the underwater caves he had discovered yesterday. The searchlight probed down through the tossing seas. The skimmercraft showed no signs of leaving, and he could not stay under forever. Determinedly, he dove and swam through one of the caves, emerging with his lungs bursting on a shallow beach *inside the coral Reef*.

He waded ashore, astounded. The cavern was lit by a twinkling galaxy of tiny blue and golden-white sparkles that gave off no heat to the hand he held to them, but glowed coolly of their own accord. Some sort of fungus, he supposed, but like the rest of the cavern, they seemed safe enough. Safer by far than the hurricane-lashed coral outside that Dunn and Cynthia—

He startled guiltily. Cynthia! Above all, he had to rescue Cynthia! Breathing deeply again, he dove through the cave for the rough, wild sea and the brave, annoying woman he liked so well.

The first skimmercraft circled. "Negative contact on the man," the pilot reported metallically. "We go back, Alain? It is not warm here."

"Stand by one. I think I see someone in the surf. I'm going down for a better look."

Alain buzzed the coral as close as he dared and saw no one. Dissatisfied, he made another pass, and another, but saw only the tortured sea, the phosphorescent plumes of spindrift, and the silver lances of the torrential rain. He felt a keen disappointment.

Dipping his wings in salute to Riker, whom he thought to be drowned, Alain broke off the search, and the two skimmers whined away toward the landing strip on the far side of the island.

Riker came up under Cynthia's timber and unceremoniously pulled her under just in time, his hand across her nose and mouth, fighting her vague attempts to free herself. The searchlight from Alain's skimmer swept the timber as he dove, pulling Cynthia with him, homing for the blue-white illumination glowing below. He surfaced once more inside the Reef with Cynthia sputtering and shaking with cold. But even as he carried her ashore, she twined her arms about his neck and began to cry.

"I knew you'd get us out of there, Ace, I just knew it," she sobbed. "I knew you'd do it."

He sat down heavily on the sand and Cynthia wrapped herself around him, sniffling into his neck. Almost without thinking about it, he slipped his arms around her and held her close. It was so nice, he thought, just to sit there in the quiet, with Cynthia growing snug and warm beside him. And the sound of the wavelets lapping the edge of the sand. And the wind and the rain far away . . . He was almost dozing when a sarcastic voice cut into his reverie.

"Well, well, well, how cozy we are, Captain! Miss Jessen." Riker's face flashed up, his stinging eyes blurry with fatigue and salt water, to see Marlowe Dunn standing above them. His clothes were shredded to ribbons and broad abrasions on his legs were bleeding, mingling with the seawater that dripped from his tattered clothes. The courier's bag was still slung around his shoulder, and he was pale and testy.

"Dunn!" Riker scrambled to his feet and pulled Cynthia up as well. "We thought you'd gone under! I'm glad you made it."

"Fortunately, I knew the lagoon entrance to this place," Dunn commented bitterly. "You would have let me drown out there!" His voice had acquired a peculiar rasping quality, as if every word was an effort. Effects of seawater, Riker surmised. Things are tough all over.

"As a matter of fact," Riker said curtly, "I would, since you left Miss Jessen to drown while you saved yourself. By the way, it's nice to know you can speak sequentially. I was under the impression you were limited to monosyllables."

"What I am limited to, Captain, is a very short period of time. I have to get out of these nesting caverns before the strumpets come back, or I am in grave danger."

"So what else is new," Cynthia groaned. "Everything is 'grave danger,' 'grave danger.' Whatever happened to 'ordinary'?" There was the distant call of a trumpet, and Dunn made an abortive jerk and grabbed his chest. Riker marked it and caught his arm.

"What's going on? What are you up to, mister?" Dunn tried to break away, but Riker pried his arm aside and ripped open his bloody shirt. There, nestled against his chest, was a skein of ramper brats, so newly spawned they were still encased in their individual balloons, like elongated sausages. Each of them was so beautiful, with its silver scales, fragile fins, and sea-horse heads, that Cynthia wanted to stroke them, but Riker struck her hand away.

"Don't touch them!" He jerked the end of the skein and revealed that the tiny rampers had chewed deeply into Dunn's chest and belly with their thousand needle-sharp ivory teeth. Behind him, Cynthia made a weak little moan and retched ominously, and Riker, revolted, muttered, "My God, man, they're eating you alive!"

Dunn wrenched away, his arms wrapped protectively around the skein. "I don't care!" he defended hoarsely. "They're mine!"

"Where did you get them?" Riker demanded thickly. "They're protected by law, you can't just take them out of here."

"Down the shingle. There were so many, nobody will miss a few." He giggled nervously, a high, hysterical titter. "I'm afraid I stepped on more than I took with me. They were thick on the ground, you see." The blood and seawater were staining the sand pink, and the cry of the ramper was closer now. They could hear fins sculling nearby.

Riker thought fast. The approaching ramper would smell the blood, and like as not, the brats in Dunn's shirt. He remembered Maing's saying a ramper would come miles for a trace of blood. What might they do if the blood was that of their own young?

"Drop them, Dunn!" he ordered. "Right here, right now! Drop them and let's get out of here. Maybe it will delay the mother." Dunn shook his head.

"Oh, no. No, all those years at the university, it was never Dunn. Never old Dunn. There was always someone ahead of me, some young upstart with a surprising find, a new idea; never reliable old Dunn. Well, now I've got this skein of ramper brats, and this"— he patted the courier's pouch— "from Mr. Mennon, and it's enough to—I mean—" He stammered to a guilty halt, then burst out defiantly, "Now I'm as good as any of them!"

"Money won't do it, Jocko," Cynthia muttered. "Take it from me."

"No wonder you hung on to this!" Riker's eyes were hard as he ripped open the pouch and held up a fistful of large-denomination credits for Dunn's close inspection. "Why would Mennon pay you off, unless—" Realization dawned.

"You sold Marik out, didn't you? Why, you filthy—!" He grabbed Dunn's jacket front, drawing back a clenched fist, but Marlowe Dunn pushed a Krail pulser into Riker's face.

"I wouldn't try that, Captain. I wouldn't try that at all." He gestured with the pulser. "Back against the wall!" As they complied, Riker keeping himself between Cynthia and Dunn, he added: "I'm taking my money and my ramper brats and I'm getting out of here! Too bad I can't say the same for you two!" He grimaced, slapping his chest as one of the brats bit deep. His eyes gleamed with a mad light. Riker tried to reason with him.

"Look, Dunn. You can still make it out of here alive if you put them down! Put them down, I tell you! I can hear the mother coming, for God's sake!"

"I don't think so, Captain Hero," Dunn smirked, wincing as the brats shifted for better purchase. "It's worth a lot to me—your lives included—to get these brats back to the mainland. I'm afraid this is where we part company." He aimed carefully at a spot dead center of Riker's forehead.

Behind Dunn, three exquisite ramper heads emerged from the water on slender necks, weaving curiously, hungrily, nostrils fluttering. Incongruously, one yawned, showing long, fine teeth like an ivory harp. Riker pointed, aghast.

"Oh, my God! Dunn, behind you! Look out!"

Dunn smirked. "Don't try that trick with *me*, Captain! I wasn't born yester——"

The first ramper trumpeted loudly in the enclosed cavern, the echoes bouncing from wall to wall to water. Dunn whirled, stricken and wild eyed, while inside his shirt, the brats responded in tiny voices like the bugles of tin soldiers. Riker drew Cynthia back against the wall and stood between her and the dreadful retribution Dunn had called upon himself.

The ramper, a strumpet, heard her brats and reared angrily. Dunn fired at it wildly, and it retreated beneath the surface. The second and third rampers rushed to the attack. Both were male, and the first snapped viciously at Dunn's face, making his pulse charge strike low on its dorsal fin. Its serpentine body twisted and writhed hugely in agony as it righted itself for another strike, and Dunn fired excitedly several times. One of the misses blasted the head off the third ramper, and a rush of blue-green blood geysered into the water, followed almost instantly by a splashing agitation across the grotto that signaled the arrival of more hungry predators.

Riker edged away down the grotto, keeping Cynthia between himself and the wall for her own protection. They were still murderously vulnerable. Up to the left, the grotto narrowed and split, the main cavern persisted at water level. A smaller branch angled away in semi-darkness, and Riker felt a faint cool breeze from that direction. He indicated it to Cynthia with a jerk of the head, and she sucked her index finger, held it up, and agreed with a surprised nod.

"The first chance we get," he muttered, "run for it. I'll be right behind you."

Dunn stared in fascinated horror at the churning water, where several rampers in their feeding frenzy were devouring their fresh meal, and was almost bitten by the beached trumpet.

Frightened now, he reached inside his shirt, tore the skein free, and flung it to the ground, smashing several of the brats in the process; but the trumpet was not so easily sidetracked. It pressed the attack with snaps and hisses and flailing fins. Dunn aimed yet another charge at the wounded ramper, but the weapon misfired.

He pressed the stud again and again in a frenzy of terror, while it clicked impotently and the ramper reared over so slowly—and then pounced, jaws agape. There was a hoarse scream and the sound resembling that of an ivory scissors shearing open, then shut, a few times.

After that, there was only the trumpet's deep blowing as it smelled at the brats lying bruised and broken on the sand. The strumpet surfaced and approached shyly, snuffed at the living brats, and nudged the dead. Her finely chiseled head lifted and swung suspiciously over Riker and Cynthia, who froze motionless against the grotto wall. She came so near that the pendant gossamer tatters on her head brushed their faces, and her dark, liquid eyes, like a seal's wide gaze, brimmed with mute anguish a scant meter away.

She blew a misty exhalation smelling of seaweed and spindrift, but neither Riker nor Cynthia smelled of blood, nor of the brats, but only of the familiar sea. And at last, she blew heavily once again and returned down the shingle to curl around her young, living and dead. Softly at first, then louder, she began a slow, sad keening that followed Riker and Cynthia far along the entire twinkling length of the grotto and up into the warm, lessening rains, and out onto the Reef below the pavilion, in the first faint light of morning.

Marik stood there in the doorway, bloody, drenched, and exhausted. There was a peculiar quality about him, a sense of barely checked power burning brightly, just under the surface.

Kles Mennon rose slowly. "Dao," he said, thinking fast. "I didn't expect to see you here."

"You should have, Kles," Marik said softly.

Mennon smiled briefly, uncomfortably. "Yes. Well. Perhaps we should drink to you, after all." He lifted the bottle. "Tarangi all right?" Marik came slowly into the room.

"Oh, yes, tarangi's fine. But first, let us talk, Kles," he suggested in a voice so quiet they had to strain to hear him. "Let us reason together." Mennon put down the bottle and glanced at the door. The lock sequence glowed softly red. There was a *viith* in the desk drawer—

"Don't even consider it," Marik warned. "We don't want weapons, do we?" He shed his *viith* sleeve, removed both *gons* from his belt at the small of his back, and laid them in Audrey's lap, paying no attention at all to Misi. "Go into the other room, Owdri," he instructed. "And stay there until I call you."

"Yes."

"And keep Misi and Jana with you."

"Yes."

Taking the baby, the weapons, and her two charges, Audrey left the room. Marik turned back to Mennon.

"You must admit," he began, "that I have been patient with you, Kles. I permitted you to share my life and education, because we swore a blood vow of brotherhood, as boys."

Flushing, Mennon retorted stiffly, "And I swore my oath of fealty to you in payment!"

"Fealty. Ah, yes." He eyed the inside of the cave, pausing at the closed door where Audrey and Misi waited. "Define *fealty, ris'Tadae*." Mennon looked away uncomfortably.

"Your choice, the oath. I wanted you as brother, and you insisted upon becoming my servant." He shook his head. "You are a poor brother, Kles, and an abominable servant."

He crossed to the desk and stared earnestly into Mennon's face.

"You must admit I have been patient with you," he repeated. "I let you work off your grief at Mishli's death, there on *Hope*, even though I was humiliated and injured by it." There was the tandem whine of skimmers putting down at the landing strip, and Mennon glanced up and smiled at the sound. He slowly poured half a bowl of tarangi and sipped it as Marik spoke.

"Yes, you were patient," he agreed, "but I was very, very angry. I hated you." He smiled again, showing all his teeth. "I still hate you. I intend to kill you, when the time comes."

"I know." Marik's head came up fast. His eyes were a tiger's eyes. "And now *I* am very angry, and while I don't intend to kill you, you may wish I had." He hit Mennon full in the face with everything he had, knocking him backward over the desk. The bowl shattered against the wall.

In the next room, Jana started toward the sound, but Audrey fired the gun, striking the doorframe next to her head. The Einai woman whirled, astonished.

"Expert marksman. Notre Dame, class of '79," Audrey said quietly. "Sit down." Jana sat.

Mennon bounced up and launched himself at Marik, but Marik sidestepped and chopped him behind the ear, and Mennon crumpled to his hands and knees, shaking his head to clear it. Scrambled to his feet, smearing his cut lip on the back of his hand.

"You've made a mistake in imprisoning my child, Kles," Marik said conversationally. "I hope you recognize that."

Mennon made no answer. He threw a left which Marik blocked, and hit him dead center in the face with a left of his own. Blood flew, and Mennon gasped and let go with a right to the body that staggered Marik, who feinted right and came up with a left uppercut that brought Mennon back to his knees. He knelt there for a moment, his nose and mouth bleeding profusely and his right eye beginning to swell shut.

"It's not to happen again—agreed?" Marik inquired, politely.

Mennon pulled himself up, hand over hand, on Marik's fatigues. When Mennon was upright, Marik hit him in his other eye, opening a nasty gash in his brow, dropped him to the floor yet again, and repeated, "Agreed?"

Mennon refused to answer, and Marik grabbed his tunic front, dragged him to his feet, and hit him in the face again, noting mentally that his nose was beginning to feel spongy.

"Agreed?" Marik repeated, in exactly the same tone and volume. When Mennon failed to answer, Marik slapped his face, back and forth with his open hand, until Mennon mumbled, half-sobbing through his split lips, "Agreed, agreed!"

"I have your *word of honor*, Kles. I'll hold you to it." Marik pushed him away roughly.

Mennon staggered back against the desk, nearly upsetting the tarangi bottle, and Marik grabbed for it and righted it, while Mennon slumped there panting.

"Careful. You wouldn't want to spill that. You offered me a drink—remember?" Mennon roared and charged him blindly with the last of his strength, and Marik, whirling, delivered a roundhouse kick to the ear that felled him like a beef. He hauled him up by the front of his tunic and spoke closely into his shockingly mangled face.

"Now hear me, and remember: you are not to touch the person of my child!—nor the personnel of my ship!—nor the memory of my wife!—for the rest of your life!" he commanded quietly, dangerously. "For if you make the slightest move in that direction, I will come after you—wherever you are!—and we will discuss this to its natural conclusion!" He let him go and Mennon dropped like a stone and lay still.

"I'll have that drink now, if you don't mind," Marik said, and, stepping over Mennon's inert body, poured himself the best bowl of tarangi he had ever enjoyed. "It's all right now, Owdri," he called. There was a faint, familiar scent in the room, a whiff of fragrance. He sniffed the air.

Jana appeared in the doorway. "Mennon!" She rushed across the room to stoop beside him and feel his heartsbeat, then rushed for the door. "Jek! Ilai!"

"Go on," Marik encouraged her, following the delicious scent around the room. "Call them. Bring them all in and let them see what an unarmed man has done to the great Kles Mennon!"

"They will kill you *slowly!*" she spat.

"Or better yet," he suggested softly, "they will go back to the nova and trade my life for Mishli's. And then he will bring her back—and marry her!—and where will you be then, lady? Where will you be then?" He found a rucksack lying behind the desk, smelling wonderfully of promise, and unstrapped it. "Go ahead, call them," he encouraged Jana yet again. "Shall I open the door for you?"

Jana turned her face away. These were new thoughts, and not pleasant ones. She knelt beside Mennon, lifted his head into her lap. Patted his face. Purred softly at him in Eisernai. There was no response. He was unconscious and probably would be, for some time. She laid his head carefully on the stained flagging and went to the door, resting her forehead against it, thinking fast.

Finally, she looked up at Marik, who had found the last fat wedge of Arbat's wonderful cheese, the wedge Mennon had stolen from him in the Preserve. He shouldered the rucksack, looking very satisfied with himself, and she hated him. But he had won.

"There are three skimmers on the strip. When I draw the men away, take your child and Missis Lassita and go." Marik touched her mind and found truth. Nodded. Jana slipped through the door and they heard her shouting orders over the sound of the lessening rain, and the men's heavy footsteps fading in the distance. In a surprisingly short time, the landing strip was deserted but for the skimmers waiting there to take them home.

Marik turned to Audrey, and his child. The same dark curls, the flyaway brows over soft little black fans on her jade cheeks; he caressed her cheek with the back of one finger and gently lifted her chin. Mishli's gold-flecked gray eyes looked back at him, evoking memories too dear and painful to name. "*Zo-ili tu' tadae, Misi,*" he told her. *I am your father, Misi.*

Misi's eyes brimmed. "Tadae?" she whispered hopefully, almost unbelievingly, touching her chest with a dimpled hand. "*Ze tadae?*" Marik's eyes smarted and he nodded, unable to speak.

She thought him a flower.

Marik shut his eyes and took a long shuddering breath, like

a man surfacing after a deep dive, or returning home after a long absence; and taking Misi into his arms at last, he hugged her hungrily, as if he would never let her go.

Sunday—4:47 A.M.

They were waiting at the skimmerport: Charles and Riker and Cynthia, along with a contingent of the PBI; a representative of Interpol; the media; Shang; and the *amah*. When Marik and Audrey, carrying the baby, alighted from the skimmer, there was scattered applause from the media, and Riker offered Marik his hand—and then hugged him unashamedly—while Cynthia rushed over to coo over the baby.

The tri-D people wanted Marik to pose with Misi, but Charles diverted their attention to Cynthia instead, who launched into a graphic, blow-by-blow account of the abduction and escape, and loved every minute of it.

The little boy Marik had found at Sofyan's house toddled around wailing, *"Botta tannich, botta tannich,"* until the old *amah* handed him one of several peanut-butter-and-jelly sandwiches in her bag, whereupon he sat down in the middle of the proceedings and began gnawing on it happily.

Riker waited until the cameras were panning the view of the sea from the Promontory, with the police cutters converging on Tagan en masse and PBI skimmers whining overhead, and took time to kiss Cynthia good-bye properly.

"You never did teach me what you said to break down that wall," she accused, and Riker meditated on that for a minute and agreed, "You're right. Tell you what. When I get back from this mission, I'll call you and we'll have dinner. And afterward, ah, I'll teach you all my magic words, how's that?" She looked at least disbelieving.

"Oh, right, Ace. I'll hold my breath." She pulled his head down again for a long moment, and then pulled back suddenly. "What if you don't come back?" she wondered abruptly.

"Shut up, Cynthia," Riker muttered, at very close range, and kissed her yet again before the woman servants led her off to bathe and change.

Charles and Audrey Lassiter made their hasty good-byes in

the middle of the confusion and promised to get together with Riker, if ever the occasion presented itself. Shook hands with Marik and made the polite remarks expected of them. Charles was deeply, almost paternally, grateful for Marik's rescue of his wife. Audrey, wrapped in a wool blanket, her injured wrist in a sling, was on her way to the rescue helo, but when Charles turned aside to attend to some sort of Interpol business, she managed a moment with Marik alone.

"Thank you, Priyam." Simply that.

"For nothing."

"I believe this belongs to you." She extended the hand with his ring on it. "I hope you don't mind. I put it on to keep from losing it." She wore my ring, he thought. And it fit her perfectly.

"It becomes you, Mrs. Lassiter." His eyes were warm.

She took the ring from her finger and placed it in his palm. "I found it in the Citadel. I thought you might have lost it." His face lit with surprise and quiet delight.

"You found the tower." She nodded and met his eyes, and they smiled, remembering the shells and the feathers and the sandals. Even with Misi in his arms, she could see the little boy Marik carefully arranging the beautiful relics on the flat stone. She could see him watching the rampers from the tower window. She could see . . . in the distance, Charles, waiting for her.

"I'm glad you have your baby back." There were dark smudges under her eyes. Such lovely eyes, he thought. Such a gallant lady. Sweet little alien lady. Owdri. Audrey.

"Thank you, Mrs. Lassiter. I hope your wrist is better soon." He rescued us, she thought. He saved us all, and nearly died doing it. He kissed me.

"Well, then." She extended her good hand. "So nice to have met you. Thank you for everything." He leaned down and kissed her fingertips, his eyes on her face.

"It was an honor," he said softly.

Charles led her away toward the rescue helo and Audrey smiled faintly to herself. He was right, she thought warmly. That was the proper word. Perhaps, in fact, it was Marik's Word. For, viewed objectively, she realized, the entire experience had been a matter of honor.

The East Terrace was all but deserted now. The tri-D people were moving out their equipment and the law-enforcement agencies had taken up stations down the Reef. Riker consulted his ticket, and the sky, which was beginning to show clearing patches between the ragged bands of cloud. "We'd better be getting back to *Skipjack*, Mister Marik," he said thoughtfully. "We'll be shipping out in a little less than four hours, if we're to make our Jumpslot."

"Aye, sir." How easy it was to slip into the familiar shipboard usage. How comfortable.

Riker patted his tunic, feeling the satisfying bulk of his orders there. "We're lucky Mennon found the wrong set of orders in my dress uniform, eh?"

Marik smiled absently and set his little daughter down on the wet glasphalt, holding her hand. "We're lucky about a lot of things, Captain. Luckier than most."

"I'll go that," Riker agreed, as the old *amah* came up to take the baby. Marik shook his head.

"Not yet, *amah*," he told her. "There's something more important we have to do first." His smile was tired and white and beautiful. "I want to show her Mishli's roses."

As they started for the fragrant rosary, Riker sauntered to the balustrade at the end of the Promontory and looked over the wide expanse of sea and sky. There was a harmless sprinkle of warm rain, quickly gone. The sky was brightening behind the island of Tagan, ragged red clouds streaking a somber dawn. The sea was gray metal, a calmer, less angry sea, with spent foam like torn lace on the swells.

Above him, a flight of *standi* wheeled, crying down the wind, and, pouring over the edge of the sea-cliffs, settled once more into their nesting places. High in the ancient trees, finiks and other songbirds began chanting their matins. The early sun glowed warmly through a rift in the clouds. A soft sea breeze touched his face.

Then, distantly, almost triumphantly, he heard the sound across the water as of medieval trumpets, two notes, low and rising, repeated twice, and coming from no particular direction.

Paul Riker, Captain, USS *Skipjack*, listened for a long, thoughtful while; then he smiled, crossed the broad, wet terrace, and went into the Summer Palace to pack.

DAVID DRAKE

__*NORTHWORLD*__ 0-441-84830-3/$3.95

The consensus ruled twelve hundred worlds—but not Northworld.
Three fleets had been dispatched to probe the enigma of Northworld. None returned. Now, Commissioner Nils Hansen must
face the challenge of the distant planet. There he will confront a
world at war, a world of androids...all unique, all lethal.

__*SURFACE ACTION*__ 0-441-36375-X/$4.50

Venus has been transformed into a world of underwater habitats
for Earth's survivors. Battles on Venus must be fought on the
ocean's exotic surface. Johnnie Gordon trained his entire life for
battle, and now his time has come to live a warrior's life on the
high seas.

THE FLEET Edited by David Drake and Bill Fawcett

The soldiers of the Human/Alien Alliance come from different
worlds and different cultures. But they share a common mission:
to reclaim occupied space from the savage Khalian invaders.

    __BREAKTHROUGH__   0-441-24105-0/$3.95
    __COUNTERATTACK__   0-441-24104-2/$3.95
    __SWORN ALLIES__   0-441-24090-9/$3.95